'All right,' she said through her teeth, 'you can come in. But only for a few minutes. And you are not to say anything to Gillie – about who you are, I mean. You're just a friend, all right? A friend, passing by and dropping in to say hello.'

He gave her a long look but didn't reply and she had no idea, as she turned to lead him indoors, whether he would obey her. She could only hope that he understood what damage any revelation might do – to her, to her family, to Gillie herself.

She heard the front door close behind him and led him along the short passage, opening the door to the living room. The children were still on the rug where she had left them, glancing up to see who the visitor was, and she felt Floyd stop behind her and heard his tiny intake of breath as he gazed down, for the first time in his life, at his daughter.

Lilian Harry's grandfather hailed from Devon and Lilian always longed to return to her roots, so moving from Hampshire to a small Dartmoor town in her early twenties was a dream come true. She quickly absorbed herself in local life, learning the fascinating folklore and history of the moors, joining the church bellringers and a country-dance club, and meeting people who are still her friends today. Although she later moved north, living first in Herefordshire and then in the Lake District, she returned in the 1990s and now lives on the edge of the moor with her three ginger cats and a black miniature schnauzer who has a fan club bigger than that of her mistress. She has a son, a daughter and two grandchildren, is still an active bellringer and member of the local drama group and loves to walk on the moors. Visit her website at www.lilianharry.co.uk

A Penny A Day

LILIAN HARRY

An Orion paperback

First published in Great Britain in 2008
by Orion
This paperback edition published in 2009
by Orion Books Ltd,
Orion House, 5 Upper St Martin's Lane,
London WC2H 9EA

An Hachette UK company

3

Copyright © Lilian Harry 2008

The right of Lilian Harry to be identified as the author
of this work has been asserted by her in accordance
with the Copyright, Designs and Patents Act 1988.

All rights reserved. No part of this publication may be
reproduced, stored in a retrieval system, or transmitted,
in any form or by any means, electronic, mechanical,
photocopying, recording or otherwise, without the
prior permission of the copyright owner.

All the characters in this book are fictitious, and any resemblance
to actual persons, living or dead, is entirely coincidental.

A CIP catalogue record for this book is
available from the British Library.

Typeset by Deltatype Ltd, Birkenhead, Merseyside

Printed and bound in Great Britain by Clays Ltd, St Ives plc

The Orion Publishing Group's policy is to use papers that
are natural, renewable and recyclable products and
made from wood grown in sustainable forests. The logging
and manufacturing processes are expected to conform to
the environmental regulations of the country of origin,

www.orionbooks.co.uk

To Philip and Christine

Chapter One

Bridge End, near Southampton, December 1952

'Goodness me,' Ruth Hodges said, opening the envelope that had just arrived in the post. 'It's a wedding invitation!'

As her husband Dan glanced up from his breakfast, Sammy came down the cottage stairs, shepherding his little half-sister, Linnet, ahead of him. Tall like his father, but as slender and fair as his mother had been, he had just finished his National Service in the RAF and would soon be returning to complete his apprenticeship with Solly Barlow, the Bridge End village blacksmith.

Ruth turned to him, her face alight with pleasure. 'You'll never guess what, Sammy. We've had an invitation to Rose Budd's wedding, in Portsmouth.'

'Rose Budd?' Dan said. 'That's Frank Budd's eldest girl, isn't it?'

'Well, you ought to know – you're the one who used to live near them,' she told him, laughing. 'Yes, she's getting married to a chap called ...' she scanned the invitation '... Kenneth Mackenzie. Sounds a bit Scottish, doesn't it? Did you know any Mackenzies round April Grove way, Dan?'

He shrugged. 'Not that I remember. How about you, Sam?'

'Well, since I only lived there for a year or two, when I was about seven' the young man grinned, 'I only *just* remember Rose. She never had much to do with me – it was her brothers,

Tim and Keith, I played with most, and that was when we were all evacuated out here at Bridge End. There's another sister too, isn't there? I seem to remember a baby.'

'That's right. Maureen. She came to our wedding – she was about six, so she'll be twelve or thirteen now. And Rose is in her twenties – there was a big gap between them.' Ruth helped Sammy to a plate of fried eggs and bacon and poured some cornflakes into a bowl for Linnet. 'Well, it'll be good to see them all again. It's a couple of years since Jess and Frank last came out to Bridge End to visit all their friends here, and I don't know how long it is since we saw the boys.'

'Are we all invited?' Dan asked, wiping the last piece of fried bread round his plate. 'Sam and Linnet as well, I mean?'

'Of course we are! You will come, Sammy, won't you? It's in January. A cold time of year for a wedding, I must say.'

'Am I going to be a bridesmaid, with a long pink frock and a bunch of flowers?' Linnet asked. There had been a wedding in the village church a few weeks earlier and Linnet, whose best friend had been given this honour, had longed for it ever since.

Ruth smiled and shook her head. 'I don't think so, sweetheart. I expect Rose will have Maureen, and maybe some other friends or relations. She doesn't really know us that well, after all.'

'I dunno really why we're being invited,' Dan observed, getting up from the table. 'It's not as if we've been all that close friends. I know Frank and me were mates for years, even before me and Nora went to live in April Grove, and Jess was good to us when times were hard, what with Nora being poorly and Sam left on his own too much. But I'm surprised they've asked us, all the same.'

'Well, we did invite them to our wedding,' Ruth pointed out. 'And they always look us up when they come out to Bridge End. I wonder if they've asked anyone else from the village? It'll be nice if there's a few of us to go together.'

2

'I'd like to go,' Sammy said, giving Linnet a piece of his bacon. 'It'll be good to see some of the April Grove people again. There's Mr and Mrs Vickers, they were good to me too, and the Chapmans and all the others. Even Micky Baxter,' he added with a sly look at his father.

Dan snorted. 'Micky Baxter! I'll be surprised if he's not in prison by now. I always thought that's where he'd end up – it's where he ought to have been years ago,' he added, his thick eyebrows coming together in a dark frown. 'I don't suppose he'll be at this wedding, anyway.' He went over to the back door and unhooked his working jacket. 'Well, I got to be going. Me and Solly have got a lot of work on, with the Hunt busy again. You'd better make the most of this demob leave of yours, Sam, because you'll be hard at it once you start down at the forge again, I can tell you.'

He gave Ruth and Linnet a kiss each and went out. Silver the parrot, who had been peacefully dozing on his stand near the range, lifted his head and observed that he was a teapot, short and stout, but nobody took any notice and he went back to sleep. Ruth poured Sammy another cup of tea.

'It's nice to have you back home. Are you looking forward to starting work again at the forge? It'll be a bit different from being in the RAF.'

Sammy buttered a piece of toast and gave half to Linnet before answering. Then he said, 'I'm not really sure, Auntie Ruth. I've done such different things in the RAF. I knew I wouldn't be doing any blacksmithing, of course – not much scope for that on an airfield! – but I didn't expect to learn so much, and get so interested in it all. I know I've got to finish my apprenticeship, but I'd really like to go on working with electronics.'

Ruth stared at him doubtfully. 'You mean mending wirelesses and things? Don't you need a lot of training for that?'

'Not wirelesses so much, no. It's radar I've been working with mostly. And I've had the training, in the RAF. That's

3

what National Service can do for you, you see – it can give you a trade.'

'But you've already got one.'

'Blacksmithing – I know. But honestly, Auntie Ruth, do you really think I'm cut out to be a blacksmith? I mean, look at me.' He stretched his arms wide. 'I'm just not built to be a blacksmith. It's hard, heavy work—'

'Your father says you're good at it. You're wonderful with the horses, and you can do lovely wrought-iron work.'

'I can *design* lovely wrought-iron,' he corrected her. 'I did the design for that weather-parrot Dad made you for your anniversary. And I can make it too, because I've been taught – but I'm really *good* at what I did in the RAF. And it's developing so fast.' His blue eyes were bright and eager. 'I'm going to find a night school in Southampton or Portsmouth and get some more qualifications, so that when I've finished my apprenticeship with Solly, I can get a job in that sort of work.'

Ruth was still looking doubtful. 'Your father and Solly will be disappointed not to have you with them.'

'I know. But it'll be another year or two before it happens, and they'll have time to get used to the idea. Solly might even decide to terminate my apprenticeship before then.'

'But then you won't get your indentures!'

'I won't need them,' he said. 'Look, I'm going to play fair with Dad and Solly. I don't want to disappoint them – but you must admit I didn't really have much say in what I did when I left school, did I? Dad was already working with Solly and he fixed it all up without even talking to me about it.'

'Well, that's what a good father does – tries to set his son's feet on a path that'll take him through life and bring him a decent living.'

'I know, and I appreciate it. It's just that blacksmithing isn't the right path for me – and electronics is. And if I hadn't gone into the RAF, I might never have found it out.'

Ruth said no more. She gathered up the plates and took

4

them to the sink. Linnet scrambled down from her chair and held out her hand to her big brother.

'Take me for a walk. We can go and see Auntie Jane.'

'All right,' Sammy said, standing up. He had grown taller than Ruth would ever have believed possible, so tall that his head almost bumped the wooden beams of the ceiling. 'We'll see if she's doing any baking, shall we? I hope she's making some of her cheese scones.'

'Honestly, Sammy!' Ruth scolded. 'You've only just this minute finished your breakfast. I don't know what else the RAF did for you, but it seems to have given you hollow legs.'

Sammy grinned and came over to give her a hug. 'I've missed the home cooking. They fed us pretty well, but it's not like going into a farmhouse kitchen and smelling fresh bread and scones. I've got a lot of catching up to do.' He looked down at Linnet. 'Go and get your coat and mittens, and that woolly bonnet with the bunny's ears. It's cold outside.' He turned back to Ruth. 'Are we having the carol singing this Christmas? That's another thing I missed, being away from home at Christmas last year.'

'Of course we're having the carol singing,' Ruth said, smiling. 'It was because of you that we started it up again during the war.'

Linnet came back into the kitchen with her outdoor clothes and Sammy buttoned her into the thick coat and helped her pull on the mittens that were threaded on a long string through both sleeves. Then he fitted her bonnet over her dark curls, pulled on his own old jacket, and clicked his fingers at the parrot.

'Goodbye, Silver, you old wretch. Take care of Auntie Ruth for me while we're gone.'

'Sammy, Sammy, shine a light,' the parrot replied, in the hoarse voice that still bore some resemblance to Sammy's more adult tones. 'Ain't you playing out tonight? Sod the little buggers. It's a bleeding *eagle*.'

5

Sammy laughed. 'You'd never believe I only said that once. I hope you're not repeating the things he says,' he added to Linnet. 'He knows more naughty words than anyone else I've ever met, even in the RAF.'

'I'm teaching him some more nursery rhymes,' she said, and waggled her hand at the cage. 'Come on, Silver, say "See-Saw, Margery Dawe".'

'Johnny shall have a new master,' the parrot replied obligingly, then fell silent, scratching his head with one foot as if trying to rack his memory.

'He shall earn but a penny a day,' Linnet prompted. 'Because he can't work any – any what, Silver? He knew it yesterday,' she added in disappointment.

'Sometimes he takes a bit longer to learn something new,' Sammy said. 'Come on, let's go.'

Ruth watched them walk down the garden path and then started the washing-up, her mind drifting back to the time when Sammy had first come to Bridge End, a frightened little boy of eight. It had been weeks before she'd discovered that his mother had died not long before he'd been evacuated from Portsmouth, and months before his father had come out to see him. She remembered the day Dan had arrived unexpectedly on the doorstep. It was almost the first time that she'd ever been cross with Sammy over some scrape he'd been in with little Muriel Simmons, and they'd all got off on the wrong foot. But things had improved after that and now here they were, a family that had seemed complete until Linnet had arrived, almost as unexpectedly as Dan, and made it all perfect.

But nothing was ever quite perfect, she thought, scrubbing egg off the plates. And this idea of Sammy's, that he might give up working with his father at the blacksmith's forge and do something quite different – something Ruth didn't really understand but was sure he wouldn't be able to do at Bridge End – looked likely to disturb the family life she loved so much, and very possibly upset Dan into the bargain.

Well, that was all in the future and might never happen. There was something nice to think about now – Christmas, with Sammy at home once more, and then the wedding in April Grove. She would have to think about what to wear – her best grey suit with a nice flower in the lapel, probably – and she could make a new frock for Linnet. Her little girl might not be a bridesmaid, but she would still look as pretty as a princess.

Chapter Two

Portsmouth

In April Grove, Jess and Frank were busy making preparations. Not only did they have Christmas to think about, but there was the wedding as well – the first in their family. Rose was twenty-five and Jess had begun to worry that she was never going to marry, but a year or so ago she had come home with a tall, dark-haired sailor who spoke with a Scottish accent, and Jess had seen at once that he was different from the other boyfriends her daughter had had.

'I think this is the one,' she'd said to Frank as they got ready for bed after he'd gone, and Frank had looked at her in astonishment.

'How can you know that? The girl's hardly known him five minutes.'

'I think she's known him a bit longer than she says – I've had a feeling for the last couple of months that there was someone a bit special. Anyway, you can tell by the way they look at each other.'

'Well, you certainly can't tell from the way they talk to each other!' Frank had observed, pulling on his pyjama trousers. 'I couldn't make out a word he said. We'd better start taking lessons in Scotch if he's going to be part of the family.' He thought for a moment and added gloomily. 'We'd better start saving too, if there's a wedding coming up.'

Jess laughed. 'Go on, we've been saving for that for years.

And it's *Scottish*, she added, 'not Scotch. You have to say Scottish. Rose told me when we were out in the kitchen making cocoa.'

'Oh.' He got into bed. 'There you are, you see. We're having to learn already.' He glanced at his wife. 'You realise what it means, don't you, if our Rose marries a sailor? He might want her to move away from Pompey. And Scotland's a long way off.'

'I know.' She slipped in beside him. 'But there's nothing much we can do about that, Frank. And plenty of sailors settle in Portsmouth, if that's where they're based. Their ships come in here so often, they don't need to move away, and by the time they leave the Navy, they're used to the area. I don't think we need worry too much about that.'

'I don't think we need to worry about it at all, until it's a bit more definite she's going to marry him,' Frank declared, switching off the bedside lamp he'd made. 'She's only brought the lad home once and you've got them up the aisle already. There's a lot of water got to flow under the bridge before we gets that far.'

Eighteen months later, Jess's prophecy had come true. Young Kenneth Mackenzie had been in Portsmouth for several months, based at the shore station HMS *Vernon*, before he'd had to go to sea again, and during that time the family had grown to know and like him. Even Frank could soon understand his accent, and by the time the young Scot had asked his permission to marry Rose (even though she was over twenty-one and he didn't strictly need to ask) they knew he would make her a good husband. The wedding had been fixed for the second Saturday in January, partly to give people time to get over Christmas but mainly because Kenneth would be at sea until Christmas and had agreed to take the second leave when he came back.

'We're getting married quarters,' Rose told her mother excitedly. 'A little flat, with two bedrooms and a proper bath-

9

room and everything! You'll be able to come to tea and maybe next year we could have Christmas there.'

'My goodness, let's get this Christmas over first!' Jess exclaimed. 'Not to mention the wedding. There's a lot of organising to do, especially with Ken's family coming down from Scotland. I don't know where we're going to put them all.'

The biggest problem was where to have the reception. If it had been in summer and just their own family, they could have had it at home, Jess thought, but with so many people having to be invited they would need somewhere bigger. The little church of St Lucy at the top of the road didn't have its own hall, so they would have to find somewhere else – perhaps the hall belonging to the bigger church in Copnor. They might even decide to have the wedding itself at St Alban's, she thought, because now she came to think about it, St Lucy's wasn't registered for weddings.

In the event, that was what they did. Rose and Ken went to see the vicar to fix the date, and booked the hall at the same time. Jess's concerns about the catering were soon dispelled by her sister Annie Chapman, who declared that she and Olive would see to all that, and no doubt Freda Vickers would lend a hand as well, and probably Gladys Shaw – or Weeks, as she was now that she'd married young Clifford.

'It's a pity it's not in summer,' she said, echoing Jess's thoughts. 'You can't do better than a nice ham salad for a wedding breakfast then. But it'll be cold in January. People will need something hot inside them.'

'But what's it to be?' Jess asked worriedly. 'We can't do a roast – there aren't the facilities. And you can't give people stew or shepherd's pie for a wedding. And what about the rations? Oh, I wish they'd waited until summer, it would all be so much easier then!'

Annie thought for a minute or two. 'Well, we could do a salad as the main course as long as they'd had a bowl of soup to warm them up. And then maybe apple pie or even rice pudding for afters ...'

'*Rice pudding*?' Jess echoed. 'Annie, we can't give people rice pudding!'

'I don't see why not. You've got to admit, rice is appropriate for a wedding.'

'Not for the meal,' Jess said firmly. 'And you can stop laughing at me. I knew you weren't serious. No, a nice apple pie would do. We could get the baker to make some and deliver them hot. And we could manage the soup somehow – they've got that little gas cooker at the hall to heat it up on. It's going to be a lot of work, though,' she finished doubtfully.

'I told you, me and Olive will see to all that. And I dare say you'll be inviting the Vickers.'

'Yes, they've been good friends, but we can't invite Freda and then turn round and ask her to spend half the week cooking for it. Honestly, if I'd known it was going to be all this trouble I'd have suggested to Rose that she and Ken might be better off eloping.' But she didn't mean that, and Annie knew it. Jess's face was bright with excitement at the thought of the coming celebration. When the two boys, Tim and Keith, married in their turn, all this would fall to their brides' parents, and it would be a good few years yet before young Maureen thought about a wedding.

Freda Vickers was only too pleased to help; indeed, she came straight down to number 14 as soon as she'd received her invitation and offered. 'Anything I can do, you know you've only got to ask,' she declared, standing at Jess's freshly-scrubbed doorstep. 'I dare say you'll be making all the dresses, so if I can give a hand there ...'

Jess thanked her and said she was well ahead with the dresses and had almost finished Rose's. 'Come in and see it, Freda. It's oyster satin and lace trim, with a long veil and train – she's going to look lovely. I just hope we don't get one of those January gales that'll blow it all to bits. And Maureen's going to be bridesmaid, of course – they're only having the one, since Ken hasn't got any little girl relations – so I haven't got too much to do. I'm making myself a costume in dark red; it'll look nice and warm for the day and do me for best afterwards. But there is something you can do, if you really want to help.' She explained about Annie's ideas for the catering. 'A good hot bowl of soup and a ham salad and warm apple pie would be about right, we thought. The only thing is, it means making a lot of soup beforehand, and then heating it up at the hall. But Annie says there'll be time while people are arriving from the service and having sherry.'

Freda nodded. 'That's what we did when Gladys and Clifford got married, if you remember.' Clifford Weeks was Freda's nephew and had come to live with the Vickers when his parents had been killed in the Blitz. 'Gladys'll give me a hand too, I expect. How many are you inviting?'

'The list gets longer every day,' Jess said. 'Half the street's coming, and we want to ask some of the Bridge End people as well. Dan Hodges and Ruth and young Sammy, and Mrs Greenaway that Rose and me were evacuated with for a while, and Edna Corner that had the boys. Tim and Keith still go out to see her now and then. She and her hubby were really good to them – it was such a shame he got killed.'

'Shame a lot of people got killed,' Freda said soberly, but their sadness didn't last long. People were trying to put the war behind them now and look to the future. It didn't do any good to harp on the past. She waited while Jess got out the flowing, creamy fabric of the dress she was making for Rose and exclaimed over its beauty. 'It's going to look lovely, Jess! You were really lucky to get it. What colour's Maureen going to wear?'

'Blue. She wanted yellow, it's her colour really, but Rose didn't think it would go with the cream and I think she's right. And Maureen will look very nice in a pale blue frock. She can use it afterwards for school parties and that sort of thing.'

'So what do you want me to do?' Freda asked as Jess carefully folded the material and put it away.

'Well, if you could make some of the soup, it would be a big help. I wish we could give people a hot meal but you just can't do it at the hall, and we can't afford hotel prices.'

'Goodness me, no!' Freda exclaimed. 'People like us don't go in for all that, anyway. Soup and ham salad and apple pie sounds ideal. I'll pop in and see Annie and she can tell me what she wants me to do. She used to do catering, didn't she?'

Jess nodded. 'She worked at one of the big houses out at Alverstoke before the war – did all kinds of posh cooking for dinner-parties and things. Mind you, it gave her a few ideas. I remember when me and Rose were evacuated and she offered to give Frank his dinner of an evening. She gave him rice instead of potatoes and he nearly died of shock! Said he thought rice was for puddings – didn't seem right to eat it with stew.'

'My Tommy would have said just the same,' Freda said. 'And how are Olive and Derek getting on? And Betty, out in the country? It must be hard for her, with her hubby being blind.'

'Oh, they manage all right – you'd never know there was anything wrong. And there's a lot Dennis can do on the farm. Betty says he's a wonder with the animals; he can milk all the cows and he knows just how to handle the sheep when they're lambing. He says his hands are as good as eyes when it comes to that sort of work. And they've got three little girls now, you know, and he'll do anything for them. Happy as Larry, the lot of them.'

She wished she could say the same for Betty's sister, Olive and her husband Derek. They'd been so much in love when they'd got married early on in the war, but then he'd been away so much and Olive had joined the ATS and somehow things seemed to have changed. And it was a tragedy that Olive had never been able to have children. Annie and Jess both felt that the couple would have been a lot happier if they'd been able to start a family.

'It's not that they're always rowing, or anything,' Annie had said once. 'It's just that they're not as *close* as they used to be. I mean, you know how Olive used to go on in the first year or so, always talking about how much she missed him and how unfair it all was. But by the time he came home, she'd changed. It wasn't that she didn't love him, I'm sure of that, but there seemed to be some sort of barrier between them.'

'And you've no idea what it is?' Jess had asked, but her sister shrugged.

'I wouldn't say that. I've got my ideas – but I don't know anything for sure. She got a bit too friendly with that young soldier, Ray something-or-other, and I often wondered ... but there, he seemed to disappear off the scene so maybe I was reading too much into it. Anyway, it's years ago now and best forgotten.'

Jess thought of it only briefly now as she saw Freda out and turned back to get on with cooking the dinner. Maureen, who went to the Girls' Grammar School, would be home soon and Tim, who was finishing his apprenticeship on the Gosport Ferry, wouldn't be long after, so Jess still liked to cook in the morning and always put up a plate-meal for Frank to take to work next day. Today, they were having rabbit stew, a favourite for them all.

Her thoughts returned to the wedding. The children were growing up so fast – Rose getting married, Keith already a Petty Officer in the Royal Navy, and Tim talking about joining the Merchant Navy. Soon it would be just her, Frank and Maureen. It would seem funny to be such a small family again.

It was the right way for life to go, she thought. Families growing up and going their own ways, making their own lives. It was what you wanted for them when they were tiny babies, what you brought them up to do. There was sadness in seeing the changes, but pride and happiness too. As long as everything went well.

Like most women, Jess wanted passionately for everything to go well for her family.

Chapter Three

Southampton

Ruth's niece, Lizzie Warren, had also had a letter, but it was not as welcome as a wedding invitation. In fact, it was not welcome at all, and she stood frozen at the kitchen table for several minutes, staring at words that seemed to have no meaning.

'Floyd ... coming *here?*' she whispered at last. 'But why? He said he wouldn't interfere – he *promised*. Why is he coming back now?'

Lizzie and her husband Alec lived in Southampton, not far from Alec's parents, who were distantly related to the Warrens at Bridge End. They had moved there from the village after the war, when Alec had decided he could never go to sea again and had found a job in the docks, working on the refitting of the great liners that were now back in service, crossing the Atlantic. They lived in a tiny house with two rooms downstairs and two upstairs, with a scullery tacked on at the back and a lavatory outside. It was very similar to the house in which Jess and Frank Budd lived, in Portsmouth.

Just lately, they'd been talking about trying to find something bigger. They needed another bedroom, with a boy and a girl already and another baby on the way, but houses with three bedrooms cost more to rent and were usually further away from the docks. Alec would have to travel to get to work.

'I can use the bus,' he said when they discussed it. 'Or go on my bike. Plenty of blokes do that.'

They had applied for a council house too, and the arrival of a new baby would put them higher up the list. There were large estates being built, and the prefabricated 'Phoenix' houses that had been erected after the war to house all the people who had been bombed out or had spent the war sharing their families' homes, were still in use. Even though they were only meant to be temporary, they were very popular and the people who lived in them were reluctant to be moved. Lizzie and Alec might have qualified for one of those if they had lived in Southampton all their lives, but since they had begun their married life at Bridge End they were at the bottom of the list when they joined it.

'It would be lovely if we could get a house before the baby's born,' Lizzie had said wistfully. 'Those council houses have proper bathrooms, you know. It would make such a difference to have a real bath instead of bringing the tin one in every Saturday night, and washing the children in the sink.'

Lizzie had plenty to think about, but the letter drove it all from her mind.

All morning, she worried about it, until eventually she could stand it no longer and decided to go out to Bridge End to see Ruth. Alec wouldn't be home until after six, so there was plenty of time. She dressed the children in the warm coats her mother had made them and caught the bus at the end of the street.

'Are we going to see Silver?' Gillie asked.

'I hope so,' Lizzie said, but when they reached Ruth's cottage there was nobody at home. She bit her lip and then walked up the track to her father's farm. She would have to talk to her mother instead and, although Jane had accepted the situation, Lizzie knew that she had never quite got over her disappointment that her daughter had behaved so badly.

'Hullo,' Jane said as she saw them open the gate. She was

out in the yard, feeding the hens, and she put down her bucket to hold out her arms for the children. 'This is a nice surprise. Have you come to tea?'

'We need to catch the bus back at half-past five,' Lizzie said, 'but I'd like a cup of tea. The children can feed the hens for you now, can't they?'

Jane gave her daughter a curious look. 'Is something the matter?'

'No. Well, yes. I don't know really.' Lizzie brushed her hair back with trembling fingers. 'I just wanted to come home for the afternoon and – and talk to you,'

'You're not ill, are you?' Jane said quickly, coming closer. 'You're looking a bit peaky.'

'No, I'm fine. It's just – let's go inside, Mum. The children will be all right out here.'

The two women went into the farmhouse and Jane settled her daughter in the old rocking-chair by the range while she filled the kettle. She kept giving Lizzie sharp little glances. Eventually, she came and sat opposite her and said, 'What's up, love? You're looking like a ghost. Is it Alec?'

Lizzie shook her head miserably. 'No, it's not, but I don't know what he'll say when he finds out.'

'Finds out what? Lizzie, what have you done now?'

At that, her daughter's temper flared. 'I haven't done anything! Why do you immediately think it's me who's in the wrong? Anyway, it's nothing like that at all.' Her flash of temper died away and she looked down at her fingers, twisting themselves together in her lap. 'I had a letter,' she said quietly. 'From Floyd.' She took the envelope from her pocket.

Jane stared at it. 'From *Floyd*? But—'

'I know. We agreed I'd write to him every Christmas and he would only write back if he had something important to tell me, like if he was changing his address or – or getting married or something. And so far he never has written. But today ...' She stopped as her voice broke a little, then went on,

'He says he's coming to England. He's travelling over on the *Queen Elizabeth*, so he'll be putting in at Southampton, and he wants to see Gillie.'

There was a long silence. The kettle came to the boil and Jane got up automatically and made the tea. She fetched the milk from the larder, poured some into two cups, and took out a tin of biscuits. She laid everything out on the table, poured the tea and handed a cup to Lizzie before sitting down again. Neither of them spoke until she had taken her first sip.

'He wants to see Gillie?' she repeated at last. 'But surely he said he'd stay away?'

'I know, he did say that. He didn't think he'd be coming back to England, anyway. But now he's got some new job and wants to come over.'

'A job in England?'

'I don't think so, no. I think he's just coming for a visit. But he'll be in Southampton, Mum, and he wants to see Gillie, and I – I just don't know what to do.'

'What does Alec say?'

'He doesn't know yet. He'd gone to work before the letter arrived. Oh, Mum ...' Lizzie looked miserably at the sheet of paper between her fingers.

'Well, Alec does know about Floyd, doesn't he,' Jane said gently. 'It's not as if it's going to come as a shock.'

'Yes, of course he knows, and he's always treated Gillie like his own daughter. But she isn't – she's Floyd's – and I don't know how he's going to feel about this. It's going to bring it all back to him – all that awful time when he'd just come back from POW camp and he was so poorly and so miserable, and he couldn't – well, you know. And then finding out that I was expecting, and the baby couldn't possibly be his. He was really good about it in the end, but it wasn't easy for him, and I'm afraid ...' She stopped. 'If only I knew why Floyd had decided to come back. If only I knew what he meant to do.' She looked at her mother with dark, fearful eyes. 'Suppose he wants to tell her he's her father,' she whispered. 'Suppose he wants to take her back with him.'

'To *America*? Oh, surely not!'

'Well, it's where he lives, isn't it? He could do that. He's never got married – he doesn't have any other children. You know he wanted her from the minute he knew I was expecting. He wanted us both,' she added in a low voice.

Jane set her cup down hard. 'You're not going to go off with him, are you?'

'Of course I'm not! I love Alec, I always have. And we've got Barry, and …' She stopped abruptly. She'd almost said 'and the new one coming along', but she hadn't yet told her mother she was expecting again. She'd wanted to save the news for Christmas.

'You can't be thinking of giving Gillie up!'

'*No!* Oh, why do you have to jump to these awful conclusions?' Lizzie put her own cup down and pulled out her hanky. Tears were streaming down her face. 'How could I possibly give up my little girl? Don't you think any better of me than that?' She scrubbed blindly at her cheeks. 'I wish Auntie Ruth had been in. She would have understood.'

There was a moment's silence. Then Jane said a little stiffly, 'So you went to your Auntie Ruth's first, then, did you?'

'I knocked on her door, yes, but there was nobody there.'

'They've gone to Southampton to buy a wedding present for Rose Budd,' Jane told her. 'I'd have thought you'd know that, you two being so close.'

Lizzie sighed. 'Don't be like that, Mum. You know I only told Auntie Ruth about Gillie coming because she was a nurse.'

'And you hoped she might help you out. You'd have given your little girl up then, wouldn't you!'

Lizzie flinched. 'I was desperate, Mum. I didn't know which way to turn.'

'And you couldn't turn to me.' Jane met her daughter's

eyes for a moment and then her face softened. 'Well, that's water under the bridge, I suppose, and it's no use harking back to it. You've come to me now, even if I am only second best.' The bitter edge returned to her voice with the last words and Lizzie's face crumpled again.

'Mum, don't go on. You're not second best. But do you blame me, when you start accusing me of the most awful things before I've even had a chance to tell you how I feel? I came out here this afternoon because I needed to talk to someone who'd understand and listen to me, not because I wanted to be accused of leaving my husband or giving up my little girl.'

Jane bit her lip. 'I'm not accusing you. But what am I supposed to think? You were unfaithful to Alec, you know you were, and just when he was away going through the most awful time. He was ill for months when he came back, and then he had to face knowing what you'd done because you were expecting and couldn't pretend the baby was his. You were very lucky he decided to stay with you, and you know it.'

'Yes, I do know it!' Lizzie blazed. 'You don't have to tell me that, and you don't have to tell me Alec was ill – I know that better than anyone. And you're not supposed to *think* anything – you're supposed to *listen* to me. That's all I wanted. That's why I'd rather have seen Auntie Ruth – because she would have listened to me.' She got up, trembling. 'I'd better go. I'll call the children and we'll catch the bus back to Southampton.' She stalked to the door, her back stiff. Jane stared at her in dismay and then ran to catch at her arm.

'No, Lizzie, don't go like that. I'm sorry – I shouldn't have said those things. I suppose I was so upset at the time and it all came over me again for a minute. Sit down, there's a love, and drink your tea. Don't let's be bad friends. Let's talk about it and I'll listen properly this time.'

Lizzie hesitated, then turned quickly and the two women fell into each other's arms. Both were crying by now, and their

21

tears soaked the other's shoulders before Lizzie drew back and pulled out a hanky. She mopped her face, and smiled shakily at her mother.

'I'm sorry, too. It's just been going round and round in my head ever since the letter came. If only I knew what's in his mind, but I don't. He just says he wants to see Gillie, and that's all.'

'Well, perhaps, it *is* all he wants to do.' Jane led her daughter back to the rocking chair. 'Look, your tea's gone cold – let me get you another cup. Honestly, when you come to think about it, what else could he want? He can't take her back with him if he's coming over for something to do with his job. All it is, is that he's coming to Southampton and thinks it would be a good chance to see his little girl, that's all. He won't cause any trouble. He's not that sort, you know he isn't.'

Lizzie didn't answer. She was remembering Floyd's reaction when he'd found out that she was expecting his baby. He had very strong feelings about families, and he'd wanted to take them both back to America then. It had taken all her strength to refuse and stay with Alec.

She didn't dare tell her mother that, though. She didn't dare tell her that, despite her love for her husband, she was afraid that she might still be a little bit in love with the American who had stolen her heart during the war.

It wouldn't, in fact, have come as a complete surprise to Jane if she had. As Lizzie and the children walked away up the lane after tea, to catch the bus back to Southampton, she turned away from the door with a sigh. Truth to tell, she'd dreaded this moment for years. She'd never been convinced that Floyd Hanson would be satisfied with a letter once a year to tell him how his daughter was. A man who had fathered a child would either cut himself off completely or he'd want to keep in touch. And that didn't give the woman a chance to forget him. Neither was Lizzie the sort to forget that easily.

Jane sat down in the rocking-chair by the kitchen fire and stared thoughtfully into the flames, thinking over the events of six years ago. Lizzie had been married before the war began, and had waited faithfully for her husband Alec all through the anxious years when he'd been at sea in the Merchant Navy, travelling in convoys escorted by warships to bring food to Britain. Eventually, Alec's ship had been sunk; he had been taken prisoner and spent the rest of the war in a grim compound somewhere in Germany.

Lizzie had been almost desperate with fear and loneliness and, looking back, it was almost inevitable that she should turn to the young American airman who had come to the house every Sunday for dinner. There had been two of them, billeted out as many were to local homes – not to sleep or live there but simply to share a meal occasionally and be given a little home life as thanks for what they were doing to help win the war. Floyd and Lizzie had been friends from the start and it was through them that the square dances had been held at the air station nearby. As time had gone on, they'd grown closer but although Jane had worried a bit about it, she knew that neither had intended their friendship to go so far. Floyd was a decent man and Lizzie a faithful wife. It was the joy and release of VE Day, when everyone had gone a little mad, that had finally proved too much for them. And it was bad luck that their one fall from grace should have resulted in pregnancy.

Jane remembered the distraught look in her daughter's eyes when she had finally confessed the truth. She'd told her aunt first, because Ruth was a nurse and, in her despair, Lizzie had begged her to help her to rid herself of the baby. Ruth had been horrified at the idea but she had felt desperately sorry for the girl, especially as Alec had returned from prison camp in such a frail state. When Lizzie, unable to hide her pregnancy any longer, had finally told her mother, she had admitted that they hadn't even been able to make love. 'If we had,' she'd said miserably, 'I might even have thought this baby was his.

But I know it can't be – and so will he. Oh, Mum, what am I going to do?'

In the end, she'd been forced to tell him the truth. It had been hard for him to accept but he'd finally come round to the idea that this might be the only child they'd ever have, and agreed to accept it as his own. But even that had had its complications.

Floyd, who had gone away the day after VE Day, had come back. Unlike many men, he hadn't breathed a sigh of relief that he wouldn't have to take on the child and its mother. Instead, he had been genuinely in love with Lizzie and wanted to take her back to America. When she'd refused, he had made her promise to keep in touch so that he would know how his baby grew up. When Gillie was old enough, she was to be told the truth, so that she would know her true heritage. And because of that, the rest of the family had had to know, too.

To everyone else in the village, Alec was Gillie's father and even the family had almost forgotten that he wasn't. But now, as she stared into the flames, Jane wondered what was going to happen if Floyd did come back.

Would he still be happy for his daughter to stay in England, thinking of another man as her father, seeing him as a stranger?

Chapter Four

Sunday dinner was nearly ready in Lizzie and Alec's small house in Southampton.

'That smells good,' Alec declared, coming into the tiny lean-to scullery where Lizzie was just taking a casserole of brisket out of the gas oven. 'I hope we've got some mustard to go with that.'

'We've always got mustard,' she said, holding the dish with two folded teacloths. 'Oh bother, I've forgotten to put a mat on the table. Get one out for me, would you?'

Alec opened the middle drawer of the dresser and took out a cork mat. He put it on the green American cloth that covered the tiny kitchen table and Lizzie set the casserole on it. She took the lid off and the rich smell of beef and vegetables wafted into the air.

'Ahhh – Bisto!' her husband grinned, and stuck one arm out sideways as if he were in the advertisement that showed the 'Bisto Kids' standing in a row. 'Got lots of spuds? I'm starving.'

'You're always starving.' She fetched the plates and dished the food up on to them so that Alec could carry them through to the back room, where the square dining-table took up most of the space. Gillie and Barry were already sitting in their chairs, waiting. They had been to Sunday School that morning and would be going again in the afternoon, leaving Lizzie and Alec to enjoy almost the only real privacy they had all week. They usually took full advantage of it, slipping upstairs to their bedroom the moment the children had set off up the road with the older children next door. Lizzie had been uneasy about letting them go without her at first, but they only had to go a short way to the primary school where Sunday School was held, and young Jean Hayward was twelve and very responsible. And as Alec pointed out, it gave them a few more minutes to be on their own.

As soon as they were out of sight, he took Lizzie's wrist in his and drew her towards the stairs. She hesitated and he looked at her in surprise.

'Aren't you in the mood?'

'Yes, of course I am, but—' She stopped, took a breath and then went on rather quickly, 'There's something I have to talk to you about.'

'Well, can't we talk upstairs in bed?' he enquired good-humouredly, and then caught sight of her expression. His grin faded. 'What is it, Lizzie? There's nothing wrong, is there?' He touched her stomach. 'You haven't had any problems?'

'No, it's nothing like that.' She was over three months gone now, and her waist was beginning to thicken. 'I'm fine. It's something else.'

'Well, let's go upstairs anyway,' he said. 'We can just cuddle while you tell me what's up, and there'll still be time for you-know-what afterwards.'

If you still want it then, Lizzie thought, following him up the narrow staircase. She would much rather have stayed downstairs to tell him about Floyd's letter. It was a long time since they had mentioned him. Alec knew that she wrote every Christmas, of course, but she never talked about it and, apart from that, they'd almost forgotten that Alec wasn't Gillie's true father. Now, the truth was about to rear its head again and she knew that it must hurt him to remember that the little girl he loved as his own was really no relation at all. And, worse, that she was the result of Lizzie's own unfaithfulness.

In the bedroom, Alec unbuttoned her blouse and slipped it

26

from her shoulders. Lizzie felt the tears come to her eyes and put her hands on his wrists to stop him. 'Don't, Alec. Let's just sit on the bed and talk.'

'Lizzie, what on earth is it? You're scaring me.' He put his arm around her shoulders to draw her down beside him. 'Something's really wrong, isn't it? Tell me.'

Lizzie looked into his eyes, then away again, hating the anxiety she saw there. 'It's not me or the baby, Alec. There's nothing the matter there. But – well, yesterday I had a letter.' Her voice quavered and she stopped, staring down at her skirt and pleating it between her fingers.

'A letter? Who from?'

'From Floyd,' she whispered, and felt his stillness. She turned her head so that she could see his face. 'Alec, he's coming to Southampton. He wants to see Gillie.'

There was a moment of complete silence. Then Alec said slowly, as if he didn't quite understand the words, 'He's coming *here*? He wants to see *Gillie*? But—'

'I know. He promised he wouldn't interfere. But he says he's got a new job and he'll be coming over to England on one of the *Queen*s. And since he'll be here ... He says that's all it is. He won't want—'

'Won't want what?' Alec said harshly when she stopped again. 'Won't want to take her away? Well, he couldn't do that anyway. She's yours – ours. He's got no rights over her at all.'

'He's her father.'

'*I'm* her father. My name's on her birth certificate. He can't take her away, whatever he may think.'

'He doesn't want to – I'm sure he doesn't. He just wants to see her.'

'He was supposed to wait until she was grown up and then only if she wants to see him – not the other way about.'

'I know,' Lizzie said miserably. 'It's because of this new job. He thinks it's a good chance.'

27

'Well, it's not. You'd better write back straight away and tell him so. He's not coming here, upsetting us all when we're all right without him.' Alec's eyes narrowed a little. 'You don't *want* to see him, do you, Lizzie?'

'No!' she exclaimed, too quickly. 'No, I don't. I really don't.' But she felt his body stiffen.

'You do,' he said in a toneless voice. 'You might as well admit it. And that's why' his voice shook a little, 'that's why you don't want to make love with me.'

'*No!*' she cried again, suddenly frightened. It was years since she had seen that look in his eyes, heard that coldness in his voice – not since those dark days when he had first come home from the war, a broken man, first unable to make love to his own wife and then faced with the evidence of her unfaithfulness. 'Alec, no, you mustn't think that. It's you I love – you know that. It always was.' She turned and clung to him, but his arms were like pieces of wood and his body unresponsive. 'You don't think I'd leave you now. You can't think that.'

'How do I know?' he asked. 'You nearly did before. And what have I got to offer you, anyway? A tiny house in a backstreet in Southampton, not even big enough for the children we've got now. Whereas he's a rich Yankee, who could give you everything you want.'

'No, he couldn't.' Frantic now, she began to unbutton his shirt, pressing herself against the rough warmth of his chest. 'Alec, please. Let's get into bed now. Let's love each other properly. You were right – it's where we should have been in the first place.' She began to kiss his face. 'Please, Alec.'

But he shook his head, and to her dismay, began to do up his buttons again; then he pushed her away and stood up. His face was averted but she could see his expression in the dressing-table mirror and it was like looking at a stranger.

'No,' he said. 'I don't reckon it's a good idea after all. I've got to think about this, Lizzie. And so have you. I thought we

28

were all right together. I thought we were safe. But we're not, are we?' He turned suddenly and stared down at her, his eyes black. 'You can't fool me, I know you too well. You *want* to see this man again. I know you do.' There was a long pause and then he said abruptly, 'I'm going for a walk.'

'Alec!' she cried as he put his hand on the doorknob. 'Alec, don't go!' And, as he went through the door, 'You – you are coming back, aren't you?'

'Of course I am,' he said, pausing to look back at her with those awful eyes. 'I live here, don't I?'

He shut the door behind him and Lizzie heard his footsteps going down the stairs. She then heard him open the cupboard door and get out his coat. Then the front door opened and closed, and the last thing she heard was his footsteps walking quickly away along the street.

She fell back on the bed, turned over and began to cry. But even in the midst of her fear, she knew that he had spoken the truth.

Deep down inside her, she did want to see Floyd again.

There was no time to talk any further until late that evening, after the children were in bed. Lizzie and Alec sat in their chairs on either side of the fireplace, listening to the music of *Grand Hotel* on the wireless, Lizzie knitting and Alex staring at the newspaper. Eventually, plucking up all her courage, Lizzie said, 'You're not reading that, Alec. You haven't turned the page once.'

'I'm reading an interesting article,' he said stiffly.

'You're not. Please, Alec, put it down and listen to me.' He didn't move and, suddenly angry, she reached out and jerked it from his hands. Alec tried to snatch it back, but she whipped it out of his reach and he scowled at her.

'What did you do that for?'

'Because you weren't listening. Alec, we can't go on like this. We've got to talk about it.'

'About what?' he asked, and she sighed impatiently.

'You know very well what I mean. About Floyd, of course. Look, I think you ought to read his letter.'

'I don't want to read his damned letter!' Alec snapped, but Lizzie went to the sideboard drawer, took out an envelope with an American stamp on it and held it out to him. After a moment he took it grudgingly.

'Go on,' she said gently. 'Read it. See exactly what he says, and then we'll talk about it.'

Alec glowered at her but took out the single sheet of paper. His expression didn't change as he scanned the few lines of handwriting, then folded the letter and pushed it roughly back into the envelope. 'All right, I've read it. Now what?'

'Well, you can see he doesn't mean to cause trouble. It's just as I told you – he's coming to Southampton and he'd like to see Gillie. And that's all there is to it.'

'Oh yes? Who are you trying to kid, Lizzie? Because you're not fooling me, and you're not fooling yourself either. He might want to see Gillie, but he wants to see you too. And you want to see him. That's the worst of it.'

Lizzie looked down at her knitting. Tears blurred her eyes and one fell on to the wool. She bit her lip hard, took a deep breath and tried to keep her voice steady.

'Alec, I don't know what I think any more. I know that when I read his letter yesterday morning, I was frightened. I knew straight away it was going to make trouble. I went out to see Auntie Ruth—'

'You went to see your aunt? You didn't tell me that.'

'Well, you would have asked why, wouldn't you? Anyway, she wasn't there – they'd gone shopping. I saw Mum instead.'

'I see. So *she* knows all about this too, does she? It was bad enough that you had to tell them all about Gillie in the first place, because *he* said you'd got to, but if you're going to go running back there every time ...' Alec was on his feet and

30

stood irresolute, half-inclined to leave the room yet unwilling to leave the argument.

'Stop it, Alec!' Lizzie felt her own temper rise. 'You know I don't do that. Look, it's six years since all that happened and I've never gone running to my mother about anything, in all that time. We've got Barry and now another baby coming – we live our own life. But you weren't here and I needed someone to talk to, someone who'd understand, that's all.'

'And did your mother understand?' he asked sceptically.

'I'm not sure. In the end, I think she did. But that was why I wanted to see Auntie Ruth, because I knew she *would* understand. This isn't easy for me, you know, Alec.'

He looked at her properly for the first time since she had told him about the letter, and his mouth creased a little. He lifted his shoulders in a sigh and sat down heavily. 'All right, Lizzie. You'd better tell me what you want to do about it. Do you want him to come here? D'you want Gillie to know he's her father?'

'No, of course I don't. She's barely six years old – how can we tell her that you're not her daddy, and expect her to understand that this strange man is, instead. He agreed that we should wait until she's grown up, so that she could decide for herself if she wanted to meet him. I still think that's best.'

'So he's breaking the agreement.'

'Well, not really.' Lizzie took the letter out of the envelope again. 'He doesn't say that, does he? He says he just wants to see her.'

'And how's he going to do that? Lurk around the street corner and wait for her to come out of school? Or does he think you ought to invite him to tea? Because I'll tell you straight, Lizzie, I don't want him in my house. It might be six years or more since it happened, but it *did* happen. You can't expect me to welcome him with open arms.'

'I know, love. I think you've been wonderful, taking to Gillie the way you have.'

'I think of her as mine,' he said shortly. 'And she thinks of me as her daddy. I hope he realises that.'

'I'm sure he does. He must do. He doesn't want to spoil things.'

'So what does he want to come here for, upsetting us all?' Alec burst out. 'He must have known it would cause trouble. I'm sorry, Lizzie, but I think there's more in this than meets the eye. If he really did want to let Gillie grow up happy in England, he'd keep out of the way. He wouldn't *do* this.'

'He just thinks it's a good chance to—'

'A good chance for him! Not for anyone else. And who's to say it's only going to be once? We don't know what this job of his is – he might be coming over regularly, maybe several times a year. Will he want to see Gillie every time? He's not going to be satisfied with seeing her come out of school, I can tell you that. He'll be wanting to talk to her – to get to know her. *He'll soon be wanting her to know who he is.*'

Lizzie could find no answer. She knew that Alec could well be right. And she knew, too, that he was right about Floyd's other, hidden motive. He wanted to see Lizzie. He wanted to know that she and their daughter were happy, and if he thought they weren't ... But that's not going to happen, she told herself fiercely. We *are* happy. Alec's a good husband and a good father. We've got a good marriage, and I'm not going to let anything spoil it.

She reached over and took his hand. 'I'll write back and tell him we don't want him to come. I'll ask him to keep to the agreement – that we'll tell Gillie when she's twenty-one. Until then ...'

'You can't do that,' Alec interrupted. 'It's too late. Your Floyd's been very clever about this. Look at what he says. He's going to spend Christmas with his sister, somewhere in New York State. By the time you write back, he'll have left home. The *Queen Elizabeth* will be on her way from New York

32

to Southampton soon after Christmas, and he'll be aboard her. You don't have any way of contacting him until he knocks on our door.'

Chapter Five

Burracombe, South Devon

Stella Simmons, the young schoolteacher in the village of Burracombe on the edge of Dartmoor, was surprised and delighted to open her own invitation for Rose Budd's wedding. She showed it to her landlady, Dottie Friend.

'The Budds were the people who were so kind to us after we lost our mother. They took me and Muriel in until Daddy could make other arrangements for us.' She laughed at herself. 'Listen to me, calling her Muriel! It's ages since I did that – it must be because I was thinking of when we were both children.' Her voice saddened a little and Dottie gave her arm a sympathetic pat.

'You never get over losing your parents, my bird, especially when you lost 'em so young. I know little Maddy used to cry herself to sleep often when she was stopping with me. Of course, she'd lost you as well, so she had plenty to cry for, poor little mite. It was cruel, the way you were separated during the war.'

'Well, we've found each other again now,' Stella said. 'We must have a guardian angel, to end up in your cottage the way we both did, years apart. We'll never lose each other again.'

''Tis a happy ending all round,' Dottie said. 'I wonder if Maddy will have been invited to the wedding as well.'

'Oh, I'm sure she will. I gave Auntie Jess her address in West Lyme so she knows where to send it. Isn't it kind of them to invite us, Dottie? It's not as if we were family, and they're not all that well off.'

'You were evacuated with their boys for a while, though, weren't you?' Dottie asked. 'At the village near Southampton, wasn't it?'

'That's right – Bridge End. We lived with the vicar. Really, we saw more of the boys than we did of Rose – more than she saw of them herself, probably. Well, it's lovely to be invited but of course I won't be able to go.'

'Why ever not?' Dottie asked in surprise.

'Because the school term will have started again. I could go by train on Saturday, I suppose, but the wedding's at two in the afternoon and I'm not sure I could get there by then. And I'd have to come back the next day.' She looked wistfully at the invitation. 'It's a shame, I'd love to see them all again.'

'Why not go on the Friday evening, after school?' Dottie suggested. 'I'm sure there'd be a train. Or you could ask Felix to take you as far as West Lyme in that little car of his, and go on from there with Maddy. She could put you up for the night in her little flat, couldn't she?'

'Well, it is a *very* little flat,' Stella said with a smile, 'but I could sleep on the sofa. That's a good idea, Dottie. I'll ask him.'

Felix was the curate at Burracombe Church, and due to be installed as vicar for the neighbouring parish of Little Burracombe at Easter. He and Stella had announced their engagement a week earlier, but it would be some time before they would be married, and meanwhile Stella was enjoying being engaged and wearing her solitaire diamond ring.

'Of course I'll take you to West Lyme,' he said when she told him about the invitation. 'We can go on Friday evening and I can stay with my uncle.' Felix's uncle was the Archdeacon of West Lyme and Maddy was his secretary. 'I wish I could come to the wedding with you, but I'll have to be back for Sunday services.'

35

'I know. Anyway, you're not invited – I haven't told Auntie Jess about you yet. I was going to put a note in with my Christmas cards. I'll tell her she doesn't have to feel obliged to invite you too, although I expect she will.' Stella looked at the invitation again. 'I'll have to think of something to buy for a wedding present.'

'Don't get a toast-rack,' Felix advised her. 'When my cousin got married she was given six! I often wonder why people don't just make out a list and pass it round so that people know just what they need.'

'Because it would look rude, I suppose. Like asking for things in return for being invited. I'll ask Auntie Jess – she's bound to know what they need. I'll have to decide what to wear, too. My Sunday costume isn't smart enough for a wedding.'

'You always look very nice in it,' Felix said. 'I like that furry bit on the collar.'

'Micky Coker says it looks as if something had crawled up my neck and died,' she said, and he gave a shout of laughter.

'Trust Micky Coker! Well, it looks as if you'll have to go on a shopping trip. Why not try the January sales? Get Val to go with you.'

'I might, at that. Anyway, the important thing is that I can go to the wedding – I'll write to Auntie Jess straight away.' She gave him a quick, excited kiss. 'It's going to be lovely to see everyone again – all the April Grove people I remember from when we lived there after we were bombed out of our own house, and perhaps even some of the people from Bridge End as well. If they've invited Maddy and me, they're bound to have invited them. I know Auntie Jess and Uncle Frank go out there quite often.'

'It's going to be a real reunion,' Felix said. 'I hope she'll invite me too. I'd really like to meet all these people from your past.'

'I'd like you to meet them too,' she said. 'Maybe at our own wedding.'

'That's ages away. I want to meet them now,' he said.

'I don't see why you shouldn't have a weekend off,' Basil Harvey, the vicar of Burracombe said when Felix told him about the invitation. 'You've worked very hard all this year. I'm sure we can get someone to come and take the Little Burracombe services – someone retired, perhaps. There's John Marchwood from Whitchurch, he likes to take a service now and then although his sermons are inclined to be a bit long.'

'You mean he goes on and on and on,' Felix said with a grin. 'Well, that's all right. It'll make them appreciate me all the more when I come back the next week. So I can take Stella to West Lyme on the Friday evening and we can travel back on Sunday. I'm not sure we can all three squeeze into Mirabelle to go to Portsmouth, though – the dickey seat's a bit cramped for a long journey. We'll have to take the train for that bit.'

Stella agreed. 'We'll be in our best clothes too, don't forget, and Maddy's bound to wear something glamorous. She won't want to be squashed up at the back. And isn't the roof still leaking?'

'Only a bit.' Mirabelle was Felix's little sports car, given to him by his uncle; the folding top had a few cracks now that let in water in just the most inconvenient places. 'Well, as long as you don't mind wearing a mac to go as far as West Lyme?'

'I don't mind at all. It'll be lovely to go away for a weekend, and to have a wedding as well and meet so many old friends – not that most of them will remember me and Maddy – but there'll be the Budds and the Chapmans, and then the people from Bridge End if they're going. It'll be such fun. I'm looking forward to it already.'

Before the wedding, however, there was Christmas to be celebrated in all three places.

In Portsmouth, the residents of April Grove went to church

and enjoyed Christmas dinners such as they had never had during the dark days of the Second World War, and then kept up their family parties until the early hours of the morning. The Budds had another party on Boxing Day, with both Tim and Keith at home and some of their friends coming round for the evening. Rose's fiancé Ken was there too, since his own home in Scotland was too far to go, and they played charades and Family Coach and Stations until they were all exhausted with laughter and lay about in chairs or on cushions in the little front room, begging for a rest.

'We'll have a drink,' Jess declared. 'Cider for anyone who wants it, except Maureen, of course. You can have orange squash.'

'Oh, Mum!' Maureen protested. 'Why can't I have cider too? It's much nicer than orange squash.'

'It's alcoholic,' Frank said sternly. He was very nearly a tee-totaller and wouldn't allow beer or spirits into the house. He and Jess, and now the older children, treated themselves to a glass of sherry before their Christmas dinner and a small glass of port afterwards, and they would probably have another one on New Year's Eve and occasionally when they had visitors, but apart from that the bottles would stay in their cupboard. In fact, he hadn't realised for a long time that bottled cider was alcoholic and all the children, even Maureen, had been allowed it with their Sunday dinner. After he'd found out, they'd had to have Cydrax, which tasted much the same but didn't have quite the pleasant, warming feeling of proper cider and didn't make Frank feel sleepy on Sunday afternoons when he wanted to be working on his allotment.

'It's not very alcoholic,' Maureen argued. 'You always used to let me have it.' But her father gave her a look and she remembered that this was Christmas and she hated being told off at Christmas, so she subsided. And Jess produced a bottle of Tizer, which was nearly as good, and Rose had a glass of that too, for company.

In Burracombe, Stella and Maddy attended the early service at St Andrews and received Holy Communion from Felix's hands, and then went across the river to Little Burracombe where he was taking Matins. As they walked across the narrow wooden bridge they could hear the bells of both churches ringing out in the frosty air and Stella thought for a moment of their own wedding, sometime in the future. The bells of both churches would ring for them then, too.

'It's lovely to be here for Christmas,' Maddy said dreamily. 'Do you know, I haven't spent Christmas in Burracombe since I was fifteen years old. Fenella started to take me to Switzerland as soon as it was easier to travel after the war, and we went skiing. We used to go to Wengen – they've got little trains there that go right up the mountain, and you can ski all the way back to the village. And the village itself is lovely – every single house looks like a musical box. I used to want to lift up the lids to hear them play!'

'That sounds wonderful,' Stella said. 'Don't you wish you were there now?'

'Of course I don't!' Maddy said, squeezing her sister's arm. 'Well, I might, if you could be there, too. But I'm happy to be here in Burracombe with all my friends.'

'I'm glad Uncle Ambrose gave you Christmas off,' Felix remarked. 'I did wonder if he'd say you had to stay in West Lyme and have a week later on.'

'Of course he didn't. He knows how much it means for me to be with Stella. Anyway, the office is closed over Christmas so there wouldn't be any work for me to do. And besides ...' she glanced at Stella and pressed her lips together in a mischievous smile, so that the dimples showed in her cheeks '... Stephen's home on leave and I can't miss the party at the Barton tomorrow night.'

Stella laughed. 'I thought there must be some other attraction. So you've been keeping in touch with him?'

'We write to each other now and then,' Maddy said off-

39

handedly, and then grinned. 'Of course I have! You don't think I'm going to let an attractive man like Stephen Napier get away, do you?'

'You'd better be careful,' Stella advised her. 'Hilary says he's still thinking of emigrating to Canada when he comes out of the RAF. I'm not sure I want you going so far away, when we've only just found each other again.'

'Oh, there's a lot of water to go under the bridge before we get to that stage,' Maddy said comfortably. 'If we ever do. All I want at the moment is to enjoy myself. I'm not going to be tied down for a long time yet.'

Stella smiled, and held Felix's hand. She was very happy to be tied down. But Maddy had lived in a different world during the years she had spent with the actress Fenella Forsyth, who had adopted her as a child. She had travelled all over Europe and met many different people. In many ways, although the younger of the two, she was far more sophisticated than Stella would ever be.

After the service they went back to Burracombe to enjoy Christmas dinner with the vicar and his family. Dottie was working behind the bar at the pub and they'd promised to go back to her cottage for tea. In the evening, they were all invited up to the Tozers' farm for a large, jolly party in the big parlour, with a roaring fire that would roast them all as they sat around, cracking hazelnuts gathered from the hedgerows in the autumn and singing the old songs of Devon that they loved so much – 'Widecombe Fair', 'Devon, Glorious Devon' and 'Drake's Drum'.

'Drake, he was a Devon man an' ruled the seven seas,
(Capten, art thou sleepin' thar below?)'

Ted Tozer sang the words in his fine baritone voice and the others joined in with the second line of each verse.

> *'Rovin' tho' his death fell, he went wi' heart at ease,*
> *An dreamin' arl the time o' Plymouth Hoe ...'*

Then they went on to 'Admiral Benbow', moved down to Cornwall for 'Trelawney' and finished up with a rousing selection of sea-shanties, during which Felix introduced them to some verses of 'What Shall We Do With A Drunken Sailor?' that none of them, even Tom Tozer, had ever heard before.

'They'm not rude, exactly,' Alice Tozer observed, wiping tears of laughter from her eyes, 'but they'm not quite what you'd expect from a vicar, either.'

'I'm not a vicar yet, though,' Felix pointed out. 'Not until Easter. I expect I'll learn to behave myself then.'

'I'll be very surprised if you do,' Stella told him wryly. 'I don't think you'll ever learn to behave yourself.'

In the village of Bridge End, the festivities had started on Christmas Eve, with half the village going out to sing carols to the other half. Sammy carried Linnet round the village on his shoulders and made sure, as they all crowded into the Knights' big farmhouse kitchen, that she was supplied with a cup of cocoa and a mince pie which she ate sitting on his knee by the fire that burned in the inglenook.

'They make a good picture, don't they?' Dan's voice said in Ruth's ear and she nodded and slipped her hand through his arm.

'I was just thinking that myself. We're lucky, aren't we, Dan, to have such a nice little family?' She saw a shadow cross his face and added quickly, 'It would be perfect if we could only have your Gordon here too.'

'I dunno that it would, to be honest,' he said. 'Gordon was always a worry to me and his mother, as you know. I dunno how he'd have fitted in out here at Bridge End. In fact, if you want the truth, I don't think he'd have even tried. I think if he hadn't got killed in the war, he'd have been one of those

41

chaps who cuts himself off from his family and goes his own way. I've said it before and I'll say it again, though it hurts me to say it – I'm glad he died a hero, because I'm not at all sure he'd have lived like one.'

'Oh, Dan,' Ruth said in distress, but he shook his head firmly.

'You don't have to upset yourself about it, love. It's all behind us now, though I don't suppose you ever really get over losing a child, but at least I know Gordon enjoyed his time in the Army. It suited him, that life, and not everyone's that lucky, you know. A lot of people have to sweat away all their lives at jobs they hate.'

Like you used to, Ruth thought. Dan had been one of the lucky ones, able to leave his job in the shipyard to come out to Bridge End and join Solly Barlow in his blacksmith's forge. The thought reminded her of Sammy and his plan to leave Solly and study for – what was it? – radar and electronics instead. She still felt torn in two directions over that – proud of Sammy for wanting to better himself, and being clever enough to do it, and worried about how Dan would take the news.

Dan moved away to talk to old Arthur Knight, and Ruth found her niece Lizzie at her side. Lizzie and Alec had come out to stay with Jane and George over Christmas. Ruth smiled at Lizzie.

'Are you all right? You look a bit tired,' she remarked, and Lizzie blushed.

'I'm having another baby. But don't say anything – we're going to tell the family at Christmas dinner tomorrow. And Mum'll never forgive me if she knows I told you first.'

'Oh, Lizzie, that *is* good!' Ruth gave her a quick kiss. 'What are you hoping for this time?'

'We don't mind. We've got our pigeon pair already, so it doesn't really matter.' Lizzie hesitated, then added, 'Well, maybe if I'm honest I'd like another little girl, for Alec. But as long as it's healthy ...'

'... that's all that counts,' Ruth finished for her, still feeling a little anxious about her niece. There was a shadow in her eyes that surely ought not to be there on such a happy occasion. 'Well, your mother will be thrilled. And so will Gillian. I daresay she'll be hoping for a sister to play with.'

'She will. She'll still want to come out here and play with Linnet, though. They're like sisters themselves. Make sure you come up to the farm as early as you can tomorrow, Auntie Ruth, she'll be on tenterhooks to show Linnet her presents. She's having a doll's pram, you know.'

Lizzie spoke lifelessly, as though reciting words that didn't really have much meaning, and Ruth's anxiety increased. She wondered if there was something wrong between Lizzie and Alec. Now she came to think of it, they did seem a little cool with each other, not standing together for the carol-singing and now at opposite ends of the room. But that was silly! Of course everything must be all right, with this good news.

'Linnet's having a doll's house,' she said. 'Dan's been busy every evening after she's gone to bed, making it in Dad's old shed at the bottom of the garden. They'll be hard put to it to know which to play with first!'

The party ended soon after that. Everyone knew they'd be up early next morning, starting on the Christmas dinner or helping children to open their stockings. Linnet was just old enough now to remember last Christmas, and had been told enough this year to be convinced that even now an old man in a red suit and white beard was flying across the sky in a toy-laden sleigh drawn by magical reindeer. Sammy himself had spent the afternoon wrapping her presents, while she was up at the farmhouse helping her Auntie Jane to make mince pies. Apart from the doll's house, they were hidden in one of Ruth's old stockings and a pillowcase, underneath his bed. The matching stocking would be hung empty on her bed that night and Dan, who insisted that this job was his, would creep in early next morning to exchange them.

43

Dan lifted the sleeping Linnet into his arms and they went out into the cold night. Ruth looked up at the stars and then smiled around at her family.

'Another happy Christmas at Bridge End,' she said softly. 'A wedding to look forward to, and then the Coronation. Nineteen fifty-three is going to be a good year – I feel it in my bones.'

But even as she spoke, she remembered the shadow in Lizzie's eyes and a shiver touched her skin. Could *any* year be good for everybody?

Chapter Six

To everyone's relief, after a cold start January turned mild and Rose Budd's wedding-day didn't bring snow or even the biting winds that Jess had feared as she sewed the long, lacy veil her daughter would wear up the aisle. Maureen grumbled that her bare arms would be all goose-pimples as she stood outside the church for the photographs, but Jess brushed aside her complaints and promised to take the new bolero that Annie had knitted her for Christmas, for her to put on afterwards. It was pale blue in a lacy stitch that looked nice over the satin dress, and Annie had knitted it specially, foreseeing that it would be needed.

Rose and Ken looked happy as they came down the aisle, and the guests filed out behind them to stand shivering (a mild day in January was still pretty cold, as Tommy Vickers remarked to his wife) while Colin Chapman took photographs. Colin had always been keen on photography, from the days before the war when he used to spend hours on the little turret on top of the Chapmans' house, snapping the streets and allotments with his Box Brownie. When he came out of the Army and recovered from his sojourn in a Japanese prisoner-of-war camp, he had decided to buy himself a good camera and set himself up as a photographer. He now had his own studio in Copnor Road, where he lived with his wife Sue and their two children.

Ruth and Dan stood with Sammy and Linnet, looking round at the other guests. There weren't many from Bridge

45

End, apart from themselves and the Greenaways, with whom Jess and Rose had been billeted in the early days of the war. Ruth hadn't really expected to see many other familiar faces. However, two young women standing at the other side of the little crowd caught her eye, and she stared at them before giving a sudden exclamation.

'Surely that's Stella and Muriel Simmons! I always thought they were separated and lost track of each other. It *is* them, isn't it?'

'I think it is,' Sammy said, following her gaze. He grinned. 'Muriel and me used to get up to all sorts of tricks.'

'You don't have to tell me that,' Ruth said tartly. 'Which is which? Muriel was the younger one, wasn't she? I always thought Stella was like a little mother to her.'

'That's right. Muriel's the one with the fair hair.' He looked again at the two girls. 'She's pretty, isn't she? I wonder who the bloke is with them. He's got a dog-collar on – must be a vicar. I wonder why he's come.'

'We'll get a chance to say hello once we get to the reception,' Ruth said. 'I dare say there are quite a few people here you know too, Dan.'

'There's Tommy Vickers and his missus. You know them, Sam – they were really good to us after your mother died. And Mrs Chapman and her old man, Ted. And that's Bert Shaw – blimey, he's aged. I suppose that young woman in the red hat's his girl, Gladys. She married Freda Vickers's nevvy, if I remember right. The other one went off to America to marry some GI.' Dan stared around, gradually recalling names and faces. It was nearly eight years since he'd left April Grove and he'd never known the street all that well, but after his wife Nora had died, a number of them had come to his aid. He hadn't appreciated their help at the time, but he realised now just what good neighbours he had had.

Sammy was still looking at the Simmons sisters and trying to remember what had happened to them after their father had been killed at sea. It had all seemed rather queer at the time. Tim and Keith Budd had told him that a woman who looked like a brown settee had come to the vicarage and taken them both away to Children's Homes. Tim had said that Mr Beckett had tried hard to get the settee woman to let them stay with him, but she'd said it wasn't suitable – why it was suitable when their father was alive but not after he'd died, Tim didn't know – and she'd also said it was better for them to go to different Homes and not even write to each other. The vicar had been really upset, and Sammy had heard Ruth say once that she was sure it had helped bring on his heart attack. After that, Tim and Keith had gone back to Portsmouth and nobody had heard any more of the two orphan girls.

As soon as they reached the church hall and had been given a glass of sweet sherry each, he made for the corner where they were talking to Olive Harker. Stella went on chatting as he hesitated, but Muriel turned and looked at him, her face puzzled. Then her eyes cleared and she exclaimed: 'Sammy! Sammy Hodges! It *is* you, isn't it?'

'Yes,' he said, feeling his fair skin blush. 'Yes, and you're Muriel, aren't you?'

'Not any longer,' she said, her dimples showing. 'I'm called Maddy now. Oh, Sammy, how lovely! I didn't expect to see you here. Haven't you grown tall?' She turned and touched her sister's sleeve. 'Look, Stella, it's Sammy Hodges. You remember him, don't you? He lived at number two, and then he went out to Bridge End to live with Mrs Purslow. Is she here too?'

'Yes, she's over there. She's my stepmother now. She and my Dad got married after the war.'

'Did they? Goodness me! And is that their little girl?'

'Linnet, yes. She's my sister,' he said proudly.

'Your *sister*! My goodness. And you had a brother too, didn't you? A big boy – I remember him in April Grove. He used to go about with Micky Baxter.'

'He got killed,' Sammy said. 'In the war. He was in the Army.'

'Oh,' Maddy said, her smile fading. 'I'm sorry about that. I suppose nearly everyone lost someone during the war.'

Sammy remembered that Maddy and Stella had lost their mother and baby brother when a bomb struck their house one night, during the Blitz. And when their father had died, they had had no one.

'I thought they took you and Stella away to different Children's Homes,' he said. 'Tim Budd told me you weren't going to be able to see each other any more, but I suppose he got that wrong. He used to get a lot of things wrong, I remember.'

'He did,' Stella said, joining in the conversation. 'He used to listen to the first half of the story and make up the rest! But he was right about that, as it happens. Maddy and I didn't find each other until just over a year ago. She'd been adopted and then billeted in the very same village where I went two years ago to be a teacher – what do you think of *that* for a coincidence?'

'Even Tim Budd couldn't have made that up,' Sammy agreed. 'So where was that, then? Anywhere near Bridge End?'

Maddy shook her head so that her gleaming golden curls danced. 'No, it's in Devon – a little place called Burracombe. Stella's still there but I live in West Lyme now.'

'Oh.' He felt a stab of disappointment and glanced at the tall young man with the dog-collar, who was talking to Ruth Hodges. 'You're married, then.'

'No, I'm a secretary. I have to work for my living. And this is Stella's fiancé, Felix Copley – it's his uncle I work for.' She smiled and looked round at the little group. 'Isn't it lovely, meeting like this? I was just a little girl then, but I remember you all so well. Olive used to be one of Mum's best friends, and Mrs Budd was so kind after the bomb – we stayed with her and Mr Budd and Rose until we went out to Bridge End. I'm really sorry we didn't keep in touch.'

'You couldn't, though,' Olive said. She was Annie and Ted Chapman's elder daughter, and her husband Derek had recently taken over his father's building business. 'You were only a little girl. I know Auntie Jess tried to track you both down but the Authorities wouldn't tell her anything.'

'They had a lot to answer for, if you ask me,' Tommy Vickers said, joining in. 'But Authorities always do.' He looked Sammy up and down. 'Well, you're a sight for sore eyes, I must say. Haven't seen much of you for the past couple of years. Shot up like a flipping weed, too. I hope you're going to come and say hello to the missus.'

He led Sammy away and Maddy looked after him thoughtfully. She turned to find her sister watching her.

'He's turned out really well,' Maddy said. 'He was always such a timid little chap when he was a boy.'

'Not after you got hold of him,' Stella said. 'The pair of you were always up to mischief, and it was you who led him into it, more often than not. I hope you're not going to lead him astray again.'

Maddy gave her a wicked grin. 'Oh, I don't know,' she said. 'I think it would be rather fun to lead Sammy Hodges astray.'

Sammy was disappointed to find that he wasn't sitting near Stella and Muriel at the long trestle tables that Frank, Ted and Tommy had set up in the church hall early that morning. He couldn't even see them from where he was and had to listen instead to Bert Shaw droning on about his daughter Diane, who lived in America and had a big fridge and a proper bathroom and a car of her own, or about his son Bob who was a fitter and toolmaker at Airspeed, the aircraft factory in Hilsea. At least he had Linnet on his other side and was able to use her as an excuse for withdrawing his attention. He made

49

up his mind to talk to Maddy again afterwards and find out where she lived now.

'Where's West Lyme?' he asked when he finally managed to capture her.

'Near Lyme Regis.' She gave him a mischievous look. 'Why? Do you know someone there?'

'Yes,' he said. 'You. But I don't know your address.'

She smiled. 'Oh, that's easy to remember. The Archdeacon's residence. That's whose secretary I am.'

'The Archdeacon?' he echoed blankly. 'You mean you live with him? I mean, as well as work with him? I mean ...'

Maddy laughed. 'I have a little flat in the house. I told you, he's Felix's uncle. Almost everyone in Felix's family is an archdeacon or a bishop or something. But they're great fun when you get to know them – not at all pompous or stuffy. Felix isn't, anyway. Stella's a lucky girl.'

'How about you?' he asked. 'Are you engaged to anyone?'

She shook her head and the curls danced again. 'No, I don't even have a steady boyfriend. I've never had time to find one, somehow. I was adopted, you see, and my new mother travelled a lot, so I went with her. We lived in France after the war. Then Stella found me again, and Fenella – that's my new mother, Fenella Forsyth – got married and I decided to stay in England.'

'And nobody's snapped you up?' he asked in amazement. 'I can't believe that!'

'Well, there are one or two who might be interested,' she said, showing her dimples again. 'But I'm not in any hurry.'

Sammy gazed at her. She had always been pretty, but now he thought she was beautiful. She could have her pick of any man – and if she'd lived in France, and travelled, and now worked as a secretary for an important man, she must have a lot of opportunities to meet them. Someone like him, an ordinary young chap just out of his National Service and apprenticed to a blacksmith, wouldn't have a chance. Even if he went into electronics, as he wanted to do, she still wouldn't look at him. He sighed.

'Now, what's that big sigh for?' Maddy asked. 'Am I boring you?'

'No! No, you'd never bore me.' He grinned. 'Remember all the things we got up to when we were kids? That time you made me take Auntie Ruth's parrot out on a picnic?'

'I didn't *make* you!'

'You did. You said I couldn't come unless I brought Silver. And then we went off to play hide and seek, and the magpies mobbed him and he fell off his perch. It was the first time Auntie Ruth was angry with me.'

'Oh dear. Was she very cross?' Maddy said, looking across the room to where Ruth was chatting to Jess Budd.

'She was furious. Well, he could have died. And it was worse than that, because it was the first time Dad came out to Bridge End to see me and he found me sitting at the kitchen table crying and eating bread and milk. He thought she was treating me badly, like that woman who had Martin Baker and used to hose him down with cold water in the garden before she'd let him into the house. I think for two pins he'd have taken me home there and then, only the Authorities had told him I'd got to be evacuated because he couldn't look after me properly at home after Mum died.'

Maddy's face softened and she laid her hand on his arm. 'Poor Sammy. You had a sad time when you were a little boy.'

'I suppose I did,' he said, thinking of the little house in April Grove which was never clean or tidy because his mother was too ill to take care of it, the hours he'd spent queuing for rations while women pushed in front of him and got all the best meat or vegetables, the nights after she had died, when he'd been alone and terrified during the Blitz until Freda and Tommy Vickers insisted he must go into their shelter. 'But it all got better when I went to live with Auntie Ruth, and it's

51

better for Dad now, too. He likes being in the country. He was in the First World War, you see, and he had nightmares for years afterwards.'

'It must have been awful for him to have to go through another war,' she said thoughtfully.

'I think it was. I always thought he was just bad-tempered – I was scared of him. But when I think about what it must have been like, having to go through all that bombing, remembering what it was like for the soldiers overseas, working on the ships and having to go to sea for days on end, leaving me and Mum and Gordon at home, never knowing if we might have been killed by the time he came back … And then Gordon getting into trouble, and Mum dying – well, I can understand it. I wonder he stood it at all.'

'I wonder anyone stood it,' Maddy said quietly, and they were both silent for a moment. Then her smile broke out again and she said, 'But it's all over now, and we've got to look forward. Our whole lives are ahead of us. What are you going to do with yours, Sammy?'

Shyly, he began to tell her about his life at Bridge End, the apprenticeship he was serving with the local blacksmith and his plans to study electronic engineering. 'There's going to be a lot of things happening in the next few years,' he said. 'Things like television, and things we haven't even begun to think about yet. It's going to be really exciting, Maddy, and I want to be part of it.'

'It sounds wonderful,' she said, her eyes shining. 'People are talking a lot about television now – everyone wants to see the Coronation on it. The Archdeacon's got one and he says I can watch it if I like. He saw the last Coronation on television, right back in 1937.'

'I didn't know they televised that,' Sammy said in surprise, and she nodded.

'You could only see it if you were in London. And in the

evening they showed a tour of the television studios. George Robey went round with Leslie Mitchell.'

'George Robey?' Sammy asked. 'I think I've heard the name, but—'

'Of course you have! He was a famous music-hall star, and he was in quite a few films too. You hear his records on the radio sometimes. He must be very old now – I'm not sure if he's still alive. And Leslie Mitchell does those Movietone commentaries. He used to do television ones so I expect he will again, when it gets properly started. Anyway, the Archdeacon saw it and he says it was fascinating.' Maddy was pensive for a moment before adding, 'Fenella, the actress who adopted me, was in a play on television, just before the war started. She didn't like it all that much – said it was nothing like being on stage, and not at all the same as making films – but I expect she would have done more, only then the war broke out and they closed it down for the duration. She told me once that the last thing people saw on their screens was the figure of Mickey Mouse being kissed by Greta Garbo!'

Sammy laughed. 'So he stayed kissed for six years, just like Pompey Football Club kept the FA Cup for six years! It was a good war for some, all right.' He thought for a moment and then said, 'I don't suppose you ever come back to Portsmouth these days. Apart from this wedding, I mean.'

'No, I haven't. I feel a bit ashamed, really – Mrs Budd was so good to me and Stella when we were bombed out and Mummy and Thomas were killed. I ought to have kept in touch. I will, from now on. Do you ever come back, Sammy?'

'I did before I got called up – Dad and me used to come once a year, to see Mum's grave. I couldn't come so often while I was away on National Service, but he did. We're going to walk round after this is over, take her some flowers, tidy her grave up a bit if it needs it. Not that it will,' he added. 'Mr and Mrs Vickers look after it for us. It'll be like a new pin. But we like to do something, to show we still think about her.'

His fair face was a little flushed, as if he were embarrassed to be talking like this, but as Maddy touched his arm her face was soft with sympathy.

'I know what you mean. Stella and I have a grave to visit, too – our mother was buried with our baby brother at St Mary's. It's a big grave, though, with a lot of people in it who were killed that night, so it's not quite the same, and I'm afraid we haven't been as regular as you in coming to see it. Daddy was lost at sea, so he doesn't have a grave at all.'

'We ought to keep in touch now we've met again,' Sammy said a little awkwardly, and she nodded.

'I'll give you my address.' She pulled a scrap of paper from her handbag and scribbled on it. 'There you are. Write to me – or come and see me if you like. I don't suppose you've got a car?'

He shook his head regretfully. 'I'm thinking of getting a motorbike, though.'

'A motorbike! Oh, how lovely – you'll have to come and take me out on it. I've always wanted to ride on the back of a motorbike.'

They looked at each other and hesitated, neither quite sure what to say next. Then Sammy opened his mouth, but before he could speak Dan came up beside them. 'Sorry to break this up,' he said, 'but I think Frank Budd wants to make an announcement. Either that, or he's standing on that chair to change a light bulb.'

They turned and looked at Frank, who was waving his arms and calling for silence.

'I'm not going to make any more speeches,' he began, and there were cheers from Bert Shaw, who looked as if he might have had one sherry too many, and Tommy Vickers. 'I just want to say thank you to everyone for coming and helping to make this day even more special for us. Like I said before, Jess and me are pleased to have young Ken as part of the family now, and we hope you've all had a day as good as we have. And now the happy couple are ready to go off on their honeymoon, so let's all wish them good luck.'

He climbed down to more cheers, which increased as Rose and Ken appeared, looking very smart in their going-away outfits – Ken in a grey suit, Rose in a deep pink costume with a small feathery hat and black patent bag and court shoes – and hurried through the crowd to the taxi that waited outside. They were not quick enough, however, to escape the confetti that was thrown over them, and Ken in particular was going to be leaving a trail of brightly coloured scraps wherever he went for the rest of the day, Tim and Keith having almost held him down as they rammed handfuls of it down his neck.

'There. They've gone,' Jess said, wiping her eyes as the taxi pulled away. 'I hope they'll be all right, Frank.'

'Well, I should think they will be. They're only going to Torquay.'

'I didn't mean that. I meant – well, you know. I hope they'll be *happy*. As happy as we've been.' She slipped her arm through his and hugged it against her side. 'I know we've had some hard times, but it's been a good life, hasn't it? And that's what I want for our Rose, too. And Tim, and Keith, and Maureen too, when their time comes.'

'Blimey, you make it sound more like a funeral than a wedding!' he said, but his voice was gruff and he squeezed her arm too. 'I don't think you need worry about them, Jess. Ken's a good lad and he'll look after our Rose. Anyway, I'm not sorry it's over. We've just got the clearing-up to do now, I suppose.'

'And you don't need to bother yourselves about that,' Tommy Vickers interrupted from behind them. 'Me and Bert and a few of the others will see to it, and Freda's already got some of the women doing the washing-up. You just go off home now and put your feet up for a bit. It's been a long day.'

'Oh, we can't—' Jess began, but her sister Annie appeared beside her and took her arm.

'Oh, yes you can. It won't take us five minutes to get this place back to normal. Everyone else is going now, see, and they all want to say goodbye, so you forget about the work and enjoy the rest of the day. Me and Ted'll pop down later on with a few sandwiches, so you don't even need to think about supper.'

Jess laughed and thanked her. She and Frank stood by the door, shaking their guests' hands and taking the chance of a final few words. When Ruth and Dan appeared, she gave them both a kiss.

'I'm ever so pleased you could come. We were worried that we might get snow and you wouldn't be able to get here, but as it's turned out the weather hasn't been too bad at all, has it? And it's lovely to see Sammy again. He's so tall now! When you think what a little scrap he was when you first came to April Grove, Dan.'

'It's the country air that's done him good,' Dan said. 'And Ruthie here – she's been the making of him. Of both of us. It was a good day for us when he was evacuated to Bridge End.'

'You must come and see us again,' Jess told them. 'Next time you come to see Nora's grave, you make sure and pop in at number fourteen. There's always a welcome for you.'

She kissed Sammy too, and told him what a fine young man he was. He blushed and grinned awkwardly and thanked her for inviting him.

'It's been good to see you all. I never expected to see Stella and Muriel again – Maddy, I mean.'

'Well, you must all keep in touch,' Jess said. 'Maddy's a pretty girl and I dare say she's got plenty of young men after her, but we always need our old friends too. Don't we, Frank?'

'Eh?' Frank had been talking to Dan about the shipyard at Camber where Dan used to work and looked round vaguely. 'Oh, yes,' he said, obviously with no idea what his wife had just said to him. 'Oh yes, we will. We'll make sure of that.'

56

The woman laughed and moved on so that the next guests in the line could make their own goodbyes. But Sammy lingered a little, hoping for a last glimpse of Maddy Forsyth, who used to be Muriel Simmons and had got him into endless trouble when they all lived at Bridge End.

In his pocket was the scrap of paper on which she had written her address. He fingered it and thought about the motorbike he intended to buy. The sooner he got it, the better.

Chapter Seven

Maddy, Felix and Stella returned to West Lyme that evening in the Archdeacon's car, which he had lent them for the day. They felt very stylish as they drove through Southampton and entered the New Forest.

'We're not far from Bridge End,' Maddy remarked. 'Did you get much chance to talk to anyone from there, Stella? I had quite a long chat with Sammy Hodges.'

'Yes, I noticed,' Stella said with a grin. 'He's turned out quite good-looking, hasn't he? You'd never have thought such a little shrimp would grow up into a handsome young man. Of course, I do rather go for the fair-haired, blue-eyed types,' she added with a wicked glance at Felix.

'I'm glad to hear it,' her fiancé said with an attempt at severity. 'Though I'm not sure I like being called a "type". I thought I was unique.'

'And so you are,' Stella said affectionately. 'Which is a good thing, really. I'm not sure the world could cope with two of you.'

'When you pair have quite finished,' Maddy said from the back seat, 'I did ask you a question. Did you talk to many people from Bridge End?'

'Well, Mrs Purslow, of course – only she's Mrs Hodges now, isn't she. And Mrs Greenaway, and Mrs Mudge, who used to be Mr Beckett's housekeeper at the vicarage. She's looking rather frail, I thought. She retired when Mr Beckett died and the new vicar came, and I got the impression that

58

she never really got over it. She'd been with him all her life, apparently.'

'Those were the days,' Felix observed, changing gear to go up the hill at Stoney Cross, 'when vicars had housekeepers. I'm afraid I won't be able to run to anything like that at Little Burracombe, darling.'

'I wouldn't know what to do with her if you did,' Stella said. 'And Dottie's teaching me to cook. But I might need a bit of help looking after that big vicarage.'

'I expect we'll be able to afford someone to come in and do a bit of cleaning once or twice a week,' he said. 'You'll need time to do all the things that vicars' wives have to do, like go to Mothers' Union meetings and organise the flower rotas. And keep me in order, too,' he added.

'That's a fulltime job in itself,' Stella said. She turned to Maddy. 'Do you know what he did last week? He put all the numbers for the hymns in the boards upside down. Nobody noticed until they started to sing the first hymn and it was number 661. The choir started to sing that and the congregation tried to sing 199. You never heard such a din.'

'Well, it wasn't really my fault,' Felix said. 'The church-wardens usually do that, but one was on holiday and the other had 'flu. And I had the board upside down on the vestry table by mistake.'

Maddy giggled. 'I think you're going to make Little Burracombe sit up when you're their vicar properly.'

'Well, they'll never dare go to sleep, that's certain,' Stella said.

They drove on through the darkness. Felix had pointed out the turning to the Rufus Stone as they had come this way during the morning, and promising to bring both girls to see it sometime. 'It's a bit of our early history – it marks the place where William the Conqueror's son was shot with an arrow. The stone was put up in 1745, if I remember correctly, but it got damaged over the years and it's all encased in iron now.

It's fascinating to stand there and think what happened all those centuries ago on that very spot.'

They passed through the little town of Ringwood and soon after that took the road for West Lyme. The Archdeacon's house was in a small square near the church. As Felix turned into the drive and drew up behind his own sports car, there was another car on the drive, too – a two-seater not unlike Felix's Mirabelle. Maddy gazed at it in surprise as she climbed out of the Archdeacon's saloon.

'It's Stephen,' she said. 'He never told me he was coming today.'

'Stephen?' Stella echoed. 'Stephen Napier, you mean? Does he come to see you often, Maddy?'

But her sister was already hurrying up the steps to the front door. It opened as she approached and a tall man in RAF uniform stepped out in the sudden rush of light, and held out his arms.

'Stephen!' Maddy cried, running into the embrace. 'How lovely to see you! Why didn't you let me know?'

Stella and Felix paused at the foot of the steps and looked at each other. Felix's brows were half-raised and Stella looked as if she scarcely knew whether to be pleased or dismayed.

'I'd no idea they were seeing so much of each other,' she murmured. 'I know they got on very well when they met at Val and Luke's wedding, but I thought with Stephen away in Germany, it had all fizzled out. And she seemed so pleased to meet Sammy Hodges again.'

'He was pleased to see her, too,' Felix said. 'She gave him her address. I hope nobody's going to get hurt over this, Stella.'

They went slowly up the steps to where Maddy and Stephen Napier were still standing close together, their arms entwined, and the front door closed behind them all as they went inside.

*

60

'Why didn't you let me know?' Maddy demanded, coming through from her tiny kitchen with a tray of tea. 'I might easily have decided to stay in Portsmouth for the rest of the weekend, and then I'd have missed you.'

'Oh, I knew my fatal charm would lure you back,' Stephen said with a grin. 'Anyway, I didn't know until today that I was coming. I got a forty-eight-hour pass so I thought I'd pop in on my way back home. I've got some news.'

Maddy felt her heart contract. She put the tray down and turned to him. 'What news? You're not going to Korea, are you?'

He shook his head. 'Better than that. I'm coming back to England. I'm going to be based at White Cheriton – near enough to come and see you whenever I get a few hours off.' He smiled at her and she turned back to the tea-tray to hide the colour in her face, fiddling with the cups for a moment before handing one to her sister.

'That'll be nice,' she said primly. 'You'll have to let me know beforehand, though. It would be a shame to come all that way and find me not here.'

'Oh, I'll let you know,' he said, taking his cup from her and brushing her fingers with his. Their eyes met and she felt her blush rise again. Stella and Felix were watching them and Maddy felt suddenly annoyed with Stephen. He had taken her completely by surprise, and she would never have run into his arms like that when he'd come to the door if she'd had warning. She'd meant to be much more circumspect about their friendship.

'Yes, so long as you do,' she said, turning away. 'I do have quite a busy life here and I like to go back to Burracombe whenever I can.'

'Well, we could go back together sometimes,' he said easily. 'My father and Hilary will expect me home occasionally. It would be much nicer if you were there too.'

61

'That sounds a good idea,' Felix said. 'We like to see as much of Maddy as we can, don't we, darling?'

Stella nodded. She liked Stephen Napier, but she didn't think he was a particularly reliable young man – he'd already made it very clear that he didn't want to take on the responsibility of the Napier estate and had even talked about emigrating to Canada. It would be a good idea, she thought, if Maddy were to see him at Burracombe, where Stella herself could keep an eye on them.

Stephen began to tell them about the RAF station where he had been posted. 'It's mostly a training station now but the main house was built years ago by some wealthy man who fancied owning a French château. It's an amazing place – dozens of little turrets and miles of corridors. I sometimes try to pretend it still belongs to the family and I've been invited to a weekend party!'

The others laughed. 'You've got some very grandiose ideas,' Maddy told him. 'Anyway, French châteaux aren't all that wonderful. They're huge and draughty and it takes ages to find your bedroom.'

'Of course – I forgot you'd lived in one yourself, when Fenella Forsyth got married to her Frenchman,' he said. 'Well, I bow to your superior wisdom. Anyway, where have you three been, all dressed up and with flowers in your buttonholes?'

They told him about the wedding. 'There was nothing fancy about it,' Stella said, 'but it was lovely, wasn't it, Felix? Very simple and down to earth and friendly. That's what you'd expect from the Budds, though. It was good to see them all again, wasn't it, Maddy? And the people from Bridge End, too. I must say, Sammy Hodges has grown into a nice-looking boy.'

Maddy said nothing and after a little more conversation Felix declared that he was going to go through to the main house and see his uncle. 'It's only polite, since I'm staying the night with him. Where are you staying, Stephen?'

'Oh, I'm on my way home to Burracombe,' Stephen said. 'I was rather hoping to persuade Maddy to come with me – I didn't realise she was going to be away. I suppose it's a bit late to offer you a lift now,' he added, looking at Maddy.

'It certainly is! It'll be nearly midnight before you get to Burracombe. Besides, Stella's staying the night here with me and I've got things to do tomorrow before starting work again on Monday. Perhaps we could do it another weekend.'

'That's a promise,' he told her, and got up, stretching his long legs. 'I'd better be off, then. Hilary won't be best pleased if I keep her up too late.' He nodded at Stella and Felix. 'Good to see you both again. Like to escort me off the premises, Maddy?'

They went out together and Stella and Felix exchanged glances.

'It looks as if you might find yourself related to the Squire and his family,' Felix remarked. 'Those two seem very thick, even though your sister did her best to hide it.'

'I know. We must have been wrong about Sammy Hodges. She did seem very pleased to see him, but I suppose it was just meeting him again like that, and reminiscing about the time we had in Bridge End. I think you're being a bit previous, though, Felix – marrying them off just because he popped in to give her a lift back to Burracombe for the weekend.'

Felix shook his head. 'Stephen Napier's got more than that on his mind. He's seriously interested in your sister, Stella – mark my words. I don't think Sammy Hodges has got a chance.'

Maddy came back at that moment, looking flushed and bright-eyed. She raised her brows at them and said, 'Sammy Hodges hasn't got a chance of what? Just what are you two talking about?'

'Nothing,' Stella said. 'And Felix is going through to his uncle now, so that you and I can have a last cup of cocoa and go to bed. I don't know about you, but I'm tired out.'

'So am I,' Maddy said, yawning.

Yet when she slipped into her bed at last, Maddy found sleep eluding her and she lay awake for a long time, listening to her sister's light breathing and staring into the darkness as she thought of two young men – both tall, both fair-haired, both good-looking, yet in other ways so very different. One from a wealthy landed family; the other from one of the smallest back streets in Portsmouth.

Chapter Eight

'So how did it all go, then?' Jane asked when the Hodges family arrived home. She had popped down to the cottage to see that the fire was still alight in the range and that Silver was all right after his day alone. The parrot was in his cage, muttering nursery rhymes to himself and squawked loudly when he saw his family come in. Sammy went over to him and opened his cage to let the bird out on to his wrist.

'It was a lovely day,' Ruth said, unbuttoning Linnet's coat. The little girl was almost asleep where she stood. 'Rose looked really pretty in her wedding-dress. And those brothers of hers – you'd never think they were those two scallywags who used to make snowmen with old Mr Beckett.'

'Tim told me that they went into the churchyard once when there was a funeral on,' Sammy said with a grin. 'They wanted to see what a grave looked like and Keith fell in! He thought he was going to be buried as well – they only just got him out in time, before the coffin was brought out of the church.'

Ruth smiled. 'The young monkeys. Well, they've both grown up fine young men. Jess Budd must be proud of them.'

'I liked Tim best,' Linnet said, waking up a bit. She had taken a fancy to the young man and followed him around like a puppy. 'He says I can marry him when I'm a lady.'

'I'm not sure that would be a good idea,' Ruth said. 'He's a bit too old for you.'

'He's not! He's only as old as Sammy, and Sammy's my brother.'

Dan changed the subject. 'He seems to be doing well with his apprenticeship on the ferry,' he remarked. 'Jess says he wants to go into the Merchant Navy afterwards, as an engineer.' He stopped, remembering that Ruth's first husband, Jack, had been in the Merchant Navy, but Ruth shrugged.

'He was always the adventurous one, wanting to see what was round the next corner. Mind you, Keith's going to do a bit of travelling too – he's in the Royal Navy. So both the Budd boys are going to be sailors.'

'Mrs Budd will miss them,' Jane said.

'And has Silver behaved himself?' Ruth asked as she prepared to take Linnet upstairs for bed.

'As much as he ever does. I gave him some sunflower seeds and fresh water at teatime and we had a bit of a gossip.' Jane hesitated. 'I'll come up with you, Ruth. There's something else I want to tell you.'

Ruth gave her sister a curious glance. 'All right. Put the kettle on, would you, Sammy? We could all do with a cup of tea, I'm sure.'

'I'm a little teapot,' Silver began obligingly, and Sammy laughed.

'So you might be, but we don't get much tea out of you. You go back in your cage now, there's a good boy.' He helped the parrot to hop back into the big cage and left the door open while he went to fill the kettle. The two women went upstairs, half-carrying the sleepy Linnet, and when she was undressed and in bed Ruth looked at her sister again.

'Well? What's this about? You're being very mysterious.'

'It's our Lizzie,' Jane said. 'She came out to see me this morning. She's a bit upset.'

'What's happened?' Ruth asked. 'Is it Alec? He's not had another breakdown, has he? I was a bit worried at Christmas, to tell you the truth, but I thought it was Lizzie who wasn't looking well.' A second fear touched her. 'It's not the baby, is it?'

66

'No, Alec's fine. At least ...' Jane stopped again, then took a breath and went on in a rush. 'It's Floyd. He's coming over to England. From America. He wants to see his daughter.' She hesitated again and then went on, 'She told me just before Christmas but we agreed not to mention it to anyone else, in case he changed his mind. But now she's had another letter. He's on board the *Queen Elizabeth* now, Ruth – he'll be here at any time and Lizzie's almost frantic. She thinks he'll want to tell Gillie who he is. She's afraid he might even want to take her away.'

By the time Ruth and Jane went back downstairs, Sammy had made the tea and brought it through to the back room where the family spent most of their time, and there was no chance to discuss this development. Ruth sank gratefully into her armchair and stretched out her feet, realising suddenly how tired she was.

'It's been a long day.' She reached for the cup of tea Sammy was holding out to her, and took a sip. 'Thank you, love. There's nothing like a cup of tea to set you to rights when you've been out all day.' But she didn't feel 'set to rights'. The news about Floyd Hanson had cooled the warm glow she had felt from their day out, and brought a little worm of uneasiness, almost dread, into her heart. She wanted to talk about it to her sister, or to Dan, or to Lizzie herself, but she couldn't. Sammy didn't know the truth – he'd been only a little boy when it had all happened – and this wasn't the time to tell him. In any case, the secret wasn't hers to tell. And, just now, he was too concerned with his own future.

'I've got something to tell you,' he said later, as they finished the cheese on toast Ruth had made for their supper. She glanced at him in dismay. Does it have to be now, she thought, when I've got this other worry on my mind? But neither of the others knew about that, and Sammy had the right to choose his own moment. He looked across the table at his father. 'You might not be very pleased.'

Dan's black brows came together in a heavy frown. 'What's this about, then? You've not gone and got some girl into trouble, have you?'

'No, of course not,' Sammy said indignantly. 'I haven't done anything wrong at all. Why do you always—'

'All right, don't let's get off on the wrong foot,' Ruth broke in swiftly. 'I think I know what Sammy's going to tell you, Dan, and there's nothing to get aeriated about. You just need to think about it, that's all.'

He stared at her. 'So he's told you already, has he? And you haven't said a word to me?'

'It's for him to decide what to say and when about his own business.' Ruth turned to her stepson. 'You'd better get on with it, Sammy.'

'All right, I will.' He looked across at Dan again and Ruth was suddenly reminded of the very first time father and son had sat at this table together. It had been a difficult evening and she would never have believed that they would, eventually, make such a happy family together.

Dan drew in a slow breath and waited. He still looked as if he thought Sammy was going to confess to something criminal.

'It's just that I've decided I don't want to be a blacksmith,' Sammy said. 'I told Auntie Ruth how I've done different things while I've been in the RAF, and I think they suit me better. I'm not like you, Dad – I'm not cut out to be a blacksmith. For one thing, I'm never going to be size you are.'

'Blacksmithing isn't all about brute strength,' Dan began, but Sammy shook his head.

'It helps, though, doesn't it? Look at you and Solly Barlow. You're both enormous.'

'You've put on a lot of muscle in the past couple of years,'

Dan said, unwilling to let it go. 'You've done weight-lifting and you're a good boxer.'

'Bantamweight!' Sammy said with a grin. 'But that's not really the point, Dad. The point is that I like electronics and I'm good at the work. I want to go to night school and get some qualifications. I think I could get a good job if I do that. It's going to be important, Dad, stuff like that.' He leaned across the table. 'Think of television, and computers.'

'Computers? What are they when they're at home?'

'They're sort of enormous calculating machines. But people say they're going to do a lot more besides. And it's not just them, there are going to be so many things that will work by electricity and electronics, and if I get in now I'll have the chance of a good job for the rest of my life.'

'And isn't that what blacksmithing is?' Dan demanded. 'That's what I thought you'd have here, when I got Solly to agree to taking you on as an apprentice – a good job for the rest of your life. You know he's got no family to pass it on to. This electronic business, whatever it is – how d'you know that's not going to turn out to be just a flash in the pan? But there's always going to be work for a blacksmith.'

'I'm not so sure there is,' Sammy said. 'Factories are going to take on a lot of the jobs a blacksmith does. Farm machinery will take over from horses and men – you'll need to be a mechanic to fix that, not a blacksmith. I reckon that in ten years' time there'll be hardly a horse left working on farms. The only work for farriers will be putting shoes on riding horses.'

'Oh, surely not!' Ruth exclaimed in distress. 'The village wouldn't be the same without those lovely shire horses.'

'Everything's changing now, Auntie Ruth,' he told her. 'It's the war – it's pushed things on quicker than they would have moved in peacetime. The backroom boys were kept busy inventing new things – jet aeroplanes, radar and the like – and they're not going to stop now. And that's were people like me will come in.'

'You're not an inventor,' Dan said, beginning to grin a bit. 'You have to be old and mad with white hair to be one of those.'

Sammy smiled too, but he shook his head. 'There are a lot of people working behind the scenes, and most of them aren't much older than me. I may not be an inventor – I'm not clever enough for that – but I can learn to make things work. I like doing it, and I'm good at it. Better than I'll ever be at being a blacksmith.' He gave his father another apologetic glance. 'I'm sorry, Dad. I don't want to let you down, but I want to do what I'm really good at.'

Dan sighed heavily and looked at his hands as they lay on the table. They were big, strong hands with thick fingers, hands that worked with iron and fire every day and never looked properly clean, no matter how hard he scrubbed them. The skin was hard and there were calluses on his palms that would never soften, but he'd always felt rather proud of them. They showed their owner did a good, honest day's toil. You never knew what to make of a man with soft hands, he always thought, and it struck at his heart to think that his own son's hands might be soft and white.

But Sam's hands would never be like his, just as Sam would never be the same build as him – he was right there. Sam was Nora's son, fair and slightly built, a bit delicate if you were truthful, with slender hands and long fingers. The boxing and weight-lifting he'd done in the RAF had built him up a lot, so that he had some good muscle on him now, but Dan had to admit that the boy had always struggled a bit with the heavier work at the blacksmith's forge.

'So what is it you want to do?' he asked, and heard a tiny sigh of relief from Ruth. She'd been worrying about his reaction, he realised, and he gave her a small, rather rueful smile. 'It's all right, I'm not going to lose my rag over this. Not unless I have to,' he added with a note of warning. 'I want to hear a bit more about it before I make up me mind.'

70

Sammy leaned forward again and Ruth got up from the table. 'Before we go any further, I think I'll make some cocoa. It always helps to have a cup of something hot beside you when you're having a talk.' It would also help to calm things down a bit while she made it, she thought, gathering together their empty plates. A little break would give them time to think it over, and then they could start again.

'Right,' she said, coming back with the tray. Neither man had spoken while she was busy and Silver was asleep in his cage. The only sound was the crackling of the fire. She handed them their cocoa and sat down beside Dan on the old settee. 'Now, Sammy, you'd better tell your father all you can about this idea of yours.'

Sammy took a breath and gave them both a straight look. His eyes were clear and his face a little flushed as he spoke. 'I want to go to night school, like I told you. I can get good qualifications there – a Higher National Certificate or maybe even more than that. There's any amount of jobs I could do once I'd got that.' He hesitated and then added, 'I don't want to let Solly down, Dad. I want to be fair to him. I've still got some time to serve on my apprenticeship, but if he didn't want me to carry on with it I'd look for something else to support myself while I'm at night school. I'm not asking anyone else to pay out for me.'

'I'd rather you finished your time, all the same,' Dan said. 'You'd have a trade then, if this other thing don't work out. You'd have your papers.'

'I think we ought to leave that to Solly to decide,' Sammy said. 'He might want to take on another apprentice – someone who'd stay with him.'

Dan sighed. 'I've always seen you and me working together in the forge, maybe even after Solly's given up. That might not be too long now, neither – he's not far short of seventy, you know, and talking lately about putting his feet up. We're going to have to do a bit of thinking if you're going to be off doing something else.'

'I know. And I'm sorry. But I really want to do this, Dad. I get on all right with the blacksmithing, I know, and I like the farrier side of it, working with the horses, but it's not really my cup of tea.' He lifted his cup as he spoke and grinned a little. 'It's not even my cup of cocoa! I've found something else that is, though, and I want to do it. You don't blame me for that, do you?'

'No, son, I don't blame you,' Dan said quietly. Ruth, glancing sideways at him, could see the disappointment in his eyes and felt sorry for him. He'd put a lot of store in having Sammy work with him, she knew. But she could see that Sammy's heart was in this new idea, and she also knew that he was enough of his father's son to hold on to what he wanted and not let go.

'Let's go to bed now and sleep on it,' she said. 'We're all tired after our long day and things tend to sort themselves out while you're asleep. We'll talk about it again tomorrow.'

As they got ready for bed, she could see that Dan's mind was still turning over this latest piece of news. She wanted, desperately, to tell him about Floyd Hanson coming back, and discuss what it might mean to Lizzie and Alec, to Jane – to all of their family. But she knew it would have to wait.

They said goodnight and Ruth lay quietly, waiting for sleep to come. Her thoughts would not leave her alone, though. They circled endlessly in her mind: Sammy and his future; Lizzie and Alec and the two children. And Lizzie was pregnant again! Somehow, that seemed to make it even more difficult.

Changes were on the way, and Ruth had a sinking feeling that they were not all going to be happy ones.

Chapter Nine

It was not until the next morning, after church, that Ruth had a chance to talk to Jane again, and she wasn't surprised when her sister drew her aside in the churchyard.

'If you ask me, she's scared stiff he'll want to take Gillie away with him,' Jane said in a low voice. 'And I'm not absolutely sure she herself wouldn't go too, if he asked her.'

Ruth stared at her in dismay. 'Surely not. Lizzie thinks the world of Alec. They've got a good marriage. She'd never leave him now.'

Jane shrugged. 'You never know what folk will do, Ruth, not even your own children. I'd never have thought she'd have got herself into such a pickle in the first place. Anyway, there's nothing we can do about it. And I have to watch my words too, I can tell you. She flew right off the handle when she came out to tell me when she got the first letter, though we parted good enough friends in the end.' She paused, then added in a slightly bitter tone, 'It was you she really came out to see, not me at all.'

Ruth sighed. She'd always known that her sister was jealous of the relationship between herself and Lizzie, and she didn't really blame her. I wouldn't like it if my Linnet went to someone else before me, she thought. But she understood why Lizzie had done it. Ruth had been the only person she could turn to in those dark days after she had discovered she was pregnant, and a bond had been forged then that would never be broken.

'It's because she doesn't want to hurt you,' she began but Jane sniffed.

'I'm not so sure about that. Anyway, we've had a good talk about it all. She's told Alec, that's one thing. It wouldn't do to keep it a secret from him.'

'No, it wouldn't, Ruth agreed. 'How did he take it?'

Jane shrugged. 'How do you think? He doesn't like the idea any more than I do, but there's nothing he can do to stop Floyd coming. What he does say, is that he's not to come to the house and he's not to tell Gillie anything. He doesn't want him to see Gillie at all, and you can't blame him for that either.'

'No, you can't,' Ruth said, feeling sorry for the young man who had taken on another man's child and been a good and loving father to her. 'Well, I suppose we'll just have to wait and see what happens. It's for them to sort it out between them, after all – we can only stand by in case Lizzie needs us. It's the same with all these young people, they have to make their own lives same as we did.'

They went on to talk about the wedding in Portsmouth. Ruth was relieved to have got over the awkwardness over Lizzie. She smiled at her sister. 'Why don't you pop in for a cup of coffee before you go home? Where's Linnet got to?'

'She's over there with Jenny Bunter. All right, I can manage half an hour before I have to get the vegetables on.' They called Linnet over and began to walk along the lane. 'Seems like there are going to be a few changes around Bridge End. I hear Edna Corner's thinking about getting married again. Some chap from Ashford. And what do you think of the new people who've moved into the old Woddis house?'

Chatting about the village and its inhabitants took up all the rest of the half-hour Jane had promised, and by the time she left, the two sisters were back to their old easy friendship. But as Ruth stood at the kitchen sink, washing up the cups and thinking about getting the potatoes into the oven to roast, her mind returned to Dan and Sammy, out walking somewhere and discussing Sammy's own change of plan and, despite her words to Jane, she felt her own doubts return.

I hope he's doing the right thing, she thought anxiously. I hope they're not going to fall out over it.

The air was mild for January but the path through the woods was quite dry as Dan and Sammy walked along. A few early snowdrops were poking slivers of white light through drifts of fallen leaves, and the bare twigs looked as if they had been pencilled against the pearly sky. A blackbird was trying out his voice from a high branch and three or four rabbits scuttered away as the two men approached.

'I like all this,' Dan remarked. 'Funny, when you come to think about it, me growing up in the worst part of Old Pompey. Used to run around the streets with no shoes on and me backside hanging out of me trousers, and get a few pennies mudlarking down by the ferry on a Saturday afternoon. And look at me now, living in the country as if I been here all me life.' He glanced at his son. 'Tell me about this idea of yours again. I didn't properly take it in last night, what with the wedding and all the travelling and everything.'

'I know. I didn't mean to let it all out then, it just seemed to come up.' Sammy explained once more why he wanted to give up his apprenticeship and study to be an electronic engineer. 'It's the way things are going to go, Dad. There are machines being invented now that will be able to do all kinds of things – solve mathematical problems all in a minute that would take a man hours to do. And there's a new thing called a transistor that's really tiny but does the same thing as a valve, so that radios and so on will be able to be much smaller'. He went on talking, his face and eyes alight, his conversation peppered with terms such as 'resistors', 'transformers' and 'oscillators' until Dan held up both hands in surrender.

'All right, you don't have to blind me with science. I can see you're really keen on it and I take it you know what you're talking about. I hope so, anyway, because nobody else round here is going to! The important thing is, is all this just a flash in the pan or is it going to give you a trade? You were only a nipper, but you ought to remember what it was like for us before the war, back in Pompey. I was one of the lucky ones, I had a job, but we had to watch every penny just the same, and there were a lot of blokes who just walked the streets, half-starving, looking for whatever bit of work they could pick up. I don't want to see you chuck away a good trade and then have it all go wrong, Sam.'

'I know,' Sammy said soberly. 'We hardly had two pennies to rub together. But this is the coming thing, Dad, it really is.' He grinned. 'I'll be earning a lot more than a penny a day, like the boy in that nursery rhyme Linnet's trying to teach Silver.'

Dan grunted. He didn't set much store by nursery rhymes, although the one Nora used to sing, *'Sammy, Sammy, shine a light, ain't you playing out tonight'* still brought a lump to his throat when he heard Silver recite it. He pulled a stick out of a young tree and swished it at the undergrowth.

'So how much time are you going to have to put in at night school? You reckon you'll get a decent job at the end of it? And what do you reckon you'll do while you're studying, if Solly decides to cut off your apprenticeship?'

'I can probably get a job in Southampton, maybe in an electrical shop or something. Or working on ships – they'll all be getting more and more equipment now. I don't think I'd have much trouble, Dad, honestly. I could even work for the Civil Service.'

'The Civil Service? That's office work.'

Sammy shook his head. 'Not all of it. They have research stations, where they work on new systems of things like radar. They have scientists and technology officers – I could be one of them. It's a good job, Dad.'

'The Civil Service,' he said thoughtfully. 'You're established in the Civil Service – you'd never get the sack. There'd be a pension as well. And you reckon you'd be qualified?'

'Yes. And I'd get more training, too. There's that place on Portsdown Hill – the Admiralty Signals Establishment. That's the sort of place where I could work.'

'How would you get there every day? On your bike? It's a long ride to do in bad weather.'

'I thought I'd get a motorbike,' Sammy said casually.

Dan turned his head and stared at him. 'A motorbike?'

'Well, it makes sense, doesn't it? There's no buses up there. There might be a works bus, I suppose, but I'd still have to get to Fareham or Pompey. Anyway, I don't know that I will work there – it's just an idea. But wherever I work, I'm going to need to get there, and even going into Southampton for night school isn't going to be easy.'

'There's a late bus back.'

'I know. But I'd really like a motorbike, Dad. I learned to ride one when I was in the RAF. It's good fun, and they don't cost much to run.'

'I don't know what your Auntie Ruth would have to say about it.'

'You don't think she'd really mind, do you? They're not as dangerous as people say, not if you ride them properly. You don't *have* to go tearing along at sixty miles an hour.'

'I should hope not.' Dan swished his stick again. 'Well, you'll be twenty-one before long and able to do what you like, so there's not much sense in us stopping you now. But I'm still a bit worried about Solly. What's he going to think when you tell him you want to cut your apprenticeship?'

'I'll do whatever he wants me to do,' Sammy said. 'I won't let him down. I don't want to let you down either, Dad. I know you were thinking we'd be working together even after Solly retired. But like I said, things are changing. There'll still be blacksmithing work for you, but there won't for me. Nobody

77

knows just what the world will be like in a few years. But I do know electronics are going to be important.'

'Maybe you're right, son,' Dan said. 'I reckon I must be getting old at last, because I can't see it meself. I just want to stay out here in the country, where it's peaceful and you can have a good life. All this dashing about's for you young 'uns now. Two world wars have left the rest of us feeling a bit tired of it all.'

Sammy glanced at him. Dan was a big man, powerfully built, with dark features that accentuated his strength. But now that Sammy looked more carefully, he could see the grey touching the black hair, and the lines that a hard life had etched into his skin. He felt a sudden pity for his father, who had known little but hardship and sorrow for years before finding happiness at Bridge End. Carefully, feeling for his words, he said, 'The second one brought you out here though, didn't it, Dad? Neither of us would ever have met Auntie Ruth if it hadn't been for the war and the evacuation.'

Dan looked at him sharply and Sammy feared for a moment that he had said the wrong thing. Then his father nodded and said, 'I reckon you're right there, son. And it wouldn't have made no difference to your mother – she'd got that leukaemia thing in her blood already, so the doctor said. We'd have lost her whatever happened.'

'I know,' Sammy said quietly, and they walked in silence for a moment, each thinking of the frail, delicate woman they had loved and lost. Then he said, 'So is it all right if I talk to Mr Barlow about the apprenticeship, then? And see about getting into night school? And a motorbike?'

Dan gave him a wry grin. 'Seems to me there's not much I can say – you've got it all worked out. Well, like I said, you're a man now and I don't see as we got the right to stand in your way. You live your life the way you think you should, son, and good luck to you. I can't help wishing I'd had your opportunities, but I don't begrudge them. I'm glad you've got

78

the brains and the chance to make something of yourself. I'm proud of you.' He stopped and held out his hand. 'And that's the honest truth.'

Sammy gripped his father's hand in his. For a moment or two, he could find nothing to say. At last he said simply, 'Thanks, Dad. thanks.' He cleared his throat. 'Let's go back now, shall we? I expect Auntie Ruth's wondering where we are. The roast potatoes will be getting burnt.'

'Blimey,' Dan said with a return to his usual robust humour, 'we'll be in real trouble then!'

They turned and walked back through the forest, and it seemed to them both that the air was a little clearer, the sky a little bluer, the snowdrops whiter and the birdsong gayer, than when they had first set out.

Chapter Ten

Solly Barlow listened to Sammy in silence. He didn't seem too surprised about the change in plans, and when Sammy had finished talking he looked at him wryly and said, 'Well, I reckon I saw this coming. There's a lot of young chaps coming out of their National Service with a trade, and you were never going to do a lot of blacksmithing in the RAF. All this newfangled stuff, it's beyond me but I can see it's going to come, and there's nothing much us old folk can do to stop it. Can't say I'm not sorry, but there it is, you got to go your own way.'

'I really don't want to let you down,' Sammy said, but Solly shook his head.

'Don't reckon you will be, lad. Young Joe Dewar's been hanging round here the past few weeks, giving me a hand now and then. He'll be leaving school soon and I reckon he's got the makings of a useful chap. I might talk to his dad about taking him on.'

'Joe Dewar? D'you really think he'd stick it?' The Dewars were well known as the most feckless family in the village, none of them keeping a job for long. Their cottage was unkempt and the front garden a trampled waste, the weeds littered with old motorbikes that one or other of the boys was trying to get to work. 'Which one is he, anyway?'

'The one that looks like his dad,' Solly said with a grin. Nobody in the village knew quite how many of the Dewar children actually had been fathered by Bert, but Joe and a couple of his sisters had the same dark, curly hair and bright eyes, and the Dewars themselves didn't seem too bothered. Even the youngest, born while Bert was away in the Army, had been accepted without comment. But none of them, as far as Sammy knew, had ever been accepted for a commitment such as an apprenticeship.

'He's not a bad lad,' Solly went on. 'Got a feel for iron and he's good with the horses. I'm not saying I'll take him on, mind, but I'll think about it. I reckon he could do with a leg up, coming from that family.'

'What do you want me to do, then?' Sammy asked. 'I'll go on working for you as long as you want – I'm not going to leave you in the lurch.'

'Well, lad, we've managed without you all the time you've been away so I dare say we could again, but I won't say I'll not be glad of you stopping on for a bit. Joe can't leave school till the summer and I dare say you'll need a job of some sort. You might as well work for me as for anyone else.'

'That's what I hoped you'd say,' Sammy said with relief. 'I can start at night school pretty soon, but I'll have a bit of catching up to do and I'll need to earn my living at the same time.'

They agreed that his apprenticeship would cease but that he would continue to work as a general assistant at the forge. He went home feeling pleased with life and thinking about the motorbike he intended to buy.

The world seemed to be opening up before him. With a motorbike, he would have freedom to travel wherever he wanted, whenever he wanted to go there. Freedom to go to Southampton for his studies; to Portsmouth for work, if he was lucky enough to get the job he wanted.

He would also be able to go to West Lyme or Devon, to see Maddy Forsyth.

'A motorbike?' Ruth said doubtfully. 'Well, I suppose it would be all right. Quite a lot of the village boys have got them now, and Sammy's got his head screwed on right. You'd have to wear a crash helmet, though,' she added, looking across the tea-table to where Sammy was helping Linnet with her tinned salmon.

He glanced up in dismay. 'Oh, you're not going to make me wear one of those things, Auntie Ruth. Nobody else does.'

'Someone must, or they wouldn't make them,' she pointed out. 'Please, Sammy. I'll never have a minute's peace, thinking of you falling off and banging your head.'

'I'm not going to fall off. I've done a lot of riding in the RAF – I know what I'm doing. Honestly, those things make you look like a man from Mars.'

'It doesn't matter what you look like when you're going along,' Ruth said implacably. 'And I've seen what a fractured skull can do, in the hospital. I'd rather see you in a crash helmet than all swathed in bandages.'

Sammy turned to his father, but Dan shook his head. 'It's no use looking at me for help, Sam. Your Auntie Ruth is right. Come off one of them things at speed and you're a goner. I know what it is, mind,' he added to Ruth. 'He thinks riding a motorbike will get him a few girlfriends but if he wears a helmet they won't be interested.'

Sammy's fair skin flushed and he started to protest, but Ruth cut across him. 'I don't care what it is, he's to wear a helmet. You won't have any trouble finding a nice girl,' she added. 'You're a good-looking young chap, and wearing a helmet when you're going along at forty miles an hour or more isn't going to change that. I'm not going to argue about this, anyway. I know we can't tell you what to do once you're twenty-one, but there's a little while to go before that. In any case, I'd hope you'd do it just because I ask you to.'

Sammy sighed. 'I suppose so. All right, then, I'll wear a helmet. I'll get a black one, with a peak, they're not so bad. It'll keep my head dry when it rains, anyway.'

Ruth smiled at him and he gave her a rueful grin in return.

They both knew that he would always give in when she used that particular tone of voice.

'What sort of motorbike is this going to be?' Dan asked. 'You're not thinking of getting one of those big ones, I hope?'

'No, just a 197cc – a two-stroke – they're big enough to take two people. I'll take you out on it, Auntie Ruth,' he added before either of them could ask who he planned to take on the pillion. 'You'll enjoy it.'

'Will you take me on your motorbike, Sammy?' Linnet asked. She had finished her salad and was eating a piece of Ruth's home-made sponge cake. She had butter icing round her mouth and Ruth reached across to wipe it off.

'No, he won't be taking you on his motorbike. You're too little.'

'Ohhh,' she began, but Sammy shook his head too.

'You couldn't hold on tightly enough. I wouldn't want to lose you, would I?'

She pursed her lips, but before she could think of any further argument Silver butted in with the information, which they had all heard a million times before, that he was a teapot, short and stout, adding that he was also a bleeding eagle. Ruth rolled her eyes and Sammy grinned. It wasn't the worst phrase the parrot knew, after all – the sailors on board ship when Jack Purslow had been bringing him home had seen to that.

They finished tea and Sammy took Linnet into the other room to read her a story before bed. Ruth washed up and Dan sat in the chair by the range, gazing thoughtfully into the hot coals.

'You reckon he'll be all right on this motorbike he's on about?' he asked at last. 'I was a bit surprised you took it so easy, to tell you the truth.'

Ruth swilled the water down the sink and dried her hands before starting on the wet dishes.

'I didn't see much point in objecting to it. He's a man now and been away from home – he's not going to take kindly to

83

being told what he can and can't do. And at least he'll be wearing a helmet.' She came over and looked down at him. 'I'm a bit surprised at you, Dan, too. You've never wanted to mollycoddle him. I'd have thought you'd be pleased about this.'

He sighed. 'I know. I must be getting old, I suppose. I seem to see the dangers more these days. And what with having Linnet ... I never had much to do with Gordon and young Sam when they were little, you see. And I can't deny Gordon always seemed more like me, a big, strong boy wanting to do the sort of things I understood. But being big and strong didn't do him no good in the end. He still got killed.' He was silent for a moment before adding quietly, 'I've just got this feeling about our Sam on a motorbike. It's daft, I know.'

'It's not daft at all,' she said gently. 'It's because you care about him. I don't really like it either, but we've got to let him make his own decisions. He'll be careful, I'm sure of that, and the rest is up to Providence.'

'Providence,' Dan repeated, and then turned to look up into her face, the beginnings of a smile on his lips. 'Well, it was Providence brought Sam and me here in the first place, so I reckon we can trust in that. Come on – let's go and see what they're doing in the other room. Maybe when Linnet's gone to bed we can have a game of cards, the three of us, and that'll be the weekend over.'

'A good weekend,' Ruth said, and he nodded. It had been a very good weekend. Except, she thought, for the news about Lizzie.

Maddy had been thinking quite a lot about Sammy, too. She, Felix and Stella had enjoyed a lazy Sunday, attending the early service and spending the rest of the morning walking on the stony beach. They took the Archdeacon's black labrador, Archie, with them and he bounced along, dashing enthusiastically into the waves to chase stones which he had no chance of finding, but coming out with a large grin on his face just the same, and repaying Felix by shaking himself vigorously all over him.

'Serves you right,' Stella told him. 'You're just teasing him. Throw his stick instead – he'll be able to fetch that.'

'I don't know how he can stand the cold water,' Maddy observed, drawing her coat closer around her. 'The wind's bitter this morning.'

'Dogs don't care. They just have fun. I'd like a dog, sometime.' Archie rushed back with the stick and Felix threw it again. 'What do you think, darling? Shall we have a dog like Archie one day?'

'Well, maybe,' she said, slightly taken aback. They had never discussed pets, although both were fond of Dottie Friend's large cat, Albert. But cats were easy – they looked after themselves, asking only a bowl of food a day and somewhere comfortable to sleep. A dog needed a lot more attention.

They strolled to the end of the bay, where a tumble of rocks at the foot of the high cliffs impeded their progress. Felix bent and picked up a rock, examining it with interest.

'Look, it's a fossil. An ammonite – a sort of prehistoric snail, I think. See how it's curled round?' He handed it to Stella. 'We'll keep it as a souvenir.'

'There are lots of fossils on this beach,' Maddy said. 'They've even found dinosaurs' bones at Lyme Regis. It was a little girl who found the first one, and people have started to come specially to look for them.'

'Yes, I've heard about her,' Felix said. 'I wish I could find a dinosaur. Just think how exciting it would be to look up and see the shape of a huge prehistoric animal in the cliff-face. Now, that *would* be something to take home as a souvenir.' He glanced up and then gripped Stella's arm. 'Look! What's that? Surely it's—'

'Stop fooling about, Felix, and be satisfied with your ammonite. We wouldn't have room for a dinosaur in the Little Burracombe vicarage anyway.'

'When is Felix being installed?' Maddy enquired.

'At Easter. Well, during Easter week actually, because the Bishop will be busy with services on Easter Day. You'll come, won't you?'

'Yes, of course. It'll be lovely to come to Burracombe for Easter.'

'I expect Stephen will have leave then as well,' Felix said a little slyly. 'He could give you a lift.'

'So he could,' Maddy said. 'And you needn't look like that, Felix. We're just friends, that's all.'

'Of course you are,' Felix said. 'We believe you.' He didn't add, 'Thousands wouldn't,' but the words were in the air and Maddy aimed a kick at him, which he dodged, grinning. Archie, sensing a skirmish, bounded up eagerly and shook icy water all over them and they ran along the beach, laughing, to get back to the house in time for Sunday dinner.

Felix and Stella left soon afterwards to return to Burracombe, leaving Maddy to get ready for her own week. She thought about Stephen, now stationed only a few miles away. He had left reluctantly last night, holding her in his arms as they stood just outside the front door. She'd returned his kiss and rested her head against his shoulder for a moment before gently pulling away.

'It's been nice to see you, Stephen. I'm sorry I wasn't here when you arrived.'

'Not to worry. We'll have lots of chances to see each other from now on.' He kissed her again. 'I'll let you know when I'm coming over next time and we'll go for a drive. We could go to Lyme Regis or Dorchester for lunch. And as the weather gets better we'll be able to explore the New Forest. We're going to have fun this summer, Maddy.'

'Yes,' she said a little doubtfully. 'It does depend on what the Archdeacon wants me to do, though. He's often quite busy on Saturdays and he needs me then.'

'Oh, I'm sure he'll understand,' Stephen said airily. He held her a little closer. 'You're very special to me, Maddy, you know that, don't you?'

Maddy didn't answer. She turned her face to his and kissed his cheek. He moved his head so that their lips met, and then released her. 'I'd better let you get back to your guests. I've got quite a long drive down to Devon anyway. And next time, I shall expect you to come with me. You know you're always welcome to stay at the Barton – Dad and Hilary are always asking after you.' He gave her a last kiss and whispered, 'Goodnight, my sweet darling Maddy.'

'Goodnight,' she murmured, and stepped out of his arms. She watched him run down the steps and leap over the door of his car into the driver's seat. It was a bigger, rather grander sports car than Felix's little Mirabelle and she thought it would be nice to go driving in the New Forest or through Dorset at Stephen's side. It would be nice, too, to have him coming over to see her and take her out to lunch or tea. They would, as he had promised, have a lot of fun through the spring and summer.

And yet ... thinking about it again, as she went about her chores after Stella and Felix had left, she knew that there had been something in Stephen's manner that disturbed her a little. Something possessive, as if he had already made up his mind that she was his property. And I'm not, she thought, hanging a few small items of washing over the bath. I'm not ready to be tied to anyone yet. I want to have fun, but not just with Stephen Napier. There are other people I want to get to know – other nice young men to make friends with.

Sammy Hodges's face came into her mind, smiling shyly as he reminded her of the day they had taken Silver out on a picnic. She'd enjoyed meeting him again. She wanted to get to know him better, without having to explain to Stephen that it was just a childhood friendship.

87

He doesn't own me, she thought, gazing out of her bedroom window at the curve of the bay and the shining sea. Nobody does. Nobody's going to own me for a long time yet.

Chapter Eleven

Alec was right. Floyd was on board the *Queen Elizabeth* as she steamed up Southampton Water a few days later, and Lizzie waited in trepidation for his knock on the door. She had almost decided to go out, but she didn't know when he would come. And where could she go? It was too cold to take the children to the park, and she couldn't keep running away to Bridge End. Besides, although she and her mother had parted on good enough terms, she couldn't talk to her as she could to Ruth, and she knew that if she did go to Ruth her mother would be annoyed. There was no point in making things worse.

I could go to the shops, she thought, but the children don't really enjoy that, and it wasn't fair to drag them around for nothing. Instead, she spent the morning doing chores and after they had had sausages and mash for dinner she lit the fire and sat down to listen to the wireless. *Woman's Hour* was on, with Jean Metcalfe talking to a woman who kept her own goats.

Barry tipped his box of coloured wooden bricks out on to the rag rug in front of the fire and began to build a castle. Gillie opened the front of the doll's house that Alec had made her for Christmas and began to rearrange the small pieces of furniture. The whole family had got together to give her this present; George had made chairs and a table for the living room, and Jane had covered them with scraps of fabric, while Ruth had papered the walls. It even had a proper bathroom, something none of the family possessed in their own homes.

'I wish the house had a garden,' Gillie said. 'It could be a farmhouse. They could have animals.'

'Perhaps when your birthday comes along,' Lizzie said. 'That's not far away.'

'The sixth of February,' Gillie said with satisfaction. 'I'll have a farm then.'

'I said *perhaps*,' Lizzie told her, and started another row of Alec's new work jumper. It would be nice, she thought rather wistfully, if their own house had a garden big enough to keep a couple of goats in and perhaps some hens. She felt so cramped sometimes, here in this tiny house in a little back street in the middle of Southampton. You couldn't even see the sky properly and there were no trees or grass for miles, except in the park. And—

The knock sounded unusually loud and sharp. Lizzie dropped her knitting. Her heart seemed to jump right into her throat and she put her hand up to her neck.

'Someone at the door,' Gillie said. 'Shall I go?'

'No!' Lizzie said sharply, jumping up so quickly that her knitting fell on to Barry's castle and knocked off the top row of bricks. 'It's all right, Barry, you can soon build them up again ... I said, no, Gillie. I'll go. You stay here.'

'But it might be—' Gillie began, but Lizzie was already closing the door behind her. She went down the narrow passage, her heart thudding, and paused to take a deep breath before opening the door. It probably isn't him, she told herself. It'll be the coalman, or Mrs Huggett from next door wanting to borrow some sugar – or almost anyone. It didn't have to be Floyd. He wouldn't come without letting her know ... she pulled the door open.

And there he was. Tall and smiling gravely, as she remembered him. The years showing a little in the dusting of grey on his dark hair, in the fine lines around his eyes. What would he be now – only in his early thirties. Too soon, surely, to be going grey? Unconsciously, she put her hand up to her own hair, staring at him speechlessly with wide eyes.

'Hello, Lizzie,' he said quietly.

There was a long pause. Lizzie could find nothing to say and didn't think her voice would have worked if she had. She looked up at him, shaken by a rush of emotion so powerful that if she had not put her hand on the door jamb, she would have fallen. Her knees felt too weak to support her and there was a singing in her ears. Her heart seemed to be banging against the wall of her chest, as if it were a bird trying to beat its way out.

'Lizzie?' he said again, and she took a deep, shivering breath and tried to speak.

'Floyd,' she said, her voice no more than a whisper. 'Floyd, I didn't think ... I didn't expect ...'

He frowned, his dark brows coming together in the way she remembered so well. 'Didn't you get my letter?'

'Yes – yes, but I didn't think ... I didn't really think you'd come here.'

'Where else would I come? This is where you are – where Gillie is.'

Lizzie flung a quick glance along the passageway behind her. The door to the back room was still closed but any minute now it might open and Gillie come inquisitively out. She said desperately, 'I can't stop out here. The children are in there by themselves. The fire—'

'Fire? You mean you've left them by themselves with a *fire*?'

'We can't all traipse to the door every time someone knocks,' she retorted. 'And there's a guard up, of course there is. But I'll have to go in.'

'Aren't you going to ask me in as well, then?' He smiled down at her and her heart, which had slowed down a little, quivered and threatened to begin its dance again. 'I've come a long way, Lizzie, and it's cold out here.'

'You should have let me know. We could have met some-where. I can't ask you in here, Floyd. This is Alec's house.'

'And Gillie is my daughter.'

'You said you'd stay away. You said you wouldn't ...' A door opened two or three houses away and a woman Lizzie didn't like much stepped out on to the pavement, glancing curiously at them. Lizzie bit off her words abruptly. 'Please, Floyd, go away. I'll meet you somewhere in town. Tomorrow, perhaps.'

He shook his head. 'Won't do, Lizzie. This is a business trip. I don't have a lot of time.' His eyes hardened a little. 'I know what I said – what we both said. But I didn't think then that I'd ever come back to England. Now I have, and I want to see my daughter.' His voice had been low, too low for Lizzie's neighbour to hear the words, but when he added, 'Either you bring her out here or you ask me in – which is it to be?' he raised his voice very slightly and Lizzie, her face scarlet with embarrassment and anger, knew that he did not mean to give up.

'All right,' she said through her teeth, 'you can come in. But only for a few minutes. And you are not to say anything to Gillie – about who you are, I mean. You're just a friend, all right? A friend, passing by and dropping in to say hello.'

He gave her a long look but didn't reply and she had no idea, as she turned to lead him indoors, whether he would obey her. She could only hope that he understood what damage any revelation might do – to her, to her family, to Gillie herself.

She heard the front door close behind him and led him along the short passage, opening the door to the living room. The children were still on the rug where she had left them, glancing up to see who the visitor was, and she felt Floyd stop behind her and heard his tiny intake of breath as he gazed down, for the first time in his life, at his daughter.

*

The children stared up at the stranger. Lizzie cast her mind around wildly, trying to decide what to tell them. Did she need to tell them anything? Couldn't she simply pretend he was someone she knew slightly who had come to – to – to what? I'm not good at this, she thought miserably. It was bad enough lying to Alec all those years ago, I can't lie to my children as well.

Floyd took matters out of her hands, as she might have known he would. He knelt down on the rug, close to his daughter, and touched her doll's house. Lizzie, who had caught her breath, let it out in a small sigh. If he had touched Gillie herself ... he was speaking and she realised she had missed his first words.

'... your doll's house? It's a very nice one. Does it have a name?'

Gillie stared at him, fascinated by his voice. She had only ever heard an American accent on the radio, or in the cartoons she had seen in the cinema. She said, in an awed tone: 'Are you a cowboy?'

Floyd laughed. 'No, honey, I wish I was. I've got a horse at home, though.'

'A horse?' Gillie was enthralled by horses and always begged to see her grandfather's shires when she went out to Bridge End. 'What's his name?'

'Tornado, and she's a mare. You know what a mare is, don't you?'

'Of course I do,' Gillie said, a touch of scorn in her voice. 'It's a lady horse. My grandad's got big horses on his farm. What colour is she?'

'She's grey. She's just had a foal.'

'That's a baby horse,' Gillie informed her brother, who had stopped playing with his bricks and was gazing at the visitor, entranced. 'Do you live on a farm?'

'No, but I've got room for a horse in my yard and there are lots of good places to ride where I live.'

'In your *yard*?' Gillie turned her head to look out of the window, which gave on to the tiny square of backyard that was all the garden the house possessed. 'We couldn't keep a horse in our yard.'

'A yard's what we call our garden,' he explained easily. 'We've got plenty of room.'

'We?' Lizzie asked before she could stop herself, and he looked up at her. Their eyes met.

'Yep, still living with Mom and Pop,' he said in a casual tone, and she bit her lip. She didn't want him to think she was interested in his life. 'How long are you here for?' she asked, wanting to divert his attention from Gillie. And then, reluctantly but driven by good manners, 'Would you like a cup of tea?'

'I would,' he said without getting up. 'I really would. Thanks, Lizzie.'

She hesitated, then went out to the scullery, leaving the door open so that she could hear what was going on. Gillie's voice sounded, telling Floyd about the doll's house – how her daddy had made it for her, Grandad had made the furniture, Grandma the cushions and how Auntie Ruth had papered the walls.

'And it's got a proper bathroom, see? I want a parrot too, like Auntie Ruth has. He's called Silver and he can talk and—'

'I know,' Floyd said quietly. 'I've seen him.'

There was a sudden silence. Lizzie came to the door and stared through it and he looked up and caught her eye. She saw the colour run up from his neck and knew that her anger was showing on her face. They held their gaze for a long moment and then he broke it.

'I'm sorry, Lizzie.'

'You said you wouldn't—' she began in a low, furious voice, but Gillie interrupted.

'You've seen Silver? When? When did you see him?'

'A long time ago,' he said, not looking at either of them. 'During the war, before you were born.'

Gillie looked at him uncertainly. 'Before the war' was a phrase she had heard quite a lot, but never quite understood. She knew, of course, that there had to have been a time before she was born, but it was in the magic fairytale time of long ago and far away, and she could never really believe that there had been a time when she did not exist. It was a matter which she often brought up: where had she been before she was born, had she been dead then, why couldn't she remember? – without ever being given a satisfactory answer. And now here was this stranger, who talked like a cowboy and had a backyard as big as a field, who said he had known Auntie Ruth and Silver before she was born.

'Did you know Mummy then, too?' she asked doubtfully. 'And Daddy?'

'I knew your mom,' Floyd said, glancing at Lizzie. 'Not your – your dad. He was away then.'

Gillie nodded. 'He came home afterwards. He was poorly and then I was born and he got better.'

The shriek of the kettle interrupted them and Lizzie turned back quickly to remove the whistle and make tea. Her hands were shaking as she poured boiling water on to the tea leaves and she felt hot with anger. This was going too far. This wasn't meant to happen. Gillie was sure to tell Alec all about it that evening, probably the minute he was in the door, and she could just imagine his face as he listened to her excited voice telling him about the American who had come to the house, who knew Auntie Ruth and Silver, who had known Mummy before Gillie herself was born ...

Oh, no, she thought, putting both hands to her face. Gillie, don't say that, please don't say that.

She poured the tea into cups and carried them into the back room. Floyd was in a chair now, Gillie on his knee, and she stared at them with a mixture of fury, love and a strange, unexpected kind of grief – almost, she thought, a yearning.

'You'll have to go soon,' she said abruptly, setting the cups on the table that took up most of the middle of the room. 'I've got Alec's supper to get ready.'

'Sure,' he said easily. 'I only dropped by for a few minutes anyway. Maybe it would be a good idea if you and I did get together – have a coffee somewhere, maybe? How are you fixed for tomorrow afternoon?'

'I thought you said you didn't have time. This is a business trip.' She added sharply, 'Get down, Gillie. How can Mr Hanson drink his tea with you on his lap?' She saw him flinch and knew it was because she'd used his surname. 'How long are you here for, anyway?'

'A month or so. I'll be in London, mostly. Got a meeting on Thursday. I was going to travel up tomorrow but it can be put off a day. So how about it?' He met her eyes and saw the refusal beginning in them. 'We have to talk, Lizzie.'

'I don't see why.'

Floyd set Gillie gently down on her feet. 'Go and play with your doll's house again, honey.' He met Lizzie's eyes. 'Of course we do. You know we do.'

'I don't,' she said stubbornly. Her heart was fluttering and she felt slightly sick. 'We agreed that we'd keep it to Christmas letters. You weren't even going to write back.'

'And so I haven't.'

'But you've *come* here instead!' she cried, and saw both children look up in surprise. With an effort, she controlled her voice and said more quietly, 'That's worse than writing. You've broken the agreement and now I want you to go away and not contact us again.'

'I can't do that.' His eyes went to the little girl's head, bent once again over her toys. 'I've seen her now. I've seen you. I can't let it rest.'

'You must. I can't meet you tomorrow, Floyd, or any other day. Not ever. You've got to leave us in peace.' Her voice trembled and she felt tears in her eyes.

'Lizzie, don't talk like that. I don't want to upset you.'

'Then go away!' she cried, her voice sharp and jagged, so that the children stared again and Barry climbed to his feet and put his hand on her knee. She put the back of her wrist to her eyes, wiping away the tears. 'Can't you see you've already upset me? You're upsetting them, too. Please, Floyd, just go away and don't come back. *Please.*'

There was a long silence. She gathered Barry against her and rested her face against his hair. She knew that Gillie was watching her with frightened eyes and she felt a surge of anger against Floyd. But it was anger shot through with something else – something bright and hot, like dark smoke shot through with flames.

'Just meet me tomorrow afternoon,' he said quietly. 'Without the children. Can you do that? Please?'

She raised her face and looked at him. He was watching her gravely and she had a sudden sharp memory of him looking at her like that before. At Sunday dinner in her mother's house, where he and the other airman (what was his name? Marvin?) had come as part of the 'friendship' exercise between the local people and the American air station. At the square dance he had organised in one of the hangars. On their walks together during those last months of the war. And on VE Day, when they had celebrated together on the village green – and, later, in the woods, privately and too well.

'All right,' she said with a tiny sigh. 'I'll do that.'

He went soon after that, and she returned to the back room after seeing him stride away up the street, seeing it suddenly with different eyes. Americans lived in big houses, with huge gardens; what had he thought of this tiny, two-up two-down terraced house with a scullery tacked on the back and an outside lavatory? He probably thinks we're poor, she thought defensively, but we're not. We've got a nice little home and anyway we're planning to move somewhere bigger soon, now that we're expecting another baby.

It occurred to her then that she had not mentioned the

new baby to Floyd – but why should she? It was none of his business. She might tell him tomorrow, when they met at the teashop she had suggested, or she might leave it until her next Christmas letter, when the baby would be here. Or she might not tell him at all. After all, why should she? It was none of his business. She would keep their conversation tomorrow focused entirely on the agreement they had made, and the need for him to keep to it.

'Has the man gone now, Mummy?' Gillie enquired, looking up from her game. 'He was a nice man, wasn't he?'

'Yes.' Lizzie went to pour herself a fresh cup of tea. 'Yes, he was.' She wondered if she should ask Gillie not to mention Floyd to Alec, but decided against it. She could not ask a child to deceive her father, even by omission. In any case, Alec had a right to know, and it was best that he knew immediately. She'd tell him herself.

In the event, however, neither of them told him. He came home late that evening, long after Gillie had gone to bed. There had been a sudden emergency on the ship he was working on at the moment and he'd be working late for the rest of the week. He wouldn't be home until ten and he'd have to leave again at seven in the morning. He was tired and preoccupied, and Lizzie knew that this was not the time to remind him of Floyd.

He didn't even see Gillie until the weekend, by which time she'd forgotten about the man who talked like a cowboy. And by that time, everything had changed anyway.

Chapter Twelve

The teashop was in Shirley, not far from the docks. The dock where the *Queen Elizabeth* lay was so close to the road that the huge liner seemed to rear up over the passing traffic. Lizzie looked up at the bow, aware that Floyd was no longer aboard but feeling a strange connection with the ship that had brought him back to her. It was three in the afternoon and already dusk was creeping in.

It had been a relief not to have to tell Alec about his visit, and an even greater relief that Gillie hadn't been able to blurt it out. I'll have to tell him tonight, Lizzie told herself, or at least at the weekend when we've got time to talk. But before that, she must sort out her own feelings. Anger was a part of them – anger that Floyd had broken their agreement, anger that he had intruded into her life. And there was fear too – the fear that he would want to increase his contact, that he would want to tell Gillie who he was – that he might even tell her without Lizzie's agreement. That he might want to take Gillie away.

He can't do that, Lizzie thought, quickening her pace as she came within sight of the teashop. He wouldn't be allowed to do that. But the fear still pulled at a corner of her mind.

And behind all that, like a shadow that faded if she tried to look at it squarely, was something else. Something to do with that unexpected leap of her heart, that warm, betraying colour in her cheeks; something that caught at her memory when she looked into his eyes.

The windows of the teashop had net curtains, so that you couldn't see who was inside. Lizzie pushed open the door and peered into the dim interior. There were half a dozen small round tables covered with shiny American cloth and at one, in the far corner, sat Floyd.

She walked over to him and sat down. There was a pot of tea already on the table, with two cups and saucers. As she shrugged off her coat, a waitress came with two plates holding hot buttered crumpets.

'Is this all right?' Floyd asked. He picked up his crumpet and stared at it. 'I've never had these things before. What are they? What are you supposed to do with them?'

'They're crumpets. They've been toasted – you just eat them as they are.' She looked at hers but didn't touch it. 'Do you want some tea?'

'I guess so.' He watched while she poured. 'We don't drink this much, back home. About the only place I've ever had it is in your mother's kitchen.'

Lizzie ignored the attempt to bring back memories. 'Do you take sugar?'

'I dunno. There wasn't much of it about in those days, was there? Didn't you have some sort of little pill you put in tea and coffee?'

'Saccharin. Try it without and if you don't like it, put some sugar in.' She handed him the cup. 'I don't have very much time, so if—'

He interrupted her. 'Where are the kids? Where's Gillie?'

'I've left them with a friend. They're all right. Floyd, you shouldn't have come yesterday.'

'Whether I should or shouldn't doesn't matter now,' he answered. 'The point is that I did. What we have to do now is decide what to do next.'

'We're not going to do anything *next*. You're going to go away and go back to America and never do this again. I'll write to you at Christmas, as I always have, but you won't write back and you won't try to get in touch with Gillie. Ever. It'll be up to her. That's what we agreed.' She heard her voice quiver, but looked him firmly in the eye.

There was a short silence. Floyd took a small bite of his crumpet and chewed, making a face as if it tasted better than he expected. 'Hm,' he said. 'Not bad.' He chewed some more.

'Do you understand what I'm saying, Floyd?' Lizzie asked at last, and he looked back at her, his expression unreadable.

'I understand. Yeah, I understand all right.' A small pause. 'I don't necessarily agree, but I understand.'

Lizzie gathered in the reins on her anger. 'Floyd, we had an agreement—'

'We also had a daughter.'

The words hit her like a shock of cold water. She caught her breath and said, 'No, Floyd. We didn't. *Alec and I* had a daughter. He's her father. His name is on her birth certificate. He's brought her up, cared for her, earned a living for her. He took me back when a lot of men would have thrown me out, and he said he'd treat her as her own, and he always has. She's his daughter now.'

'She's mine,' Floyd stated. 'And she always will be. Nothing can change the truth, Lizzie.'

'Maybe it depends which truth you're trying to change,' she said swiftly. 'There's only one way she's your daughter – '

' – a pretty important one, I'd say. She wouldn't exist at all without me.'

Lizzie shivered. Her anger was increasing, fuelled by her fear. 'Floyd, please.'

'Please what?' he asked when she paused, unable to think of the words that would make him do as she wanted.

'Please – just leave us alone. Go away. Stay away. It won't do any good, coming here and saying you want to see her again. It'll just cause trouble. Please, Floyd. If you ever ...' She stopped again.

'If I ever what?' he asked quietly, and she looked down at

the shiny green American cloth, biting her lips, unable to say the words yet unable to think of any others.

'If you ever loved me,' she said at last, her voice so low that she could barely hear it herself. 'If you ever loved me, Floyd, even for a minute, please go away now.'

There was another long pause. Then he said, his voice not much louder than hers, 'It's because I love you – because I couldn't forget you – that I came. And it's because I'll never be able to forget you that I can't go away. Not now.' He paused and then, his voice lower than ever, said, 'I never stopped loving you. Never.'

Lizzie raised her eyes slowly. He was gazing at her with a darkness in his eyes that took the breath from her lungs. She shivered, and he put his hand across the table and gripped hers before she could take it away.

'Did you hear me, Lizzie? I said—'

'No,' she whispered. 'Don't say it again, Floyd. Please.'

'Don't I have the right to say what I feel?' he asked. 'Don't I have the right to talk to you, of all people, about what the past six years have been like for me? I went away because you wanted me to, I stayed away, I kept to our agreement, but have you ever given a thought to what that meant to me? You've lived your life with another man—'

'Not another man! My *husband*. He was my husband before I met you.'

'Another man,' he repeated. 'You've got my daughter and a son of your own – yours and his. Have you ever wondered what *I* had? What *my* life was like?'

'We said goodbye—'

'And now,' he said, 'we're saying hello again.' There was another short silence. He looked at her hand, still gripped in his, and turned it over. With the forefinger of his other hand, he traced a pattern in her palm and she quivered. 'It's the same for you, Lizzie, isn't it?' he said quietly. 'You feel it too. I knew it the minute you opened the door to me yesterday.'

'No,' she whispered. 'No.'

'Yes, Lizzie. *Yes.*'

She pulled her hand away roughly. 'I've got to go now. I said I wouldn't be long.'

'Not yet,' he said. 'We haven't even begun to talk yet.'

'There's nothing to talk about.'

'There is. There's a lot to talk about.' He glanced around. The other customers had gone and they were alone apart from the waitress, who was watching them curiously. 'Let's get out of here.'

Lizzie was on her feet, dragging her coat around her shoulders. Panic rose and swirled inside her, like bubbling water from a whirlpool deep inside. 'No!' she hissed. 'No, Floyd – no! I don't want to talk to you. There's nothing to say, nothing. Leave us alone. Please – just leave us alone.' She stumbled across the room, bumping into tables and chairs as she went and almost knocking two over. The waitress started forward but Lizzie pushed past her and out into the cold, darkening street. Behind her, she was aware of Floyd throwing money on to the table, dragging the door open again. But she was running now, into the darkness that lay between the pools of yellow gaslight, and as she turned a corner she found a bus just pulling away from its stop. She leaped aboard, neither knowing nor caring where it was heading, and left Floyd standing on the pavement, staring after her.

The bus took her all the way to Bassett Green, where she got off and waited in the dark for another one going back to the centre. It was bitterly cold on the road and she stood with her hands thrust deep into her coat pockets, tears almost freezing on her cheeks. Her heart was in turmoil and her mind seemed to be like treacle poured on to a table, spreading uncontrollably with thoughts slipping in and out of her grasp. Floyd loved her – he wanted her – and ... but she skidded away from the thought, knowing it was too dangerous to put into words.

'I love Alec,' she repeated over and over again. 'I love Alec, I'm married to him, I want to spend my life with him. Alec, Alec, Alec ...'

But Floyd would not go away. For six years, she had pushed him out of her mind, for six years she had given herself entirely to her marriage, her husband and her children. She had thought herself safe for ever from the American who had stolen her heart and given her a child. Yet now, after only two brief meetings, she knew that she had never pushed him away – not entirely. He had remained there, hidden in some deep recess, waiting for the right moment to come out.

This isn't the right moment, she told herself frantically. There's never going to be a right moment. He's got to go away. I've got to *make* him go away.

A bus came along and she climbed aboard, shivering. The conductor looked at her curiously.

'You looked shrammed, love. Been waiting long, have you? We don't often pick up people at that stop, this time of day – it's a bit lonely by the Green.'

'I'm all right. I've been to visit someone and it's turned colder than I expected.' She made her way to a seat and sat down, staring out of the window, seeing her own reflection look back at her. Her face looked pale and her eyes wide, almost frightened.

There's nothing more between us, she thought fiercely. There can't be, ever again. I don't want it.

I won't see Floyd again. If he comes to the door I won't open it. I won't answer his letters and when we move I won't let him know the address. I won't let him see Gillie, ever, and I won't tell her she's got another father.

I'm going home now, back to Alec and the children. Back to my own life. That's what I want – and it's *all* I want.

Chapter Thirteen

Once Sammy's plans were out in the open, he saw no reason to hesitate and went into Southampton the very next day, coming home triumphant on a small motorcycle with a blue petrol tank and black saddle, and a pillion seat fixed over the back wheel. He stopped outside the cottage and heaved it up on to its prop stand, removing his new black helmet and grinning as the family came down the path. Linnet was first, pulling the gate open and dashing over to cling to him.

'Sammy! You've got your bike! Oh, let me have a ride on it, please, *please*!'

'Now, you know what you've been told—' Ruth began, and Sammy shook his head.

'You're not allowed to until you're twelve. Anyway, you haven't got a crash helmet.'

'I could get one. I could have it for my birthday. Oh, please!'

'Not until you're twelve years old,' Sammy repeated, having been told this by his father as a condition to his having the bike at all. 'And they don't make helmets your size.' He had no idea if this was true, but Linnet wasn't going to be allowed to ride the bike and was more likely to accept this if she was given good reasons why she couldn't. Otherwise, she would never stop pestering. Now, she wrinkled her face and pursed her lips but said no more. She watched a little sulkily as her parents examined the machine and Sammy proudly showed off all its good points.

'DMW have only just started making these bikes. There's a 122c.c and this one – the 197c.c De Luxe. It's got a Villiers engine, see. They're really good. They're going to be shown at Earls Court this year. It's brand new.'

'Must have cost a bit,' Dan said. 'I hope you haven't got it on Hire Purchase.'

'No, I saved up for it. It was a hundred and sixteen pounds.'

'A hundred and sixteen pounds?' Ruth echoed. 'However did you manage to save that much, Sammy?'

'I just didn't go out drinking like the other erks on the station,' Sammy grinned. 'And look what I've got to show for it. I'll be able to go anywhere now. And I can do all my own repairs. I haven't been a blacksmith's apprentice for nothing.'

'So long as you treat it sensibly,' Dan said, still unwilling to give it his wholehearted approval. 'Don't go racing all over the country. Some of those main roads are getting proper dangerous these days.'

'I'll be careful, Dad,' Sammy promised. 'I've got too much to live for to want to do anything daft. Anyway, will it be all right if I keep it in the shed? I can always move it out if it's in your way when you want to work in there.'

Dan nodded. He and Sammy had spent the previous evening clearing out the shed to make room for the motorcycle, removing a lot of clutter that he'd been meaning to get rid of for some time anyway. He stood with Ruth and Linnet, watching as Sammy carefully wheeled his new acquisition along the path and round the cottage to the shed in the back garden. They looked at each other a little ruefully.

'He's really grown up now, isn't he,' Ruth said sadly. 'I know it sounds silly, since he's been away from home in the RAF all this time, but you sort of felt they'd look after him for us. Now, he's making his own decisions and the bike's giving him his freedom. There's hardly any point in waiting for his birthday to give him the key of the door – he might as well have it now and be done with it.'

Dan shook his head. 'No, we'll keep that until he's twenty-one. He can come home late if he wants to, but until then he's got to ask for a key – it's a sort of symbol. It'll mean all the more to him if he gets it on the right day, and it's not all that long – just another couple of months, that's all. But I know what you mean, Ruthie. Seeing him today with his bike – well, he does look more grown up, somehow. It's daft, but he even looks a bit taller!'

Ruth laughed and squeezed his hand. 'He's a young man now. A lovely young man, and a credit to his dad.'

'A credit to you, you mean,' Dan said gruffly and then, in his normal tone, 'Blimey, what's the boy doing in that shed? Wrapping the flipping bike in a blanket and telling it a good-night story? He'll be taking it a cup of cocoa next.'

'He's just thrilled he's got it,' Ruth said with a smile. 'But he'd better come in soon. I've got a meat pie in the oven and I don't want it burning. Go and tell him tea's nearly ready, Linnet, there's a love.

The little girl ran off and Dan and Ruth stood in the garden a moment longer. Then Dan seemed to rouse himself from his thoughts and gave her shoulders a quick squeeze.

'Come on, love. Our Sam might be growing up, but we've still got Linnet to keep us green. It'll be a good few years yet before she's ready to fly away.'

'And by then,' Ruth said, 'you could be a grandfather! There'll always be kiddies round us, Dan. We don't have to have any worries about that.'

The thought of having children of his own had never even entered Sammy's head. He was entirely absorbed in the present: the joy of owning his own motorbike and the freedom it would give him, the excitement of being able to go wherever he like and – most of all – the anticipation of going to see Maddy Forsyth at West Lyme.

He had already sent her a postcard asking if she would like to go out with him the following Saturday, and to his enormous delight she had written back saying yes. He'd even managed to intercept Bill Watkins, the postman, in the lane the day her card had arrived, so neither Ruth nor Dan knew about this – not that they'd have minded, but he just felt he wanted to keep it to himself for a while. Bill knew, of course, because he always read postcards – it was legal to do that, he had told Sammy once, and if you wanted things to be private you ought to put them in an envelope – but he wouldn't tell anyone. He didn't know who Maddy was, and her message had been so brief that even Bill probably didn't understand it.

He had bought a road map and already worked out his route. It would take him, he reckoned, not much more than an hour to get there, mostly along the wooded roads of the New Forest and then along the Dorset coast. He wondered if she would consent to coming for a ride on the back of the bike – they could go anywhere they liked then. But this first time, it might be best if they just walked somewhere or caught a bus. Anyway, she wouldn't be likely to have a crash helmet and he knew Ruth would be annoyed if he took a girl on the back of his bike without one.

The weather, which had been cold at the beginning of the month, was still mild and Sammy was impatient for the weekend to arrive. He wanted to try out his bike with a trip somewhere before that, but Ruth was anxious about his going out in the dark before he was used to it. In the end, however, she agreed to his going as far as Southampton for his night school classes.

'Why don't you pop in and see our Lizzie?' she suggested. 'She's been feeling a bit under the weather lately, what with the new baby coming and Alec doing a lot of overtime. She'd welcome your company. You could have your tea there before you go to the Institute.'

Sammy thought this was a good idea. Solly had agreed to his leaving work early on the three nights a week he would be attending the Institute, and he could ride over before it got dark. He sent another postcard to let Lizzie know he was coming, and the next afternoon he arrived on her doorstep just as the street lights were coming on.

'I hope it's all right for me to come like this,' he said, as she answered the bell. 'There wasn't time to get a reply. You can tell me to go away again if you're busy.'

'Don't be silly,' she said. 'Come in and get warm by the fire. So that's your new bike, is it? Very posh!'

'It's smashing,' he said, stepping into the narrow passageway and starting to take off his motorcycling clothes. He was wearing a thick jacket over two jumpers and had a long navy-blue scarf wound several times around his neck. He unwrapped himself and bent to take off his heavy boots. 'You don't mind my socks, do you? They were clean on this morning.'

Lizzie laughed and led him into the back room where the fire was burning brightly behind its guard and both children were playing on the rug. 'Sit down. I'll make a cup of tea. You're going to night school, aren't you? Have you got time for something to eat? It's beans on toast tonight.'

'Smashing,' he said. 'Are you sure you don't mind?'

'Of course I don't. It's nice to see you, Sammy.' She went out to the tiny scullery and Sammy sat down in one of the two small armchairs and looked around him. He'd never been to Lizzie's house before; he'd always seen her at Bridge End, either at the farm or in Ruth's cottage. Here, the rooms were much smaller and like little boxes, without any of the beams or stone walls that made the country cottages so cosy. It was very similar, he realised, to the house he had lived in when the family were in April Grove. He had a sudden vivid memory of being in a room just like this when he was only six or seven years old, sitting beside his mother as she lay back, exhausted, in an old armchair, and then going out to the scullery to make her a cup of tea. The memory was so sharp that he felt almost faint and Lizzie, coming in with tea, looked at him in consternation.

'Sammy! Whatever's the matter? Have you got too cold on that bike?'

'No,' he said, shaking his head as if to clear the memory away. 'No, I'm all right. It was just a funny feeling I had for a minute – as if I'd gone back into the past. We used to live in a house just like this in Portsmouth.'

'I suppose there are houses like this in most big towns,' Lizzie said, handing him the cup. 'Drink this, it'll make you feel better. It's quite a nice little house,' she went on, rather defensively. 'A bit small for us really, but we're hoping to find somewhere a bit bigger before the baby comes. But there are plenty of families who manage, even with four or five children.'

'I know.' Sammy thought of the Budds, who had four children and used a Put-U-Up bed settee in the downstairs front room. A lot of the time when the war was on, the two boys Tim and Keith had been evacuated, so they hadn't had everyone at home all the time, but it must have got quite crowded when they came back. And even though they'd both gone into the Forces after a while, there were plenty of times when everyone was there. Yet Jess Budd had always kept the house looking tidy and comfortable – unlike the Hodges' house, which had been like a slum.

'It's nice here,' he said, looking at the bright colours of the rag rug, the polished dining-table and sideboard, neither of them new but looking cared for, and the pictures on the walls. 'It's a real home.'

'Well, I should hope so!' Lizzie said with a laugh. 'We've been here three years now. But I'd like to move soon. We need another bedroom and it would be nice to have a bit of garden for the children to play in. I can't help admitting I miss the countryside, but we've got to live where Alec's work is.'

'Auntie Ruth says he's doing a lot of overtime,' Sammy said, sipping his tea. He was feeling better now. Maybe Lizzie was right and he'd just got a bit cold. He looked at Lizzie properly and noticed that she was rather pale. Probably that was because of the baby, he thought. Sammy knew very little about babies and what it was like for a woman to be expecting one, but he remembered that Ruth had often been tired while she was expecting Linnet. But Ruth had looked happy and excited as well, and Lizzie didn't. There was a shadow in her eyes that worried him; maybe Ruth was right, and she did need some company with Alec working such long hours.

'So what's this night school you're going to?' Lizzie asked. 'Mum said something about you not working for Solly Barlow after all. Don't you want to be a blacksmith?'

Sammy told her about the electronics training he'd had in the RAF. 'It's going to be important,' he said. 'Nobody really knows how important, but I think it's going to change things a lot.'

'I don't know what the difference is between that and electricity,' she said, frowning, and he tried to explain about television and the new computers.

'There aren't many of them yet, and they're very big – they take up whole rooms. But we're only at the beginning, Lizzie. There's no knowing what we'll be able to do with them in a few years.'

'I'd like a television set,' she said wistfully. 'They're going to show the Coronation on it, you know. I'd really like to see that.'

After a while, she got up again and started to get the tea ready. The children left their games and sat up to the table, a plate of beans on toast in front of each of them, and Lizzie poured more tea.

'Alec won't be home until after they've gone to bed. He

hardly sees them these days, he's so busy in the dockyard. You know, Sammy, you're welcome to come to tea any time while you're at night school. I'll be pleased to see you.'

'I don't want to impose on you,' he began, but she shrugged.

'Honestly, I'd like it. I don't see enough of Bridge End people these days. You pop in whenever you like – there's always a welcome for you.'

Sam grinned at her, a little embarrassed. He'd always liked Lizzie – she'd been a frequent visitor at Ruth's cottage when he'd been evacuated there as a small boy, and she'd been kind to him in those early weeks when he'd been so unhappy and scared of everything. Between them, she and Ruth had given him confidence and helped him to grow into an ordinary little boy, and he still had a special feeling for her.

'All right,' he said. 'Thanks.'

Lizzie cleared away the empty plates and brought in the remains of a sponge cake she'd made the day before. 'So tell me what else you're doing with yourself. Have you got a nice girlfriend to go out with?'

Sammy's fair skin blushed. 'Not really. There was one at the RAF station – she used to come to the dances – but it fizzled out after a while. I think she found someone else.'

'That's a shame.'

'Not really. It wasn't serious.' He thought of Maddy. 'Actually, there is someone I'd like to get to know better. You might remember her – Muriel Simmons, she was called; she stayed at the vicarage for a while with her sister.'

Lizzie frowned. 'Weren't they orphans? I seem to remember something about their father being lost at sea.'

'That's right. They were split up after that and sent to different Children's Homes. They found each other a year or two ago. Muriel's called Maddy now, and she lives at West Lyme. I met her at the wedding we went to last week.'

'And you're going to go and see her on your motorbike,' Lizzie said with a smile.

Sammy's blush deepened. 'I thought I might, yes.'

'Well, why not? You used to play together, didn't you? And it's not all that far to West Lyme.'

Sammy grinned at her again. 'I know. I've looked at the map. In fact, I'm going on Saturday.'

'Good for you,' Lizzie said. 'I tell you what, Sam, you've got to take your chances in this life. They don't always come again.' She paused, then added in a slightly different tone, 'I'm not saying you should rush into anything, mind. You're too young to get tied down just yet.' She got up suddenly and started to clear the table. 'Look at me, going all bossy on you! Anyway, you'll need to be going soon if you're to be at the Institute in good time. I dare say you'll need to find your way about if this is the first time.'

'Yes,' Sammy said, a little bemused. He had the feeling that Lizzie was thinking about something quite different while she was talking to him and he'd seen that shadow cross her face again. She's really lonely, stuck here in this little house with the children and hardly ever seeing any of her old friends, he thought. Maybe it would be a good idea to drop in once or twice a week. 'Yes, I need to find out where to leave the bike, and which room I'm going to be in and all that. I'd better go soon.' He stood up, a little awkwardly. 'Thanks for the tea, Lizzie. It's been really nice seeing you again.'

'That's all right.' They stood looking at one another for a moment. 'And I meant what I said. You're welcome to drop in any time. Make it a regular thing, if you like.'

She saw him out and then came back to finish clearing the table and do the washing-up. The children went back to their games for the last half-hour before bed. Once again, it was unlikely that Alec would be home in time to say goodnight to them.

All the time Sammy had been here, Lizzie had been on

hot bricks in case Floyd knocked on the door again. She'd half-wanted him to go, in case the American did arrive, and half-wanted him to stay so that she could tell Floyd honestly that she had a visitor and he couldn't come in. When she'd invited Sammy to come two or three times a week, she'd been genuinely pleased at the thought of seeing him so often – but she'd also been aware that she was using him as a protection.

Since she'd left Floyd at the café the previous afternoon, she'd lived in terror of his coming to the door. She'd been sure he would come again this afternoon and wondered if perhaps he had and then, seeing the motorcycle outside, had gone away again. Even now, it wasn't too late.

On the other hand, he might have realised that she meant what she said – that she didn't want to see him again. That it was no use his trying to force her to meet him or to let him see Gillie. He might have decided to forget them both, and go on with his life as he had done before.

I hope he has, she thought, standing at the sink and washing tomato sauce from the plates. I hope he's decided not to bother us any more. I hope he never comes back.

Chapter Fourteen

Floyd came back the next afternoon.

Once again, Lizzie answered a knock on the door to find him standing there, grim and unsmiling. Once again, her emotions began to swing as if on a trapeze and she felt as sick and dizzy as if she were indeed flying high about the earth, suspended by a wire too thin to bear her weight. She pressed her hand against the wall and stared up at him wordlessly.

'Are you going to let me in, Lizzie?' he asked quietly.

'No,' she whispered through suddenly dry lips. 'No – you can't come in, Floyd. You can't. Please, just go away.'

'You know I'm not going to do that. We haven't finished our talk.'

'There's nothing to talk about. Nothing.'

'I think there is.' She could hear the determination in his voice. 'If you won't meet me somewhere, and stay with me while we talk this out, then I'm going to do it here. On the doorstep, if that's what you want.'

A door opened further along the street, and she bit her lip.

'I don't care how long I wait,' he said. 'I'll stand here until *he* comes home, if that's the way you want it. But you're going to talk to me, Lizzie, make no mistake about that.'

Lizzie drew in a deep, ragged breath. Her mind raced and leaped about the possibilities – of her mother turning the street corner on an unexpected visit; of Sammy roaring along on his motorbike; of any one of her neighbours appearing suddenly and glancing curiously at this tall stranger, hearing his

American accent; of Alec, coming home early . . .

'Go away,' she said in a low, angry tone. 'I can't have you standing on the doorstep like this.' She looked into his eyes again and knew she would have to give way. 'All right. I'll meet you. But not at the same place. On – on Bassett Common, tomorrow afternoon. We'll go for a walk. But I can't stay long – not more than half an hour. You can say all you want to say in that time, can't you?'

'I'll say some of it,' he said. 'Tell me where, then, and what time. And make sure you're there, Lizzie, or I'll be back. And I'll keep on coming back, until you face this thing properly. I'm not going to be brushed aside, you understand?'

Lizzie stared at him. 'You've changed, Floyd,' she said. 'You've changed a lot.'

'I've had time to change,' he replied. 'I've had six years without you, and without my child. That can change any man.' He looked at her for a moment and then stepped back, still holding her eyes. 'I'll see you tomorrow.'

Lizzie stood at the door and watched him stride away. Dusk was already gathering, and he was little more than a shadow as he passed the gas lamp and turned the corner at the end of the street. Little more than the shadow he had been in her mind and her heart for so long.

Yet he was no shadow now. He was here, real and angry and unpredictable, and she felt another shadow touch her heart.

The shadow of fear.

'Are you sure you don't mind having them again?' Lizzie asked her friend June the next afternoon. The two young women had met while they were in hospital giving birth to their first babies and had stayed friends ever since. June, however, had no other children and was always pleased to have Gillie and Barry to play with her Jimmy.

'Of course I don't. It gives Jimmy some company. To tell the truth, I'll be glad when he goes back to school next week.

Christmas holidays are all very well but the kiddies spend the first week getting over-excited about Santa Claus and the next two grizzling over broken toys or because the weather's too bad for them to play outside.' She glanced curiously at Lizzie. 'Where are you off to this time? Got some money to go to the sales?'

Lizzie shook her head, then wished she hadn't. 'No, I'm just meeting someone for a cup of tea. An old friend from war-time, just in Southampton for a few days.' She could feel her colour rising, even though she had spoken the perfect truth. 'I shan't be late back,' she went on hurriedly. 'I've got Alec's tea to get ready – he said he might not be so late tonight – and Barry's been a bit tired lately. I think he might be sickening for something. Someone told me there's chicken-pox about.' She was talking too fast, she knew, but she didn't seem able to stop. 'Mind you, I'd be pleased if he got it, if they both got it; it would be one more thing over and done with.' And it might keep Floyd away too, she decided, wishing she'd thought to tell him that the children had that, or some other infectious disease. Measles, perhaps, or mumps: men never liked to be around kiddies with mumps ... 'I don't suppose he will, though. They never do, when it's convenient, do they?' Her tongue stopped at last and she gazed helplessly at her friend, unable to think of anything else to say.

'No, they don't,' June said, and Lizzie could tell that she was now more curious and maybe even a little suspicious. She thinks I'm telling lies, Lizzie thought miserably. She thinks I'm carrying on with someone. But I'm not.

'I'll get off, then,' she said in a depressed tone. 'Thanks again, June. I'll see you in about an hour. Bye-bye Gillie, bye-bye, Barry – be good.' She looked at them, wishing suddenly that she were going with them into June's warm, cosy living room with its clutter of toys and sewing and newspapers, wish-ing that she could turn her back on Floyd and all the problems he brought with him, and that he would simply vanish from her life. But it wasn't going to happen like that. Whatever was going to happen, she would have to face and deal with – if being swept along as if by a swift tidal current could be called 'dealing with' her problems.

I don't feel as if I've got any choice, she thought, walking away into the chilly grey afternoon. All I can do is go with the stream, wherever it takes me, and hope I don't drown.

Floyd was waiting in the spot she had chosen and they began to walk across the common. Once again, Lizzie's heart was hammering and once again she wished she could have stayed with June, drinking tea and watching the children play.

At last, he said, 'Have you thought any more about all of this, Lizzie? About you and me and Gillie?'

'Of course I have,' she retorted. 'I've hardly thought about anything else. Floyd, you've got to stop this. You've got to forget about seeing Gillie or having any part in her life. We had an agreement – you've got to stick to it, like I have.'

'I've told you, I can't do that any more. Now that I've seen her—'

'You shouldn't have come,' she interrupted. 'You ought to have known it could only cause trouble. Seeing her was bound to upset you. Well, I'm sorry, but that's your own fault and you've got to put up with it. Don't you think you've upset me too? But I'm not having Gillie upset. Nor Alec. It's not fair, Floyd, it's not fair on any of us and I want you to stop now and go away, and not come back. Ever.'

There was a long silence. She stole a look at him and saw that his face was hard and cold, his eyes shuttered. Her heart sank. 'Floyd,' she began pleadingly. 'Floyd, you must realise what you're doing to us. I've got a home – a family. We're *Gillie's* family. How can she understand that this strange man, all the way from America, is her father? How can she understand that Alec isn't? And there's Barry, too. What's he going to make of it all? You can't just come in and break it all up – all that Alec and me have worked for, all that we've put together. You can't.'

'Can't I?' he asked. 'Not even when you're the woman I love and you've got my child? Don't I have the right to fight for what I want?'

'No,' she said tersely. 'No, you don't. You gave that up six years ago. You don't have the right to come back and demand it now.'

'You made me give it up! You sent me away.'

'What else could I do?' she cried. 'Alec was in a terrible state when he came home. He'd been in a prisoner-of-war camp and he wasn't even a fighting man – he was in the Merchant Navy. They were unarmed, did you realise that? His ship was sunk – he spent hours in the sea before they picked him up; he nearly died, and he had a dreadful time in the camp. How could I tell him I was leaving him for another man – an American airman? It would have destroyed him.'

'You told him you were having my child.'

'I had to,' she said tiredly. 'He knew it couldn't possibly be his. But we got over that. He took Gillie as his own. It's his name on her birth certificate. You can't think of taking her away now, Floyd. In any case, you wouldn't be allowed to.'

'I would,' he said, 'if you came with her.'

'No! No, I won't! I won't leave him, Floyd, and it's no use you keeping on at me about it. Leave us alone. Leave us *all* alone. We don't want you here. *I* don't want you here.'

He stopped suddenly and gripped her arm, swinging her round to face him. Before she could pull herself away, he had dragged her into his embrace, holding her tightly. Her own arms were pinned to her sides, making struggle futile, and as she looked up at him and opened her mouth to remonstrate, he brought his lips down hard on hers, crushing her protest.

'Now,' he said roughly, letting her go so that she staggered and would have fallen had he not caught her again. '*Now* tell me you don't want me here.'

Lizzie raised her hand to her mouth, touching her lips with her fingertips. Her eyes burned with tears. She looked up at him and saw a brief flash of regret in his eyes, swiftly replaced by the hard anger she had felt in his kiss.

'I'm sorry, Lizzie,' he said, his voice still raw. 'I didn't mean to do that. But you don't seem to understand what this is doing to me. You talk about what it's doing to you, but you don't give a thought to the way I feel.' His voice was quieter as he said, 'Doesn't that matter to you at all, Lizzie? Don't *I* matter to you, any more?'

Her hand was still at her mouth, feeling the tenderness of her bruised lips. She looked down, away from his gaze, and shook her head blindly. Her voice came in a whisper. 'Don't ask me that, Floyd. Please.' Helplessly, she turned away, took a few steps into the darkening afternoon. 'This has got to stop.'

'It can't.' He caught at her arm again, more gently this time, and turned her to face him once more. His eyes were dark shadows in the pale oval of his face. 'It can't stop, Lizzie, not now. We've gone too far. I've been here, I've seen you again, living in that hovel you call a home, I've seen my daughter. How can I walk away and pretend it never happened? You're asking the impossible, and you know it.'

'I don't live in a hovel!' she exclaimed indignantly. 'It may be a lot smaller than the big houses you Americans live in but it's not a hovel. We've got gas and electricity and running water, and it's warm and dry – it's our *home*, and it's good enough for us. Or perhaps you don't think so? Perhaps you don't think it's good enough for *your daughter* to live in.'

'As a matter of fact, I do think that,' he said. 'I can see you've done your best, Lizzie, and it's a cosy enough little place, I'll give you that. You're a homemaker, like your ma. But I can give you so much more. A house with more than four tiny rooms – a house with a proper bathroom. Two bathrooms. A big garden for the kids to play in. Countryside all around, space to grow up and run free, plenty of good food to eat. We don't have rationing in the US, Lizzie, and we don't have all this utility furniture, poor stuff made of not much more than cardboard, nor all the bombsites in every street and the re-building you've hardly started. I tell you, seeing Southampton shook me rigid – it's almost as if the war's still going on. Why is it? Why hasn't Britain got back on her feet again?'

'Probably because we've been too busy helping Germany to get back on to hers,' Lizzie said bitterly. 'And I'm sorry you think we're in such a poor way, Floyd, but as it happens we think we're doing quite well. Everything's looking up. We *are* rebuilding, and it's all going to be better than ever before. Didn't you hear about the Festival of Britain? That showed the world that we're still here. And now we've got a new Queen, it's like a whole new age is starting.'

'You're getting off the point, Lizzie. I didn't come here to talk about Britain's future. I came to talk about ours. And I reckon you ought to be pretty clear about that by now.'

'I'm talking about the future, too,' she retorted. 'Mine and Alec's. And as for living in a hovel, Alec and I are going to move soon anyway. We'll need another bedroom because—' She stopped abruptly, remembering that she hadn't meant to tell Floyd about her pregnancy, but to her relief he didn't seem to notice. Instead, he nodded.

'So you should, with a boy and a girl. But it's *our* future we're here to talk about now, Lizzie, and I'm not letting you get away from it.'

'I shall, all the same,' she snapped, a flash of spirit still sounding in her voice. 'And so should you. There's no future for you and me, Floyd, and none for you and Gillie either – not until she's grown up, anyway. And that's another fifteen years away.'

'I'm not prepared to wait that long,' he said quietly.

Lizzie lifted her chin. The indignation which had fired her was still there, giving her a strength she hadn't realised she had. She met his eyes.

'You're going to have to,' she said. 'I'm not going any further with this, Floyd. I'm not meeting you again and if you come to the house I shan't let you in. You can stand outside and shout the place down if you want to. I don't care what my neighbours think. We're not going to be living there much longer anyway. All I care about is my family – Alec and my children. You're not going to destroy that.'

'Lizzie, Lizzie, don't talk like that. I don't want to destroy anything.'

'Then that's all right, isn't it?' she said, beginning to walk away. 'You'll go away and stop tormenting me.'

He stood still for a moment, then called after her. 'And Alec? Are you going to tell him about this – about meeting me, not once but twice? *Are you going to tell him how you felt when I kissed you?*'

Lizzie stopped and turned. He had moved soundlessly to catch up with her and stood closer than she had expected.

'What do you mean?' she asked, her voice not quite steady. 'How do you know what I felt?'

'I know all right,' he said tersely. 'We never did a lot of kissing, Lizzie, and we only made love that once – but I know you as well as if we'd been married for years.' He reached out and laid his hands on her arms. 'If I'd thrown you down on the grass and made love to you then and there, you wouldn't have done a thing to stop me.'

'*Floyd!*'

'Not a thing,' he repeated. 'You felt it on VE day, when we did what we ought to have been doing for months, and you felt it again just now.' His tone deepened with urgency. 'Lizzie, we were made to be together. We *belong* together. Something – someone – meant us to meet and fall in love, and it's still there. *It's all still there.*' He shook her, as if desperate to make her understand. 'You're my woman, Lizzie, and I'm your man. Nothing else matters but that. *Nothing.*'

'Floyd, stop it!' She could feel terror rising within her – a terror she couldn't analyse. 'Of course other things matter. I have a home, a family, a husband – they all matter. And my family at Bridge End, they matter too. I'd be letting them all down if ...' She stopped and tried to turn away but he held her where she was, twisting her back to look into her face.

'If what, Lizzie? *If what?*' He waited but she bowed her head and said nothing. 'If you came away with me,' he said quietly. 'That's what you were going to say, wasn't it? You're thinking about it, aren't you? It's not quite so impossible as you say.'

Lizzie shook her head again. The tears that had been threatening for so long overflowed now and ran down her cheeks. She raised her arm to wipe her face on the sleeve of her coat, aware that Floyd was watching her. He made a slight sound and then gathered her into his arms and held her close, one hand stroking her back.

'Oh, Lizzie, my love,' he murmured. 'Come now, I didn't mean to make you cry. It's all right. Everything will be all right, I promise you.'

Lizzie rested her head against his shoulder and let the tears flow. They stood there for a moment, then she drew back and looked up at him again.

'How can you say that?' she asked shakily. 'How can everything be all right now? Nothing can ever be the same again!'

Chapter Fifteen

'Nothing can ever be the same again!'

Lizzie's cry to Floyd had come straight from her heart. With that simple movement of taking her into his arms, with the sudden tenderness in his voice as he murmured in her ear, all her resistance had vanished and she knew that he was right. There was a part of her that still belonged to him, a deep reservoir of love that had long been buried and now welled up; unbidden, unwanted – and undeniable. Whatever happened now, someone was going to be hurt, and hurt badly.

'Oh, Floyd,' she wept, 'what are we going to do?'

'We're going to talk about it,' he said firmly. 'We're going to meet somewhere warm and quiet where we can talk it through, without interruption, without having to rush back to get Alec's tea or collect the children. We can't leave it now, Lizzie. We've got to have time to do that.'

'Yes,' she said. 'I know.' She looked up at his face. 'Floyd, I've got to go now. I really have.'

'But we'll meet again?' he asked urgently, and she nodded. The spirit had gone out of her, leaving her drained and exhausted. She felt as if she were being swept along by a powerful tide, like those that sometimes surged up Southampton Water on the head of a winter gale, with no strength to resist.

'Tomorrow?' he asked, but she shook her head.

'I can't ask June again. She's already beginning to think there's something odd going on.'

'I'm going to London soon,' he said. 'I'll be away for three days. Can you arrange something before then? Could your mother have the children for a day?'

'I don't know. Perhaps. I'll have to think of something to tell her.' Already, she was drowning in lies. She met his eyes again and felt the tide pull at her heart once more. 'Yes. I'll meet you tomorrow, if I can. Or the day after.'

'Come to my hotel,' he said. 'We can talk in my room. Nobody will disturb us.'

'In your room?' Immediately, she felt alarm. 'Floyd, I don't think that's a good idea.'

'Why not?' But he knew why not. 'Look, where else can we be sure of being private? Where else can we be sure no one will see us together?'

'Oh, God, I hate this!' she cried. 'It's all turning into lies and hiding and pretending. I don't think I can do it. I can't!'

'You have to,' he said, holding her by the arms. 'You know you have to.'

They were both silent for a moment. Then she said dully, 'All right. I'll come to your hotel. I'll come as soon as I can. But please, Floyd, promise you won't do anything. It will be just to talk. Please?'

Again, he was silent, as if weighing up his own powers of resistance. At last he said, 'I promise,' and let go of her arms. She stepped away.

'I'll go now. There'll be a bus along soon – I can catch it if I hurry.'

'Lizzie.' She turned back to look at him. 'You will come, won't you? You'll keep your own promise?'

She sighed. 'Yes, I'll come. And you keep yours, too.'

She walked away from him, back towards the road where a bus stop stood like a dim beacon against the darkness of the trees. She knew, although she did not look back, that he was watching her every step. And she wondered if he felt as cynical about the promises they had made, as she did.

We're not famous for keeping promises, she thought bitterly. Either of us.

Finding a reason to ask her mother to have the children for a day wasn't easy. For a start, Lizzie would have to take them out to the farm in the morning and collect them later. How could she explain needing to leave them for that long? Alec would have to know, too. In the end, it was June who gave her the answer.

'Is everything all right?' she asked when Lizzie knocked on the door that afternoon. 'You're looking as white as a sheet.'

'I'm just a bit tired. The new baby, you know. Seems to be taking it out of me a bit more than the others did.' She smiled faintly. 'I must be getting old!'

'Well, you're five years older than when you were expecting Barry, I suppose, but I wouldn't have said you were over the hill,' June said with a grin. 'But honestly, Liz, you do look a bit washed-out. If you ask me, you need a good rest. Why don't you go out and stay with your mum for a few days?'

'How can I do that, with Alec needing to be looked after? He's working so hard these days, he needs his breakfast to start him off, and a good supper inside him when he gets home. He'd never look after himself properly if I wasn't there – you know what men are like.'

'Well, maybe you could ask her to have the kiddies for the last few days of the holidays,' June suggested. 'That would give you a break.'

Lizzie stared at her. 'Yes,' she said slowly. 'It would, wouldn't it? That's not a bad idea – not a bad idea at all.'

She walked home thoughtfully, the children skipping beside her. The idea, which would have been unthinkable not long ago, now presented possibilities that were both exciting and frightening. Without the little ones to consider and to order her days, she would have a freedom she had never known before. She would be able to go anywhere, do anything – and nobody would know. Nobody would know if she met Floyd. Nobody would know how long they spent together, or what they did ...

Her heart lurched. She must stop these thoughts at once. Determinedly, she turned her mind away, walking a little faster through the cold dusk and thinking of what she must do when she reached home. Light the fire ... give the children their tea ... put them to bed ... get Alec's supper ready ... darn socks, mend the hole in Barry's shorts, turn one of Alec's shirt collars ... There would probably be something to listen to on the wireless, too – *Take It From Here*, which always made her laugh, or Wilfred Pickles with his quiz programme *Have A Go*. And she had a new library book – *My Cousin Rachel*, a Daphne du Maurier she hadn't read, which looked gripping. There was plenty to take her mind off Floyd.

All the same, she had promised she would meet him. June was certainly beginning to wonder why she was so secretive and she had to do something about the children. What harm could it do, to take them to her mother for a day or two? They'd enjoy it, Jane and George would love to have them, and she really was feeling tired. The break would do her good ...

Alec raised no objection to the plan when she finally broached it, just before they went to bed.

'Sounds a good idea to me. You do look a bit tired. But why don't you go too, let your mum fuss over you a bit?'

'And leave you to eat out of tins and never make the bed? You need looking after just as much as the children do. Anyway, I don't want fussing over. I just want to be able to spend the day as I please. Stay quietly at home.' She could feel her colour rising and bent quickly to sort out the darned socks from the undarned ones.

Alec grinned at her. 'We can have some time on our too. It'll be like a honeymoon.'

'Not if you're still working late. It won't be any different from what it is now anyway – you only see the children at weekends.' She looked up at him suddenly. 'I wish you didn't have to work such long hours, Alec.'

'I don't have any choice, do I. We need all the overtime I can get, to pay for a bigger house. We'll have to start looking properly soon, Lizzie. We need to be settled before the baby comes along.'

'I know.' She felt a great weariness settle over her, like a cloud. 'I can't worry about that just now though. There seems to be so much to think about.'

'Does there? What?' His tone had sharpened and she gave him a quick look, afraid that she had given herself away.

'Oh, I don't know. Just winter, I suppose – all the extra work it brings, like fires and cooking different meals. And Christmas, and the holidays.'

He looked at her more closely, frowning a little. 'That American bloke. He was supposed to be on the *Queen Liz*, wasn't he? Have you heard any more from him?'

Lizzie hesitated. Until now, there had never been a moment when they had time to sit and talk. If she was ever going to tell him about Floyd, it should be now. A few days ago, I could have, she thought miserably, but now things have gone too far.

She said, trying to keep her voice uninterested, 'No. Perhaps he's decided against it, after all. Anyway, I've got more important things to think about – you, and the new baby and everything.' She concentrated on winding up a small ball of grey wool. 'I really do feel tired, though. That's why I want to take the children out to the farm for a few days. It'll be a break for all of us.'

'All except your mum,' he said with another grin. 'Well, you go ahead and ask her. Like you say, it's not going to make much difference to me, except that you might feel better. That could make a difference. It seems a long time since we had a nice long afternoon together.'

'I know. I'm sorry.' She finished sorting the socks and stood up. 'I'm going to bed now. Are you coming up soon?'

He nodded. 'I'll just finish my cocoa first. Don't go to sleep too quickly, Liz.'

'I'll try,' she said, feigning a yawn. But she knew, as she climbed the stairs, that by the time Alec slipped in beside her she would be asleep – or pretending to be.

That was another thing Floyd had done to her. Even before she'd begun to admit her feelings for him, she hadn't been able to make love with Alec. She'd used her condition as an excuse, but she knew now that it wasn't the reason. It was Floyd's arms she wanted around her, and Floyd's lips she wanted on hers.

I do love Alec, though, she argued hopelessly as she pulled back the blankets. I *do*. And I'm not going to be unfaithful to him again.

She knew, in her heart, that she was playing with fire. But it was possible – surely it was possible – to play with fire and not get burned.

She walked up the road to the telephone box as soon as the children had finished their breakfast next morning. Jane answered and listened to her halting request as if wondering why Lizzie was making such an elaborate explanation for it. I'm saying too much, Lizzie thought, sure that her mother knew she was blushing. She's bound to suspect there's something up.

'Of course you can bring them out here for a few days,' Jane said. 'I don't know why you even bothered to ask – you could have just turned up. You know that, Lizzie.'

'Well, it might not have been convenient,' Lizzie said lamely, and her mother snorted.

'When is it not convenient for me to look after my own

grandchildren for a while?' It's not as if I'm going anywhere. You bring them out straight away, Lizzie. They can stay as long as you like.'

'All right. They'll have to come back when school starts.' She came out of the kiosk, feeling as though she had committed herself now. The children looked up at her questioningly.

'Are we going to Granny's to stay?' Gillie asked, and Lizzie nodded.

'Just for a little holiday. You'll like that, won't you? You always like going to the farm.'

'You'll be there too,' Barry said, slightly anxious but stating it as fact. Lizzie smiled and took his hand as they walked back down the street to the house.

'No, you're going to stay there on your own like big children. You can help Granny and Grandad with the farm.'

'Where will you be?' His small hand tightened around her fingers.

'I'll be here, where I always am. At home, with Daddy. I've got to stay and look after him, haven't I? I've got to cook his dinners and wash his clothes.'

'But how long will we be there?' Barry's voice had risen another notch and Lizzie felt a spasm of guilt.

'Just a few days. Perhaps till Gillie goes back to school, that's all. Maybe not even that long if I miss you too much.' She smiled at him but wished she hadn't mentioned 'missing'. His lip wobbled.

'But *we'll* miss *you*.'

'Only a little bit. You'll be too busy to miss me much. And you'll be able to go and see Auntie Ruth, and Uncle Dan, and Sammy and Silver. And you can play with Linnet and the other children at Bridge End. You'll have a lovely time, you know you will.'

Gillie, who had said nothing until Lizzie was opening the front door, said, 'Will you be all right here without us to look after you?'

Lizzie bit her lip, then smiled at her daughter. 'Of course I will. Now, let's go in and get your things ready and then we can catch the bus. We'll be at the farm by dinner-time.'

Jane was waiting for them when they arrived, festooned with shopping-bags and the small suitcase that Lizzie had bought to take on her honeymoon. Despite her stipulation that only the smallest and lightest toys could be taken, Barry had set up such a howling at the idea of leaving his wooden bricks behind that she had been forced to give in. They weighed her shoulder down as she trudged up the track leading to the farm.

'Goodness me, you look as if you're coming for the duration!' Jane exclaimed, hurrying to take some of the bags. 'You shouldn't be carrying all that in your condition.'

'What's a condition?' Barry asked, standing with stiff arms in his winter coat, with at least two jumpers underneath, and looking like an advertisement for the Michelin Tyre Man.

'It's like being poorly,' Gillie said. 'Are you poorly, Mummy?'

'No, of course she's not,' Jane said quickly. 'I just meant because it's cold and you're all wrapped up. Now, take some of these things upstairs out of the way while I make some cocoa.' She watched them go, then turned to her daughter. 'Now, what's this all about?'

'It's not about anything,' Lizzie said, feeling her colour flare up at once. 'I just need a rest, that's all, and I thought while Gillie was on holiday ...'

'You've never asked me to have them before, at short notice like this.' Jane examined her face. 'Are you sure you're all right? There's nothing wrong with the baby, is there? You're keeping well?'

'I'm as fit as a flea. Never better. Honestly, Mum, if it was anything like that I'd tell you.'

'So it's something else. It's no use trying to pull the wool over my eyes, Lizzie. You ought to know that by now. I'm

131

your mother – I can tell when you're trying to hide something from me.'

Lizzie sighed. 'And I'm a grown woman and entitled to my privacy. Look, if I'd thought I was going to be subjected to an interrogation, I'd never have brought the children out here. If you'd rather I took them away ...'

'Don't be silly. That's got nothing to do with it – you know I'm glad to have them any time. I never really understood why you and Alec had to leave the village and move to Southampton anyway. You'd have been far better off stopping here, with your family. But you can't tell me there's not something the matter. You've got that look in your eye – that look you used to get when you were a girl and had done something you didn't ought to have done.'

'I haven't done anything like that now,' Lizzie protested, guiltily aware that her mother would take the view that meeting Floyd at all was something she ought not to have done, and that planning to meet him in his hotel room was most definitely something she ought not to be doing. 'And there's nothing wrong with the baby. I just need a bit of time to myself, that's all. *Alec and me* need time to ourselves.'

'And you'll not get much of that, with him working all the hours God sends,' Jane retorted. 'Well, if you won't tell me, you won't. I can't force you. But I hope you're not thinking of doing anything silly, our Lizzie. Anything you'll come to regret.'

'I'm not.' But Lizzie turned away as she spoke, unable to meet her mother's eye and aware that this made her look even more guilty. She braced herself for a question about Floyd, but at that moment the children clattered back down the narrow atairs and she heaved a sigh of relief. The moment of danger had passed – for the time being.

It was only as Jane saw her off, after a dinner of beef stew and dumplings, that she asked the question Lizzie had been dreading.

'Did Floyd ever turn up after all?' she enquired casually, handing Lizzie her scarf. 'The *Queen Lizzie*'s been in for a week or two now, hasn't she?'

'Been, gone back and come in again, I think,' Lizzie answered, equally casually. She wound the scarf round her neck. 'Perhaps he changed his mind.'

'That's strange. He seemed so set on it in that letter he wrote.' Jane was watching her daughter closely. 'I wouldn't have been surprised if he'd just turned up at the house one day.'

Lizzie shrugged. 'Maybe he did, and we were out.'

'So you haven't seen him? Or heard any more?'

Lizzie took refuge in exasperation. 'What *is* this, Mum? The Spanish Inquisition?'

'I just wondered, that's all. You were so upset about it. I wondered if he'd been pestering you and that's why you're feeling a bit under the weather.' Jane paused. 'You know, if it's anything like that, you've only got to say. Alec would soon see him off. Or your father. I'd give him the rough edge of my tongue myself, if he's been upsetting you.'

'He hasn't,' Lizzie said tightly. 'I tell you, Mum, everything's all right. I just need a few days to myself, that's all. Why won't you believe me? Honestly, if I'd known it was going to cause all this trouble, I'd never have come out here.'

'I'm not causing any trouble,' Jane said quietly. 'Just asking a few natural questions, that's all, becaue I'm your mother and I don't like seeing you look so pale. But there, it's nothing to do with me. You go home and rest, if that's what you need, and I hope you'll be looking better when you come to fetch the kiddies home again. But remember, we're your family here and we care about you. We don't want to see your life go wrong.'

'Well, it's not going wrong!' Lizzie caught herself up and made herself calm down. 'I know. I'm sorry I snapped.' She kissed her mother and then stepped away, aware that there were tears in her eyes that might fall at any moment, and that if they did she might not be able to stop the whole story tumbling out with them. She turned away quickly, biting her lips, then called back through the doorway, 'Mummy's going now. Be good for Granny and Grandad, won't you?'

The children appeared at the door. Gillie was looking anxious again but Barry, who had made the most objections, was cheerfully dragging on his Wellingtons.

'I'm going to help Grandad,' he announced importantly. 'We're going to do the afternoon milking.'

'Well, don't get trodden on,' Lizzie said, and bent to kiss him. She hugged her daughter. 'Look after your brother, won't you, and I'll be back soon. What are you going to do this afternoon?'

'Make flapjacks,' Gillie answered. 'I wish you were staying here too, Mummy.'

'I've got to go and look after Daddy. You know that. And you're going to have a proper, grown-up holiday by yourselves with Granny and Grandad. Now, I must go or I'll miss the bus.' She gave them both a last kiss. 'Bye-bye, now.'

Without looking at her mother again, she hurried away down the track. The bus would be along in a few minutes and it would take her all the way to the centre of Southampton and close to Floyd's hotel. Even as she settled in her seat, her heart was beginning to bump with excitement at the thought of seeing him again.

I'm going to keep my promise, all the same, she thought. I'm not going to let Alec down. Not a second time.

Chapter Sixteen

'I was scared you wouldn't come,' Floyd said, holding her a little distance away from him and looking into her eyes.

Lizzie looked down. 'I promised I would.'

'Promises aren't always kept,' he said, with an uncanny echo of her own thoughts.

'I know.' There was a small silence. They were standing just inside the door of Floyd's room. Lizzie, scarlet with embarrassment, had asked for him at the reception desk and waited while the perfectly made-up young woman had telephoned his room, casting a curious glance at Lizzie as she did so. She's wondering whether to get someone to throw me out, Lizzie thought, trying to shrink further into her old winter coat. She thinks I'm a call-girl. If Floyd says he doesn't know me ... But after listening for a moment, the receptionist put down the phone and said politely, 'Mr Hanson will be down in a moment.'

'Thank you.' Lizzie hesitated, and the girl pointed to two or three leather armchairs round a small table.

'Why don't you sit down?'

'Oh – thank you,' Lizzie said again, and walked over to one, feeling the young woman's eyes on her back. When she turned to sit down, however, the other girl was busy, her head bent over some papers, and seemed to have lost interest in Lizzie.

Lizzie perched on the edge of the chair, staring nervously at the stairs. The hotel was quite a smart one, although she had nothing to compare it with since she had never been in one before. She'd seen them in films, however, where they seemed to veer between luxurious palaces in America or dingy, narrow-halled Victorian houses in London, sandwiched between other tall, thin houses in windy back streets. This one seemed to have been built as a hotel and escaped the bombing; its walls were painted a smooth cream, the wooden floor highly polished. There was nobody else in the hall, although while she sat there two men passed through, talking together, and a young girl in a black frock with a white pinafore and maid's hat hurried by, looking anxious.

I wonder what it's like to work in a hotel, Lizzie thought. Much the same as any other form of service, probably. Cleaning up after people. Making their beds. Taking them drinks and food, bowing and scraping, all just as if they were royalty when a lot of them were probably not much better off than you were yourself. Well, they'd have to be better off than Lizzie and Alec, who couldn't have afforded more than a few days in a seaside boarding house, but that wouldn't make them rich. And it certainly wouldn't make them *better*.

Her musings were interrupted by a shadow falling across her. She jumped to her feet.

'Floyd!'

'Come upstairs,' he said quietly, taking her arm. The girl at the desk looked up and watched them thoughtfully, but Floyd ignored her. 'We can talk better in private.'

The room was bigger than Lizzie's bedroom at home, but it still seemed to be filled by the large double bed. Lizzie glanced at it quickly, then looked away. There was a small armchair and a dressing-table with a stool in front of it. A big mahogany wardrobe with a long mirror between its doors took up most of one wall. The window looked out towards the old walls.

'I'm glad you kept this promise,' he said after a moment, and slid his hands up her arms.

'Floyd.' She twisted away from him and went to stand by the window, fiddling with her gloves. 'Floyd, you mustn't think—'

'What mustn't I think? Look, why don't you take off your coat? It's warm enough in here.' He came towards her and she backed away, holding her coat more tightly around her. 'It's all right, Lizzie, I'm not going to bite you.'

'I'm not afraid of being bitten,' she said with a little laugh, and he grinned.

'Maybe you should be. So what *are* you afraid, of, Lizzie?'

She looked at the floor. 'I'm not afraid of anything. Only,' she paused, then shrugged and lifted her head, 'yes, I am. I'm afraid of what we're doing, Floyd, and where it's going to lead. I don't want anyone to get hurt.'

'Lizzie, we've been through all this before. You can't have a situation like this without someone getting hurt. Someone already *is* hurt. Two people, I'd say – wouldn't you?' His eyes held hers. When she didn't answer, he went on. 'I know damn well I'm hurting and I'm pretty sure you are too.'

'That's different,' she said. 'We deserve to be hurt. Alec doesn't, and neither do the children.'

'*Deserve* to be hurt? How d'you make that out? Because we gave way once – and only once – to what we both really wanted? Because we've got a beautiful little girl? Because we behaved in the most natural way a man and a woman can behave together? *That* means we deserve to be hurt?'

'Yes, it does,' she said. 'Because I was married and we knew we shouldn't be doing it.'

'And on the other hand,' he said, 'we loved each other and it's exactly what we should have been doing.'

'*No!*' she cried. 'Floyd – *no!* It wasn't like that. I was *married*. I still am. That's what made it wrong, and you know that. You knew it then. Why else would you have gone away, without another word?' she demanded bitterly. 'Why else would you have left me like you did?'

'Is that it? You're punishing me because I tried to do the *right* thing? Come on, Lizzie, you can't have it both ways!'

'I can,' she said. 'Because you brought love into it, and that should have made all the difference. If you really had loved me, you'd never have left me the way you did.'

'I had no choice. I was in the American Air Force, for God's sake.'

'You could have written. You could have let me know you were coming back. You could have *told* me.'

'And what if I had? What difference would it have made? You'd have sent me away anyway.'

'Yes, I would,' Lizzie said tiredly. 'But at least I'd have known.'

'You knew when I did come back. It wasn't that long, Lizzie. You could have left him then.'

'He was *ill*! He'd had a dreadful time in the POW camp. How could I have left him then? Oh, it's no use going over and over it all.' She began to pace up and down the narrow space. 'It's over, and that's all there is to it. You went away and I stayed with Alec, and I still want to stay with him. There's nothing more to talk about.'

'There is,' he said. 'There's Gillie.'

Lizzie turned on him. 'You're not using Gillie as an excuse! She's my daughter – '

'And mine.'

' – and I'm not having her made a part of this. She's only six years old, Floyd. I won't have her upset by it all.'

'I don't aim to upset her. Look, all I wanted when I came here was to see her – that's honestly all I meant to do. But when I did, I knew I couldn't just walk away again. And when I saw *you* ...' He paused for a moment, then went on in a quiet voice, 'I knew what I'd tried to hide from myself all these years. God knows why, but it's you I want, Lizzie. You're my woman. I want to spend the rest of my life with you.'

There was silence in the room as they stared at each other, Lizzie feeling suddenly disorientated. His eyes held hers and she felt drawn towards him, as if there were some magnetic force between them. She closed her eyes and shook her head blindly, putting her hands up to her face.

'Floyd – please. Don't say such things.'

'Why not? They're true. They have to be said. We've got to be honest with each other, Lizzie.' He came close to her and took her hands, holding them up to his chest. 'Don't you think we owe each other that?'

'I owe it to Alec too,' she whispered.

'Sure you do. I'm not asking you to lie to him, Lizzie.'

Their eyes met again and held. Lizzie was trembling. She could feel the swelling in her throat that meant tears were coming again, and a second later they stood hot in her eyes. She looked down and they began to fall.

'It would hurt him so much ...'

'And suppose you stay with him?' he asked quietly. 'Won't that hurt him just as bad, in the end?'

'Why should it?'

'Because you'll never be able to love him again. And he'll know it.'

Lizzie gasped and twisted away from him. 'That's not true! I *would* love him – I do now. That wouldn't stop.'

'Wouldn't it? Not during the hard times, when he's working those long hours in the shipyard and you're struggling to bring up two kids virtually on your own? With not enough money – always worrying about how to pay the rent, buy food and clothes, all the other things you need? And you lie there in the dark, thinking of me and how it might have been – a good life in America, with a decent house and garden for our daughter to grow up in? And Barry too, if you like – I'm not asking you to leave him behind. Will you still go on loving him, when you think of that and wonder why you stayed?'

'You're reducing it all to money,' she said scornfully. 'A marriage is more than that.'

'I know. And ours would be, too. I promise you, Lizzie, ours would be full of love.'

'And guilt,' she replied. 'How am I supposed to live with that, Floyd? How can I take everything away from him – me, the children, everything he lives for – and go off and live in a big house in America with you, being given all I want, and not feel guilty? How could I ever be happy?'

'You don't have to take it away just like that. It can be talked over in a reasonable manner until he comes to understand—'

'Oh, you're talking nonsense!' she exclaimed, moving away again as he came towards her. 'Alec would never understand. I don't understand myself – I don't know why I'm here at all.'

'You do know,' he said, watching her. 'You know it's because there's a cord between us that can't be broken. It's because you feel the same as me. Admit it, Lizzie.'

She met his eyes, opening her mouth to deny it, but the words died in her throat and she turned away once more, her eyes filling with more tears.

'I've got to go. Alec will be home soon.'

'And you've got to be there to give him his tea. You talk about honesty, but you'll go home now and lie to him. You'll lie about where you've been, what you've been doing ...'

'I won't! I'll tell him about taking the children to Bridge End. He knows that's where I was going.'

'But you won't tell him about coming here, will you? You'll give him his supper and listen to him talk about his day, and later on you'll go to bed together. You might even make love.' There was a bitter note in his voice now. 'You'll let him think there's nothing wrong, and yet you talk to me about *honesty* and *guilt*. Don't you think you're being the tiniest bit *dis*honest, Lizzie? And don't you think you'll even feel a little bit guilty?'

'I've never been dishonest with Alec. Not until you came back. And what else can I do anyway?' she demanded, wheeling to face him. 'You keep pestering me – you threaten to come to my house if I won't come to you. What else can I do but come here and try to persuade you to leave me alone?'

'Are you sure that's what you came here for? Didn't you think for even one second about what else might happen? In this room? In this *bed*room?' He came towards her, his hands held out, and Lizzie backed away again, terrified.

'No! No, I didn't! If I did, I didn't want it to happen – not really. Floyd – please – please don't touch me!'

'Why not? Are you afraid of what might happen if I do? Are you afraid of me, Lizzie – or of yourself?'

'It mustn't happen,' she whispered. 'We mustn't let it happen.'

He let his hands drop and watched her for a moment. Then he said in a different voice, 'All right, Lizzie. We'll leave it at that – for the time being. I'm not going to force you. How long are the children staying with your mother?'

'Three or four days. Till the end of the week. Gillie starts school again on Monday.' Her voice was little more than a thread of sound.

'So we've time to meet again. Tomorrow.'

'Floyd, it isn't any use.'

'I think it is,' he said. 'Look, I've managed to put off any business in London until next week. It suited them anyway. We can spend all day together. Not here, if you don't want to. We'll go out somewhere. I'll hire a car. We'll go where nobody you know will see us.'

'I can't do that.'

'Please,' he said. 'For old times' sake. And if you still want me to go away after that, I will.' She looked up at him and he held her eyes gravely. 'That's a promise, Lizzie.'

'All right,' she said after a moment. 'But it won't be any good, Floyd. I'm not going to change. I'm not leaving Alec.'

He nodded, and took her hands, and this time she didn't resist him. 'We'll see,' he said quietly. 'But if you don't – well, I'll have one last day to remember, and I hope you won't begrudge me that.'

Chapter Seventeen

The evening out with Stephen had been a success as he set out to show Maddy what a good time she could have with him.

As darkness had fallen, the drawing room had been lit only by the glow of the fire. The radio was on, playing soft music, and after her afternoon on the beach Maddy was half-asleep, her head resting on Stephen's shoulder, when the door opened and the Archdeacon came in, switching on the light. The two on the sofa sat up quickly, blinking in the sudden brightness.

'Goodness,' Maddy said, brushing back her hair. 'I must have dozed off. Whatever time is it?'

'Just after six,' the Archdeacon said, regarding them with some amusement. 'I must say, Maddy, you're something of a witch. I'd no idea you had a friend here.'

Maddy smiled, 'Stephen was here when I came back from my walk. He came to invite me out to dinner before he goes back to camp.'

'I've been to Burracombe for the weekend,' Stephen explained easily, 'and ran into Felix while I was there. I'm hoping to persuade Maddy to come down with me next time I go – she could stay with her sister and we could make up a foursome.'

'Felix is busy at the weekends,' Maddy reminded him, 'and there really isn't room for me at Dottie's cottage. Stella lodges with the woman I used to live with in Burracombe,' she explained to the Archdeacon, 'but it's a tiny cottage and I usually stay just across the road.'

'Well, let's do it during the week sometime, when I'm on leave. You'll come and stay then, won't you? Hilary would love to have you at the Barton. And so would I, of course.'

'We'll see. I'd better go and get ready now, anyway, if we're going out. That will be all right, won't it, Archdeacon? Or is there anything you want me to do this evening?'

'No, you go along, my dear, and enjoy yourself. I'll keep this young man entertained.' He went to the side table where glasses and bottles were set out. 'We'll have a drink and talk men's talk.'

Maddy grinned and went up to her own small flat, where she had a bedroom, a tiny sitting room and a bathroom. She'd thought of inviting Stephen up there but had decided that the Archdeacon really wouldn't approve of that. Taking him into the drawing room, where anyone might come at any moment, and curling up on the sofa together as dusk fell, was perfectly respectable.

Maddy was aware that Stephen might not always be as respectable as he should be. There was a wicked glint in his eye at times, and some of his words seemed to have another meaning, one she couldn't quite grasp. Despite her travels with the actress Fenella Forsyth, Maddy had remained rather naive – Fenella had seen to that – and living in an Archdeacon's household wasn't doing much to advance her education in that respect.

All the same, she was well aware that Stephen considered her his own property – he'd more or less said as much – and although she had denied this, the thought gave her a pleasurable feeling inside. But then there was Sammy. Brief though their meeting had been, she had a strong sense that he could be important in her life. And Sammy, she knew, was much less experienced than Stephen, and could be much more easily hurt.

There's no need for either of them to be hurt, she thought staunchly, looking through her wardrobe to decide what to wear, as she waited for her bath to run. We're just friends having fun, all of us. There's nothing serious with either of them and there's not going to be for a long time.

She picked out a blue dress which matched her eyes and went to have her bath.

After her life with Fenella Forsyth, it was nothing unusual for Maddy to go to dinner at a smart hotel, but since returning to Burracombe and then taking up her post with the Archdeacon, life had been much simpler. It seemed quite strange to be walking into a discreetly lit restaurant again, and to be greeted by a respectful head waiter and shown to a table laid with crisp white linen and sparkling cut glass.

'I hope you're hungry,' Stephen said, picking up the menu. 'I've been told the food here is really good.'

'You haven't been here before, then?'

'No reason to, until now.' He grinned at her. 'I hope I'll have plenty of reason to in the future, though.'

Maddy smiled back. Someone was playing softly on a white grand piano in one corner of the room, and people were talking quietly. It was very relaxing, yet somehow she felt a little wistful as she thought again of Sammy Hodges. Being with someone you felt completely at ease with gave you a warmth that no stylish restaurant and gourmet meal could ever quite achieve. It had to be the right company, she decided.

Stephen set out to be entertaining. He talked about his life in the RAF and his desire to emigrate to Canada and set up his own flying business. She was surprised to find just how clear he was about these plans – Stella had mentioned once that she'd heard a vague reference to them, but even Stephen's sister Hilary didn't seem to know just how advanced they were.

'Flying's going to be really important,' he said. 'The big airlines will see to passenger transport – but piloting someone else's plane, full of people, that's not for me. I want to run my own freight company, and Canada's the place to do it. Taking stuff to outlying areas, to islands or lake settlements – that's what I want to do. And in time, I could build up a whole fleet of transport planes, operating all over Canada. The world's an exciting place now, Maddy, and I want to make the most of it.'

She listened, fascinated. It was a whole new world.

'Men are so lucky,' she said pensively. 'You can do so much with your lives. Women are still supposed to stay at home and bring up the children, even though they did so much during the war.'

'That's what my sister Hilary says,' Stephen said. 'She was in the WAACs during the war and went to Egypt and drove generals and people like that about. She had quite a responsible job – I'm not at all sure she didn't do something quite secret as well, only she'd never talk about it, of course. When she came home to look after our mother, she didn't intend to stay – she wanted to make her own life. But then Dad got ill as well, and she started to take over the estate, and she really likes doing it. Except that Dad's brought in an estate manager,' he added. 'She was furious about that, although she seems to have accepted him now.'

'Doesn't she want to get married?'

Stephen shrugged. 'No idea. She was engaged, you know, before the war, but he got killed and she's never seemed all that interested in anyone else. And she's always going on about how women ought to be more independent and get better jobs, and not just be pushed back into the kitchen. I asked her to come to Canada with me, but she won't have it. Says I just want her as a housekeeper.'

'And don't you?' Maddy asked with an impish look, and he grinned.

'Well, perhaps. Look, are you going to have any more of this venison? Because if not, I might as well finish it.'

'No, I don't want any more,' Maddy said, hiding a smile.

Stephen really did seem very young at times. She could remember Tim Budd doing exactly the same at meals in the vicarage at Bridge End during the war – gazing longingly at the last sausage or scrap of bread-and-butter pudding and asking, in a polite voice that left nobody in any doubt, if it was going to be wasted if he didn't eat it, and reminding them that waste was wrong in wartime. She watched as Stephen piled the last few roast potatoes on to his plate as well, and cleared the vegetable dish. 'You've got almost as much there as you had the first time,' she pointed out.

Stephen looked abashed. 'Am I being very greedy? Only if we don't eat it ...'

'It'll be thrown away,' she agreed, thinking once more of Tim and, from Tim, going on to thoughts of Sammy again. He would be eating supper in Ruth Hodges' warm kitchen where she had often gone herself as an evacuee. She wondered what they were having. Nothing so smart as haunch of venison, she was sure. Rabbit, perhaps, or sausages and mash, or something like beans on toast since Ruth and Dan would have had their main meal at midday. 'Anyway, I couldn't eat another thing. We had shepherd's pie for lunch.'

'Nothing? Not even a pudding? They do some wonderful trifles here and pavlovas, so I've been told. They'll bring the trolley round in a minute, I expect – you'll change your mind then. And if you can't eat it all, I'll help you.'

Maddy did find that she would probably have room for a pavlova, although when she saw the enormous mountain of meringue the waiter piled on to her plate she had a moment of doubt. Stephen's encouraging expression told her that he would be able to carry out his own promise, even after a helping of chocolate fudge cake, and so it proved. She eyed him, wondering how he stayed so lean, and he grinned.

'It's growing up on boarding-school food. You live on stodge for your formative years, and spend the rest of your life making up for it. And you never get fat at school, even with all the stodge, because they keep you on the go all the time. If you're not playing cricket or rugger, you're boxing or jumping or running for miles across country. We had games every afternoon. *Every single afternoon.*'

Maddy laughed. 'Am I supposed to feel sorry for you?'

'Not really. I liked games. But it got a bit much sometimes, when it was snowing or hailing, or blisteringly hot. I'd quite like to have just lain down in the long grass, stare at the sky and think about flying.'

'Have you always been keen on aeroplanes, then?'

'Always,' he said simply.

Maddy knew that Stephen had had an older brother, Baden, who had been expected to run the estate when his father died. But Baden had been killed during the war and Colonel Napier had automatically assumed that Stephen would step into his brother's shoes. The disputes between father and son about this had never been completely resolved, and even Hilary's willingness to take over hadn't helped all that much.

'I used to go up to the local aerodrome and watch them,' Stephen went on reminiscently. 'There was one chap who had a Tiger Moth and he took me up in her a few times. It was amazing, being up there, looking down on Burracombe and everything I knew so well on the ground. And he could do anything with that plane. He could turn it round like a corkscrew. I learned a lot from him. He's dead now.'

'Was he killed in the war?' Maddy asked, assuming that anyone fairly young would have died in combat. 'I suppose he joined the RAF, did he?'

'No, he flew the Moth into the ground one day. Didn't come out of a dive quickly enough.' Stephen helped himself to the last of Maddy's pavlova while she gazed at him in horror. 'Plane burst into flames – he didn't have a chance – but he probably died on impact.'

'Stephen, that's awful. Did you see it happen?'

'Partly. I was watching him from the 'drome and we saw

him go down and then the flames, but he was out of sight over a hill when he crashed. The chaps scrambled to get to him, but it was all over before we got there.'

'But didn't it put you off flying? It would have me.'

Stephen shrugged. 'Not really. One of the other chaps took me up straight away so I didn't have time to think about it. It's the best way, you know, like getting on a horse again after you've fallen off. D'you want some coffee?'

'Yes, please.' She still felt a bit shaken at the thought of the crash, and Stephen – presumably still a young boy then – witnessing it. 'I think you must have been very brave, all the same.'

'It happens, you know,' Stephen said gently, seeing her face. 'It's not that much different from being killed in a road accident. And he was doing what he enjoyed doing most.'

'Mm.' She wasn't sure about this, however. She'd heard it said before, about people dying when they were mountaineering, or sailing, or even just working in the garden. She had a feeling that if you'd asked any of those people if they would like to die now, please, while they were enjoying themselves, they'd have said, 'No.' She thought you would really rather die when you weren't feeling very well and didn't expect ever to feel better.

'Let's talk about something more cheerful,' Stephen suggested. 'When are you going to come out with me again? I could get over one afternoon and we could go to the cinema.'

'That sounds nice. A weekday would be best, though. The Archdeacon needs me on Saturdays sometimes.'

'What about Sundays?'

'Well, he does expect me to go to church in the morning, but the rest of the day is all right. Only …' She hesitated, then went on, 'I don't really want to be committed every weekend. And it's probably better to let me know in advance.'

He frowned at her. 'You mean you've got another boyfriend? More than one?'

'No – I just don't want …'

'Go on,' he said. 'I bet you've got strings of fellows after you.'

'Not at all. I don't know what sort of a girl you think I am!'

'A very nice one,' he said. 'And a very pretty one. And I don't want to let you slip through my fingers, so why don't we make a regular date for Sundays? At least, when I can manage it?'

'*No*,' Maddy repeated, more forcefully. 'Honestly, Stephen, I don't know why you should expect me to keep every weekend free just in case you can manage to get down here. You let me know when you can come, and I'll tell you if I'm free. What's wrong with that? It's not as if we aren't on the telephone here.'

His frown deepened. 'There *is* another fellow, isn't there? That's what you really mean. You want to keep Sundays free for him.'

'I want to keep them free for myself,' she said haughtily. 'Honestly, Stephen, I don't want my time spoken for weeks in advance. I just want to enjoy myself and take life as it comes.'

'And of that,' he said, screwing up his napkin, 'I heartily approve. It's my own philosophy exactly. So shall we agree that whenever I have a free evening or weekend, I'll pop down and see if you feel like coming out? Or would you rather I phoned?'

'It would probably be best,' she said, smiling at him, because she really did like Stephen and enjoyed his company, especially when he was being light-hearted and frivolous. 'But if you don't mind taking the chance, you can always drop in like you did today, on your way back from Burracombe.'

'And that's another thing,' he said. 'Burracombe. You will come down with me for a weekend sometime, won't you? You can see your sister and all your friends and we could have fun, spinning round the moors in the jalopy. We'd really like to have you stay. You used to stay at the Barton, when Miss Forsyth came to visit Ma.'

'Yes, I did. That was before Stella went to teach in the school and found out that I used to live with Dottie.' She smiled at him. 'I'd like to come. It would be good to see them again.'

'Why not make it next week, then?' he suggested. 'If I can wangle another forty-eight-hour pass, we could go down on Friday evening and come back on Sunday. You could give your sister a surprise.'

Maddy looked at him, about to say no, she couldn't manage it, the Archdeacon was bound to need her, but the words wouldn't come. Instead, she found herself saying quite opposite. Yes, she thought she would be able to do that, and if the Archdeacon needed anything in particular, she was sure she would be able to get it done on Friday. He rarely did need her much on Saturday, after all. And it would be lovely to surprise Stella ...

'That's wizard!' Stephen said, beaming at her, and she laughed, feeling rather astonished at herself. I didn't mean to say any of that, she thought. But now it had been said, she was rather pleased and excited. Perhaps life had been getting a little dull lately, without her noticing.

Stephen waved his wallet and the waiter came over with the bill. He went away again and Stephen put a five-pound note on the silver tray. Another waiter fetched their coats and soon they were out in the cold night air, walking towards the car.

'You won't mind if we don't go straight home, will you?' he murmured as she took his arm. 'I can't let you go without a proper kiss.'

And Maddy, looking sideways at the tall, handsome young pilot at her side and feeling a flicker of excitement somewhere low down in her stomach, agreed that she wouldn't mind at all.

Chapter Eighteen

Ruth was making pastry, with Linnet kneeling on a chair on the other side of the kitchen table, watching her absorbedly, when Gillie and Barry ran in through the back door. She straightened and turned to them, beaming with pleasure.

'Well, you're a sight for sore eyes, I must say! Having a little holiday with your granny then, are you?'

'Yes, and she's coming as soon as she's finished making butter.' Gillie dragged up another chair, while Barry peered over the edge of the table. 'What are you making, Auntie Ruth?'

'Pastry for a plum pie.'

'Little Jack Horner,' Barry said, and recited the nursery rhyme, stopping in astonishment as Silver joined in with the last line. '*And said, "What a good boy am I".*'

'You!' Ruth said to the parrot. 'You don't know how to be a good boy. Do you like plums, Barry?'

'Yes, but there aren't any now. It's winter.'

'These are bottled plums, off my tree in the garden.' She arranged them on the pastry liner in the dish. 'And what have you been doing this morning?'

'We helped Grandad milk the cows. I squeezed her titties,' he said proudly. 'And then we collected eggs, only Granny says the chickens aren't laying many now. And then we went indoors again because my fingers were cold.'

'And are you staying to play with Linnet for a while?'

'I'd rather go with Grandad,' he said. 'He's taking the horses to the forge and Sammy's going to put new shoes on them.' He turned as Jane let herself in. 'Has Grandad gone without me?'

'No, love, he's just coming down the track now. You can go outside and wait for him if you like.' She wrapped his scarf a little more firmly round his neck and watched him run outside before shutting the door. Ruth put a china blackbird in the middle of the plums and draped the pastry lid over the top. She pricked it with a fork and then brushed it with beaten egg.

'I'll put this on the windowsill to relax. There are a few scraps for you two girls to roll out, and here's some jam – you can make jam rolls with it. Come into the other room, Jane, I've got the fire alight and we'll have a cup of tea.'

Linnet and Gillie shared the pastry between them and began rolling it out until it was almost as thin as paper, then forming it into balls before doing the same again. Ruth's lips twitched as she made the tea. They would entertain themselves like this for a good twenty minutes before finally making their jam rolls with pastry that would by then be a grubby grey, and bake as heavy as lead. Nobody else would want their jam rolls, but they would eat and pretend to enjoy them.

'What's this all about, then?' she asked Jane, going through to the other room and shutting the door. 'Lizzie's never left the children with you like this before. Is she all right?'

'If you mean in herself, yes, I think she is,' Jane said a little grimly. 'I'm not sure that everything's as it should be, though, all the same.'

'Why, what do you mean? That American's not come back again, has he?'

'She hasn't said so,' Jane sighed. 'But between you, me and the gatepost, I wouldn't be at all surprised if that's not what's at the back of it. She wouldn't look me in the eye when she brought them over yesterday. *Couldn't*, if you ask me. Too ashamed.'

Ruth stared at her sister in dismay. 'Oh, Jane! You surely don't think there's something going on, do you?'

'Well, what else can I think? She was open enough about it at the start – well, more or less,' Jane said, remembering that Lizzie would have chosen to speak to Ruth rather than herself. 'But now, she's just like a clam. Couldn't wait to get away in case I started asking awkward questions. I would have done, too!'

'D'you think that's the best thing?' Ruth asked doubtfully. 'Isn't it better just to leave her alone and wait until she's ready to tell you? That's if there *is* anything to tell.'

'I don't know what's best, Ruth, I don't honestly,' Jane said in exasperation. 'She doesn't seem the same girl any more. I mean, when all that happened before, with Floyd, she kept it to herself for a long time, but when she had to come out with the truth she was honest enough. But now – oh, I don't know. I just hope she's not going to do anything silly, like going off with him, or something daft like that. I mean, look at the way she's left the kiddies with me. Why's she done that? She said she needed a rest, but she don't look tired to me. In fact, if I was asked I'd say she looked like a volcano about to go off!'

Ruth lifted the poker and stirred the fire, her face thoughtful. She had had a similar impression the last time she'd spoken to Lizzie herself – as if the girl were hugging some secret to herself, a secret which threatened to burst out of her.

'I can't believe she'd do that,' she said at last. 'She'd never leave the kiddies, and she couldn't take them away. Alec wouldn't let her.'

'You've got to remember that Gillie isn't Alec's daughter,' Jane pointed out. 'She's Floyd's.'

'But he's always looked on her as his! He's been a lovely father to her. You'd never know, from the way he's behaved, that she was some other man's child. To tell the truth, I'd more or less forgotten it myself, and I think he has too, to all intents and purposes.'

'He's been reminded now, though,' Jane said with that grim tone back in her voice. 'And no mistake about it.'

There was a slight sound at the door and they both turned. To their dismay, Gillie stood there, with Linnet close behind her. Her face paper-white, she stared from one to the other and then asked in a frightened voice, 'Why isn't Daddy my daddy?'

There was a moment of silence. Then Jane said sharply, 'You shouldn't be listening, Gillie! Go back into the kitchen at once.'

Ruth gave her sister a horrified glance. 'Jane!' She turned back to the child, whose face was now distorting with tears. 'Gillie, come here, pet. It's all right. Granny didn't mean to sound cross, but we didn't know you were there.'

The child came forward slowly, keeping a wary eye on her grandmother. Ruth saw Jane's expression change as she recovered from her reaction, but her first concern was for Gillie, and for Linnet who was looking almost as afraid. She drew the little girl into her arms, and held her closely, beckoning to her daughter.

'I've done it again,' Jane said bitterly. 'Spoken too sharp and out of turn. I'm her grandmother, but it's you she goes to – just like Lizzie goes to you.'

'It's just the way it happens,' Ruth said, keeping her voice quiet and steady. 'You were surprised – we both were. We shouldn't have been talking about it, with them only in the other room.' She rested her cheek against Gillie's hair. 'Go to Granny, sweetheart. She's not cross with you.'

Gillie was sobbing against her shoulder. Linnet leaned against Ruth's other side, her eyes wide and anxious. After a moment, Gillie said in a muffled voice, 'You said Daddy's not my daddy. *Why* isn't he?'

Ruth spoke gently. 'Of course he's your daddy. He's looked after you all your life, hasn't he? You live in his house with him and your mummy and Barry. Granny didn't mean it.'

Gillie lifted her face away and looked at her aunt. Then she turned and looked at her grandmother. 'You said the cowboy man is my daddy.'

'The ... cowboy man?' Jane said faintly.

'Yes. He came to see us one day. He talks like a cowboy and Mummy called him Floyd. He told us he used to come to the farm for his dinner and he knows everyone here. He even knows Silver. You said he was my daddy.' Gillie's eyes were fixed on Jane's face. 'Is it true? *Is* he my daddy? Is he Barry's daddy as well?'

'No!' Jane exclaimed before she could stop herself. 'No, he's not Barry's daddy. He's – Gillie, you're not old enough to understand all this yet. It's grown-up talk and you *shouldn't* have been listening. Look how it's upset you.' Her voice softened. 'Come here, pet. Come on.'

Gillie glanced at Ruth and Linnet and, reluctantly, went to her grandmother. Jane, tears streaming down her own face, pulled her on to her knee and cuddled her close. She looked across at Ruth. 'I wouldn't have had this happen for the world.'

'I know,' Ruth said soberly. 'But it has happened, and the question now is, what are we going to do about it?'

'Perhaps she'll just forget about it,' Jane said hopefully, but Ruth shook her head.

'I don't think it's going to be that easy. And quite honestly, Jane, I don't know that we should be deciding it anyway. It's Lizzie's business, and Alec's. It's not really for us to interfere.'

'I suppose you're right. But I've got the children here for the next two or three days. I can't just pretend nothing's happened. Oh, that naughty girl!' she exclaimed with sudden anger, and then cuddled the child more closely against her. 'No, Gillie, it's all right, I don't mean you. You couldn't help hearing what we were saying.' She spoke to Ruth again. 'For two pins, I'd send Lizzie a telegram and tell her to come out here and sort it all out. She can't expect me to know what to say to them.'

'She didn't expect you to need to say anything. But I think

155

you're right, it's the best thing to do. What was she planning to do, while they're here – rest?'

'Rest?' Jane echoed acidly. 'I don't suppose she'll be doing much *resting*. She'll be off with that American, that's what she'll be doing. You mark my words, that's what this is all about – give herself a bit of free time for some fun and games.'

'Jane, surely not. Lizzie wouldn't do that.'

'I don't think,' Lizzie's mother said sourly, 'that we have any real idea about what Lizzie would or wouldn't do. I sometimes wonder how she came to be my daughter, and that's the honest truth.'

Gillie raised her head. 'But you *are* Mummy's mummy, aren't you?' The fear was in her voice again, and Ruth felt a pang of compassion. The child's world was falling to pieces around her ears. She looked warningly at her sister and opened her mouth to speak, but Jane was already clearly regretting her words.

'Yes, of course I am, pet. I didn't mean that. Why don't you and Linnet go and finish making your jam rolls and forget about all this? It's grown-up talk.'

'We have finished. That's what we came to ask you – if we could put them in the oven.'

'I'll come and help you,' Ruth said, getting up. 'And I must put my pie in as well or it won't be cooked in time for Uncle Dan's dinner. Jane, why don't you leave the children here while you go back to get George's meal ready? You can talk it over with him then, and I'll take them for a walk or something. There's plenty of stew in the pan.'

'Yes, I think I will. We'll have to decide something.' Jane looked uncertainly at her granddaughter. 'Will you be all right with Auntie Ruth, pet? You can look out for Barry when he comes up the lane, and tell him you're having your dinners here.'

'All right,' Gillie said, and turned to Ruth. 'Can we go

to the forge? I like watching Uncle Dan put shoes on the horses.'

'Yes, of course we can.' Ruth gave a little sigh of relief and met her sister's eye as Jane put on her coat. It looked as if the immediate crisis was past.

But as Jane walked up the track to the farmhouse, she felt a deep unease creep over her. It might be past for the moment, but Gillie wouldn't forget. The question of who was her daddy, too enormous for her six-year-old mind to contemplate, would nevertheless recur. She was likely to ask again. She was all too likely to ask Alec.

And where was Lizzie while all this was going on? Jane asked herself savagely. Off with her fancy-man, that's where. The naughty, *naughty* girl.

'I don't know,' George said as she recounted all this to him over their dinner an hour or so later. 'I reckon meself it might be better just to lay low and say nothing until we see if Gillie remembers it. You know what kiddies are – the world's coming to an end one minute, and before you can look round they've forgotten all about it. If Ruth keeps them busy this afternoon it'll probably go out of her mind altogether.'

'Or I'll go out of mine,' Jane said darkly, passing him a large helping of steak and kidney pie. 'I mean to say, George, what does our Lizzie think she's doing? She can't really be planning to go off and leave poor Alec. And if she's just having a bit of a fling, well, I'm sorry to say it but if it wasn't for the children I'd have nothing more to do with her. And her carrying Alec's baby, as well! It's disgusting.'

'D'you really think that's what she's doing?' George asked, helping himself to potatoes and cabbage. 'I don't think we ought to judge the girl till we know for certain.'

'Why else did she bring the children out here? She didn't look tired, I can tell you that! She looked as excited as a kiddy at Christmas. She's having a few days with Floyd, that's what she's doing. She might be going home at night but to all intents and purposes she's living with him. And he's just as bad!' Jane exclaimed, her voice rising with fresh anger. 'After all the times we welcomed him to our house and gave him Sunday dinner during the war! I thought he was such a nice young man, too. Decent and honest, that's what I thought, and so I told anyone who passed remarks about the Americans and what they were like. Well, it seems they were right and I was wrong and that's all there is to it.'

George sighed. 'I must say, it does look as if there's something going on. The question is, what do we do about it? It's not our place to interfere, you know.'

'It might not have been, as long as Lizzie didn't involve us,' Jane retorted. 'But she has now, hasn't she? She's brought the children here and she's told me lies. I've got a right to know the truth now, and when I know it I shall give her a real piece of my mind. And it's not just that,' she went on, ignoring her own meal. 'It's the children. Poor little Gillie – you should have seen her face. White as a sheet, she was, and asking if Alec was her daddy – and if he wasn't, was it the "cowboy man". The *cowboy man* – I ask you. And that's another thing. He's obviously been to the house and met the children. *Alec's* house. It's downright disgraceful.'

'You don't know that Lizzie invited him there,' George pointed out. 'Perhaps he just called round one day and she had to ask him in.'

'Well, she shouldn't have. She should have sent him away with a flea in his ear. I don't want this,' Jane said, pushing away her plate. 'I'm too upset to eat. I'll have to say something to her, George. I can't let it go like that.'

'All right, but wait until she comes back for the children. If you start sending telegrams the neighbours are going to take notice, and you know what'll happen then, she'll have a string of them at the door wanting to know if there's anything wrong. And Alec's bound to find out. Seems to me, we ought to let them deal with it in their own way. I'm not saying you can't talk to her, mind,' he said, pointing his fork at her. 'But you've got to wait until she comes here. You can't risk causing worse trouble than they've already got. And it's not going to help anyone if you waste good food and make yourself bad.'

'I suppose not.' Jane picked at her plate again. 'I don't know how I'm going to keep my temper with her though, I tell you that. I don't think I've ever been so angry with her, ever. I mean, we never brought them up to act like this, none of them. Sent them to Sunday School, took them to church, tried to teach them to know right from wrong. What happened to all that? Doesn't she have a conscience?'

'Oh, I think she knows right from wrong,' George said. 'And she's got a conscience too. She's just not taking any notice of it. And only Lizzie knows why that is.' He paused for a moment, chewing a piece of meat. 'How did you think she and Alec were getting along, before all this blew up? They seemed all right to me, I must say.'

'They did to me, too. I don't think there was anything wrong at all between them. It's Floyd coming back that's set the cat among the pigeons. But she ought to have known *better*!' Jane cried, thumping her fist on the table. 'Oh, if I had the two of them here I'd bang their heads together, I would really. And I'd show him the door in no uncertain fashion – but only after I'd made sure he knew just what I thought of him.' She pushed her plate away again and then got up. 'I'm sorry, I just can't swallow it. And if you've finished, there's jam sponge pudding and custard for afters but I don't want any. I'm too upset and too cross to eat another bite. I'm going to clear out the small bedroom. It's been wanting doing for weeks.'

She served George his pudding and went upstairs. He heard her overhead, shifting furniture, carrying boxes out on to the landing, banging about with a broom. He sighed and ate his jam sponge without much enjoyment. George liked a quiet life, without all these arguments and rows, and family arguments and rows were the worst sort of all.

Like Jane, he wondered what Lizzie was thinking of. And what on earth was going to happen next.

Chapter Nineteen

On Sunday, Sammy took Linnet for a walk in the woods, pointing out to her the signs of spring – a patch of snowdrops, like a drift of snow which had forgotten to thaw, the tight catkins on a hazel bush, waiting to break out into lambs' tails, the golden beak on a male blackbird singing in a tree.

'They're still yellowish, but they only start getting really bright again in January. They start to sing again properly then, too.'

'Why?' asked Linnet, who seemed to have rediscovered this word lately.

'Because they'll be starting to think about nesting soon and they've got to find a mate.'

'But it's still winter!'

'I know. But it takes them quite a while to get ready properly. And it's been mild so far, this winter, so perhaps they think spring's nearly here and they'd better hurry up.'

They were busy in the forge that week. The local Hunt was in full swing and horses were forever casting shoes and coming in for new ones, and Solly had an order for a large pair of wrought-iron gates for one of the big houses in the neighbourhood. Ruth brought Linnet down one afternoon, and Sammy was surprised to see Gillie and Barry with them but accepted without comment the explanation that Lizzie had been feeling a bit tired and brought them over to stay with Jane for a few days. They were going back soon, Ruth added, because Gillie was starting school again next week.

After work, Sammy came home and washed hastily to go to Southampton for his night school classes. Remembering Lizzie's invitation, he dropped in to see her at the end of the week, and she told him he ought to have come before to have supper with her.

'I don't like to take it for granted,' he said. 'You don't want me treating you like a café.'

'Don't be silly. You're always welcome. I like the company, and the children like to see you too. Why don't we set a couple of days for you to come to tea? Tuesdays and Thursdays, perhaps. Honestly, Sam, I'd like you to.'

'All right,' he said. 'I'll do that. Thanks, Lizzie.' He remembered what Ruth had told him and thought she did look tired, and not very happy. She was probably lonely, with Alec working such long hours. He knew she was pregnant, of course, although he was vague about its effects, but Ruth had passed one or two remarks about some women feeling quite ill with it. 'So long as you're sure it's not too much for you,' he added anxiously.

Lizzie gave a little chuckle. 'Of course it's not. I have to get a meal for us anyway. You make sure you come, Sam.'

'I can always do any little jobs you want doing,' he offered. 'I'll get the coal in, for a start. And you can tell me if there's anything else.'

'I will.' She went to make a cup of tea. Sammy had already eaten his supper at home, and hadn't time for more than a quick cup, but Lizzie was the sort who couldn't let anyone in the house without offering them sustenance. She supposed she got it from her mother and Ruth, who both always had a kettle on and, as often as not, some scones or rock cakes just about to come out of the oven. She took the biscuit tin into the back room with her and found Sammy playing *Sorry* with the children.

'I'd forgotten what a long game this was,' he said, shaking the dice and groaning as he found himself sliding backwards on the board. 'I'm never going to get Home at his rate.'

Lizzie smiled. 'We usually only play that on wet Sundays when there's plenty of time. You shouldn't have got it out, Gillie. You know how long it takes, and Sammy'll have to be going soon.'

'Oh, why?' Gillie said, in the plaintive bleat that all children seemed to employ when they thought they were being hard done by. 'Where's he got to go?'

'To school,' Sammy said, helping Barry to decide which man to move. 'Look, if you move that one you can get into the safe place and he'll be nearly home.'

'School's in the daytime.'

'Not mine. It's night school, so I have to go at night, see? And I'll have to go soon, too.' He drank his tea and stood up. 'Thanks, Lizzie.'

'So you'll come next Tuesday?' she asked, seeing him to the front door.

'Yes, please.' He buckled on his helmet and kicked the bike's engine into life. 'And don't forget, if there's anything I can do ... And don't go lifting heavy coal-buckets.'

'I won't,' Lizzie said. She stood and waved as he turned the corner, and went back indoors. Sammy was a nice boy, and she'd had a soft spot for him ever since he had first come to live with Ruth. And it was good to have a visitor she didn't have to feel guilty about.

She took the cups out to the kitchen and started to wash them up, thinking about the last time she had seen Floyd. That third day of the children's stay with their grandparents, when Floyd had hired a car and they'd gone out together, pretending they were any innocent young couple on an outing. Pretending, at first, that they were single.

Pretending, later, that they were married.

She hadn't meant it to happen, Lizzie told herself. Although she had an uneasy, niggling feeling that in some dark, unacknowledged recess of her mind, she might have meant it to happen. Or, at least, not meant to stop it if it did. Anyway, it *had* happened, and now she had an added burden of guilt.

The day had been fine and mild, almost like early spring. Lizzie had refused to allow Floyd to call for her in his hired car, knowing what a flurry of excitement and curiosity this would cause in the street, and had met him at the bus stop before the one she normally used to go into town. That way, she thought, she'd be unlikely to run into anyone she knew. She'd stood demurely, as if waiting for the bus, feeling as though she had a whole flock of butterflies inside her, and when the car drew up and he leaned over and called out, 'Hi there. Want a lift?' she'd opened the door and got in quickly, still afraid that someone might see her and ask questions later or, worse, mention it to Alec. But that was one good thing about Alec's long hours – he hardly ever saw the neighbours and even if someone did notice them, they were unlikely to go out of their way to tell him.

Floyd had pulled away from the kerb as soon as she was in her seat, and within a few minutes they were on the road heading out of Southampton, towards Romsey.

'I thought we'd go this way,' he said, his hands resting lightly on the wheel. 'It's a pretty little town, from what I've heard.'

'Yes, it is. I've only been there a few times. We went on a Sunday School outing when I was about twelve, and Dad took us to the market there once.'

'I'd like to see the Abbey,' he said. 'It's nearly a thousand years old, so I've read. I can't imagine a building as old as that. A thousand years!' He shook his head, whistling.

'I suppose it is pretty old,' Lizzie said. 'I've never thought about it much. A lot of our buildings are old. The cottages at Bridge End, for instance.'

'But not a thousand years! Although, even two or three

hundred is older than anything we've got.' He shook his head again. 'This country – it's just amazing.'

Lizzie hadn't ever thought of Bridge End, or any of England for that matter, as 'amazing'. She looked at Floyd's long fingers, resting so easily on the steering wheel, and said, 'I suppose you've got a car at home.'

'Oh, sure,' he said in a casual tone. 'Everybody does. I don't know how you Britishers manage the way you do.'

'We have buses and trains,' Lizzie said, feeling a little affronted. 'Or bikes. Or we use Shanks' pony.'

'Shanks' pony?'

'We walk,' she said briefly. 'And some people do even have cars.'

'Yeah, and I guess a lot more will too, in the next few years. It's the only way to travel, Lizzie. Better than having to wait around for trains or buses. You can go in your own time, in your own way, and not have to struggle about in bad weather. Don't you and Alec ever think about getting one?'

'We're thinking about getting a house at the moment,' she said shortly, and looked out of her window.

Floyd glanced sideways at her. 'Sorry, Lizzie. I didn't mean to talk about you and Alec. Let's forget all that today and just pretend we're the only people in the world.'

'I wish we were,' Lizzie said wistfully. 'I wish there was nobody else but you and me. Nobody to care what we do, nobody to tell lies to, nobody to stop us being just ourselves – you and me, for ever.'

Floyd looked at her again. Then he drew the car into the side of the road, beneath some trees, and turned to her, pulling her into his arms.

'Floyd,' she whispered, feeling all her resistance slip away from her like silk. 'I've wanted you so much. Oh Floyd, I love you.'

He pressed his lips to hers and she felt the leap of desire, as fierce and as hot and as overpowering as it had been on

VE Day. For a few moments she lost all reason in a whirl of emotion and longing; and then, as he pulled reluctantly back from the kiss, her sense reasserted itself and she murmured, 'Not here, Floyd. Please – not here.'

'Later,' he said, looking into her eyes. 'We'll go back to my hotel.'

'No, we can't do that,' she said quickly, fear licking at her mind. 'They'll know. That receptionist gave me a funny look last time.'

'Well,' he said, 'we'll think about that later on. We promised ourselves a real day out. Let's have that first.' He kissed her again, quickly and firmly, and once again she felt that leap of excitement. 'There's nobody in the world but us today, Lizzie. Nobody else matters.'

The thought of her children slid into her mind, but she pushed it away. They were safe with her mother and need never know about this day out of time that she was taking. Tomorrow, or the day after, she'd go to Bridge End and bring them home, and everything would be just as it had been before. All she wanted was this one day. Could anyone really begrudge her that?

Floyd started the car again and a short time later they found themselves in Romsey. He parked the car in the square and they set off to explore on foot.

'It's all so old,' he said, gazing around at the Georgian houses. 'Let's go and look at the Abbey.'

They went into the big stone church and stood in the dim nave, lit only by the sun which streamed through the tall windows. Floyd rested his hand on one of the massive pillars and stared up at the roof.

'They sure knew how to build. And to think it's been standing here, just the same as it is now, for a thousand years.'

'Well, I'm not sure it all has. I think there's been an abbey here all that time, but some of it might be a bit later.' Lizzie

166

dredged her memory for old school lessons. 'I think most of it is Norman. About eight or nine hundred years.'

He glanced at her. 'Well, that's still pretty ancient. You make it sound as if it was just yesterday.'

'I've never really thought about it much,' she confessed. 'Are there really no old buildings in America?'

'Well, not this old. How could there be? Nobody settled there until the seventeenth century, and I don't reckon they started to build straight away. I don't know anywhere more than a hundred years old. If that.'

'So everything's new and modern?' she said thoughtfully.

'I wouldn't say that. There are poor areas too – shacks and old wooden houses that aren't in too good condition. But where I live, things are pretty nice. Dad's got a big block of land and I'm planning to build my own home on it.' He looked at her again: 'It could be your home too, Lizzie. You could have it just the way you want.'

She laughed. 'I don't think I'd even know how to begin to think about that. The farmhouse is quite big, but it's old and rambling – it's been added on to through the years. I don't know how you go about designing a new house from scratch.'

'You don't have to,' he said easily. 'You just say what you want and an architect does the rest. Every bedroom could have its own bathroom, if you wanted it.'

Lizzie tried to imagine such a house. In the little two-up, two-down house with a scullery tacked on the back that she and Alec lived in, there wasn't even one bathroom. They still dragged the tin bath in from the back yard every Saturday night and filled it with hot water from the Ascot. She dreamed of a house with just one proper bathroom – one for each bedroom seemed excessive.

'I don't see how you could ever need that many. And it would have to be a very big house.'

'Well,' he said, 'it could be.' He took her hand and stroked her wrist with one finger. Lizzie shivered. 'It's cold in here,' she said abruptly. 'Let's go outside.'

They went out and gazed at King John's Hunting Lodge, the oldest building in the town apart from the abbey. Then Floyd declared that he was hungry and led the way to the White Horse Hotel. Lizzie hung back a little.

'I can't go in there, Floyd. It's much too smart.'

'Don't be silly. Of course you can. This is a special day, remember?' He took her hand again and led her firmly through the door and into the restaurant. 'We're going to have a really good lunch, and some wine to go with it.'

'I've never had wine.'

'Then today's a pretty good day to start.' He spoke to the waiter who came forwards, and they found themselves seated at a small table in the window. Lizzie sat down and looked around her nervously.

'At least I'm not likely to meet any of the neighbours here,' she said with a giggle, and Floyd grinned.

'That's better. I like to see you smile, Lizzie. It spreads all over your face.'

She blushed and looked down at the crisp white tablecloth. 'All this cutlery.'

'You start from the outside and work in,' he said. 'So they tell me, anyway! We keep things a bit simpler back home.'

They had brown Windsor soup to begin with, then roast mutton with boiled potatoes, carrots and cabbage, and finished with treacle pudding. Lizzie sipped her wine tentatively at first, then found that she liked it. 'It makes the food taste better, and the food makes the wine taste better.'

'That's the general idea,' he said with a grin. 'We'll make a toper of you yet.'

'Oh no,' she said hastily. 'We only ever have cider at home – at the farm, I mean. Alec has some beer from the Bottle and Jug sometimes.'

'Is that your local pub? I haven't noticed it.'

She shook her head. 'It's a door round the corner of the pub where they sell beer for you to take home. People take their own jugs.'

'Or bottles,' he said, and she laughed.

'I suppose so. It's easier to fill a jug, though.'

Floyd shook his head. 'I shall never understand you English.'

Lizzie looked down, noticing with some dismay that she had managed to drop a shred of cabbage on the tablecloth, She moved her plate a little, hoping that it wouldn't be noticed when the waiter cleared the plates.

'Sorry,' Floyd said quickly. 'I didn't mean you, of course. You're different.'

Lizzie looked up and met his eyes. 'I'm not, you know. I'm not any different from anyone else. You'll be disappointed if you think I am.'

'I'll never be disappointed in you, Lizzie,' he said quietly. 'The only way you could disappoint me is by not saying you'll come with me.'

Alarm flickered through her. 'Floyd, we said we wouldn't talk about it today.'

'No more we will,' he said, putting his hand over hers. 'Say, why don't we take a room here? We don't need to go any further, do we?'

Lizzie stared at him. '*Here?*'

'Sure. Why not? It's a pretty comfortable-looking place. I'll see if they've got a room, shall I?'

'But I can't!' Alarm turned into panic. 'I've got to go home – I can't stay away all night.'

'Who said you should? Sure, I'd rather you stayed, but if you won't, we'll have all afternoon.' His fingers stroked hers. 'Love in the afternoon, Lizzie. Doesn't that tempt you?'

Her mind flashed to Sunday afternoons with Alec, while the children were at Sunday School. But Alec seemed very small and very far away, as if seen through the wrong end of a telescope. She looked at Floyd helplessly, aware of his finger-tips like small, white-hot flames stroking the backs of her own fingers, so lightly and gently that they could have been feathers. They could equally, for all the strength she had to move away from them, have been manacles.

'Love in the afternoon,' he whispered, and his eyes burned into hers.

'But we can't,' she breathed. 'We haven't got any luggage.'

He smiled. 'I put a suitcase in the car this morning.'

Lizzie drew back at once. 'Floyd! You meant this to happen.'

'Well, OK, so I did. We both knew it, didn't we? What did you want – a cold, open field? At this time of year?'

Lizzie glanced out of the window. It was not long after two, yet already the afternoon was closing in, the dark clouds pressing down on the town. She looked at Floyd again. 'I thought we were going to go for a long drive.'

'Would you rather? If you can say yes – and mean it – then that's what we'll do. But you'd better be sure, Lizzie.' He waited a moment. 'Well?'

She felt her skin colour and gave him a quick, shy smile. 'Well . . .'

Floyd laughed delightedly. 'I knew it!' He took her hand more firmly and drew her to her feet. 'Maybe I should confess right now – I booked a room yesterday. Just in case. Nobody will suspect a thing, Lizzie, and if they do look at you, you just stare right back.' He led her through to the reception area and approached the desk. The smartly dressed woman at the typewriter glanced up and said, 'Yes?'

'I've booked a room for tonight,' Floyd said easily. 'Name of Hanson. We thought we'd check in early, get a bit of rest before going out for the evening.'

'Oh yes. You'll need to register.' She passed over the book and he signed it confidently. The woman glanced at Lizzie without curiosity. 'I'll call the porter to take up your luggage.'

'It's in the car,' Floyd said. 'We're parked right outside.' He turned to Lizzie. 'Wait here, sweetheart, while I see to things. Sit down for a minute or two – you're looking tired.'

Lizzie sank into a chair. Events seemed to have moved beyond her control. She glanced at the receptionist, then away again and watched the revolving door fixedly, wondering what she was doing here and why she had come. This is the moment when I could get up and walk out, she thought. I could catch a bus back to Southampton and tomorrow I could go and fetch the children. I don't need to do this. I don't need ever to see Floyd again.

But she knew that she could no more get up out of her chair and walk out of the hotel than she could sprout angels' wings. And that's something I'm never going to do, she thought ruefully.

Floyd came back, accompanied by a boy of about sixteen in a dark blue uniform with a red stripe down his trousers, who was carrying a suitcase. She stared at it, wondering what Floyd had packed. Did he intend to stay here tonight after he'd taken her back to Southampton? Wouldn't they think it strange that she wasn't with him? And a little dart of terror pierced her heart. He *did* mean to take her back tonight, didn't he?

'Room seventeen,' the woman said, handing the boy a large key, and Floyd smiled at Lizzie.

'Coming, hon?'

'Yes,' she said, getting up to follow him; and knew that she had sealed her fate.

Chapter Twenty

Dawn had not quite broken on the following Saturday when Sammy revved up his motorbike outside the cottage at Bridge End and set off on his first long ride to West Lyme. He waved a gloved hand at his father, Ruth and Linnet, who were standing at the gate watching him and, as soon as he turned the corner out of the village, he twisted the throttle a little harder to increase his rather sedate pace to a more satisfying speed.

The air was cold against his face and he was glad of the goggles which covered his eyes. He was even glad of the black crash helmet he had bought and privately admitted he quite liked the look of it, with its peak that gave it a more dashing look that the plain round ones. In his black waterproof riding suit, he felt that he looked smart and self-assured, and hoped that Maddy would think the same.

Sammy had sent her a postcard a day or two before, to let her know he was coming. There hadn't been time for her to reply, but he was confident that she would be there and pleased to see him. He wouldn't offer to take her on the bike on this first visit, but if she seemed keen to ride it, he would buy her a crash helmet of her own. As he buzzed along, he dreamed of spring and summer days when they would explore the lanes and byways of the New Forest and Dorset together. There could be days on the beach too, at Lyme Regis or Charmouth, or even as far as Devon. Once you had wheels, he thought, you could go anywhere you liked. The only restrictions were time and distance, but even those could be overcome.

I'd like to travel one day, he thought. Go abroad – to France and Italy and Spain. I could do all that on a motorbike. You can go anywhere, now that the war's over. I could go even further – maybe right around the world. Down to Australia and New Zealand – across to America. What an adventure that would be! And even better if Maddy could go, too.

But that would only be possible if they were married, and that was a dream he didn't even dare to contemplate, just yet.

Soon, the grey January light crept across the sky, revealing grey January clouds. There was very little traffic on the road, and he was able to keep up a good, steady speed. He was confident on the bike by now and increased his speed until he was going at sixty miles an hour. It wouldn't go much faster than that, and he wasn't sure he wanted it to – sixty miles an hour was a mile a minute and rather alarming. The hedges and banks seemed to blur as he passed them, and after a little while he slowed down to just under fifty.

The road led him past Bournemouth and Poole and through Dorchester before turning closer to the coast. As it swooped across the high Dorset downs, Sammy felt as if he was riding across the top of the world. A sense of exhilaration swept over him and he let the bike run faster again, shouting aloud with sheer joy at the power and freedom of being able to speed across the wild, open countryside. Away to his right, he could see the rolling hills, the fields, the hedges and the woods, with villages dotted amongst them and in the distance the smudge of a larger town. On his left lay the expanse of the English Channel, glittering and grey, with a few ships passing on the horizon. The sense of space seemed to open out his heart and mind, and he thought again of travelling far and wide, seeing the world and all its glories, all from the seat of a motorcycle. I'll do it, he told himself. One day, when I've got my qualifications, I'll do it. This is why we fought the war – so that we could live our lives in freedom to go where we please. This is what life is *for*.

A herd of cows, emerging suddenly from a field, brought him back to earth and he slowed down to follow them for a short distance until they veered into another field. Well, that would all be a part of it. Unexpected sights, interesting things to see and learn about. He felt his excitement rise again. And if Maddy would go with him ... but again, he shied away from that idea. It was too big, too overwhelming. He could go at sixty miles an hour on his motorbike, he could plan to travel the world, but this was a dream he dared not dream. Not yet.

The signpost to West Lyme took him by surprise and he turned without slowing down enough, so that he almost went into the ditch. His heart thudding, he righted the machine and proceeded a little more slowly. He would have to take more care if Maddy did agree to ride pillion. No daydreaming then. He put away his thoughts and concentrated on the road, slowing down for each junction and reading the signs carefully. Excitement gripped him again. He had been almost two hours on the road and was nearly there. In only a few minutes he would see her again.

The last mile took him to the edge of West Lyme, where the Archdeacon's house stood in its own grounds overlooking the sea. Feeling suddenly nervous, Sammy turned into the drive, wondering whether the Archdeacon would object to a motorcycle buzzing up to his front door. Perhaps he ought to get off and push. But before he could make up his mind, he had rounded a corner between a shrubbery of rhododendron bushes and found himself on a large gravel circle with the house before him. He stopped and looked up uncertainly, half-inclined to turn the bike round and ride away before anyone knew he was there.

'Sammy!'

He looked up. A window was open above the front door and Maddy was leaning out dangerously far, waving her arm. Sammy grinned and waved back rather self-consciously and she blew him a kiss.

'Wait there! I'll come down and let you in.' She disappeared and the window closed. Sammy propped his bike on its stand, still feeling rather conspicuous on the wide driveway, and a few moments later the door at the top of the steps opened and Maddy came flying out, accompanied by a large black dog. Both flung themselves at their visitor, who staggered back and almost collapsed on the gravel.

'Archie! Get down at once, you great lolloping idiot!' Maddy scolded, and the dog obeyed reluctantly, sitting on its rump and gazing up at Sammy with large, brown, expectant eyes. 'He hasn't got anything for you – he didn't even know you were here.' She twinkled at Sammy and then flung her arms around him. 'Oh, it's *so* good to see you. I got your card. How long did it take you to get here? And just look at your lovely motorbike! Are you going to take me for a ride?'

'Well – if you like.' He was breathless from her hug and the torrent of remarks and questions she was flinging at him. 'But not unless you can get a crash helmet. Auntie Ruth made me promise to wear one and she'd be really angry if I took you out without one. I thought maybe today we could just go for a walk, or something.'

'Oh, yes! We'll take Archie on the beach. He loves playing with the waves. Come in while I get my coat.' She whirled up the steps, leaving Sammy to follow. By the time he went through the door, she had disappeared and he stood uneasily in the big hallway, looking round at the dark panelling, the even darker pictures and a hallstand festooned with coats and hats. Archie leaped about him, released from Maddy's command, and Sammy put out his hand and stroked the labrador's head. Immediately, the dog collapsed in a heap of ecstasy, pedalling its legs in the air.

A door opened and a tall man with silvery hair and a grey beard emerged. He looked at Sammy questioningly.

'I'm sorry. I didn't realise anyone was here. Were you waiting to see me?'

Sammy felt his face burn. 'No – um – actually I'm waiting for Miss Simmons – Muriel – I mean, Maddy. She's just gone to get her coat. I can wait outside just as well.' He started back towards the door but the man put out a hand to stop him.

'By no means. You're welcome to wait here. Sit down.' He indicated a settle which looked remarkably like a church pew and then stood regarding Sammy. 'I'm Archdeacon Copley. You must be young Sammy Hodges. Maddy's talked about you.'

'Has she?' Sammy said, surprised.

'Indeed she has. You were friends when you were children, in Portsmouth and at Bridge End. That's right, isn't it?'

'Yes. We used to play together. But then Maddy was taken away and I didn't know where she'd gone.' He remembered the bewilderment he had felt at that time, when Mike Simmons had died and a woman Keith Budd had said looked like a brown settee had come to remove and separate the sisters. 'None of us knew.'

'So she's told me. A cruel thing to do. But she and Stella have found each other, and now you have as well. So all is ending happily.' He smiled at Sammy. 'It's kind of you to come all this way to see her. And is that your motorcycle on the drive?'

'Yes. I hope you don't mind me leaving it there. I didn't know where else—'

'It's perfectly all right where it is. Why don't you show it to me? I used to ride a motorcycle myself when I was young. I had a Sunbeam. Not as modern-looking as yours is, of course!' He led the way outside and Sammy followed him, slightly bemused by an Archdeacon who could ride a motorcycle. Before long, they were both kneeling on the gravel as he explained the design of the engine and the Archdeacon compared it with the one he had ridden thirty years earlier. Maddy, now wrapped in a bright red winter coat with a black fur hat and gloves, found them there.

'I might have known it! You're just like little boys. Stephen and Felix are just as bad with their sports cars. I sometimes think they'd rather just take them to pieces and oil them than actually go out in them.'

Sammy straightened up at once, looking abashed, and she laughed and slipped her arm through his. 'I'm only joking, silly. And I'd really love to ride on your motorbike one day – when I've got a helmet. But we've promised to take Archie for a walk on the beach now, so we'd better go. Are you staying for lunch? That would be all right, wouldn't it, Archdeacon? I'd better let Mrs Sellers know.'

'Certainly, my dear, and I'll tell her, otherwise this poor dog will die of anxiety. You shouldn't have mentioned the word "walk".' They all looked at the labrador, who was now rushing round them in circles and leaping up and down with excitement. 'Go along, now. You won't mind if I take the bike for a spin, will you?' He laughed at Sammy's expression and said, 'That's a joke, too. Though if I didn't have work to do . . .' He cast a longing eye over the blue machine and turned away with evident regret, while Maddy pulled gently at Sammy's arm to lead him down the drive.

'He doesn't seem much like an archdeacon, does he?' Sammy observed as they walked away. 'Not that I really know what an archdeacon is, except that it's more important than a vicar.'

'None of the family seem like vicars or even bishops,' Maddy said. 'Not when they're at home, anyway. They can be perfectly proper when they're being official, of course. Except for Felix,' she added thoughtfully. 'I'm not sure he's ever really *proper*. You remember Felix from the wedding, don't you? He's engaged to Stella.'

'I remember.' He followed her along a narrow path through the bushes, with Archie barging past him to go first. 'When are they getting married?'

'Oh, not for ages yet. They only got engaged at Christmas.

Felix is going to be vicar of Little Burracombe – that's the village over the river from Burracombe.' She came to the edge of the bushes and paused. 'Here we are. Isn't that a wonderful view?'

Sammy came to stand beside her. They were on the edge of the cliff, looking down at a shifting sea of glimmering pewter. The beach was no more than a narrow strip of rock and pebbles, frothed with surging white foam, curving to the shape of the cliffs which swooped away to east and west. Seabirds dived all about them, screaming and cackling, and on some of the rocks far below he could see cormorants shaking their dark green wings as if holding them out to dry.

'That's smashing,' he said. 'I didn't know it was like this here. Round Pompey, it's just shore.'

'I know. I love the cliffs. Look, that's Portland Bill you can see that way – and if you look the other way you can see how the cliffs go red in Devon. Except for Beer, where they're white chalk, like Portsmouth, which always seems rather strange to me. It would be nice to walk along the cliffs, all the way to Land's End, wouldn't it?'

'Can we get down to the beach?' Sammy asked, looking down at the surging sea. 'Or isn't there any beach?'

'Oh yes. There's a nice little cove down that way, and a path leading down to it. Come on.' She began to lead the way along the cliff top. 'I expect it was used by smugglers – there were lots along the coast. You know the old poem:

> *Five and twenty ponies*
> *Trotting through the dark –*
> *Brandy for the Parson.*
> *'Baccy for the Clerk;*
> *Laces for a lady, letters for a spy,*
> *And watch the wall, my darling,*
> *While the Gentlemen go by!*

'The Archdeacon would have probably had the brandy!'

'Would he? But it was a crime.'

'I don't think they looked on it quite like that,' Maddy said. 'It was the only way they could get their luxuries in those days, and smuggling was the only way a lot of people could earn any money – a lot of them would have starved without it, when fishing was poor. We don't really realise these days how desperate they must have been. Desperate enough even to cause wrecks deliberately.'

They scrambled down a narrow path and eventually found themselves on the beach in a small, secluded cove the shape of a horseshoe. Archie immediately tore down to the edge of the waves and Maddy ran after him and bent to pick up a stone. She threw it into the water and Sammy did the same, while Archie stood and barked.

'You've got a better throw than I have,' she said with a laugh. 'Can you do ducks and drakes?'

'Yes, but not in these waves. You need calm water for that. The water's really clear here, isn't it? I'd like to come back and go swimming in summer.'

'Well, so you can,' she said, tucking her hand into his arm. 'We'll go swimming together. You'll come again, won't you, Sammy? Lots of times?'

'Yes,' he said, looking down at her upturned face. 'Yes, I'd like to. As often as you'll let me.'

They stood very still for a moment, gazing at each other. Then Maddy's face broke into laughter and she squeezed his arm tightly against her side before breaking away and running off along the beach. Sammy and Archie ran after her, but she dodged them and scampered like a puppy up on to some rocks, where she stood laughing before jumping down again. They caught her finally at the edge of the bay, where the cliffs ran right down into the water, and Sammy captured her by the waist as she stood above the foam.

'I thought you were going to fall in,' he said, pulling her back to safety, and she laughed again.

'I've got perfect balance. I had ballet training when I was a little girl. I thought of going on the stage, like Fenella, but I wasn't really good enough. Anyway, I'm not going to go swimming today, it's too cold.' She glanced at the watch on her wrist. 'Shall we go back? Mrs Sellers will be cross if she's made more specially and then we're late. Anyway, she makes such wonderful meals that nobody's ever late for them, not even the Archdeacon.'

They spent the afternoon walking around the country lanes surrounding the house. Mrs Sellers had provided fish pie and cabbage, followed by apple tart, for lunch, which Sammy would have called dinner (lunch, to him, was a snack you had in the middle of the morning), and the Archdeacon had insisted that he have two helpings of each. He had been very welcoming, but Sammy was glad when it was over and they could escape outside again.

'I'm not used to big houses and posh people,' he told Maddy as they strolled along. 'I'm always scared I'm going to do the wrong thing or drop something on the tablecloth.'

'You're all right,' she said. 'Your Auntie Ruth made sure you knew your manners. They're the same anywhere, except when there are lots of knives and forks, and then you just work in from the outside. As long as you remember that, you won't go far wrong.'

The clouds had thickened and a few spots of rain were beginning to fall as they returned to the house. Maddy, walking ahead along the drive towards the house, suggested a cup of tea but Sammy shook his head. 'I ought to think about getting back. It's going to get dark soon and I haven't done much riding at night.' He hesitated. 'Is it really all right if I come again?'

'Of course it is,' Maddy said. 'It's been lovely to see you. And maybe next time I'll have found myself a crash helmet.'

'I'll bring you one,' Sammy promised. 'Once the weather gets better, we can go all over the place.'

'We can take picnics with us.' Her face was glowing. 'Archie won't be too pleased, but he gets plenty of walks anyway. And in the summer, we can go down to the beach and he can come with us then. And – oh!'

'What is it?' Sammy began, but as he followed her past the clump of rhododendrons he saw the small red sports car which had caused her exclamation. 'Someone you know?'

'Yes.' She sounded a little flustered. 'Yes, it's a – a friend of mine from Burracombe. He drops in sometimes on his way back to camp at White Cheriton.' She quickened her pace towards the tall young man who had just emerged from the house and was coming down the steps towards them. 'Hello, Stephen. I didn't know you were coming today.'

'I telephoned just after lunch.' He sounded slightly aggrieved and gave Sammy a suspicious glance. 'The Archdeacon said you were out with a friend. An *old* friend,' he added, as if he'd expected Sammy to have a long white beard and be hobbling along with a stick.

'Yes, this is Sam Hodges. Sammy, this is Stephen Napier. He's in the RAF. Sam was in the RAF too, Stephen.'

'Really?' Stephen said coolly. 'National Service, I suppose?'

'That's right,' Sammy said. 'I was a radar technician.'

Stephen nodded uninterestedly and turned back to Maddy. 'I thought we might go out to dinner this evening. I don't have to be back until midnight. Unless you have something better to do?' His glance flicked briefly over Sammy.

'No – that is, Sammy's off soon – he's riding back to Bridge End on his motorbike. I'm not sure about dinner, though. It depends if the Archdeacon needs me for anything. Sunday's his busy day.' She was talking disjointedly, as if embarrassed, and Sammy began to feel he was in the way. He made an effort to say something, but Stephen talked over him.

'It's all right – I've already asked, and he doesn't need you. So how about it, Maddy? Dinner somewhere nice? I thought the White Hart – we can dance there, as well. You've got time to have a bath and change. You did say you were just leaving?' he said to Sammy in an offhand manner.

'Yes.' Sammy looked rather miserably at Maddy. 'Thanks. I've enjoyed it. And I'll see you again, won't I?'

'Of course you will. Lots of times.' She came closer and stood on tiptoe to kiss his cheek. 'And don't forget that crash helmet!'

'I won't.' He turned to walk over to his motorcycle, still standing on the drive next to the sports car. He couldn't help giving the car an envious glance as he passed it. The bike seemed less impressive now, and he wondered whether Maddy really would ever ride on the pillion with him. Conscious of them both watching him, he pulled the bike off its stand and swung his leg over the saddle. The engine started with the first kick and he gave Maddy a wave and set off down the drive.

The ride back to Bridge End was like a roller coaster of mixed emotions. Elation at Maddy's welcome had faded to disappointment at the way they had said goodbye. Her kiss had been friendly but cool, not at all like the one he'd hoped for. And although the day had been a happy one and he was sure she'd meant it when she'd said he could come again, his mind was filled with pictures of her standing beside Stephen waving him goodbye. And then going on to some grand hotel, all dressed up, to eat an expensive dinner and dance in the other man's arms.

I haven't got a chance, he thought dismally. I might as well forget Maddy Forsyth.

'So who was the erk?' Stephen asked as he and Maddy went into the house. 'Bit young for you, isn't he?'

'Not at all. We're roughly the same age.' Maddy tried to remember just how old Sammy was. 'Well, there's not much difference anyway. And we knew each other as children. His mother looked after Stella and me when our mother was killed.'

'So you've been having a little stroll down Memory Lane together. Well, so long as that's all it was.' He smiled at her and Maddy felt a flicker of irritation.

'What do you mean, *so long as that's all it was*? What business is it of yours anyway?'

Stephen raised his eyebrows. 'Bit touchy, aren't we?' Then he grinned and pulled her towards him. 'Come on, Maddy, you know you're my girl. It's only natural I should feel jealous. And you haven't given me a kiss yet, you know. Aren't you even a little bit pleased to see me?'

'Yes, of course I'm pleased to see you,' she said, not sounding pleased at all. 'I was pleased to see Sammy, too – especially as he had the courtesy to send me a postcard asking if he could come. And I'm not "your girl". We're friends – that's all.'

'Is it?' He pulled her closer still and nuzzled her ear. 'I thought we were a bit more than that, Maddy.'

'Stop it, Stephen.' She jerked away crossly. 'Anyone could come into the hall and see us. You'd better go into the drawing room and I'll get Mrs Sellers to bring some tea. Go on.' She gave him a little shove.

Stephen made a face but allowed her to push him through the door. 'You will come out with me this evening, though, won't you? I promise to be good – well, *fairly* good.' He gave her a wicked grin. 'You're not going to send me back to camp with nothing to cheer me up through the long, lonely week, are you?'

'That remains to be seen,' Maddy said primly. 'I'll think about it after tea. Now wait there, like a good boy.' She watched him go into the drawing room, where Archie had already ensconced himself in front of the fire, and her lips twitched, recognising the words and tone as ones she had often used to the dog.

She returned about ten minutes later with a tray of tea and freshly baked scones. Stephen was stretched out on the sofa. He sat up and patted the seat beside him but Maddy ignored him and took the chair by the fire, setting the tray on a small table between them. Archie lifted his head, gave the scones a hopeful look, then flopped back and moved over with a heavy sigh.

'So tell me more about the erk,' Stephen said, buttering a scone. 'Is that home-made strawberry jam? Good.'

'Stop calling him that. It's a horrible word.'

'It's not. It just means someone who works on aeroplanes in the RAF. He wouldn't mind.'

'Well, I do. Anyway, what do you need to know? We knew each other as children and we met again at the wedding I went to the other week – you know, the one in Portsmouth that Stella and Felix went to as well. You were here when we got back. That's all.'

'If that's all, why did he come here? *I* don't go rushing off to see every person I knew when I was a kid.'

'You probably didn't lose touch the way we did,' she said shortly. 'I don't know all that many people from that time. Only Stella and the Budds, and I hadn't seen them until the wedding. It was good to meet them all again, and it was good to meet Sam too. We were friends.'

'And obviously you want to go on being friends,' Stephen commented, and she set her cup down with a small clash against its saucer.

'And why shouldn't we? I like him – I always did. We had a lot of fun together. Look, Stephen, if you're going to carry on being childish – '

'I'm not being childish!'

' – then you may as well go. I've already told you, I'm not "your girl" and you've no right to question me about my friends. I won't have it.'

Stephen opened his mouth to retort, then thought better

of it. With a sulky look on his face, he took another scone and spread it with butter and jam. At last he said, 'All right, if that's the way you want it, I won't even mention his name again.'

'Good.'

'He's of no interest to me anyway,' Stephen went on. 'Looks a bit namby-pamby, if you ask me, with his pretty yellow curls and blue eyes. And you certainly won't be wanting to go out on that tin-can of a motorbike. I don't suppose it's capable of carrying two people.'

'I shall go on it if I want to.'

'Come on, Maddy,' he coaxed her. 'Don't let's squabble. Come out with me this evening and I'll take you to have a nice dinner and some dancing. And I promise I won't say any more about the er— about Sam Hodges.' He put his head on one side and smiled at her in his most winning fashion, and she laughed reluctantly.

'All right. Since you've come all this way. But you've got to keep your promise, mind,' she warned him. 'One word out of place and I shall ask you to bring me straight back home.'

'Cross my heart,' he said, placing both hands on the wrong side of his chest, and Maddy laughed again. 'Now, why don't you come over here and sit beside me on this comfy sofa and watch the fire until it's time to go and get ready? And you still haven't given me a kiss, you know.'

Maddy shook her head at him, but she did as he had asked. As she settled down beside him amongst the cushions, he stretched out an arm so that she was already in his embrace. He pulled her closer and nuzzled her cheek, and she turned towards him so that their lips met.

Stephen sighed with satisfaction.

'There,' he said. 'That's better, isn't it?'

Chapter Twenty-One

'And you can't tell me,' Jane had said when Lizzie went back to the farm to collect the children, 'that you've been stopping at home with your feet up all this time.'

Lizzie stared at her, feeling the hot colour flush up her neck. 'I don't know what you mean.'

'Oh yes, you do,' her mother said sharply. 'Don't come the innocent with me, Lizzie, I know you too well. Only as it turns out, maybe I didn't know you as well as I thought,' she added bitterly. 'If anyone had ever told me you'd play fast and loose with your man and leave your children to do it, I'd have slapped their face, I would really. But then I'd have had to eat humble pie and apologise – wouldn't I!'

Lizzie shook her head. 'Mum, you're not making sense.'

'I am, though, and you know it. You know very well what I'm talking about. While I've been looking after your children, you've been gadding about with that American, haven't you? Floyd. You've been carrying on with him, our Lizzie, and I don't like it.'

Lizzie turned towards the door. She had only just begun to take off her coat when her mother had started, telling her first that the children were with Ruth and she wanted to have a few words before Lizzie collected them. 'Well, you've had your few words,' she said now. 'I'll go and pick up the kids and go home. Thanks for having them, Mum, but I won't bother you again.'

She took one step and found Jane barring her way. 'Oh no

you don't, my girl. I haven't finished with you yet, not by a long chalk. And you might as well take off your coat and sit down because we've got a lot of talking to do.'

'Not while you're in this mood,' Lizzie retorted. 'You might remember I'm a grown woman now. I don't have to be talked to like that by anyone.'

'You might be a grown woman, but you're behaving like a spoiled baby. You're not thinking of anyone but yourself, taking what you want, never mind who gets hurt. And it's your husband and your children who are going to suffer. Well, I'm not prepared to stand by and see you throw away everything you and Alec have worked for.'

'It's none of your business,' Lizzie said, quivering with rage and humiliation.

'It *is* my business. You're my daughter and the children are my grandchildren – no matter who their father is. I've a right to say my piece.'

'Well, you've done that, so—'

'I told you,' Jane said, giving Lizzie a gentle push so that she sat down suddenly in George's armchair, 'I've got a lot more to say before we're done. And you, miss, are going to listen to me.'

'And suppose I say I'm not?'

'I'll call your father,' Jane said inexorably. 'He's only out in the cowshed. And if you won't listen to either of us, we'll come back with you and talk to Alec.'

The colour left Lizzie's face. 'You wouldn't.'

'Don't try me,' her mother warned. 'I'm pleased to see that he still matters to you a bit, anyway.'

'He matters to me a lot!' Lizzie cried. 'I love him – I don't want to hurt him.'

'Well, you could have fooled me,' Jane said, using an expression she'd heard Sammy using once or twice. 'Because the way you're going on, you're going to hurt him worse than he's ever been hurt before. Worse, even, than when he came home from POW camp and found you carrying another man's baby.'

Lizzie stared at her and then, without warning, covered her face with her hands and burst into tears.

'Oh, Mum,' she wept, but although Jane's instinctive reaction was to go to her daughter and take her into her arms, she held back and stood quite still, watching her. She felt curiously detached, as if she were watching a not very good film.

'You needn't turn on the tap,' she said coldly. 'There'll be plenty more tears to cry before all this is over.'

Lizzie took her hands from her face and stared up at her. Her eyes were magnified by the tears that swam in them and her face was already blotchy. 'Mum, you don't know what it's been like.'

'Thank goodness for that. I shouldn't like to be in your shoes – betraying my husband for the second time with the same man. But then, I always stayed faithful to your father.'

'Mum, please don't.'

'Don't what? Tell the truth? Have you gone so far, Lizzie, that you'd rather talk in lies? Because if so, I'm afraid you've come to the wrong shop. And what's more, you'll stop here until you do start telling the truth. I mean to get this mess sorted out, one way or the other, before you leave here today.'

'You can't,' Lizzie said wearily. 'Nobody can. It's gone too far for that.'

Jane stared at her. 'What do you mean?'

Lizzie met her eyes. 'I mean that Floyd's asked me to go to America with him.'

He had asked her while they were wrapped in each other's arms in bed together, drowsy with love. It wasn't the first time he'd asked her that, but it was the most serious and Lizzie knew that she had to give a serious answer. She had lain quite still, her face hidden by a curtain of hair, her mind in a sudden panic.

'Lizzie?' he whispered. 'Did you hear me? Are you awake?'

I could pretend to be asleep, she thought. But he'd only ask me again. And I'm afraid – so afraid I'll say yes ...

'Lizzie?'

'Yes.' She rolled back a little, so that she could look up at him. He was propped on one elbow, gazing down into her eyes and she felt a tremor pass through her body. 'Floyd, I don't know.'

'Don't know? How can you not know, after ...' He gestured with one hand. 'Lizzie, we belong together, you know we do.'

She hid her face again but he laid one hand on her cheek and turned her head back so that she was forced to meet his eyes. Their look was long and deep, until she slid her glance away as he said, insistently, 'You know we do, don't you?'

'Floyd, it's not that easy.'

'I know. There's Alec and there's Barry. Gillie's mine, so I don't count her. All right, I know what you're going to say.' He held up his hand as Lizzie began to speak. 'He's been a father to her, looks on her as his own and all that. But she's not his. She's mine. And I want her, Lizzie. I thought when I left you before that I could manage my life without either of you – but I was wrong. I need you.'

'Look, we've been through all this before. I can't just walk away. And he wouldn't let me. He'd go to court to stop me, I know he would. Anyway, I haven't got a passport, none of us have, so how could we just leave? It would all take time, and time would be on Alec's side, not ours.'

She realised that she was talking of herself, Floyd and the children as a unit, not herself and Alec, and stopped suddenly. Floyd narrowed his eyes.

'He doesn't have to know, then. Not until the last minute. Look, Lizzie, I'm returning to the States soon but I'll be coming back. You can be making the preparations while I'm gone – getting passports and so on. It can't be that difficult. And then, when I come back, you'll be ready and we can just leave. It'll be better that way. A clean break is better than a long-drawn out argument. Just live as normal.'

'You don't know what you're saying,' she said. 'It would be like telling lies every day. Every minute. I couldn't do it.'

'You can do anything,' he said, 'if you really love me.'

Lizzie rolled away, feeling the same old frustration well up within her. 'But I love Alec, too. Oh, Floyd, please, *please* don't keep on at me. I don't know what to think any more, I don't know what to say or what to do. I wish I'd never come today. I knew I shouldn't – I knew it was wrong – but I thought we'd have this one day to remember. That was all I wanted – just one lovely day – and now it's spoiled. It's all spoiled.'

The room was silent. She could feel Floyd, cold and still, beside her. At last she rolled back and looked at him.

He was lying on his back, staring fixedly at the ceiling. Tentatively, she put out a hand to touch him, but he flinched away. She felt stabbed, and said in a small, broken voice, 'Please don't look like that.'

'How do you want me to look?' he asked in a tired voice. 'Happy and excited because you've smashed all my dreams to pieces?'

She winced. 'But you had no right to dream them, Floyd.'

He turned his head towards her. 'So what "rights" *do* I have? None, apparently. No rights over my daughter, no rights over the woman I love. And who loves me.' He moved so suddenly that she cried out, leaning over her again, his hands pinning her wrists to the pillow. 'You do, Lizzie – don't deny it. You *do* love me.'

'Yes,' she whispered. 'Yes, I do.'

'So what's stopping you? How can you love me and love Alec, both at the same time? And how can you deny yourself and your children – *both* your children – the life I can offer you in America? A better life than you'll ever have here.'

She struggled for the words and then knew that she must tell him. Her eyes still on his, the tears forming in her own, she said quietly, 'Because they're not the only children, Floyd. There's another one to think about too.'

'Another one?' His brows came together in a frown. 'What do you mean? I don't understand. Are you saying you've had another child, one I don't know about?'

Without saying a word, she pulled back the sheet and laid his hand on her belly, still only very slightly swollen by its new life.

He stared, first at her face, then at their two hands. Then his eyes came back to hers again. When he spoke, his voice was little more than a thread of husky sound.

'You're *pregnant*?'

She nodded. 'It doesn't really show yet, but I thought you'd be sure to realise now.'

'I've never made love to a pregnant woman before,' he said soberly, and she felt the colour run up her body into her face. 'Don't you think you should have mentioned it before?'

'I didn't know what to do. At first, I thought you'd be going away again soon and you needn't know. And then there never seemed to be a right moment. And today – things seemed to happen so fast, and I almost forgot about it.'

'You almost forgot about it,' he said slowly, and lay down again.

Lizzie waited fearfully. 'Does it make any difference?' she asked at last, hardly knowing what she wanted the answer to be.

'D'you want it to? What sort of difference do you think it should make? D'you want me to say I'll accept this baby, just as Alec accepted Gillie – or d'you want me to say I'll have nothing to with it? And what would you say if I did?'

'I couldn't give it up, if that's what you're saying,' she said. 'I couldn't give up any of my children.'

'Yet that's what you're asking me to do, with my daughter.'

'It's not the same!' she cried. 'It's nothing like the same!

You've never known Gillie – you've never lived with her. She's never been your daughter in that sense. But she *has* been Alec's, and you're asking him to give her up. *And* Barry. And this one, too. And they're *both* his.'

Floyd sat up, the sheets falling from his lithe body. 'I know. My God, Lizzie, don't you think I've been through all this in my own mind, over and over again? It's not the way I was brought up, you know. It's not the way I want to be – stealing another man's wife, even his kids. But I want you so much – it's as if I'm being driven. I just can't help it. I've got to go on asking you. Lizzie,' he turned to her swiftly, 'isn't there some way we can work this out? There's got to be a way.'

'I don't know,' she said tiredly, and crossed her arms over her face, covering her eyes. 'I just don't know.'

There was a long silence. At last, Floyd said, 'We can't go on like this. We've got to make a decision, one way or another. And it's got to be all or nothing. If you come with me, you come with all your children – including this one.' He touched her stomach briefly. 'There's no other way.'

'And if I don't?' she whispered. 'What will you do about Gillie then?'

'That,' he said, 'is something I'll have to think about.'

There was no further lovemaking. They got up and dressed, and went downstairs as if they were simply going out for the rest of the afternoon. The streets of Romsey were lit by gas-lamps and the shops were closing. They walked back to the car and got in, and Floyd drove back to Southampton in silence.

'Let me get out at the same place as you picked me up,' Lizzie said. 'I don't want anyone to see me.'

He nodded and slowed down. 'Will I see you again tomorrow?'

'I don't know. Perhaps it would be better not. I've got a lot to think about.'

She expected him to argue, to point out that she only had three days free of the children, that they should make the most of every moment, but he simply nodded and said, 'The next day, then. Same time, same place, OK?' and didn't even look at her as she opened the car door.

Lizzie watched him drive away, feeling that she had lost something but didn't know what it was. It wasn't over, after all – he was coming back, he still wanted her to go with him. Yet something had gone that afternoon, something she hadn't even known she possessed, and her heart was strangely heavy.

She walked slowly home to get Alec's supper.

She was waiting on the third day, half-afraid that he wouldn't come, but the car drew up beside the pavement and he leaned across to open the door. Lizzie slipped in quickly, still anxious about being seen, and kept her face hidden as they drove away. After a few moments, she glanced at him and said tentatively, 'Are you all right, Floyd?'

'Any reason why I shouldn't be?'

She flinched. He had never been curt with her before. 'Quite a few, I should think,' she answered ruefully. 'What did you do yesterday?'

'Went down to the New Forest and walked about. Thought a lot. Had a sandwich at a pub in Lyndhurst. Watched the wild ponies – they come right into the village, you know. One of them had his nose in a box of apples outside the greengrocer's shop. Had a lotta fun, I can tell you.'

Lizzie said nothing. She looked down at her hands, folded together in her lap, and felt tears come to her eyes at his biting tone. After another pause, she said, 'You didn't have to come this morning.'

'Oh, didn't I? And what should I have done instead?'

Suddenly angry, she flashed, 'Stayed away – like you should have done in the first place. Then none of this would have happened and everyone would have been perfectly happy, just as they were already.'

'Not everyone,' he said. '*I* wasn't.'

Lizzie looked down again. 'It took you long enough to find out. Six years.'

'Oh no,' he said. 'I knew from the start. I knew from the minute I walked away from you after VE Day and got posted to Germany. I knew then, and I knew when I came back and found you carrying my baby. *That's* when it all went wrong, Lizzie. That's when you should have come away with me.'

'I couldn't do that! I told you then – Alex was in a dreadful state. He needed me, I couldn't possibly have left him.'

'He'd have gotten over it.'

Lizzie looked at his profile. He was staring straight ahead at the road, his mouth set grim and his brows drawn together.

'You've changed,' she said quietly. 'You're not the Floyd I thought I'd fallen in love with then.'

'And what's changed me?' he demanded. 'Six years without you and without my daughter, that's what's changed me. Six years living thousands of miles away, knowing you were here, living your life without me. *That's* what's changed me, Lizzie, and if you don't like it I'm sorry, but it's your doing just as much as mine.'

'It's not! I know we were wrong to do what we did that day, but for me that was all there was to it.'

'You said you'd fallen in love with me.'

'I thought I had. But afterwards, I knew it had been wrong. I was married – and when Alec came home I knew I loved him. It really was all there was to it, Floyd – a moment of madness. It was VE Day – none of us were in our right minds. That really was all it was.'

'I don't believe you.' They were out of Southampton now, heading towards the New Forest. 'All those months before that, when I was coming to your house on Sundays, when we went for walks in the afternoons – there was something building up between us then, you know there was. We were falling in love all that time. Godammit, I only held back because you were married. And then, when I met you in the woods that day ... Lizzie, you loved me then, you know you did, and you love me now. You can't hide it from me and you can't run away from it. It's too strong. We've *got* to be together!'

Lizzie stared at him, too shaken by the tone of his voice to make an answer. Floyd too was silent, until they had come into the Forest itself and he could pull off into a clearing under the trees. He stopped the engine and turned to her.

'This is what I've decided, Lizzie. You have one chance, and one chance only, to put a stop to all this and come with me to America. I've got all the forms you need for getting a passport. We'll fill them in together. You've got to get a photograph and you've got to get them signed by a doctor or lawyer or someone. As soon as they come through I'm buying the first tickets I can get. It takes five days to cross the Atlantic and if I can't be in England to go back with you, I'll meet you in New York. You can ask Alec for a divorce, and as soon as it comes through we'll be married.'

He looked into her eyes and she saw the curtness melt away and tenderness take its place. His voice softened. 'Say you'll do it. Please, Lizzie, say you'll do it.'

Chapter Twenty-Two

Jane stared at her daughter.

'He's asked you to go to America? And what have you said?'

Lizzie bowed her head. 'I haven't said anything. I can't—'

'So you haven't said no,' her mother interrupted sharply. 'Lizzie, what on earth are you thinking of? You must be out of your mind to even let him get to the stage of asking you. Whatever's been going on?'

'I told you he wrote to me,' Lizzie said wearily. 'I told you before Christmas.'

'Yes, and that's all you've told me. It's obviously been more than a few letters. He's been to see you, hasn't he? He's the "cowboy man" Gillie was talking about.'

Lizzie looked up quickly. 'What have you been saying to Gillie?'

Jane coloured. 'Nothing. She just heard something Ruth and I were saying, that's all.'

'Something about Floyd, obviously. You and Ruth have been talking about Floyd and me, and Gillie heard you.' Lizzie was on her feet. 'Just what did you say, Mum? What did Gillie hear?'

'Sit down again, for goodness' sake,' Jane said, but her voice was less certain now. 'It wasn't anything much and she's forgotten all about it anyway. She hasn't mentioned it since. The point is, Floyd's been coming to the house and Gillie and Barry have seen him. You're lucky they've said nothing to their father.'

'I'll be even luckier if they don't say anything now,' Lizzie said bitterly. 'How *could* you talk about it when they were there, Mum? And Auntie Ruth, too – I'm surprised at her. You shouldn't have been gossiping about me to start with.'

'We weren't gossiping! We're worried about you. We love you.'

'Well, you've got a funny way of showing it. Nagging at me all the time, accusing me of I don't know what.'

'I think you know very well what I'm accusing you of,' Jane said steadily. 'And I'm pretty sure I'm right. Aren't I?'

'Oh, Mum. Please don't look at me like that. I know I've been stupid, and I know I'm a bad wife and mother – but when he came back and I saw him again ...' She covered her face with trembling hands, and her shoulders shook. 'I really don't know what to do,' she whispered.

Jane watched her for a minute, then sat down beside her daughter and laid her arms across the heaving shoulders. Bending close, she murmured in the younger woman's ear.

'All right, Lizzie. Don't go getting yourself in a state. It won't do you no good, nor the baby neither. Look, I'll make a cup of tea and we'll have a proper talk. Perhaps I did go on at you a bit too much. It's just that I've been worrying myself sick the past few days – the past few weeks, if truth be told. Now, you sit there and have your cry out and I'll make that tea. Here's one of your dad's hankies. Blow your nose and mop yourself up, there's a good girl.'

Lizzie did as she was told and by the time her mother came back with a tray of tea, she was sitting up again, her face more or less dry and the handkerchief clutched in a sodden ball between her fingers.

'That's better,' Jane said, setting the tray on the table. She lifted the brown teapot and poured a steady stream into the two cups. 'Now, you drink that. I've put plenty of sugar in.'

Lizzie sipped and made a face. 'It's too sweet.'

'You drink it,' her mother ordered. 'It'll do you good. Sugar's good for shock.'

'I haven't had a shock.'

'I don't think this is much different.' Jane sipped her own tea. 'And I certainly have! Now, you'd better tell me the whole story right from the beginning and we'll see if we can sort something out. But don't go getting yourself upset again. Remember, nobody can make you leave your husband if you don't want to. And you don't, do you? Not really.'

It was halfway between a statement and a question, and she looked almost pleadingly at Lizzie. But Lizzie didn't answer.

'I don't know if I can tell you, not just like that. I'm muddled about it myself. I didn't know where to start.'

'Well, he came to see you, didn't he? He must have done, for Gillie to know who he is.'

At mention of Gillie's name, Lizzie flushed and Jane feared for a moment that she was about to start another tirade about allowing Gillie to hear her conversation with Ruth. But after a brief hesitation, she said, in a weary voice, 'Yes. He came one afternoon just after Christmas. I didn't know he was coming, honestly. I thought perhaps he'd decided not to. But he just knocked on the door one afternoon, and there was nothing I could do about it.'

'You didn't have to ask him in,' Jane said, guessing that Lizzie had done so.

'I did. Mrs Bratchet from number twelve was looking out of her door, and you know what a nasty-minded gossip she is. All ears, she was, and he wasn't keeping his voice down. I had to ask him in.'

'And that didn't give her anything to gossip about, of course.'

Lizzie sighed. 'Mum, are you going to listen to me or are you just going to pick me up on everything I say?'

'All right, all right,' Jane said hastily. 'I won't say another word. Go on.'

'Well, he came in and I made him a cup of tea and he talked to the children. I didn't want him to, but I didn't see what I could do about it. I thought that would be enough. But then he said he wanted to see me again – to talk about Gillie. I met him in a teashop next day.'

'You met him in a teashop?' Jane cried, and bit her lip as Lizzie's eyes snapped at her.

'Yes, I did. It was that or have him come to the house again, and I didn't want that. Is that what you'd rather I'd done? He wasn't going to go away, Mum. He wasn't going to give up. I had to see him again.'

'And what did he say – in this teashop?'

'He said he still loved me,' Lizzie said in a low voice. 'He started to talk about Gillie being his daughter and about wanting her back. And wanting me back.' She flashed another look at her mother. 'I didn't say I wanted to go. I got up and walked out and left him there. But he won't leave me alone, Mum. He keeps on asking to see me. He keeps telling me what a good life I could have in America with him. Me and the children.'

'The *children*? But Barry's Alec's child! And so's the new one – you can't take them away.'

'I've told him that, Mum, over and over again. He didn't even know about the new baby until – until the day before yesterday.' Her eyes dropped again, and she felt her colour rise and knew that her mother had seen and understood it.

'You've been with him, haven't you?' Jane said flatly, and Lizzie nodded. 'Oh, you wicked, *wicked* girl!' Her hand came up with a sharp, involuntary movement and she slapped Lizzie's head. Lizzie, knocked almost out of her chair more by the surprise than the force of the blow, cried out and cringed away, and Jane caught herself up and brought her hand to her own mouth in a fist, biting her knuckles. Through tears of dismay and anger, she said jerkily, 'I'm sorry. I didn't mean to do that. But – oh, how could you be so *stupid*?'

'I knew you wouldn't understand,' Lizzie said. 'I knew it

was no use talking to you.' She raised her eyes accusingly to her mother. 'Even though you should – considering you were expecting me when you and Dad got married!'

Jane caught her breath. 'You've no right to drag that in.'

'Haven't I? Why not? It's to do with me, isn't it? And it does show that even *you* had feelings once, even if you've forgotten what they are.'

'I've got feelings now,' Jane said quietly. 'And most of them are taken up with worrying about you. And if it makes me angry when I think how silly you've been, risking everything that's important to you, then I'm sorry, but I can't help it. And if you want me to respect your feelings, maybe you ought to respect mine.' She waited a moment, then said, 'Are you going to tell me any more? You said he'd asked you to go to America. Are you thinking of going?'

'No,' Lizzie said in a tired voice. 'I'm not thinking of going. He spent all day yesterday trying to persuade me. He'd got the forms for a passport and everything. But I can't leave Alec and I couldn't take the children away. I don't even want to go to America – not really.' She crumpled in her chair, her face buried in her hands, and began to cry again, great heavy sobs that shook her from head to foot. 'I don't know if me and Alec will ever get over this – I do love him, Mum, whatever you might think – but I love Floyd, too, and I feel as if I'm being torn apart.'

Jane stared at her for a minute or two, then pulled Lizzie into her arms and rocked her gently as she had when Lizzie was a baby, and she murmured the same, soothing words as she had then.

'There, there, sweetheart. Don't cry, now. Everything will be all right – you'll see. Everything will come right.'

But even as she spoke the words, her heart knew that this was something a mother could not put right for her child. It was something that might never come right at all.

Chapter Twenty-Three

As January turned to February, the mild weather changed and a storm raged over the whole country. The inhabitants of Bridge End were kept awake by the roar of the gale and the hammering of rain on their roofs and windows. On the morning of 1 February, it was almost impossible to walk against the wind, and when Jane reached Ruth's cottage door after battling her way down the track, the latch was jerked out of her hand by the force of the draught as she lifted it.

'Come in, quick!' Ruth exclaimed as she staggered into the kitchen. 'I'd just opened the front door that very minute and the wind's going straight through the house. That's better,' as Jane slammed the door behind her. 'My goodness, what a gale! I'm surprised you came out in it.'

'I wanted to talk to you,' Jane said breathlessly, unbuttoning her coat. 'There are trees down all over the place and half the houses in the village have lost slates.'

'I know. Sammy and Dan have been out since first light, helping to clear the road. I didn't want them to go until it had died down a bit – you don't know what other trees might be going to fall down – but they wouldn't take any notice. How are you up the farm?'

'A bit of damage to the milking parlour but nothing too bad. The postman told me it was like a hurricane in Southampton – the sea came rushing up the Water like a tidal wave. It was an extra high spring tide, he says, and the wind came on top of it. I reckon there'll have been some bad damage round the coast in some places.'

'There has,' Ruth said soberly. 'All over East Anglia. It was on the wireless just now. It's flooded all across all those low-lying areas and they reckon there must be hundreds drowned. It happened too quick for them to get away, you see. It's the worst storm anyone can remember.'

'Oh, that's awful.' Jane sank into a chair. 'Those poor souls. It must have seemed like the end of the world.'

'Well, I suppose it was, for them.' Ruth put the kettle on the stove. 'We'll hear more about it at one o'clock, I expect. What was it you wanted to talk to me about, then?'

'Where's your Linnet?' Jane asked, glancing round. 'I don't want any more little pitchers with big ears.'

'She's next door, playing with the new kittens. Come on, Jane, I can see you've got something special on your mind.'

'I don't know if special's the right word,' Jane said ruefully, unwinding her scarf. 'It's our Lizzie again. She's told me a bit more about her and Floyd.' Her face crumpled and she rested one elbow on the shelf beside her and leaned her head on her hand. 'Oh Ruth, I don't know how all this is going to end. He's asked her to go to America with him. Got the passport forms and everything.' Her eyes closed and tears trickled down her cheeks.

Ruth came over quickly and put her arms round her sister. 'Jane, that's terrible. I'm so sorry. She's surely not going to go?'

'She says not. But who's to know she won't change her mind? She says she loves him, and it's tearing her apart.'

'And what about Alec?'

'She says she loves him, too. I don't see how she can, Ruth. How *can* you love two men at once? I never looked at anyone else, once I knew George was the one for me. and we've been through our rough patches, same as anyone else, but I've still never thought of carrying on like this.'

'I don't know,' Ruth said thoughtfully. 'I loved Jack and now I love Dan, but I *still* love Jack. There seems to be room for them both.'

'That's different, though. Jack's dead and he'd been dead for a long time before you met Dan. There wouldn't have been anything between you and Dan if he'd still been alive.'

'No, perhaps not. I don't think I'd have looked at him in the same way, so it probably wouldn't have happened. But it's hard to tell, isn't it? And neither of us has been in the same position as Lizzie.'

'A lot of other young women were in her position during the war,' Jane said tartly, 'but they didn't do what she did.'

'And a lot of others did, and worse,' Ruth pointed out. 'You know she wasn't really carrying on then. It was just a moment of madness on VE night. We were all a bit out of our minds that day. It was her bad luck to fall for a baby.'

'I might have known you'd stick up for her,' Jane grumbled, and Ruth sighed.

'I'm not. I'm just trying to understand. Don't you feel even a bit sorry for her, Jane?'

'I do, to tell you the truth,' Jane admitted. 'I could have slapped her to start with – I did, as a matter of fact, though I'm not proud of it – but then she started to cry and I could see she's really upset about it all and – well, you know what it's like, they're your kiddies however old they are and whatever they've done, and you don't like to see them so upset. Anyway, we made it up before she left. But I still don't know what's going to happen and there doesn't seem to be anything I can do about it.'

'I don't think there is,' Ruth said. 'She's a grown woman and she's got to make her own mistakes. We can't go interfering.'

'That's what George says. I just needed to talk to someone about it.' Jane watched as Ruth made the tea. 'I must have drunk gallons of that stuff,' she said with a little laugh. 'They say it's good for shock, don't they. I think the effect's wearing off a bit as far as I'm concerned.'

'It'll do you good, just the same.' Ruth went to the larder for milk and the wind surged through the wire window and into the cottage once more. 'However long is this going to go on for? I don't remember a storm like it, ever, not even back in 1947 when we had all those blizzards. It's been so mild up till now, too.'

Jane watched her pour the tea. Making little pleats in her skirt with her fingers, she said, 'I've been wondering if someone shouldn't let Alec know what's going on.'

'Jane!' Ruth turned, the jug still in her hand. 'You couldn't do that. It would cause no end of trouble.'

'Well, don't you think he's got a right to know? It's his marriage that's being broken up. It won't do him any good to come home one day to find a note on the table telling him she's gone and taken the children with her. It'll be too late then.'

'But you said she wasn't going.'

'She *told* me she wasn't going – it doesn't mean she won't. She seems to change her mind with the weather these days.' Jane glanced up as a fresh gust of wind howled down the chimney. 'If you ask me, this isn't the only storm that's brewing round these parts.'

'I still don't think you ought to tell Alec,' Ruth was beginning, when they were both startled by a sudden urgent pounding on the door. They glanced at each other in alarm and Ruth got up quickly and pulled it open.

'Solly! Whatever's the matter?' Fear flared up inside her and she clasped her hands to her mouth. 'Has something happened to Dan? Or Sammy?'

'Another tree's come down,' the blacksmith gasped, his big chest heaving. He leaned one hand on the table, struggling to get back his breath. 'We were just sawing through that big oak that fell across the road and there was this almightly crash and – look, you'd better come, Ruth. The whole road's covered in branches and stuff. There's half a dozen blokes there now, trying to get them out ...'

'*Them?*' Ruth was already scrabbling in the cupboad for her First Aid box. 'How many are there?' Fear clenched her heart. 'Are – are Dan and Sammy trapped too?'

'You'd better come,' he repeated, and looked at Jane. 'My missus is ringing up for the doctor now. And the hospital. They – they might need to be ready.'

'Oh, my God!' Ruth flung her coat around her shoulders and pushed past him. He lumbered after her, still panting, and Jane, dragging on her own coat, followed. Together, they ran down the lane towards the blacksmith's forge and, as they ran, they were joined by neighbours from the other cottages along the road. By the time they reached the forge, there were nearly two dozen of them.

There was a crowd around the fallen trees as well. The men were struggling to lift away the smashed branches and the women were standing by, their hands at their mouths and tears in their eyes. Ruth shoved her way through the crowd and stared in horror.

'Are they under there?' she asked in a whisper. 'My Dan, and Sammy – are they under there?'

One of the men turned. 'They were just sawing up the trunk of that oak,' he said. 'They were right in the way. They never had a chance to get out.'

Stephen collected Maddy on Friday evening and bundled her into his car, wrapped in rugs and furs. The car was unheated and, although the hood was up, draughts found their way through all the gaps. By the time he had finished, only her eyes and nose were visible.

'You look like a little Arctic squirrel, peeping out of there,' he said, bending to kiss the tip of her nose.

'Oh, and how many Arctic squirrels have you seen?' she asked, laughing. 'I'm not sure there even is such an animal.'

'Well, if there isn't, they'd look look like you if there were,' he replied, and walked round to the other side of the car. He crammed himself in beside her. 'Now I'll give you a proper kiss, to be going on with until we get there.'

Before he could do so, the Archdeacon appeared beside Maddy's window, with Archie standing mournfully at his side. 'You wouldn't like another passenger, would you?'

'I'd love to take him,' Maddy said, wriggling a fur-gloved hand out of her rugs to reach out and pat the labrador's gleaming black head. 'But there's not an inch of space. You wait there, Archie, and look after your master. I'll be back on Sunday evening.'

'Not too late,' the Archdeacon said, and Stephen shook his head.

'My pass runs out at ten o'clock so I'll have to get Maddy back here by eight at the latest. She won't turn into a pumpkin then, will she?'

'Come earlier, if you like, and have some supper with us,' the Archdeacon suggested. 'We usually have a high tea on Sundays. You could do most of the journey in daylight then.'

'Thanks. We'll do that.' Stephen let in the clutch and revved the engine. 'All right, darling? Got everything?'

'Yes, thanks, and if I haven't, I'll manage without.' She wound up her window, wondering if the Archdeacon had noticed that 'darling'. It was quite nice to be called that, of course, but she wasn't sure she was quite ready to hear it on Stephen's lips yet. Probably people in his circle called each other 'darling' all the time – like Fenella and her friends, she thought – but she hadn't heard him use it before. She wondered if Sammy Hodges ever called anyone 'darling'. Probably not. It wasn't his sort of word.

'... be nice, wouldn't it?' Stephen was saying, and she looked at him, realising in dismay that she hadn't heard a word he was saying. 'Or don't you think so?'

'Um – I'm sorry, I was miles away. What did you say?'

'I said, why don't we stop on the way for a drink? Honestly, Maddy, you might at least start the weekend by listening to me!' But he didn't sound really offended and she gave him a rueful smile and patted his knee.

'Sorry,' she apologised again. 'I suppose we could, but wouldn't it be better to go straight to Burracombe? Or do you need a break?'

'Yes, I do,' he said positively. 'It's a good three hours' drive and I'll need to stretch my legs, and I'll need refreshment too. I know a nice little hotel on one of the villages we go through – we'll stop there.'

'So long as we don't keep your sister up,' Maddy said. She didn't know Hilary very well and felt slightly nervous about meeting her. 'And there's your father, too, he shouldn't be staying up late.'

'Oh, Dad's a law unto himself,' Stephen said with a laugh. 'If he wants to go to bed before we arrive, he will. Or Hilary will make him – she rules him with a rod of iron since he had his heart attack. Not that it does her much good as far as the estate's concerned,' he added thoughtfully.

'What d'you mean? I thought she ran that too.'

'She does – or at least, she did, till he insisted on bringing in that manager chap. I told you about him, remember? Not a bad sort, and they seem to be getting on a bit better now. They were in the village pantomime together – but you must know all this. You saw it, didn't you?'

'Yes, and Stella told me about Mr Kellaway, but I don't know much about him. He made a very good Black Knight.'

'The baddie part suited him very well,' Stephen observed. 'Anyway, don't let's waste time talking about him. What do you want to do while we're there? Go for walks? Ride? Or shall we go for jaunts on Dartmoor in the car?'

'I want to spend some time with Stella,' Maddy said firmly. 'And that means Felix, too. I'd like to go to church with them on Sunday. And I want to go and see Dottie, of course, and some of my other old friends – the Tozers, especially. I must see Joanna's gorgeous twins again. They must have grown so much since Christmas.'

'It doesn't sound as if you'll have much time for me,' Stephen said mournfully, and she laughed.

'Of course I will. Lots. You can come with me to see some of them, after all. And I expect your father and Hilary will want some time with you on your own.'

'Shouldn't think so. Dad'll just make a lot of pointed remarks about me not going back to run the estate, and Hilary will be too wrapped up in whatever the current argument with Kellaway is. They won't be very interested in what I'm doing.'

'I'm sure they will. I thought you just said she and Mr Kellaway were getting on better now, anyway?'

'I did. I didn't say they were getting on *well*. Hilary doesn't want him there at all, that's the trouble. But look, here we go again – talking about them when I want to talk about *us*. I really do want to spend as much time with you, on our own, as we possibly can, Maddy. Away from your Archdeacon and everyone who might be watching you there. I want us to be able to get away from *everyone*.'

'Oh.' Maddy felt slightly breathless. 'And can we do that in Burracombe? Won't everyone be watching *you* – and don't forget, they all know me as well.'

'We can get away in this little beauty,' he said, patting the steering-wheel. 'Over the moor, or down to the coast – Dartmouth, perhaps, or Salcombe. Or into Cornwall. Let's have tomorrow out on our own, Maddy, just the two of us. And then you can spend as much of Sunday as you like, going to church and catching up with your friends. But let's have just one day – can't we? Please?'

Maddy remembered the kisses they had shared the week before. The delicacy of Stephen's hands, moving tenderly over her shoulders, his fingers tracing the lines of her neck and the hollow of her throat. She felt a quick surge of excitement and nodded.

'I'd like that,' she whispered, and put her hand on his knee again.

Chapter Twenty-Four

It was still mild on Saturday, although the sky was threatening and there was a fresh wind blowing. Maddy was up early but declined Hilary Napier's suggestion of a ride before breakfast.

'I'd like to go to Dottie's as soon as possible, in case Stella's going out anywhere. It would be awful to miss her.' She accepted a cup of coffee and drank gratefully. 'Mm, that's nice. You know, I'm never really sure it's a good idea to surprise people.'

'Not many of Stephen's ideas turn out to be good ones,' Stephen's sister remarked drily. 'But I'm sure Stella will be thrilled to see you.'

'So long as she hasn't got plans she can't put off. She could be doing something with Felix. Like – oh, I don't know, like going to see the Bishop.'

'You'd better get there early then, as you say,' Hilary advised. 'But didn't Steve say you were going to spend today together on your own?'

'Yes, but I still ought to let Stella know I'm here. She'd never forgive me if I didn't. Look, if breakfast's not going to be ready for a while I'll slip along to the cottage now. I might even have something there, so don't wait for me. You go for your ride.'

'Right. There are one or two things I need to see Travis

about too.' Hilary frowned a little, and Maddy wondered briefly if things were going as well there as Stephen seemed to think. But it was none of her business, and she was more interested in seeing her sister. She collected her winter coat and boots, and strode briskly along the drive to the village road.

'Well, if it isn't young Maddy,' a voice greeted her as she came through the big gates, and she turned to see Jacob Prout, already busy clearing out a ditch. He pushed his cap to the back of his head and beamed at her, and she smiled back. She had known Jacob since she'd first come to Burracombe at the age of seven, and he had always looked like an old man to her. He still looked the same: stocky and toughened by the outdoor work he had always done, white hair curling out from underneath his cap, blue eyes twinkling from a face reddened by the weather, and a grin of welcome showing teeth his dentist must be proud of. His voice was the same too, with a Devon brogue it had taken Maddy some time to learn to understand but which now sounded in her ears like an echo of home. 'And what be you doing here, maid? Us didn't expect to see you again till Easter.'

'I'm staying the weekend at the Barton,' she said. 'I'm just going down to surprise Stella – she doesn't know I'm coming. How are you, Jacob?'

'Oh, not so bad. Funny old weather we be having, mind. 'Tasn't been a bit like winter so far. Too mild to kill off the pests.' He glanced at the lowering clouds. 'There be summat on the way, though, take my word for it. Us be in for a real blow if I'm not mistaken.'

'I don't know how you can tell,' Maddy commented. 'I mean, it does look as if it's going to rain, but I couldn't guess any more than that.'

'Ah, that be because you'm not out in all weathers like I am. You gets to know the smell of the weather, see, and what it means when the wind changes. Anyway, I mustn't keep you here gassing, you'll be wanting to get off to your sister.' He turned back to his ditch. 'Good to see your pretty face again.'

Maddy smiled and went on her way, passing the village green with its ancient, spreading oak tree before coming to Dottie Friend's cottage in the lane leading to the little hump-backed bridge and ford. Stella had lodged with Dottie ever since she had come to Burracombe as assistant schoolteacher, and Maddy herself had lived with Dottie during the war. It was only by chance that Stella, who had lost touch with Maddy when they'd been separated as orphaned evacuees, had discovered this and found her sister again.

Maddy knocked on Dottie's door and then turned the handle. As usual, it was unlocked and she peeped through to find both Dottie and Stella having their breakfast. They stared in astonishment and Stella leaped to her feet.

'Maddy! Whatever are you doing here? Why didn't you let us know?'

'I wanted to surprise you. I came down with Stephen last night.' Maddy hugged her sister and then turned to Dottie. 'It's lovely to see you. You're looking as rosy as an apple. Haven't you had any winter here at all?'

'Not much,' Dottie said, bustling to the dresser for an extra cup and saucer. 'Now, you'm having your breakfast with us, aren't you, maid? I'll make some more porridge, and there's plenty of bacon and eggs.'

'Are they expecting you back at the Barton?' Stella enquired anxiously. Maddy shook her head and slipped into a spare chair.

'I told Hilary I might stop here. They won't mind. Well, Stephen might,' she added with a mischievous grin. 'He wants me to himself but I told him I wanted to see everyone here as well – especially you two, of course.'

'Felix will be pleased to see you too,' Stella said, thinking of the time when she had thought Felix would prefer her sister to herself. 'Do you and Stephen have any plans for the weekend?'

'He wants us to go out somewhere today.' Maddy picked up the cup of tea Dottie had placed in front of her. 'But I've told him I want to go to church with you tomorrow. I'll be able to see lots of other people then, as well.'

They chatted together in the cosy kitchen, with Dottie bustling about producing bowls of porridge, plates of bacon and eggs and a rack of toast. 'That's my own marmalade, fresh made – they had Seville oranges in the shop last week. I'll give you a pot or two to take home as well.'

'Oh, thank you, Dottie. I might have known there'd be something home-made here. I suppose the bread is, as well.'

'Is there any other kind?' Dottie enquired haughtily, and they all laughed. 'Mind you, George Sweet can make a pretty handsome loaf when he puts his mind to it. And now tell us how you'm getting on up-country, Maddy. How d'you like Dorset?'

'It's nice. I like being by the sea and the Archdeacon is very pleasant to work for. His wife's very kind too, and they've given me a lovely little flat. I'm quite independent but they look after me as well.'

'Well, I'm glad someone does,' Dottie observed. 'You were always a bit headstrong as a little tacker. Led all the other kiddies into mischief, she did,' she told Stella, 'and then she'd look at you with them big blue eyes as if butter wouldn't melt in her mouth, and get away with it! Still, it wasn't never nothing harmful. There was no malice in her.'

'Well, thank you,' Maddy said. 'I'm glad you cleared that up. Is there any more tea in the pot?'

Stella passed it over and said to Dottie, 'Did she ever tell you about the time when we were at Bridge End, and she made Sammy Hodges bring Ruth's parrot out on a picnic? I've never seen Mrs Hodges so cross, and that was the day—'

She was interrupted by a knock on the door. They glanced at each other and Stella got up to open it.

'So this is where you're hiding,' Stephen Napier said, coming in. 'I thought you were coming home for breakfast?'

'I am home,' Maddy said, smiling at him. 'I used to live here with Dottie, remember? And I did tell Hilary I might stay.'

'Haven't seen Hilary. She's out on Beau. Mrs Benson told me you'd gone out for a walk and I guessed where you'd be, so I decided to come and collect you.'

'Well, I won't be collected. Not just yet,' Maddy said sweetly. 'Why don't you stay and have a cup of tea, Stephen? Dottie won't mind, I'm sure.'

'Sit down and welcome,' Dottie said briskly, fetching another cup and saucer. 'There's plenty of bacon and eggs in the bottom oven, and I'll do you some fried bread if you like. Gentlemen always like fried bread.'

'I'm not so sure I'm a gentleman these days,' Stephen observed, helping himself to a slice of toast, 'but I'll have the fried bread just the same. Not too much, though, Dottie, because I'll have to eat another breakfast when I get back, or Mrs Benson will be mortally offended.'

'And us mustn't offend Annie Benson,' Dottie agreed. 'Her's always been a bit quick off the mark, but 'twouldn't be fair to let her cook a breakfast that's not going to be eaten. Maybe you shouldn't have any fried bread after all, Master Stephen.'

'Oh, I'll manage it,' he said hastily. 'After all, if I refuse your cooking I might offend you too. It's a hard life, trying to get by without offending people,' he added with a heavy sigh, and both girls laughed.

'I've never noticed you trying,' Maddy said. 'You don't give it a thought. You just breeze through life without worrying a bit about whether you're offending people or not.'

'That's because I am so charming I never do,' he said, and

picked up the knife and fork Dottie had handed him. 'My goodness, Dottie, am I supposed to eat all that? I hope you've left some for yourself.'

'I said there was plenty.' She sat down to her own, rather smaller, plate. 'And how be the RAF treating you, then?'

'Pretty well, thanks. I'm hoping to be a Squadron Leader soon. Shan't stay in for ever, of course. I want to be my own boss. Run my own show. Napiers aren't much good at being employees.'

'Your father seemed to like being in the Army,' Maddy said.

'Yes, but he had the estate as well. He was boss here. And he was pretty well boss in the Army, once he made Colonel. But I shan't stay in the RAF long enough to get that high. Anyway, never mind all that, what I want to know is what plans you two girls have been making behind my back.' He looked at Stella sternly. 'I'm taking Maddy out today *on our own*. You can have her tomorrow, if you like, so long as I come too. I didn't bring her all the way down here just to hobnob with her old pals and leave me out in the cold.'

'We haven't made any plans,' Maddy said. 'Except for church in the morning. You can come with us or meet us afterwards, whichever you like.'

'I might give church a miss,' he said. 'We get enough of that on the station. All right, why don't we all go out for Sunday lunch somewhere, the four of us? I'll book a decent place.'

'Won't your father want you to be at home?' Maddy asked. 'It seems a bit rude to be out all day both days we're here.'

'Well, Stella and Felix can come up to the Barton then,' he said. 'I promised to get Maddy back by about six anyway, so we'll have to leave pretty early. Dottie, that was the best breakfast I've had for years,' he added, pushing away his plate, 'only don't tell Mrs Benson I said so. And to think I've got to go home now and eat another one!'

'I hope she won't expect me to eat another one too,' Maddy

said, draining her cup. 'I don't think I'm ever going to need to eat again.'

'Go on, you'll change your mind by lunchtime,' Dottie told her. 'Off you go, now, the pair of you, and have a nice day out, though what you'll find to do with yourselves in this weather, I do *not* know. 'Tis getting worse.'

They went to the door and looked out. The wind was whipping the trees about and singing in the telegraph wires. Someone's dustbin had escaped and was rolling noisily down the road to meet them.

'That's the Cullifords',' Dottie said, regarding it with disfavour. 'Why they can't ever take it in like everyone else, I don't know, but that's Maggie Culliford all over. Well, off you go, then.'

'See you tomorrow,' Maddy said, giving Stella a kiss. 'You don't mind us going off today, do you?'

'Heavens, no,' Stella said, though she would rather have had Maddy to herself for a few hours. 'You go and enjoy yourselves. Dottie's right, though – what are you going to do? It's not the weather for walking on the moor. Those clouds look as if they mean business, and the wind's enough to blow you over.'

'We'll drive down to the cliffs at Portwrinkle,' Stephen said, 'and watch the waves beating on the rocks. Come on, Maddy. We'd better hurry – the coffee will be going cold.'

They strode away along the lane together, Maddy with her arm tucked into his, her laughing face turned up. Stella and Dottie watched them.

'I hope she'm not making a mistake,' Dottie said at last. 'He's a charmer all right, Master Stephen is, but he've got a lot of growing up to do before he'm ready to settle down. And I reckon there've been quite a few hearts broken by that smile of his.'

'Maddy'll be all right,' Stella said, a little doubtfully. 'She's not ready for anything serious either. And I thought she was quite interested in the boy we knew when we were little – Sammy Hodges. We met him again at that wedding we went to.'

'Well, 'tis not for us to say,' Dottie said. 'Right or wrong, they'll make up their own minds, same as the rest of us. And now come inside, do, before the cold gets into the cottage. I must say, I don't like the look of that sky,' she added, glancing up at the scudding clouds. 'There's a change on the way, and it's not going to be for the better. I reckon we might be going to get a bit of winter, after all.'

'Jacob was right about the weather,' Maddy observed as she and Stephen sat in the car on top of the cliffs, watching the sea. It was pewter-grey, topped with foamy white horses, and the waves were crashing and swirling on the rocks. 'I've never seen the sea so rough.'

'Neither have I,' Stephen said. 'Those waves must be twelve feet high or more. And look how far up the beach it's been. It's a good thing the tide's going out, or some places would be getting flooded.'

'Perhaps it's a spring tide,' Maddy said. 'I remember when I was little, living in Portsmouth, my father took us out to Southsea once and showed us how high it was. And then we went back a few hours later and it was lower than I'd ever seen it. He said it was a spring tide, even though it wasn't spring, and they're higher and lower than any others.'

'What a little fount of knowledge you are,' Stephen said, grinning, and she slapped his arm.

'Don't be cheeky. And someone told me once that the seventh wave is always the biggest. I wonder if that's true.'

'We'll count. Where are you supposed to start from?'

'I don't know. Look for a big one and go from there, I suppose. Look, that's a whopper. One. Two.' They counted in unison, finishing with a slightly disappointed, 'Seven. Oh well, perhaps we started with the wrong one. Let's try again.'

This game lasted them for about fifteen minutes, during which time the waves eased off a little. 'It's because it's going down,' Stephen said. 'They're still pretty big, though.' He glanced up as a gust of wind rocked the car. 'I'm not sure it's all that safe here, to be honest. Maybe we'd better move.'

They drove down the road to the hotel where Stephen had booked lunch. There were only a few other guests and they were given a table in the window, overlooking the bay. The waiter settled them with sherry for Maddy and pink gin for Stephen, and they smiled at each other.

'We've got as good a view here as we had in the car,' Maddy said. 'And it's warmer, too. I'm really enjoying this, Stephen.'

'Good. We'll do it again, shall we? Have a weekend away?'

'Mm. It's nice to come to Burracombe and see everyone.'

'I wasn't thinking of just coming to Burracombe,' he said, meeting her eyes.

Maddy felt her face colour. 'I don't—'

'Come on, Maddy. You've travelled about with Fenella Forsyth, you can't be quite the innocent you like to make out. We all know what theatre people are like.'

Her face grew hotter. 'I don't know what you're suggesting, but Fenella wasn't like that.'

'If you don't know what I'm suggesting, how do you know what I think she was like?' he asked, and she bit her lip. He changed his tone. 'Maddy, I'm sorry. I didn't mean to upset you. I don't mean anything against her – or you. I just thought you'd understand what I was saying. You've lived in a different world from your sister, for instance. It doesn't mean there's anything wrong with it.'

'I'm glad you think so,' Maddy said tightly. 'As it happens, Fenella was always very careful with me. I probably lived a more sheltered life than Stella, if anything.'

'All right, I take it all back. I was being very clumsy and I'm sorry.' He reached for her hand. 'Let's start again, shall we?' He gave her his boyish smile and her lips twitched.

'All right, but you'd better be careful what you say in future. I was brought up very nicely and I won't have anyone thinking otherwise.'

'I never doubted it for an instant,' he said solemnly, and at that moment the waiter brought their menus and they studied them, both thankful for the respite.

'I'm having the roast beef and Yorkshire pudding,' Stephen declared, and Maddy agreed that she would have that too. He gave their order and they sat gazing out of the window again, watching the waves whipping into a frenzy far out to sea. A fishing boat went by, its bow rising high on the crest of the waves before dipping deeply into their troughs, and Maddy said a little anxiously, 'I hope he makes it to harbour before it gets any worse. It's really frightening.'

'It'll blow itself out soon,' Stephen said. 'Now, about these weekends. When can you next get away?'

'Well, I ought to stay in West Lyme next weekend,' she said. 'I don't know about the one after that. I'd have to ask the Archdeacon.'

'I wouldn't be able to get another pass as soon as that either,' he said regretfully. 'But the very next one we can both get away, we will, won't we? And where would you like to go?'

Maddy stared at him. 'Stephen, we've been through all this.'

'No, we haven't. We got at cross-purposes, that's all. Look, it's very nice coming to Burracombe, and we can do it again, of course we can, but we don't always want to come here, do we? We can go anywhere we like. Find some nice little country inn and stay a couple of nights, all by ourselves. To be honest, Maddy, I don't really want to share you. I want you all to myself.'

'But I'm not yours,' she said, the tight feeling in her voice again. 'And I can't go away with you for the weekend. What would the Archdeacon say?'

'That reminds me of a joke,' he said, grinning. '"*To the woods, to the woods!*" . . . "*No, no, the vicar wouldn't like it.*" . . . "*The vicar's not getting it.*"' He saw Maddy's face. 'Oops. I've done it again, haven't I? Put my foot right in it. Oh, come on, Maddy, it's just a joke.'

'Yes, well, I don't happen to find it very funny,' she said stiffly, wondering what was the matter with her. At any other time, she'd have laughed and probably responded with a joke of her own, but a cold knot of anxiety was forming inside her and she didn't know how to react. I wish we weren't so far away from home, she thought. It's at least twenty or thirty miles and I've no way of getting back without Stephen. 'I can't do it, and that's that,' she said at last. 'Please don't ask me again, Stephen.'

'Look,' he said. 'I'm not asking you to do anything wrong. Just have a weekend away. In separate rooms. No funny business.' But it wasn't what he'd had in mind at all, and they both knew it. 'Just so that we can get to know each other a bit better. What's so terrible about that?'

Maddy felt wrong-footed. She shrugged and said in a rather sulky tone, 'Nothing. I just don't want to do it, that's all. You're talking as if I've got nothing else to do but come out with you. I do have other friends, you know.'

'I know that. But you did say you'd like to come away again – when you thought it would be to Burracombe.'

'That's different. I can see Stella then, and Felix and Dottie and everyone else. Why don't we just do that, Stephen? You can see your family as well and we can still spend lots of time together.'

'Like tomorrow,' he said. 'Church in the morning for you, and Sunday lunch at home with Dad and Hilary. A laugh a minute that'll be, with him quizzing me about what I'm going to do with my life.'

Maddy sighed. There didn't seem to be anything else to say. They looked at each other for a moment, then his grin broke out and he took her hand again.

'All right, Maddy. We'll do it your way. It'll be a lot better than nothing, and maybe by the summer you'll be ready for something more. The next weekend we both have free, we'll come to Burracombe again. Is that a pact?'

'It's a pact,' Maddy said, and she smiled at him.

The wind continued to rise all that afternoon and evening, and by the time Stephen kissed Maddy goodnight at her bedroom door it was howling round the house. She went in and stood at the window for a few minutes, staring into the darkness and imagining what it must be like up on the moors, and out at sea. I hope that little boat's safe, she thought, and felt a moment of sick fear. The idea of ships in peril always reminded her of her father, a merchant seaman, lost at sea during the war. Her worst nightmares had come from her imaginings of him and his shipmates, struggling to stay afloat miles from land, realising that they were never going to be saved, gulping in more and more water, feeling it fill their lungs until they choked their lives away. I hope that's not happening to anyone tonight, she thought, and closed the curtains quickly before getting into bed.

The storm raged all through the night. When morning came, Maddy found the others in the kitchen, bleary-eyed from lack of sleep. Hilary was at the stove, cooking breakfast, talking anxiously to her father. She turned as Maddy came in.

'Hello, Maddy. We're having breakfast in here this morning. There are a lot of things to see to on the estate. Travis has been round already, and he says there are some trees down and some damage to some of the cottages. Slates off, fences blown over, that sort of thing.'

'Is there anything I can do to help?' Maddy asked, standing

by the half-laid table. 'Just tell me where things are and I'll get them out.'

'It's all right, Stephen's doing it. Will you be coming round with us, Steve? We might be glad of an extra pair of hands.'

'I'll come too,' Maddy offered, but Hilary shook her head.

'You may as well go to church with Stella as you'd planned. We don't want your weekend spoiled. And Steve was just saying, it might be a good idea to set off fairly early this afternoon in case there's any problems on the road. According to the wireless this morning, it was even worse further east.'

'Let's see if there's any more news,' Stephen said, switching on the kitchen radio, and after the usual burblings and twitter, the announcer's voice came through. They listened in dismay.

'A tidal surge, together with torrential rain and exceptionally strong winds, has brought extensive flooding to the east coast of England. Canvey Island and many of the low-lying areas of East Anglia are underwater. A rescue operation has begun to save families who have been driven to take refuge on the roofs of their houses, but many people are feared drowned. There was no warning of the disaster, which brought a tide of around nine feet higher than normal, driven by the gales. In the Netherlands, the situation is even worse ...' Stephen switched it off and they stared at each other in horror.

'That's dreadful,' Maddy said in a shaking voice. 'Just imagine what it must have been like for them – the sea suddenly rushing into their houses in the middle of the night. The poor, poor souls.'

'Yes, it's awful,' Hilary said soberly. 'Even worse than when Lynmouth was flooded last year. And we're worrying about a few fallen trees!'

'We've got to deal with them just the same,' her father pointed out. He was sitting at the table, still in his dressing-gown, his thick mane of silver hair combed back from his forehead. 'There's nothing we can do to help them, God rest their souls, but we can help our own people.'

'I know.' Hilary set a large platter of bacon and eggs in the middle of the table. 'Help yourselves, will you? I'll made some tea and toast. It's a bit of a scratch breakfast, I'm afraid, but as you can see we're not in our usual leisurely Sunday-morning mood today.'

'It doesn't matter a bit. I just wish I could do something to help. Couldn't I stay at home and cook the lunch?'

'It's all right, Maddy. The meat's in the Aga already and the vegetables won't take long. You go off with Stella, you've hardly seen her this weekend. She and Felix are coming back to lunch, aren't they?'

'Well, they were going to, but if it's a nuisance—'

'It's not a nuisance at all,' Hilary said firmly. 'You just carry on with what you'd planned. Stephen will give us a hand with anything that needs doing this morning, and we've got Travis and the tenant farmers and everyone. And Jacob Prout's out already, clearing away fallen branches and things.'

Maddy met him later, as she walked down to the village to meet Stella for church. He shook his head when he heard where she was going.

'Don't know as you'll get across the Clam, maid. I haven't been down there yet, mind, but I wouldn't be surprised if there's not a few trees down. And if you ask me, tidden a good idea to go walking under them that's still standing on their roots. I'd stay in Burracombe, if I were you.'

'Oh dear,' Maddy said in disappointment. 'I wanted to hear Felix take the service. I wonder if he'll be able to get there himself. We were going to walk over together.'

'He'll probably go round by road in that little old sports car of his,' Jacob suggested. 'I don't reckon he'll let the weather stop him, but there's been a master lot of damage done.'

Stella and Felix were waiting at Dottie's gate when Maddy arrived and, as Jacob had surmised, Felix's red sports car,

Mirabelle, was waiting there too. They greeted her with hugs and kisses and exclamations about the storm, and then piled in with Stella in the front seat and Maddy perched in the back. Outside the village there were a number of fallen branches and trees but none blocked the road and they were able to reach the village of Little Burracombe without too much delay.

The church was filled with people who had heard about the devastation and wanted to offer up prayers for those who had been killed or injured or lost their homes. Felix preached a sermon about how disaster can strike at any time, yet good can often come out of bad. Afterwards, he stood at the door shaking hands and Maddy heard several of the parishioners thank him for his words. She watched their faces and noticed how much they seemed to like him. He'll be a good vicar here, she thought. He's full of fun and not at all as you expect a clergyman to be – a bit like his uncle, the Archdeacon, although the latter was older and not so flippant – but when he needs to be serious, you feel he really means it. Stella is a lucky girl to have found him.

She thought of the two men in her own life – Sammy Hodges and Stephen Napier. They were as different as chalk from cheese, yet she liked them both. Stephen had some of Felix's happy-go-lucky attitude to life, but she wasn't sure he shared the curate's more thoughtful side. He'd had an easy life too, with everything provided for him, and had never had to struggle. Sammy's childhood, on the other hand, had been desperately poor and tragic, and it was only when he had come to live with Ruth Hodges as an evacuee that he had begun to lose his fears. She remembered the first time she had seen him, as a pale, grubby and frightened little eight-year-old, and thought of him as he was now – still slightly-built and not particularly tall, but straight and strong, his hair still as fair as it had ever been and his blue eyes direct and honest. He took life seriously, but he had learned to enjoy it as well, and he was gentle and kind.

I don't know how to choose between them, she thought, and then reminded herself that she didn't have to. They weren't the only two men in the world, and she wasn't looking for anything more than friendship. Although she had to admit, she did enjoy their kisses!

'What are you dreaming about?' Stella enquired, coming up beside her and taking her arm. 'I've spoken to you twice and you haven't heard a word.'

'Sorry.' Maddy grinned at her sister. 'I was just thinking how lucky you are and wondering if it isn't too late to make Felix fall in love with me instead. I think I could be quite happy being a vicar's wife in Little Burracombe.'

'You haven't a chance,' Stella said firmly. 'Mind you, I was rather afraid he would when he first knew you. You're so pretty. I wonder every man you meet doesn't fall for you.'

'Oh, they do. I just don't take any notice.' Maddy turned as Felix, now divested of his cassock, came over to them. 'Are you ready to come back to the Barton for lunch?'

'I'm looking forward to it. Hilary's a wonderful cook.'

'I don't know if she'll have had time for much cooking today,' Maddy said as they walked down the church path towards Mirabelle. 'She and Stephen and Mr Kellaway were going round the estate to look at the storm damage.'

'We're lucky it's not as bad here as in the east of the country,' Stella said. 'That was a very good sermon, by the way, Felix, and all done without notes too.'

'Well, I didn't really have time to write any, did I? But I don't have much problem with preaching *extempore*, even though some people don't approve of it. I suppose I'm just naturally gifted at speaking,' he said modestly.

'Naturally gifted at chattering, you mean,' his loving fiancée told him as they got into the car. 'And it's easy to see why some people don't like preachers not using notes – some of them don't know when to stop. I may have to buy you a stopwatch if you're going to do it too often.'

'I think,' he said in a dignified tone, 'that I may fall in love with Maddy, after all.'

The two girls stared at him. 'You heard what we were saying!' Stella accused him. 'You shouldn't eavesdrop – you know listeners never hear any good of themselves.'

Felix negotiated his way round a particularly large fallen branch. 'I wasn't eavesdropping – I just happened to hear you as I came along the side aisle. Anyway, I didn't hear anything bad.'

'That's because you interrupted us before we got to that bit,' Stella told him. 'Now, for goodness' sake behave yourself at the Barton. You know what Colonel Napier's like. He's never been quite sure he was right to agree to you having the living at Little Burracombe.'

They arrived without mishap and Felix did his best to behave as instructed, but lunch was a merry one after all. Stephen and his father were in accord for once after their morning on the estate, Stephen apparently having proved himself much more useful than expected. Gilbert Napier did murmur a comment at one point that it was a pity he insisted on wasting himself in the RAF, but Hilary quickly changed the subject, and the moment passed. Shortly afterwards, as they sat over their coffee, Stephen turned to Maddy and said it was nearly time for them to leave.

'With all this debris on the roads, it would be best to get there before dark, and I've still got to get back to the station after that. I probably won't stay for high tea after all.'

Maddy nodded and went to fetch her bag. She came down, swathed in furs again, and Stephen appeared with the rugs they had used on the way down. They kissed all round and then went out to the car.

'It's been a lovely weekend,' Maddy said sincerely to Hilary and her father. 'Thank you very much for having me.'

'Come again soon,' Hilary said. 'And you don't have to

226

wait for Stephen to bring you – you can come by yourself, any time, if you want to see Stella.'

They drove away, waving until they turned the corner at the end of the drive, and then Maddy settled back in her seat and smiled at Stephen.

'It really has been lovely. I'm sorry I was cross last night.'

He took his hand from the steering-wheel and patted her knee. 'That's all right. I shouldn't have rushed you. I'm sorry. I promise not to do it again – not until you're ready for it, anyway.' He paused, and then said quietly, 'I really do think a lot of you, Maddy. I'd like to hope that we might have a future together, one day.'

Maddy looked up at him. He was gazing straight ahead at the road, as if afraid to meet her eye, and after a moment she said in the same tone, 'I really don't want to hurry, Stephen, and I can't make any promises. But I won't forget. I promise you that.'

They drove the rest of the way in easy companionship, and arrived at the Archdeacon's house just before dusk. Stephen drew up before the door and turned to her.

'One little kiss before you go in?' he whispered. 'Just to remind you not to forget your promise?'

Maddy turned her face to his. Her eyes were glowing in the glimmering light, and her lips were slightly parted. He slid his arms around her and she moved closer; just as their lips met, the front door opened, Archie came bounding down the steps and the Archdeacon hurried down after him.

'I'm glad you're back,' he said breathlessly as Maddy opened her door and looked up at him in consternation. 'I'm afraid there's been some bad news from Bridge End. Ruth Hodges has telephoned. There's been an accident and young Sam has been hurt. He's in hospital and he's asking for you.'

'For *me*?' Maddy stared at him in shock, then turned to Stephen. 'Stephen, did you hear that? Sammy's been hurt. I must go at once. Where is he?'

'He's in Southampton General. I've got the car out. I'll take you as soon as you're ready. You'll need to go indoors first, I'm sure – there's some tea and sandwiches ready for you. And you too, of course,' he added to Stephen. 'I'm sorry about this, but you can see that she needs to go at once.'

'Yes,' Stephen said, a little blankly. 'Yes, I do see.' He got out of the car as Maddy scrabbled for her bag. 'It's all right, darling, I'll bring that in for you. And there's no need for you to worry,' he said to the Archdeacon. 'I'll take Maddy to Southampton. *I'll* look after her.'

Chapter Twenty-Five

It had taken a good half-hour to clear the tangled mass of branches and release the two men. They lay a little apart from each other, sprawled beneath the debris and covered with dirt, crumbled dead leaves and twigs. As soon as the last splintered branch was lifted away, Ruth ran forwards, hardly knowing which to go to first.

'Blimey, Ruth,' Dan croaked, sitting up cautiously and brushing fragments of bark out of his eyes, 'I thought I was a goner that time and no mistake.'

'Oh, Dan.' She knelt on the rough metalled road and flung her arms around him. 'Thank God you're all right.'

'Well, I think I am. I ain't too certain yet, not till I've felt meself all over. But where's our Sam? I ain't heard a sound from him all the time since it happened.'

'He's over here,' Solly Barlow said. He was leaning on a branch, breathing heavily. 'He needs to go to hospital.'

Ruth leaped up and dropped to her knees again beside her stepson. He lay white and still on the road, covered as Dan had been by scraps of dead leaf and twigs as well as dirt that had been thrown up from the road by the tree's impact. Swiftly, she felt all over his body, looking for broken bones, and gently parted his hair where blood was staining his curls. For a brief moment, her memory flashed back to the day when she had first brought Sammy into her home and bathed him, discovering with some surprise that he was fair under the grime. Tears sprang to her eyes as she gazed down at him, seeing again the frail little eight-year-old, and it was all she could do not to snatch him up into her arms and clasp him against her.

'How bad is he, Ruthie?' Dan had staggered to his feet and was beside her, staring down at his son. 'He – he's breathing, ain't he?'

'Yes, he's alive. I don't know how bad he is, though. We've got to get him to the hospital but I'm afraid to move him. We need to be very careful.'

'I'll go down and get a stretcher,' George Warren offered. The Cottage Hospital was only just across the green from Ruth's cottage, less than a quarter of a mile away. But she shook her head.

'I'm not sure a stretcher's the right thing. If his back's broken and he isn't kept perfectly straight, it could ... well, anyway, has anyone got a plank we could use? A door would do.'

'I'll get our living-room door off its hinges,' Solly said, already heading for the forge. 'It's good, solid oak, that is. I'll need a bit of help,' he added, but already George and two or three other men were going with him. It took some doing to get the heavy old door off its hinges for the first time in more years than anyone could count, but Solly ordered them not to be over-careful and soon they were staggering back into the road with the solid slab of wood held between them. Sammy had already been covered with blankets and Ruth, together with Dan and Jane, lifted him very carefully on to the makeshift stretcher, doing their utmost not to let his body sag or bend in any way.

'Blimey, he don't make much difference to the weight, do he?' Solly remarked as they began to proceed along the lane towards the Cottage Hospital. 'I thought he was putting a bit of muscle on him, too, since he come out of the RAF.'

The procession moved slowly, with Solly, Dan, George and Ian Knight looking frighteningly like coffin-bearers as they carried the door with its white, still burden covered with blankets, and Ruth and Jane walking beside it. The tears Ruth had held back until this moment were now pouring steadily down her cheeks and Jane glanced at her anxiously.

'He's going to be all right, isn't he? You couldn't find anything broken?'

'I don't know. I didn't like to turn him over. That knock on the head's worrying me, Jane. There's not much blood, but you don't know what's been damaged inside. I don't know that we're going to be able to do much for him here, to be honest. I think he needs to go to Southampton, where he can be X-rayed. They've got all the best equipment there.'

'Well, I reckon Doctor'll be waiting for him,' Jane said, trying to offer comfort. 'He'll know what's best and he can get an ambulance out if he thinks that's where Sammy should be.'

Dr Jenkins was waiting, as Jane had said, and came out as soon as he saw the little cavalcade approaching. He looked doubtfully at the door.

'I don't think we're going to be able to get that inside. It's wider than our doorways. He'll have to go on a stretcher. Why didn't you come up for one in the first place?'

'I was frightened to move him too much,' Ruth explained. 'I couldn't find any bones broken, but I couldn't turn him over and feel his back and I was afraid something might get damaged inside. And there's blood on his head, see?'

'Has he regained consciousness at all?' He looked at Dan. 'You were in the accident too, were you?'

Dan nodded. 'That's why I'm in this state. I reckon Sam was knocked out the minute the tree come down on us. That's getting on for three-quarters of an hour now. He never made a sound once the noise had stopped.'

The doctor nodded. 'You'd better lay the door down. I'll look at him here.' He made a brief examination and nodded again. 'He'll have to go to Southampton. I'll get an ambulance out here as soon possible. But he can't stay out here in this weather – the rain's starting again. We'll have to get him on a trolley and bring him inside.'

With Ruth helping and the others watching anxiously, they managed to transfer Sammy to a hospital trolley and take him indoors. As they came to a gentle stop just inside the door, he moved his head slightly and moaned. Ruth was at his side at once.

'Sammy? Sammy, can you hear me? It's Ruth. You've had an accident, dear; you're in the hospital, but you're going to be all right. I promise you you're going to be all right.'

He moaned again and opened his eyes. Ruth drew in a sharp gasp of relief, but his eyes were clouded and unfocused, and when he spoke at last it was in a thin, strange whisper quite unlike his normal cheerful tones.

'Silver,' he muttered. 'I've got to take Silver.'

'Where?' Ruth asked, as a loss. 'Where have you got to take him, Sammy? Silver's at home, in his cage. He doesn't need to go anywhere.'

'Picnic,' he mumbled. 'Muriel says ... got to take Silver ... Maddy wants Silver ...' His eyes cleared suddenly and he looked straight at Ruth and said, quite loudly, 'I'm sorry, Auntie Ruth. I didn't mean to hurt him. I just wanted to go on the picnic ...' And then his eyes closed and he turned his head to one side and lay quite still.

'Sammy,' Ruth breathed, her heart like a stone in her breast. 'Sammy, it's all right now. It's all over. Silver's all right and nobody's cross with you.' Her voice rose in panic as she stared at the still, ice-white face. 'Sammy – speak to me, Sammy – for God's sake, *speak to me*!'

'Don't be silly, Stephen,' Maddy said, pulling her bag out of the car. 'How can you take me? You've got to get back to White Cheriton. Southampton's miles out of your way. And how would I get home again?'

'It doesn't matter about me,' he said. 'I'm coming with you, Maddy. I'll stay there with you for as long as you want to stay but I'm going to be with you.'

'You can't. You'll get put in junkers—'

'Jankers.'

'Whatever it is,' she said irritably. 'Look, we can't stand here arguing. We're wasting time. Sammy's in hospital and he wants me, and that's all that matters.'

'Yes,' Stephen said quietly. 'I can see that it is.'

They stared at each other for a moment, then he turned away. 'All right, Maddy. Have it your own way. But you know where I am when you want me. *If* you want me,' he added in a voice so low she barely heard it. And then he turned back, gripped her arms and leaned close to kiss her swiftly and hard on the mouth. 'Thanks for the weekend, Maddy.'

He got into the car and started the engine. Maddy watched, feeling baffled and dismayed, as if a favourite toy had been suddenly taken away from her without explanation. And then a vision of Sammy, lying white and still in a hospital bed, flashed into her mind, and she ran into the house. In a few minutes she was out again, a box of sandwiches in her hands. The Archdeacon's car was already in the drive, where Stephen's had stood.

'We can eat these on the way.' She scrambled in beside him. 'Are you sure you don't mind taking me? I could have gone with Stephen.'

'Of course I'm sure. There's no point in him getting into trouble. And I'll wait to bring you home, unless you need to stay longer. I can always come back for you tomorrow, or send someone else.'

'I'm being such a nuisance,' she said. 'I didn't think ... I just wanted to get there. Sammy – well, we knew each other as children, you see. We were always friends, until they took me away from Bridge End. And since we met again at the wedding ...'

'It's all right, my dear. I understand. Are you going to have any of those sandwiches?'

'I don't feel hungry. We had a huge lunch at the Barton.'

She gazed miserably out of the window at the darkness. 'It seems like another world now.'

The Archdeacon glanced sideways at her. 'And how's my nephew?'

'Oh, Felix is fine. Just the same as ever. He preached a very good sermon about the floods.' But she spoke absently and, after another quick glance, he decided to leave her to her thoughts.

They drove in silence for a while and then she asked, 'What kind of accident was it? Was he on his motorbike? Where was he?'

'Goodness, I didn't tell you that, did I? Not, it was in the village that it happened and it was nothing to do with his motorcycle. He and his father were helping to clear a fallen tree when another one came down. It could have killed them both, but fortunately the other men were able to get them out. Mr Hodges was all right, apparently, apart from some nasty bruises, but Sammy ... well, they took him straight to the Cottage Hospital but the doctor said he ought to go to Southampton. They have better facilities there.'

Maddy stared at him with frightened eyes. 'So he's badly hurt then?'

'Well, he must be conscious, mustn't he?' the Archdeacon pointed out. 'Or he couldn't have asked for you. You mustn't worry too much, my dear. I'm sure by the time we get there he'll be sitting up and taking notice, and he'll be back at home in Bridge End before those sandwiches have had time to go stale.'

'I hope so,' she said dismally.

The drive to Southampton took nearly an hour. The Archdeacon parked the car close to the main doors and Maddy scrambled out and ran inside. By the time he caught up with her, she was being directed along a corridor by a nurse, and they walked swiftly together towards the door of the ward.

'It must be visiting time,' Maddy said, glancing at the other people making their way through the corridors. 'Here it is. Ward Seven.' They walked in and she hesitated. 'Where is he? I can't see him.'

A nurse came forward. 'Who are you looking for?'

'Sammy Hodges,' Maddy said, her voice quivering. 'He was hit by a falling tree. They said he was here.'

'He's over there, in the end bed. His parents are with him.' She looked doubtfully at the Archdeacon. 'We only allow three visitors, but seeing as you've a vicar, I suppose it's all right.'

The Archdeacon smiled and said, 'We won't ask you to break the rules. The young man doesn't actually know me – I'm just a chauffeur this evening. I'll wait outside, Maddy.'

Maddy nodded, hardly hearing him, and quickened her step. As she drew nearer, Ruth and Dan looked up and Ruth's face brightened. Maddy saw that she looked white and anxious, and her own dread increased. She sat down in the chair that Dan offered her, and looked fearfully at the figure lying so still in the bed.

'How is he?' she asked in a whisper. Sammy was almost as white as the sheets that came up to his chin. His eyes were closed and his head was bandaged.

'They took some X-rays but we haven't heard the results yet,' Ruth said quietly. 'They think he's cracked a rib but there don't seem to be any more bones broken. It's his head that's the worry. Until he wakes up properly they won't know how bad the damage is.'

'You mean his brain might be damaged?' Maddy felt a wave of horror. She saw that Ruth was holding his hand and touched it herself, very gently. 'But I thought he'd come round. The Archdeacon said he'd been asking for me.'

'He did. But he was wandering too. He seemed to think he was going on a picnic with you – and taking Silver.' Their eyes met and Maddy knew they were both remembering that day, so many years ago, when she had persuaded him to bring the parrot outside. 'He kept on talking about it and asking when

235

you were coming. In the end, we thought he was getting so agitated that we'd better ask you to come. I'm sorry to be so much trouble,' Ruth ended apologetically.

'It doesn't matter a bit. It's no trouble.' Maddy looked at the ashen face again, trying to hide her disappointment. It wasn't really her, as she was now, that Sammy wanted. It was the child she had been – little Muriel, who had led him into all sorts of scrapes when they'd both been evacuees at Bridge End. She blinked away her tears, scolding herself for being selfish, and wondered if it was really any use her being here at all. Suppose he woke up and didn't recognise her. Suppose he looked into her eyes and asked piteously for Muriel …

As she sat there, holding his hand and gazing at his face, she began to think about their friendship. Rooted in their childhood, it had been so recently renewed that it was still very fresh, yet she felt as if Sammy had always been a part of her life. They had slipped back so naturally into their old easy companionship, and although she'd told herself repeatedly that she didn't want any serious relationship just yet, she'd felt, deep down, that when she was ready, Sammy would be there.

Now, sitting in the hospital ward with all the smells and sounds of illness and even death around her, she felt a quiver of panic that it might already be too late.

A sound made her turn. Dan was on his feet, following a young nurse along the ward, and Ruth whispered, 'The doctor wants to talk to us. Will you stay here?'

'Yes, of course.' Maddy felt torn – she wanted both to stay with Sammy and to hear what the doctor had to say. But it was Dan and Ruth who had that right, and at least she now had Sammy to herself for a few moments.

'Sammy,' she whispered. 'Can you hear me? It's Maddy – Muriel, who made you take Silver into the woods, re-member? You came down to see me in West Lyme, on your motorbike. We went on the beach with Archie. It was such fun, Sammy, and I want you to get better so that we can do it again. Sammy, I don't want to lose you. Please don't go away from me. Please.' Tears filled her eyes and spilled on to her cheeks. 'I want to go out with you on the motorbike, and walk along the beach with you, and go swimming and have picnics, and do ordinary things with you. I want us to be together, always. Sammy, please wake up. Please speak to me. Please tell me you can hear me. Please.'

She paused, her throat too thick with tears to go on. Sammy's hand lay cold and flaccid within hers. She looked down at it, stroking his fingers, thinking how brown and strong they had seemed only a week or so ago. And then, so slightly that she was scarcely sure it had happened, they moved and gave hers the faintest possible squeeze.

Maddy caught her breath. She leaned closer. 'Sammy – can you hear me? Do you know what I'm saying to you? Squeeze my hand again – tell me.' There was a tiny pause and then, as if with a great effort, his hand moved again in hers. 'Do you know it's me?' she asked in an urgent whisper. 'Do you know I'm Maddy?' And again, barely perceptibly, his fingers tightened.

Maddy looked round wildly for someone to tell. Dan and Ruth were at the end of the ward, in a small office whose window looked out on to the beds. They were still talking to the doctor and Ruth looked as if she were crying. She glanced through the window towards the bed and, with her free hand, Maddy signalled urgently, Ruth said something to the two men and came hurrying back.

'What is it? What's happened?' Her voice was frightened.

'He squeezed my hand!' Maddy told her. 'He heard me talking to him. He knows who I am.'

'Oh, dear God.' Ruth leaned over the bed and Maddy relinquished the hand she had been holding. 'Sammy, it's Auntie Ruth. Can you hear me? Do you know who I am?' She waited a moment, then her face lit up. 'He does! Oh, Dan!'

The two men were beside the bed now. 'He can hear us. He understands. Oh, thank God, thank God!'

The doctor eased her gently aside and bent over the bed himself. He took out his stethoscope and glanced at them. 'Draw the curtains, please, and step outside for a moment while I examine him. This may be just what we've been waiting for.'

Reluctantly, they did as they were told and stood in a little cluster near a vacant bed. A nurse hurried down the ward and went into the little enclosure and Maddy looked at Ruth.

'What did he tell you?'

'He says the X-rays showed a hairline fracture. It might not be serious at all – it just depends on whether the brain itself was damaged. It could have been shaken, or bruised – the X-rays wouldn't show that. He said it all depended on how long Sammy stayed unconscious and whether he was lucid when he came round. Some people ...' Ruth choked a little '... some people never do come round.'

'But you said Sammy had.'

'Yes, and that was good, but he wasn't lucid then, and he lost consciousness again. This time ...' Ruth gazed at Maddy. 'He really did know who you were? Who you are now, I mean – not years ago?'

'Yes. I'm sure he did.' She didn't repeat what she had said to him. Had Sammy heard those frantic words? Would he remember them? It doesn't matter, she thought, as long as he gets better. We'll have all the time in the world to talk, then – only I won't waste it next time. I won't waste a single minute of it.

Chapter Twenty-Six

Once he had fully regained consciousness, Sammy's recovery was steady. The cracked rib gave him some pain, especially if he laughed or coughed, but the hairline fracture seemed to have done no serious damage and the doctor was at a loss to explain why he had been unconscious for so long.

'I expect I was just tired and wanted a rest,' Sammy said. 'Or maybe there isn't much brain there to damage.'

'Well, at least you haven't lost your sense of humour,' the doctor observed. 'And I don't see any reason why you should stay any longer, cluttering up our wards. You'd better get your aunt to bring your clothes in tomorrow morning, and you can go home.'

'Smashing,' Sammy said, and waited for Maddy and Ruth to come in for visiting that evening so that he could give them the news.

The Archdeacon had suggested that Maddy should stay at Bridge End for at least a couple of days, until they could be sure that Sammy really was on the mend. 'It seems as if you're quite important to his recovery,' he'd said. 'It was you he asked for, and your voice he first responded to. You'd better make sure he doesn't slip back.'

'It was probably just a coincidence,' Maddy protested, anxious not to offend Ruth, but Ruth laughed and shook her head.

'I don't think so. Haven't you seen the way his face lights up when you walk into the ward? I think you're rather more

239

important to him than you realised, Maddy.' She paused. 'I hope he's important to you as well. I don't want him to be hurt. If you don't feel the same, you will let him down gently, won't you?'

'I won't let him down at all if I can help it,' Maddy said soberly. 'I didn't realise until the accident just how important he was – I thought we had all the time in the world. But nobody has that, do they?'

'True,' Ruth agreed. 'We never know what's round the corner, or when we're going to say goodbye for the last time. I found that out when my Jack died. And poor Dan did too, when he lost his other son in the war. I don't know what he'd do if he lost Sammy as well.'

Maddy had enjoyed being in Bridge End again. It was funny, she reflected, that in the space of one week, she had been in both the villages that had been home to her during her childhood. They were alike in so many ways. Ordinary people – farmers, blacksmiths, shopkeepers, gamekeepers – doing the kinds of jobs that they'd done for generations, jobs that were important to the whole country. City-dwellers, she thought, so often looked down their noses at those who lived and worked in the country, referring to them as 'bumpkins' and 'yokels', yet where would they be without the cowman or the shepherd to bring them milk and meat? Where, without the farmer to grow the wheat for their bread and the vegetables for their dinner? I like being here, she thought, walking along the lane to fetch bread from the village baker. I like seeing the fields and the woods about me, even in winter. I've lived enough in cities with Fenella. I want to stay here now, in a village somewhere in England – with Sammy.

The storms had died down but the floods along the east coast had barely abated, and in the Netherlands people were still being rescued from homes turned into islands by the water. Over two thousand people had been drowned; even in England there were more than three hundred deaths in that one night when the sea had invaded the land. Maddy walked along by the forge, where the tree that had fallen on Dan and Sammy had been cleared away now, and stood looking at the torn and broken hedges, shivering as she thought how close the two men had come to death. As Ruth said, you never knew what was round the corner.

When they went into the hospital that evening to visit him, Sammy was sitting up in bed beaming.

'I'm being allowed out tomorrow,' he said, as soon as they came near enough to the bed. 'You can bring my clothes in any time after ten o'clock. The doctor says I'm cluttering up the wards and they can't wait to get rid of me.'

'I'm sure he said nothing of the sort,' Ruth protested, but Maddy laughed.

'I bet he did! Well, at least I'll be able to go back to work now. The Archdeacon said I'd got to stay until you were out again, and I was beginning to feel guilty about taking so much time off.'

'I was hoping you'd be around for a while after I came home,' Sammy said in disappointment, and Ruth added, 'You'll be welcome to stay longer, my dear, you know that.'

'I'd like to, but I really ought to go back. Perhaps if I stay just one more night.' She had been sharing Linnet's bedroom. 'Just to make sure you're properly well again.'

'Oh, I'm not sure about that,' Sammy said at once, and put his hand to this forehead. 'I think I may be getting another headache. You probably ought to stay a bit longer.'

'Maybe we'd better tell the doctor,' she suggested, and he shook his head at once.

'It's not that bad. I'm sure I'm well enough to go home, but I'll probably need lots of looking after when I'm there. Soemone to sit and talk to me and hold my hand, that sort of thing. And Auntie Ruth's too busy.'

'It's no use,' Maddy said severely. 'I'll stay one more night and that's all. But I could come back next weekend,' she added, and he brightened.

'All right, then. As long as you promise. Or I may have a relapse.'

She shook her head at him, but inside she was feeling a glow of pleasure. He really did seem to want her there. It's probably just because he feels a bit weak and poorly still, she thought, but even that's something. And she wondered for the umpteenth time whether he had really heard, or remembered, the things she'd said to him while he was unconscious.

Ruth was quiet as they went back to Bridge End on the bus that evening, and as they walked along the lane towards the cottage, their way lit by a pale glimmer of moonlight, she said, 'So you're going to stay on for a day or two, are you?'

'Well, only if it's all right with you,' Maddy said, discerning a note of reserve in Ruth's voice. 'It's been very good of you to put me up, but I know I must be making extra work. And with Sammy coming home ...'

'Oh, it's not the *work*,' Ruth said. 'You give a hand round the place as good as anyone, more than I'd expect really. I just thought you'd be wanting to get back to West Lyme. It's not what you're used to, making do in a little cottage, I know that.'

Maddy turned her head and stared at her, but Ruth's face was in deep shadow and she couldn't see any expression. 'I lived all my childhood in a small cottage,' she said. 'Apart from while I was at the vicarage, anyway.'

'I know. But it's not what you've been accustomed to for the past few years, is it? Travelling all over the place with Fenella Forsyth – living in smart hotels and that French château or whatever it is. It's a sort of castle, isn't it?'

'Yes,' Maddy said. 'But you can still only be in one room at a time.'

'A bit bigger than my poky little rooms, I dare say,' Ruth said, and Maddy was startled to hear a tinge of acid in her voice.

'Your rooms aren't poky. They're lovely and cosy. And I like your cottage better than any great, draughty château where you have to go miles to get to your bedroom. I was always a bit scared there, to tell you the truth.'

Ruth said nothing and Maddy wondered if she believed her. She remembered that Sammy had told her that his aunt and father were uneasy about his friendship with her, but she'd thought they'd forgotten their fears since his accident. They'd certainly been kind enough to her while she was staying with them.

'I know you think I've lived a different sort of life from you,' she said after a minute or two, 'and of course you're right – I have. But I honestly do feel more comfortable in a cottage like yours or Dottie Friend's – where I lived in Burracombe – than in all the smart hotels and big houses Fenella and I used to stay in. They're *home*. French castles and huge mansions are never home, not in the same way. Honestly.'

Ruth sighed. 'I know you say that, and I'm sure you believe it, and I'm not saying you haven't been goodness itself to Sammy. You obviously think a lot of him, and he thinks the world of you. Anyone can see that. But I still can't help worrying. He's not got the experience you have, and it's bound to make a difference. I just don't want him to get hurt, that's all.'

They were at the cottage gate, and as Ruth laid her hand on the latch Dan opened the door and light flooded down the path. The two women paused and looked at each other.

'I won't hurt him,' Maddy said quietly. 'And I do know what you mean. If it's any help, I won't let things go too fast. I promise that. I can't do any more.'

Ruth nodded. 'That's the most I can hope for, I know. We can't order people's lives for them or tell them what to feel. But I do think I can trust you, and I'm grateful for it. You're welcome to stay on as long as you like.'

'Thank you,' Maddy said. 'I'll go back the day after

243

tomorrow. I've got a job to do and I've taken enough time off. But, if it's all right with you, I'll come again next weekend. You don't have to put me up – I'll stay somewhere else. There's bound to be someone in the village who can offer me a bed.'

'And that's something Sammy would never forgive me for,' Ruth said warmly. 'No, Maddy, you'll stay with us and welcome. So long as you don't let Sammy get the wrong idea in his head. He's only a boy still, whatever he might think, and he needs time.'

Time, Maddy thought. The one thing we can't be sure of. She remembered how she'd sat at Sammy's bedside, thinking of the time she'd already wasted and how she'd determined not to waste any more, and she sighed. It didn't seem as if she was to be allowed the choice.

She did have some choices left, however, and she exercised her right to one of them the following week, when Stephen appeared on the steps of the Archdeacon's house. He swept her into his arms before she could even speak, and kissed her thoroughly.

'Stephen!' she gasped when he finally let her go. 'Whatever do you think you're doing? Why are you here?'

'We had a pact, remember? We're going to Burracombe for the weekend.' He beamed down at her. 'Are you ready?'

'Of course I'm not ready! I didn't agree to go this weekend. Did I?' She brushed her hand across her forehead, pushing back her blonde hair. 'Oh, I don't remember now. It's been such a week – but I can't possibly go away, anyway. I only came back to work yesterday, and there's masses to catch up on.'

'Oh yes, how is the boy?' Stephen asked, without much interest. 'I gather he's out of hospital or you'd be there at his bedside, smoothing his fevered brow.'

Maddy eyed him coldly. 'There's no need to talk like that.

Yes, he is back home as a matter of fact, but he has to take things quietly for a bit. He had a cracked rib and a hairline fracture of the skull. There doesn't seem to be any brain damage, but—'

'That's all right then,' Stephen broke in, sounding bored. 'Well, if you can't go away for the whole weekend, I suppose you can at least come out for a few hours? The Archdeacon's not a total slave-driver, is he?'

'He's not a slave-driver at all. And of course I can have some time off. But I'm not sure I want to go anywhere with you, if you're going to go on talking in that nasty way.'

Stephen raised his eyebrows. 'Me, nasty? Look, Maddy, I don't know if you've any idea what this is like for me, but you might try to see my point of view occasionally. I take you away for a nice weekend, staying with my family, and (a) you insist on spending one of the only two days we have with other people, and (b) when we come back you go rushing off to see another man with barely a thank you. And not a single word from you since then. It's a bit rude, don't you think? Aren't I entitled to feel somewhat put out?'

Maddy sighed. 'If you put it like that, yes, perhaps you are. I hoped you'd understand, but since you don't ...' She dropped a curtsey and spoke in a little-girl voice. 'Thank you very much for the lovely weekend, Stephen. I enjoyed it very much, especially the jelly and the cake and everything.' She reverted to her normal tone. 'As it happens, I did write to Hilary and your father, thanking them. I'm not completely bereft of good manners.' She lifted her chin and met his eyes. 'And now, if you don't mind, I've got work to do. I can go out for a few hours this afternoon, if you care to come back.'

'And suppose I don't care to?' he asked, and she shrugged.

'That's up to you.'

They stared at each other for a minute or two, then he said in a more conciliatory tone, 'Come on, Maddy, don't let's squabble. I admit I didn't put things very well, and I'm sorry if I upset you. What about this evening? Couldn't you come out for dinner somewhere?'

'I don't know,' she said. 'I'm rather tired. I thought I'd go to bed early.'

'We needn't be late,' he cajoled. 'I'll call for you at seven and have you back here by ten. How would that do? And I promise not to be nasty.'

'I'm not sure.'

'Tomorrow, then? Lunch somewhere, after church if you like. Or were you planning to go over to Bridge End and see how young Sammy is?'

'It's what I'd like to do,' Maddy said honestly. 'But I can't ask the Archdeacon to take me and I don't think there's any other way, on a Sunday.'

'All right,' he said. 'How about this? You come out to lunch with me and I'll take you to Bridge End, drop you off for an hour or so and then bring you back home again. That way, we all get what we want. Though why I should take my best girl to minister to another bloke, I'm not sure,' he added gloomily. 'I must be even more smitten than I thought.'

Maddy looked at him for a moment, unsure how to take his last remark, then decided to treat it as a joke and smiled. 'Don't be such a fool, Stephen. You're not smitten at all. You're just jealous. Are you sure you mean it – about taking me to Bridge End, I mean?'

'Would I have offered, if I didn't? Is it a deal, then?'

'It's a deal,' Maddy said, and gave him her hand. 'And thank you, Stephen. Thank you very much.'

Sammy was sitting in Dan's armchair by the fire when Maddy arrived at the cottage. Ruth let her in and glanced hesitantly towards the lane, where Stephen was sitting in the car with the engine running.

'Does your friend want to come in too? I was just going to make some tea.'

246

'No, it's all right,' Maddy said. 'He's going to come back for me at about four. It's all right, Stephen,' she called. 'Sammy's receiving visitors. See you later.'

'Well, he'd better come in for a cup then,' Ruth said. 'If he's brought you all this way he'll deserve one. Unless he's going to see friends of his own?' she added.

'No, he'll just go for a drive.' Maddy followed her into the small living room. 'Sammy! You're out bed! And you look so well. Nobody'd ever guess you'd been hit by a falling tree only a week ago.'

She went over to kiss him, but Ruth touched her arm. 'Don't forget he's got a cracked rib. He doesn't want to be hugged or anything, do you, Sammy?'

'Oh, I *want* to,' he answered, grinning. 'I just know it'll hurt too much. But I'm saving up all the hugs I don't get now to have when I'm better.'

Maddy bent and kissed his cheek. 'I shall keep a note of them too.'

Ruth went into the kitchen to make tea, and they looked at each other.

'You really are all right?' Maddy asked. 'I've been worried about you.'

'No need to be. Takes more than an old oak tree to finish me off. Couple of weeks, and I'll be as right as rain. The doctor says at my age broken bones heal almost overnight. You'll see me riding up to your door on the bike in time to bring you a Valentine's card, don't worry.'

Maddy laughed. 'You're not supposed to know who Valentine cards are from. They're a secret.'

'Mine won't be,' he said, suddenly serious. 'I want to be sure you know I've sent it, so that you know who's saying those words to you. I don't want you thinking some other chap's saying them. That fellow from Devon, for instance.'

Maddy blushed. 'You mean Stephen,' she said, trying to

keep her voice casual. 'He's all right, Sammy. He brought me here this afternoon, as a matter of fact.'

'Did he? And I suppose you had your dinner on the way?'

'Well – yes. Otherwise I couldn't have got here in time, after going to church first. And he'll have to be going back to White Cheriton after he's taken me back – it's a lot of driving for him.'

'I suppose so. Seems to me he's seeing much more of you than I am, though. Dinner in some swanky hotel – an hour or more in the car, each way. And didn't I hear you say he's coming back for you at four?'

'It's very good of him to do it,' Maddy said quietly. 'He didn't have to, after all.'

'No, I suppose not.' Sammy reached for her hand. 'Maddy – those things you said to me in the hospital ...'

Maddy was suddenly conscious of Ruth, the other side of the kitchen door. 'What things d'you mean?'

'*You* know. About not wanting to lose me. About wanting to go out on the motorbike, and walk along the beach, and go swimming and have picnics.' He paused, then went on in a slightly shaky voice, 'About wanting us to be together, always.'

Maddy cast a quick, nervous glance at the door. 'Did I say those things?'

'You know you did.' His grip on her hand tightened. 'Don't say you didn't mean them, Maddy.'

'I – I can't – I don't know ...' She looked again, agonised, at the door. 'Sammy, we can't talk about this now. Let's wait until you're better. Properly better. It's too soon.'

'It's not too soon,' he said, gazing at her intently. 'You know it isn't. Maddy, what's the matter? What's happened?'

She couldn't tell him that Ruth had warned her off. She said, 'Nothing's happened. It's just – I need more time. I know I said things, and I did mean them. I think I still mean them. But I've got to have more time before I say them again. We've both got to have more time.'

'I don't see why—' he was beginning, when the door opened and Ruth came in, bearing a tray. She gave them a swift glance and Maddy felt sure that even if she had not heard, she had a good idea what they'd been saying. She watched as Ruth set down the tray and poured the tea, half sorry that the conversation had been interrupted and half grateful.

At that moment, the back door opened and Dan came in, ushering Linnet before him. And after that, there was no more chance for Maddy and Sam to talk privately. They played Ludo together until Stephen returned punctually at four, when Ruth made more tea, and by half-past he and Maddy were back in the car, on their way back to West Lyme.

'Well?' Stephen said. 'Was it a successful visit?'

Maddy sighed. 'He's a lot better,' she said. 'He'll be fit to go back to work in a week or so.'

But that wasn't what Stephen had asked, and they both knew it.

Chapter Twenty-Seven

As the doctor had predicted, Sammy's recovery was steady and quite quick. Both his injuries – the rib and the skull fracture – were minor, and he was young and healthy enough to heal rapidly. By the time St Valentine's Day – which was a Saturday – arrived, he was fit enough to go out, although Ruth put her foot down firmly at the idea of his riding the motorbike to West Lyme to meet Maddy.

'You may feel well enough, and you may even *be* well enough, but it's not worth the risk. That rib's barely had time to mend itself properly, and if you slipped on some ice or mud on the road you could open up the crack and make it even worse. And I don't like to think what would happen if you banged your head. Why don't you ask her to meet you in Southampton? She can get there by train, she said so when she was here.'

'Your auntie's right,' Dan said. Strictly, Ruth was Sammy's stepmother, not his aunt, but the habit of calling her 'auntie' had been too ingrained to change when she and Dan had married. 'It's not worth the risk. You can have a day out in town, can't you? Get some dinner somewhere, go to the pictures.'

'I suppose we could,' Sammy agreed, although he was disappointed not to be able to use the bike. He went off on the bus to Southampton and made his way to the railway station where Maddy jumped off the train glowing with pleasure at seeing him.

'Sammy! How lovely to see you. You're looking really well.'

'I am. I'm going back to work on Monday. And I'm starting my classes again. I've missed a fortnight so there'll be a lot of catching up to do.'

'Will you be having supper with Lizzie on those nights?'

'Probably. She came over to see me last week and said I'd got to be sure to call in. I think Auntie Jane would like me to do that, too; she seems a bit worried about Lizzie.'

'She's probably a bit tired,' Maddy said. 'Expecting another baby and with two little ones already. And they've only got a small house, haven't they?'

'It's not a bad house,' Sammy said. 'It's a bit like the ones in April Grove and October and March Street.'

They were quiet for a moment, each thinking back to the days when they had lived in the small back streets in Portsmouth during the war. They both had memories of the fierce bombing of the Blitz; nights when the scream of the air-raid warning had rent the air and everyone had hurried out of bed and down to the Anderson shelters at the bottom of their gardens – little more than corrugated iron roofs over holes dug in the ground. Maddy's own little brother, Thomas, who had only lived a few months, had been born in one of those shelters, with Maddy and her sister Stella huddled together, terrified, on one of the canvas bunks.

Their moment of introspection didn't last long, however. In a few minutes they were laughing again, strolling along the street and stopping to look in shop windows, dropping into a café for a cup of coffee, and feeling as if they had been together all their lives. It was while they were in the café that Sammy brought out his card and shyly handed it over.

'Oh, Sammy,' Maddy said, opening the envelope. 'That's lovely.' She read the words and blushed.

'I know I didn't write them myself,' Sammy said, watching her face intently, 'but I mean them. I hope you always will be my Valentine, Maddy – all our lives.'

Maddy coloured again. 'You know we agreed not to talk about that just yet.'

'But it's Valentine's Day,' he said. 'We can talk about whatever we like. And I don't care what you say, Maddy, I've just got to ask you . . .' He saw a look of surprise cross her face. 'What's the matter?'

'Over there,' Maddy said in a low voice. 'Look – surely that's Lizzie. But who is she with?'

Sammy followed her glance. The street door had opened and two people were coming in. Lizzie was certainly one of them. But the other was a tall man, whose clothes and bearing marked him out as someone different from most of the people you saw around the streets of Southampton. He's an American, Sammy thought. And in that instant, he knew exactly who the man was.

'It's Floyd,' he said in astonishment. 'He was stationed at the airfield near Bridge End during the war. He used to come over to Auntie Jane's for Sunday dinner and he got up dances and things in the hangars. He showed me and another boy round an aeroplane once. What on earth is he doing here, with Lizzie?'

'I don't know,' Maddy said, watching the two make their way to a corner table and sit down close to each other. 'But they seem awfully friendly. You don't think there's something going on, do you?'

'With him and Lizzie? Of course not. She's married to Alec.'

Maddy gave him an odd look. 'That might not stop her. Not everyone sticks to their marriage vows, Sammy.'

'They do where I come from,' he retorted. 'Auntie Ruth and Aunt Jane would have a fit if they heard you say things like that about Lizzie. Just because you've been all over the place with theatre people and that sort, doesn't mean everyone else behaves the same way. I don't know what he's doing here, but there's nothing like that. They're just friends.'

'Look,' Maddy said quietly, laying her hand on his arm and nodding slightly towards the couple in the corner. 'It doesn't look to me as if they're just friends.'

Sammy looked again. Floyd's hand was covering Lizzie's on the table, and as Sam and Maddy watched, he leaned over and kissed her on the mouth. It was only a fleeting kiss, but when he drew back Lizzie's eyes were closed and there was no mistaking the expression on her face.

'I'm sorry, Sam,' Maddy said. 'I can see this is a bit of a shock for you.'

'I don't believe it,' Sammy said in shaking voice. 'Not Lizzie. There's some other reason. There must be.' He got up. 'I'm going over.'

'No!' Maddy caught his sleeve. 'Don't do that. You'll only make things worse. The best thing would be for us to go outside, without them seeing us. We'll pretend we never saw them. It will only cause trouble if we do anything now. Come on – let's go.'

'But we haven't ordered anything.'

'All the better,' she said, and stood up, pushing him gently towards the door. They passed an astonished waitress and she said, 'My friend doesn't feel well. He had an accident a couple of weeks ago – he needs some fresh air.' And then they were out on the pavement.

'Thank goodness for that,' Maddy said. 'Now look, Sammy, this is none of our business. You may be quite right, there might be an innocent explanation for what we saw, and we don't want to go stirring up trouble. And if there isn't – well, it's even more important that we don't get involved. If he's American, he's probably going back soon and it will all blow over. Nobody ever need know.'

'But they saw us,' Sammy said miserably. 'I looked back just as we were coming out and Lizzie was looking right at me. They know we saw them, Maddy, and I can't just pretend it never happened.'

Somehow, the rest of the day seemed spoiled after that and Sammy never did find the right moment to say the words he had meant to say when he gave Maddy her Valentine card. They walked around Southampton for a while, looking at the old walls, and thought about going to the cinema, but there was nothing on that they fancied. In the end, Maddy said, 'Why don't we go on the ferry to the Isle of Wight? It'd be a nice trip down Southampton Water and across the Solent to Cowes. Almost like going abroad.'

'It'll be a bit cold,' Sammy said doubtfully, but she took his arm and snuggled against him, laughing.

'I'm sure we'll think of a way to keep warm.'

Sammy grinned down at her, feeling better, though he was still upset about seeing Lizzie and Floyd together. They went down to the ferry and bought tickets, and Sammy bought a huge bar of milk chocolate to nibble on the journey.

'You're not expecting to get shipwrecked, are you?' Maddy asked, eyeing it. 'We'll never eat all that.'

'Well, what's left we'll share to take home with us. And we'll have something to eat in Cowes. I meant to take you to have some dinner somewhere – lunch, I mean,' he added, recalling that Maddy always referred to the midday meal as 'lunch', whereas he had grown up calling it 'dinner'. 'I'm sorry, Maddy you must be starving.'

'Not really. But I expect you are. It doesn't matter – we'll be in Cowes in time for a slap-up high tea.' They started to board the ferry and Maddy immediately made for the upper deck. 'We don't want to be inside, do we?'

After that, the afternoon passed quite quickly and for a lot of the time Sammy was able to forget his dismay about Lizzie. He didn't know really why he was so affected, except that she was a member of his family and he knew just how upset Ruth and Jane would be if they heard about it. As for Alec ... Sammy could remember how ill Alec had been when he came home from the war, and how even now he sometimes seemed desperately unhappy for no apparent reason. It would kill him if he knew Lizzie was carrying on with another man.

'You're brooding again,' Maddy said quietly when they were on their way back. 'I can tell by the look on your face. There's no sense in worrying about it, Sammy. There's nothing we can do.'

'I know. I just feel so miserable, thinking of what might happen. They're such a nice family, Maddy, and I like Alec. I like Lizzie too. I don't know what she can be thinking of.'

'You don't know that she's thinking of anything,' Maddy said firmly. 'We might be making a huge great mountain out of a tiny little molehill.'

'I suppose so.' He thought for a minute, staring out over the expanse of grey sea. 'It's just the way she was looking. I've never seen anyone look like that, except in a film.'

Maddy gave him a quick glance. There was a wistful longing in his voice, and she knew that he was wishing he could see that look on her face. For a moment she was on the verge of telling him what he wanted to hear, but something held her back. Not only the warning Ruth had given her, she thought, but the memory of too many other people she had seen look like Lizzie, when she lived with Fenella Forsyth. People who were in love, or thought themselves to be, and whose lives were disrupted, or who disrupted other people's lives because they were too willing to give way to it.

I'm sure I'm in love with Sammy, she thought. But is it just because he was hurt and asked for me to come? And there's Stephen, too. I could so easily be in love with him as well.

'You'll see someone look like that, some day,' she said gently. 'Someone will look at you in just that way, and when she does you'll know she's right for you.'

He turned his head and met her eyes, and she knew that he was on the edge of saying the words he had been prevented from saying earlier. Gripped by sudden panic, she pointed wildly out to sea. 'Look! Isn't that one of the big liners? The *Queen Elizabeth*, or the *Queen Mary*?'

Sammy turned back to look. The moment was gone, and Maddy breathed a sigh of relief. All she had to do now as get through the next hour, until he saw her on to her train, and she would be safe. They would both be safe – for the time being.

She knew that the moment would come again. But by then, perhaps she would be ready for it; by then, she would know what her answer must be.

Sammy went back to Bridge End feeling rather blank and dissatisfied. Nothing had gone quite to plan. Maddy had seemed pleased to see him, and he'd felt more in love with her than ever, but then she'd seemed to withdraw, somehow, to keep him at a little distance when all he wanted was to be close to her.

He'd really thought that today, when he gave her the Valentine card, would be the day to tell her how he felt and to ask her to marry him. Not straight away, of course – it would be two or three years before they could afford to do that – but at least they could be engaged. Then people like that Stephen Napier would know Maddy was promised to him, and there'd be no risk of her being stolen away.

It had all gone wrong when Lizzie and that American had walked into the café. Seeing Lizzie like that, with a man who wasn't her husband, had upset them both. It seemed to jar the world slightly, tipping it a little sideways, so that nothing seemed to be as you'd believed. Sammy had always liked Lizzie. He'd looked up to her, and since he'd come home from the RAF, they'd begun to develop a real friendship. Now, it all seemed sullied, and today hadn't been the right day to propose to Maddy, after all. He'd thought once or twice that the moment had come, but each time something else had happened – like Maddy seeing that ship, which hadn't been one of the *Queens* after all. He'd even wondered for a minute if she'd done it on purpose, to stop him speaking.

That thought made him feel even more depressed. It could only mean that she didn't feel the same way about him. That she just wanted them to be friends, and didn't want to hurt him by refusing. He remembered her reaction to the card. She'd seemed pleased enough, but he thought she'd been a bit embarrassed as well. He wondered if he'd made a fool of himself, after all. He was sure Maddy wouldn't be laughing at him – she was much too nice for that – but it made him feel hot and uncomfortable to think that she knew he'd been going to ask her to marry him and wanted to avoid it to save hurting his feelings.

He sat on the bus back to Bridge End, staring dismally out of the window, and he didn't feel much better by the time he got off and walked down the lane to the cottage.

It was warm and cosy inside. Ruth was knitting a new jumper for Dan, who was in his chair on the other side of the fireplace, reading the *Daily Mirror*. Linnet was sitting on the rag rug in front of the fire, wrapped in the blue dressing-gown Ruth had made her from an old winter coat, and eating an orange. The music of the 'Knightsbridge March' was sounding from the wireless, which meant *In Town Tonight* had just finished. Linnet would be going to bed soon and then they would listen to *Music Hall* and probably the play, unless Dan suggested a game of cards. It was comfortable and homely, and he'd always liked it, but tonight he felt out of sorts and irritated.

I want to have my own home, he thought, to share with Maddy. I know it couldn't be yet, but I want to be able to look forward to it. I thought I'd be doing that tonight – coming in with good news to tell the family. Or maybe just keeping it to myself for a bit. But I thought it would be there, inside me, the feeling that me and Maddy would be together always. And instead of that, it's all been spoiled.

Lizzie had spoiled it.

He didn't really feel like going to see her as usual on the night of his class, but he couldn't think of any reasonable excuse not to, so after finishing work at the forge he set off as usual on his motorbike. Ruth and Dan had agreed that if he could do a day's work he could ride the bike as well, and it wasn't far to Southampton. All the same, he thought there was a funny look on Ruth's face as she said goodbye to him.

'Be careful, won't you?' she said, tucking his scarf into the collar of his jacket. 'And give our love to Lizzie. I thought she was looking a bit peaky last time I saw her.'

'Yes, all right.' He almost said that she'd looked well enough when he'd seen her on Saturday, but he caught back the words just in time. It wouldn't do to get involved in explanations now. Ruth would want to know where he'd seen Lizzie, what they'd said to each other and why he hadn't mentioned it before. And she'd think it very strange that he hadn't actually spoken to Lizzie. He knew that he'd end up telling her about the American, and there'd be goodness knows what sort of trouble after that. She'd be bound to tell Jane. They might even think Alec should know.

Sammy still didn't know what he ought to do – if anything – but it seemed to him that the best thing would be to keep quiet. Even that was probably wrong, but didn't Ruth herself often say 'Least said, soonest mended'? If ever there was a time when it was best to say nothing, this must surely be it.

He pulled up outside Lizzie's door, wishing he could be anywhere else but here. He knew she'd seen him and Maddy in the café. Should he say anything about it, or leave her to bring up the subject? Suppose she did – what could he say? He knocked on the door, his heart in his boots, and waited for someone to answer.

To his dismay, it was Alec. He grinned at Sammy and stood back to let him in.

'Hiya, mate. Lizzie said she thought you'd be round tonight. Night school started again, has it? How's the head?'

Sammy followed him into the narrow passageway, feeling slightly disconcerted. Alec was always pleasant to him when they met, but he'd never been so welcoming as this. He took off his jacket and hung it on the usual hook, then hesitated.

'Is it all right for me to stop? You don't get home early that often – you might not want visitors.'

'No, that's all right, chum. You come on in. Lizzie's frying up some liver and bacon and then we're having bread-and-butter pudding. Lizzie!' he shouted through to the kitchen. 'Your boyfriend's here!'

Sammy, just going through to the living room, cast him a look of horror which was mirrored exactly in the scarlet flush staining Lizzie's cheeks as she came to the other door. For a moment, they stared at each other, and in her expression he saw the guilt that proved all his suspicions were correct. He tore his eyes away and went over to Gillie and Barry, who were sitting in front of the fire, playing tiddlywinks.

'Goodness me, Alec,' Lizzie said with a forced little laugh. 'I wondered whoever you could be talking about. Hello, Sammy, how are you feeling now? Is your head better? And your ribs?'

'Pretty well, thanks,' he said, taking a large green counter and flipping a red one into the pot. 'Auntie Ruth's letting me ride my bike again anyway, so long as I don't go too fast.'

'You must be on the mend, then. She'd know what's best for you, being a nurse. It'll be ready in a minute, if you all like to sit up,' she added, going back to the kitchen.

'Come on, you two,' Alec said, picking up Barry and seating him at the table. 'You can play again afterwards. So what have you been doing with yourself, Sam? Apart from getting knocked out cold by falling trees.'

'Oh, this and that,' he said uneasily. Alec's jollity still seemed forced and he wondered if he'd walked into a row.

'Auntie Ruth's been treating me like an invalid; she's hardly let me out of the house.'

'You had a day out with Maddy on Valentine's Day though, didn't you?' Lizzie said, coming in with plates of liver and bacon with mashed potatoes and cabbage. 'At least, so Mum said,' she added hastily.

'Oh?' Alec raised his eyebrows. 'When did you see your mum, then? I thought Valentine's Day was the day before yesterday.'

'It was. I haven't seen her.' Sammy could see that Lizzie was floundering and he looked down quickly at his plate. 'She told me last week that Sam was going to see her, so I assumed he did. What did you do, ride your bike down to West Lyme?'

Sammy could feel his face flaming again. 'No,' he mumbled, still staring at his plate. 'We met in Southampton.'

'Funny you didn't bump into Lizzie, then,' Alec said pleasantly. 'She was out shopping on Saturday morning, weren't you, Liz?'

'Yes, but I'd hardly have been likely to bump into Maddy and Sam. Southampton's a big place.' She went back to the kitchen and returned with two more plates for the children, then fetched her own. 'Come on, everyone, eat up while it's hot.'

'Nothing wrong with yours, is there, Sam?' Alec enquired. 'You're looking at it as if it's going to bite you. Don't you like liver and bacon?'

'Yes, I do.' He picked up his knife and fork. 'Sorry, I was thinking about something else.'

He could feel Alec's eyes on him all through the meal, and when he caught Lizzie's glance it was worse. He could see she was silently pleading with him not to say anything – but how could he have done so, when she had virtually lied to Alec already? So now she's making me a liar too, he thought miserably. And it's not fair. It's not fair on me, or on Alec.

'So what else did you do?' Alec persisted, and Sammy was

thankful to be able to give a truthful account of their trip to Cowes.

'We're going again when the weather's better. We might go from Lymington as well, and see what Yarmouth is like. We could even take the bike over and have a ride round.'

'I went to the island a couple of times before the war,' Lizzie said reminiscently. 'Mum and Dad took us over for a treat. We hired a rowing-boat and went on the river.' She laughed. 'Dad caught a crab and fell over on his back.'

'Did you eat it?' Barry asked, and she shook her head.

'No, catching a crab is when you miss the water with your oar. We ought to take the kiddies over sometime, Alec. It would be a nice thing to do in the summer.'

He nodded, but his good humour seemed to have diminished and he didn't speak again for the remainder of the meal. Lizzie and Sammy kept up a rather stilted conversation, mostly directed at or through the two children ('Eat up *all* your liver, Barry.' ... 'I can see that piece of cabbage you're trying to hide under your potato, Gillie') until at last she served out the bread-and-butter pudding and Sammy was able to say truthfully, 'That was good, Lizzie. Thanks. I ought to go soon, though, or I'll be late for my class.'

'That's all right,' Alec said, coming to life again. 'You go off and learn how to be an electrician or whatever it is you're going to do. It's posher than that, isn't it? Radar or something?'

Sammy glanced at him doubtfully, wondering what was meant by the edge to Alec's voice, but before he could say anything Lizzie replied quickly.

'It's been nice to see you, Sam, and I'm glad you're better. It was an awful shock for everyone when you had that accident. Now, you be careful on that bike of yours – we don't want any more upsets like that.'

'No, we don't,' Alec said, with a pleasant smile, but there was still an undertone to his voice that Sammy didn't like.

He put on his motorcycling gear and helmet again and waved goodbye to the children.

'I want to ride a motorbike when I grow up,' Barry said. 'Gillie likes horses, but I don't. I like motorbikes.'

'I'll take you for a ride one day, when you're bigger,' Sammy said, glad to be escaping from the uncomfortable atmosphere. 'When your mum and dad say I can.'

He managed to get out at last, and Lizzie waved him off. When she went back indoors, her face and pale and determined.

'And just what was all that about?' she demanded, facing her husband. 'Poor Sammy didn't know where to put himself. You were downright rude to him.'

'Me – rude?' Alec echoed. 'I thought I was being very nice to him, considering.'

'Considering what?' she asked in amazement, and he gave her a caustic look.

'Considering that you've been carrying on with him for the past three months. Don't try to deny it, Lizzie – I'm not a complete idiot. All those times he's been coming here, getting his feet under the table, all innocent and above board – oh yes, you think you've been very clever, don't you? I've known all about it, so I wouldn't suspect a thing. But what about the other times, eh? Those romantic walks on the common – the cosy little meetings in teashops. And those three days when you took the children to stay with your mother.' She hadn't heard such bitterness in his voice since those early days when he had first found out about Gillie. 'You've even been to a hotel with him. You're nothing but a slut.'

Lizzie stared at him, appalled, and knew that the moment of truth had come at last. She couldn't let him go on thinking she had betrayed him with Sammy – it would split the family in two. It was going to be bad enough as it was. But she still had to make one last effort to save herself and Floyd.

'You're wrong,' she said. 'I haven't been carrying on at all. I don't know who's been telling you these lies, but—'

'Well, I can tell you that,' he said. 'Mrs Smith along the street for a start. She's seen him here, at times when he wasn't supposed to be. And she saw you getting into a car as well and going off with him, when the children were away. She told me a whole lot more too, when I happened to run into her the other day.'

'*Happened* to run into her?' Lizzie repeated scornfully. 'I bet she made sure you ran into her. She's nothing but a nosy old woman and you ought to have told her to mind her own business.'

'I would have done,' he said, 'if it hadn't been mine as well.'

They stared at each other and then Lizzie turned away.

'We can't argue like this in front of the children,' she said in a shaking voice. They were sitting on the rug, their game forgotten, staring up with frightened eyes.

'It's all right. Mummy and Daddy are just getting a bit cross, that's all,' she told them. 'It's nothing to worry about. And look at the time! You ought both to be in bed. Come on now, put your tiddlywinks away.'

Reluctantly, they did so, and she washed them and helped them change into their pyjamas. When they were ready at last, she brought them back into the living room where Alec was gazing unseeingly at the newspaper.

'Say goodnight to Daddy,' she said, and Barry went forward for his kiss. Gillie, however, hung back.

'It wasn't Sammy who came here when Mrs Smith saw him,' she said. 'It was the Cowboy Man. It was my other daddy. Wasn't it, Mum?'

Alec raised his head and stared at his daughter. He lifted his eyes and met Lizzie's, and understanding dawned at last.

'So it was him,' he said in a dry, quiet voice. 'It was that bloody Yank. You told me he'd gone back where he came from – and I believed you.'

Chapter Twenty-Eight

'It's true, isn't it,' Alec said tonelessly.

Lizzie stared at him and knew that she couldn't deny it. She could see in his eyes that he could read the truth in her face. As she turned away, feeling the tears burn her cheeks, Alec took a quick step towards her and gripped her chin in one hand, twisting her head back so that she was forced to meet his angry gaze.

'It's true,' he repeated. '*Isn't it?* Don't lie to me, Lizzie. Not now. All that's over – all the lies and excuses and cheating.' His fingers were bruising her chin. 'All these weeks, you've been sneaking off to meet him on the sly, even though this time you're carrying *my* baby. Does that make you feel good, Lizzie – making love with one man while you're carrying another man's kid? You did it to me, remember, when I came home from Germany, and now—'

'No!' she cried. 'I didn't! You knew about Floyd and the baby by the time you—' She could almost feel the heat of his rage, and faltered into silence. Alec's body went rigid, and for a moment she feared he would strike her.

'Oh yes,' he said at last in a slow, cold tone. 'Rub that in. I couldn't make love to you when I came home, could I? So you couldn't pretend the baby was mine. You had to tell the truth. But that's not what you meant to do this time, is it? You just meant to have your fling with him, without me knowing a thing about it, until he went back to America. Well? Isn't that true?'

'No! I mean – I don't know. I ...' Again, she could find no words to continue. She rubbed her eyes with the back of one wrist and looked at him pleadingly. 'Alec, let go. You're hurting me.'

'And you haven't hurt me, I suppose!' But he dropped his hand away from her face, still staring at her as he took in her words. 'And how can you say "no"? You *have* been carrying on with him, haven't you?'

'If that's what you like to call it,' she whispered. The joy and tenderness of her meetings with Floyd seemed soiled by Alec's words. And she knew that this was how it would appear to everyone – to her mother, to Ruth, to Sammy. They would all think she had been 'carrying on'.

In that moment, it was how it seemed to her, too.

'Well, then? Did you mean to go on meeting him until he went back to America, or didn't you?' Once again, she knew that he could read her eyes before she had a chance to speak, and his expression changed. 'My God,' he said in a low voice, 'you weren't thinking of going away with him? Not to America?'

'Alec, don't look like that,' she cried. 'I don't *know*! I don't know what to do! You don't understand what it's been like for me, all these weeks. I've been going through torment—'

'Am I supposed to be feel sorry for you?' he cut in. 'You tell me you're thinking of leaving me for some over-sexed GI and I'm supposed to *understand*? What the hell sort of cloud cuckoo land are you living in, Lizzie? You're my wife. You've had my children!' He stopped suddenly. 'You weren't thinking of taking them as well? Not Gillie, and Barry, and ...' His glance fell to her stomach and he drew in a ragged breath and said harshly, 'You can't do that. You can't take my children away from me. I won't let you.'

'Gillie is Floyd's child,' she whispered, and his eyes narrowed.

'Oh, yes? Let him prove it, then! She was born in our

265

marriage, Lizzie, and she's got my name on her birth certificate. *I'm* the one who's brought her up and supported her and been a father to her. He has no claim on her at all. And there's nobody in the land who can say a word differently.'

'There are blood tests.'

'They still can't prove it. There's no way of doing it, Lizzie, and you know it. It's your word against mine. You'll never be allowed to take Gillie out of the country, nor Barry. I won't stand by and see you take away everything I have – everything that makes life worth living.'

His voice shook on the last words and Lizzie gazed helplessly at him. She wanted to reach out and take him in her arms, to comfort him, but she knew that he would reject her. A great weight of misery descended over her and she shook her head blindly.

'Oh, Alec,' she whispered. 'How did we ever come to this?'

'You tell me,' he said bitterly. 'You're the one who's been carrying on behind my back. I'm just the poor idiot who trusted you and believed in you.'

'Alec!'

'Well, isn't it true?' he demanded. 'I *did* trust you. I *did* believe in you. And what for? You're nothing but a cheating, lying, shallow little bitch – and I wish I'd never married you. I wish I'd never even met you.'

When Lizzie burst into tears, he sneered, 'And now you'll turn on the waterworks and expect me to feel sorry for you. Well, I don't. I've got enough to do, feeling sorry for myself.'

'Alec – please . . .'

'Please what?' he asked, turning back. 'Please forgive you for wrecking my life? Please help you to pack so that you can go away with your Yankee boyfriend, taking my children with you? Perhaps you'd even like me to pay your fare. A nice luxury cabin on the *Queen Elizabeth*, would that do you?'

'Alec, there's no need to be like that.'

'Oh no? I think there's every need,' he shouted, suddenly raising his voice so that she jumped in alarm and backed away from him. 'You've broken every vow you've ever made, you've made a fool of me for the second time, and if you weren't already carrying my baby, you'd probably be carrying his. Just tell me what I'm expected to "be like" about it all, woman!'

Lizzie pulled out her handkerchief and wiped her eyes. Still shuddering with sobs, she said, 'Alec, it's no good going on like this. We've got to think about it – decide what to do.'

'Have we? I thought you'd already decided. You're going off to America, aren't you? I didn't realise I was going to be allowed any say in it. I thought I'd just come home from work one day and find a note on the table and all three of you gone.'

'I wouldn't have done that.'

'Wouldn't you?' He stared at her, his eyes as cold and hard as if she were an unwelcome stranger. 'I don't know what you'd do or not do any more, Lizzie. I don't feel I know you any more. All I know is, you're not the woman I thought you were. You're not the Lizzie I loved and married. Maybe you never were.'

'It's not true, Alec. I still love you – I always did.'

'*You still love me?* Oh, come off it, Lizzie! How can you stand there and say that, when you've been having an affair with this bloke, when you're planning to go off with him? Funny sort of love that is. So funny, I'm laughing, see?' He glowered at her with no vestige of humour. 'Laughing all over my face.'

'I know it sounds stupid,' Lizzie said miserably. 'But it *is* true. I do love you. If I didn't, I suppose I'd have left long ago. As it is, I've been going through torment.'

'Yes,' he said, sounding bored, 'you've already told me that.'

'Well, I have! I never meant it to happen, you know. I told him to go away – I told him not to come here any more.'

'*Any more?*' Alec interrupted. 'You mean you were carrying on in my own house – with my own children here?'

'No! He came once, that's all. Well, he came twice but I only let him in once. That first time was soon after we – I – got his letter. And we didn't do anything. I didn't want him here; I didn't want to see him again. I told him that – I told him to go away.'

'Obviously, he didn't think you meant it,' Alec said cuttingly. 'And obviously, you didn't.'

'I did. But he went on and on about how Gillie was his daughter and he wanted to see her, and I said I'd meet him somewhere to talk about it. And I did, the next day, in the teashop – '

'Oh, very cosy. Hot buttered toast and dainty little cakes, I suppose?'

' – but I walked out and left him there. That's why he came here again, but I wouldn't let him in that time. And I had to meet him again, or – or he'd have made a fuss and everyone would have heard him. and I didn't want the children to be upset.'

Alec regarded her stonily. 'So you had to meet him again. You didn't think of telling me, I suppose? You didn't think of asking me to see the bastard off? Because I would have done, and you know it.'

Lizzie was silent. To her surprise, she realised that she had indeed never thought of asking Alec's help in sending Floyd away.

'I thought you'd be angry,' she said lamely, and he snorted.

'Damned right, I would. I'd have been bloody furious. I'd have knocked him all the way back to America, that's what I'd have done. Strikes me that's just what you didn't want, Lizzie. You didn't want me seeing him off.'

'I thought you'd be angry with *me*,' she said. 'And I did mean to tell you, that first week, but you were working so hard, doing all that overtime, and you were so tired, and by the time I got the chance ... well, everything had moved on, and it didn't seem a good idea.'

'No, because by then you were having your affair,' he said. 'Secret meetings, in his hotel, I suppose. Cosy afternoons having tea. *In bed*.' His lip curled and then a fresh thought struck him. 'And where were the kids all this time? You didn't take them with you, I hope.'

'Of course I didn't!' She realised what she'd said as soon as she saw his eyebrows go up. 'I mean, it wasn't like that at all – not at first, anyway. I just went to – to talk to him. To try to convince him that I wouldn't leave you. And I left the children with June. I never let them see him again. But – and I honestly don't know how it happened – things changed. I – didn't seem able to help myself.' She paused, her voice fading. 'I'm sorry,' she whispered. 'Truly sorry.'

'So you did go to his hotel,' Alec said in the same dead tone he'd used earlier. 'You left the children with someone else and went to meet him at his hotel, and you went to bed with him. And you were planning to leave me and go away with him. Weren't you?' Lizzie was silent and he raised his voice again. 'Well? *Weren't* you?'

'I don't know,' she whispered. 'I hadn't planned anything. I didn't know what to do.'

'You shouldn't even have been wondering,' he told her. 'You knew from the start what you were doing, and you shouldn't have let any of it happen.'

Lizzie said nothing. She could find no answer to his words; she knew they were true. She should have told Floyd to go away, and she should have confided in Alec, no matter how tired or overworked he was. She should have left it to him to deal with Floyd.

'But Gillie *is* his daughter,' she said at last. 'He may never be able to prove it, but we all three know it's true. And how

269

could I tell you, knowing how upset you'd been before? I was afraid you might be ill again.'

'Oh, don't come that one!' he exclaimed scornfully. 'You didn't mind the thought of me being ill again when you started your shoddy little romance. What the hell did you think it would do to me if I found out? What the hell do you think it's doing to me now?'

'I don't know,' she said miserably. 'I don't know what it's doing. I only know I'm sorry. So sorry.'

Alec stared at her. 'Yeah. Sorry. Well, sorry's not enough, is it? And since you don't seem to have any idea what you've done, I'll tell you, shall I? It makes me feel like walking out of here and under a bus, that's what. It makes me feel like jumping off a high bridge. Because what I said just now is true – you've wrecked my life. If you go away and take the kids, there's nothing left for me and I might as well be dead.'

'Alec!' Lizzie cried, real fear in her voice, and she ran to him and caught his arm.

He shook her off as if she were an insect. 'Leave me alone. It makes my skin crawl to feel you touch me, knowing what you've been doing with *him*.' His face twisted. 'I don't even want to stay in the same house as you. I'm going out.'

He grabbed his overcoat from the hook and jerked open the door. Lizzie ran after him along the narrow passage. Once again, she caught at his arm but he pulled open the front door and stepped out into the cold wind. 'Where are you going?' she cried. 'When will you be back?'

'I don't know where I'm going,' he snarled. 'And I don't know when I'll be back. Never, probably.' And then he struck her arm and strode off along the street.

Lizzie stared after him, knowing that it would be useless to follow. Even when he turned the corner and disappeared from her sight, she remained there, begging him silently to come back. But at last she pulled her cardigan around her shivering body and went slowly back indoors.

She got no further than the living room before, leaning against the door-jamb for support, she collapsed in a storm of bitter weeping.

Alec stalked through Southampton like a heron, his coat flapping about his legs. He hardly saw the people he passed and had little idea of where he was going. He only knew that if he had stayed in the house a moment longer, the fury inside him would have erupted into violence.

How could he and Lizzie go on after this? He would never be able to forget this double betrayal, and certainly he'd never be able to forgive her. Their marriage could never be the same again.

He couldn't believe how much this was hurting him. It was as if he had been hurled back into the misery and depression he'd felt after the war, when he'd come home almost broken by his experiences in the POW camp, to find that his wife was pregnant by another man. He hadn't found out straight away, of course – he wasn't sure she'd even known about it herself then. But because he was unable to make love to her for several months, she had had no chance of hiding her condition or passing the baby off as his. She might never have known for sure herself.

But they did know. She'd been forced to confess and it had almost torn them apart. It had almost torn Alec himself to pieces, but eventually he had come to terms with the situation and, thinking that this might be the only child he'd ever have, he had agreed to take Gillie as his own daughter.

And now this American bastard had come swanning back into their lives, expecting to take that daughter away – *Alec's* daughter. And not only his daughter, but his wife as well. He wanted Lizzie. And if Lizzie went, taking Gillie with her, wasn't she going to want to take Barry as well? And the new baby – not even born yet?

His whole body ached with anger and grief. Yes, he thought

271

– grief. Grief for the wife he had loved and believed loved him, and for the death of that love; grief for the child he'd always treated as his own; grief for the son and the new baby who really were his own, and might even so be ripped away from him.

Alec stopped. He was on Cobden Bridge, the arched bridge that spaned the River Itchen, one of Southampton's two main rivers. He leaned against the wall and stared down at the muddy waters. The tide was coming in, flowing over the thick, deep mud and floating the boats that had been lying at crazy angles at their moorings. Some of those, he thought, must have been at Dunkirk. Hundreds of boats had gone from along the South Coast, to bring back the besieged Army. He had been at sea himself then, in the Merchant Navy.

He would never go back to sea. The horror of being sunk by enemy fire, the hours spent in cold, deep water, the years in POW camp, had changed him for ever. He had come home to nightmares and a deep depression. Lizzie – and Gillie, too – had brought him out of it at last, and he'd managed to keep the darkness at bay ever since. But now, he could feel it encroaching upon him like a black, threatening cloud, and he was suddenly terribly afraid that it would overwhelm him.

I can't go through that again, he thought, staring at the river swirling beneath. I can't ...

Chapter Twenty-Nine

Sam and Maddy were walking in the forest, near Bridge End. In the weeks since the great storm, the weather had turned fine and dry again, and the first primroses were beginning to show their creamy yellow faces. Leaves were already beginning to break through their buds on the horse-chestnut trees, and the birds were busy with nest-building. Some were probably already sitting on eggs.

'Isn't it lovely,' Maddy said with a sigh. 'After all that terrible flooding, it's so good to think that spring is coming at last, and things are drying out. I feel dreadfully sorry for all those poor people in East Anglia and the Netherlands.'

'I know. Dad says it's the worst storm anyone can remember.' They strolled on, hand in hand, and when they came to a clearing with a fallen log in the middle, he said, 'Let's sit down for a bit.'

'All right.' Maddy inspected the log and brushed it with her hand, then sat down. Sammy sat beside her and slipped his arm round her shoulders. She turned her face to his and kissed him.

'Oh, Maddy,' he said. 'I love you so much.'

'Sam—'

'I know you don't want me to say it,' he said quickly, 'but I can't help it. It's in my mind all the time and there's nobody I can talk to about it – only Lizzie, and she's got enough to think about at the moment.'

'With the new baby coming, you mean? It can't be easy in

that tiny house, with two children already – although we all seemed to manage well enough in April Grove. She's all right, though, isn't she?'

'I think so.' He frowned. 'I mean, she seems OK as far as the baby goes – not that she'd tell me if there were any problems, I suppose. But she seems a bit strange, somehow – as if she's not quite there, you know. As if there's something on her mind all the time.'

'Well, I expect that's the baby. And they're looking for a new house, aren't they? It all takes time and energy.'

'Yes, I suppose that's it.' But he didn't feel convinced. Lizzie had always seemed able to cope with everything and remain her bright, happy self. Now, it was as if that brightness had been switched off and she was trying to find it again. Her smile looked forced these days and her voice had lost its lilt.

'She's been really good to you, hasn't she,' Maddy observed after a minute or two, and he nodded.

'Lizzie's always been like a big sister to me, ever since I first went to live with Auntie Ruth. And it's been really nice to be able to go and see her a couple of times a week and have tea with her and the kids. Alec works long hours, and she's glad of the company. And I can talk to her. I can talk to her about you.'

'It's a pity you can't talk to Mrs Hodge about everything,' Maddy said thoughtfully. 'You've always got on so well with her up to now.'

'I know.' Ruth and Dan's objection to his friendship with Maddy was still upsetting him. He knew they had nothing against Maddy herself – how could they? – but they just thought that, with her background of travel and sophistication with Fenella Forsyth, she was out of his class. They thought that he was bound to get hurt.

'Never mind,' she said, snuggling against him. 'They'll get used to the idea.'

Sam turned his head and looked down at her. 'Used to what idea?'

'Why, the idea of you and me, of course. What else d'you think I mean?'

He hardly dared believe his ears. 'You and me? You mean – you've decided? You'll be engaged to me?'

'A lot more than that, I hope, eventually,' she laughed. 'Come on, Sammy, I know you've asked me before, but I'd quite like you to do it again – so that I can give you a proper answer.' She glanced around the quiet clearing, with the soft grass under their feet and the sunlight falling in dappled pools beneath the trees. 'And this is quite a romantic place for it, don't you think?'

'Yes!' he said. 'Oh, yes!' He slid off the log and knelt on one knee before her. The excitement that had surged up within him ebbed away as he realised that this was going to be one of the most important moments of his life. Solemnly, he took both her hands in his and looked into her face.

'Maddy,' he said, his voice only slightly trembling, 'I love you very, very much. Will you – please – marry me? Will you be my wife?'

The laughter was no longer uppermost in Maddy's face as she gazed down at him. Her eyes were huge, almost black, and there was a slight flush on her cheeks. The tip of her tongue came out and licked her lips, and then her smile broke out once more.

'Yes,' she said. 'Oh yes, Sammy, please!' And she flung her arms around his neck and hugged him tightly against her.

The rest of the afternoon was taken up with making plans. The log in the clearing seemed as good a place as any in which to do this, so they stayed there until the sun moved round and no longer spread the little glade with flickering light. Then they walked slowly back along the forest path towards the motorcycle, which they'd left at the edge of the trees.

'We'll go and buy the ring next Saturday,' Sam said. 'I want you to choose something you really like. Shall I come to West

Lyme or will you come to Bridge End again? We could go to Southampton.'

'I really ought to go to Burracombe next week,' Maddy said regretfully. 'I haven't seen Stella for ages, and I promised I would. You could come with me, if you like.'

'And *I've* promised to work at the forge on Saturday,' he said, shaking his head. 'So that's no good. It'll have to be the week after, then. And I shan't see you at all next week. I shan't see you for another fortnight.' He looked so woebegone that Maddy couldn't help laughing.

'It's not for ever! And I'll come to Bridge End the next weekend, I promise. We can go and buy the ring in Southampton, and perhaps Ruth and Dan will realise we're serious and be happy for us. You'd better tell them beforehand, though, to prepare them. In fact, we could tell them today, together.'

'You'd better tell Stella, too,' he said. 'She might not be too pleased. I expect she thinks you'll marry Stephen Napier.'

'And so I might,' she said solemnly, 'If you weren't here.'

Sammy gave her a startled glance and she chuckled again. 'I like Stephen. I'm really fond of him. But it's you I love, Sam. It's your ring I'm going to wear.'

They stopped just inside the woods and Sammy took her in his arms again. He looked down seriously into her bright face.

'I really do love you, Maddy. I might not ever be very rich, but I'll do all I can to make you happy. I want to spend my whole life with you.'

'And I love you too, Sammy,' she said quietly. 'I always will.'

Ruth and Dan were not surprised by the news. As soon as Sam and Maddy came through the door, their cheeks flushed from the cold wind, Ruth could see what had happened. She bided her time, however, and said nothing, although when

Dan came into the scullery to wash his hands after working in the garden, she told him privately what she suspected.

'Those two are engaged. I'd stake my life on it.'

'What?' He turned a startled face towards her. 'Are you sure?'

'As sure as I can be without hearing it out of their own mouths. You've only got to look at them. I must say, I was hoping they'd wait a bit longer and realise the difference between them – I thought Maddy was showing a bit of sense over it – but I reckon he's asked her and she's said yes.'

'She's a nice girl,' Dan said. 'She'll make him a good wife. And Sam's a decent young chap.'

'Yes – and young's the word,' Ruth said. 'That's my objection. He's barely twenty-one. That's far too young for a man to commit himself for life.'

'Well, there's not much we can do about it,' Dan said, drying his hands on the towel that hung behind the back door. 'Anyway, it's not as if they'll be in a hurry to get married. They'll have to save up a bit before that, and Sam's got to finish his night school and get himself a job. I reckon it'll be a good two years at the least, and a lot can happen in that time.'

They went back into the living room, where Sammy was mending the fire and Maddy was on the small sofa, helping Linnet with some colouring. It was a cosy family scene and Ruth felt her heart warm as she looked at the little group. She was fond of Maddy, she had to admit that, and had liked her from a child – even when she'd encouraged Sammy into all kinds of scrapes. She hadn't changed much, after all, despite her life with the famous actress Fenella Forsyth. She might have lived in grand hotels and travelled abroad and met all kinds of famous people, but at heart she was still the little girl from April Grove who had come to Bridge End as a lost and motherless evacuee. That was something she and Sammy had in common, Ruth realised suddenly – both had lost their mother at the age of eight. Maybe that was part of the bond between them.

'You're staying for tea, aren't you, Maddy?' she asked. 'We're not having much, just egg and chips and some baked beans. It's Sammy's favourite meal.'

'I know. I like it, too. Yes, please, Mrs Hodges, I'd like to stay, but I have to catch the seven-fifteen bus back to Southampton, to get my train.'

'I told you, I'll take you on the bike,' Sammy said. 'I'm not letting you go on the bus on your own.'

'Why, what d'you think's going to happen to me?' she asked with a grin. Then she looked at Ruth and Dan and said, a little shyly, 'We've got something to tell you.'

'Oh yes?' Ruth asked casually, although she knew very well what was coming. She busied herself with laying the table, removing the red chenille cloth that covered it between meals and spreading a clean white one in its place.

'It's quite important, actually,' Sammy said, and she turned and looked at him. He was on the sofa now, beside Maddy. 'It might be a good idea if you sat down.'

'I hope it's not bad news,' Ruth said, taking her armchair by the fire. Dan sat beside her on an upright kitchen chair and they looked at the two expectantly. Linnet glanced up from her colouring-book at their serious faces, and Sammy knew he had to tell them quickly, or she would be frightened.

'Maddy and me are getting engaged,' he said. 'I asked her weeks ago and she said no, not yet, but this afternoon we decided we wanted to do it now. We're getting the ring the weekend after next. Maddy's got to go to Devon to see Stella next week.'

'Well!' Ruth said, as if it had come as a complete surprise, and in a way, she felt as if it had. After all, she could have been wrong ... 'Well, this is something to think about and no mistake.' She looked at Maddy. 'Are you sure about this, love?

You're both very young. And you only met each other a few weeks ago, to all intents and purposes.'

'We're old enough to know we love each other,' Maddy said. 'And we did know each other well as children. It's all right, Mrs Hodges, we're not rushing to get married. We just want to be engaged – so that everyone knows.' She hugged Sammy's arm against her side.

'Well!' Ruth said again, feeling rather helpless. She looked at Dan. 'Haven't you got anything to say about this?'

'I reckon you've said it,' he said. 'They're young now, right enough, but if they can wait two or three years they'll be of a reasonable age. They've got plenty of time to find out if they're making a mistake, and an engagement can be broken and no harm done to no one – not like a marriage.' He gave the pair a direct look from beneath his shaggy brows. 'All I want to say is, don't be too disappointed if it don't go right for you. There's many a slip 'twixt cup and lip, as they say. And good luck to you both – Sam's a fine young chap, and you're as sweet a girl as ever I met, Maddy – saving for my Ruthie here, that is!'

They all laughed and Linnet said, 'Are Sammy and Maddy getting married?'

'Yes!' the newly engaged couple said together, and Ruth added, 'We hope so. But it won't be for quite a while, so don't start getting excited.'

'Will I be bridesmaid? Will there be a lot to eat and drink, like at Rose Budd's wedding?'

'I expect there will,' Maddy said, laughing. 'And you'll certainly be a bridesmaid. I wouldn't have anyone else, except for my sister. But she might be married herself by then, so she'd have to be matron-of-honour.'

'You could have Gillie as well,' Linnet observed, without noticing the sudden silence that fell at her words. 'Then there'd be two little ones and one big one.'

'Yes,' Ruth said absently, and looked again at Sammy.

'You'll be going to see Lizzie again next week, I expect. Are you going to tell her then or wait until you've got the ring?'

'I shan't see her this week,' he said. 'There's no night school – they're doing up the rooms that got damaged in the storms. We'll go and see her and Alec together, next Saturday, as soon as we've got the ring. And then we'll come home and show you.'

'And we'll have a bit of a party,' Dan declared. 'We'll ask your Jane and George down, and have a real old knees-up.'

Suddenly, the atmosphere lightened and they all began to talk and laugh at once. Dan got out the bottle of sherry for a celebration drink and Ruth added some tinned ham to the eggs, chips and beans. Soon after seven, Sammy and Maddy put on their outdoor clothes again and roared away into the darkness on their way back to Southampton.

'Well, that's that,' Dan said, closing the front door. 'I reckon they'll be all right, don't you? If they're half as happy as we are, they will be, anyway.'

'I hope so,' she said. 'And now that it's in the open, I'm not really worried about them at all. It's Lizzie I'm worried about – her and Alex. There's something very wrong there, Dan, and God only knows how it will all end.'

Chapter Thirty

The week passed uncomfortably for Lizzie and Alec. He had returned late after his long walk through Southampton, but Lizzie had not gone to bed. She had kept herself busy by embarking on a thorough house-clean, starting as soon as the children had gone to bed. She had washed down the walls in the outside lavatory, scrubbed the scullery floor and brushed the square of carpet in the back room to within an inch of its life. She had polished the linoleum round the edge of the carpet until it was like a mirror, and had dusted all the ornaments and pictures, as well as the picture rail. All the chairs had had a damp cloth wiped round their legs, and she'd washed the skirting boards and paintwork with soda and warm water. The house was tidy and smelled clean, yet she felt no pleasure in it. Her mind was filled with pictures of what Alec might be doing, and every now and then they overwhelmed her and she stopped whatever she was doing and collapsed again, weeping her heart out with fear and regret.

When she heard his key in the door, she heaved an enormous sigh of relief and then, as he came into the room, she burst into tears again and ran to him, flinging her arms around his unresponsive body and pressing her face against his chest. The fabric of his coat was cold and rough against her skin, but at that moment it felt like silk.

'Oh, Alec,' she wept, 'I'm so glad to see you. I've been thinking such terrible things.'

'No more terrible than the things I've been thinking,' he

replied in a grim voice, unpicking her hands from his coat and pushing her away. 'Let go, Lizzie. I'm cold and tired and I want a hot drink.'

'I'll make you some cocoa.' Still trembling, she moved away and went through to the kitchen. The tears were still rolling down her cheeks, and every few seconds her body was shaken by a long, shuddering sob. After she had filled the kettle, she stood waiting for it to boil with one hand on her belly, where the baby was making small fluttering movements. What sort of a family am I bringing you into? she asked it silently. What sort of a life will we be living when you arrive?

She made the cocoa and carried the cups into the back room, where Alec was slumped in his armchair, his head back and his eyes closed. He looked white and exhausted, and there was rain on his face and hair. Lizzie put the cup down beside him.

'I didn't realise it had started raining.'

'There's a lot of things you didn't realise,' he said without opening his eyes.

Her heart sank. 'Alec, we have to talk about this.'

'I thought we'd said all there is to say. Anyway, I'm fed up with talking about it. I'm fed up with *thinking* about it. Do you realise, it's going round and round in my head the whole time – I can't think about anything else. And I never get any further with it. I come up against a brick wall, whichever way I turn. I'm worn out with it. I just want to go to sleep and wake up and find it never happened, any of it.'

'What do you mean?' Lizzie asked in a small voice. 'Me – Gillie – Barry? Do you really wish none of that had ever happened?'

He opened his eyes suddenly and looked straight into hers, and she cringed at the bitterness she saw.

'Yes,' he said. 'I wish none of it had ever happened. I might have met some decent girl then, and married her, and had kids in the proper way.'

Lizzie shrank back until she was on the edge of her own

armchair, on the other side of the fireplace. She could find no answer. Eventually, in a shaking voice, she whispered. 'Your cocoa's there. Don't let it go cold.'

'Like everything else has gone cold?' he asked, and lifted his cup. He looked into it for a moment then, with a sudden jerk of his arm, he flung it at her. Lizzie cried out and ducked, and it shattered against the wall behind her, spattering cocoa everywhere. She felt the heat of the drops on her skin and through the back of her blouse, and gasped with shock. For a moment or two she felt real fear, wondering if Alec was capable of true violence. He had never been the same since he'd returned from POW camp. In those early days, his gentleness and ability to laugh seemed to have deserted him. She had feared his anger when he had found out about Gillie, but she had never really feared that he would do violence. Now, she was not so sure.

I've pushed him too far, she thought miserably. If he does anything now, to me or the children or himself, it will be all my fault. All of it *is* my fault.

'Alec,' she said, striving to keep her voice steady. 'You must stop this. You must try to understand—'

'Oh, I *must*, must I?' he broke in. 'You're pretty fond of telling me that, aren't you? Well, I think it's time *you* started to think about what *you* must or mustn't do. Do you want me to give you a list?'

'No,' she said tiredly. 'No, you don't have to do that. Look, I know how you must feel ...'

'Must again! And how would you know, anyway? You've never been in the position I'm in now, let down and betrayed, told you're going to lose your whole family.'

'I've never told you that.'

'You have – as good as. Anyway, it's what's going to happen, isn't it? You're going to leave me and go to America, taking my kids with you. At least, that's what you think you're going to do.'

283

'I've told you – I haven't decided to do that. I haven't decided anything.'

'You haven't decided not to do it either,' he said. 'Well, let me help you decide, Lizzie. Let me tell you what I think will happen. You say we've got to talk, so let's start talking.' He paused and she stared at him, her eyes huge, still not sure that he wouldn't suddenly lunge at her. 'This is what's going to happen if you leave me. For a start, you won't take the kids. Not Gillie, not Barry, not even the little one. You won't go to America – or anywhere else – while you're carrying my baby. I won't allow it. I'll go to court if necessary, and they'll stop you. And after that, I'll divorce you.'

Lizzie drew in her breath. 'Divorce?' she whispered. 'But – nobody in our family has ever been divorced.'

'There's a first time for everything,' he said. 'And you know what will happen then, don't you? I'll say that you're unfit to be a mother and the court will agree. They'll take the kids away from you. They'll be mine for good – Gillie included – and you'll never be allowed to see them again.'

'You wouldn't do that,' she breathed, sick now with fear of something worse than violence.

'Wouldn't I? D'you want to try me?' His narrowed eyes challenged her. 'And don't forget the newspapers, Lizzie. They'll have a field day with this. A nice, juicy scandalous divorce case involving an American. Remember that phrase "over-paid, over-sexed, and over here" that people used to say about the Yanks during the war? I reckon that's going to be brought out again. Wouldn't be surprised if it doesn't appear in one or two headlines.'

'Alec, you can't do that. It would kill my mother. And Dad too. And Auntie Ruth, and – and your parents as well. None of us would be able to hold up our heads again.'

'And it would be all your doing, Lizzie,' he said. 'Not mine. Yours.'

There was a long silence. The clock on the mantelpiece,

a wedding present from Jane and George, ticked loudly and then struck twelve. Lizzie looked at it without registering the time.

'You can't take my children away,' she said at last, her lips trembling so much that she could scarcely get the words out. 'You can't take them away from their mother.'

'I think I can,' he said. 'And do you really want to risk it?'

'Who would look after them? You have to go to work.'

'I'm sure the family would rally round. My mother. Yours. Your Auntie Ruth.' His eyes narrowed again. 'You don't think they're going to be on *your* side, do you? Not when they find out what you've been doing these past few weeks. Not when they find out you're planning to take the children across to the other side of the world.'

'But I'm not!' she cried. 'I don't *want* to do that. Oh, I don't know *what* I want any more.' She covered her face with both hands and rocked to and fro, her sobs rising with hysteria. 'Alec, please – let's just talk about this.'

'I thought that's what we were doing. Only you don't seem to like what I say. You only want to talk when it's all going your way, don't you? When you can decide what you want, and everyone else will agree with you. But it's not going to be like that, Lizzie. If we're going to talk, you've got to listen to *me*, and think about what *I* want. And what the children want.'

'Children want to be with their mother.'

'Not when the mother's unfit to have them.'

'I'm not unfit!' she cried, stabbed to the heart. 'I've never been a bad mother. I've always looked after them properly, made sure they were fed and clean, and loved them.'

'And left them with other people while you went off canoodling with your fancy man.'

Lizzie fell silent under his sardonic eye. Even in the midst of her distress, she had to admit that this was how it would be seen. And June, who had always been so ready to look after Gillie and Barry, might not be so ready to help once she knew the truth. She might not even want to be Lizzie's friend any more.

'What have I done?' she whispered, seeing a different life stretch before her – a life of isolation and friendlessness, with no children and no family to turn to, instead of the rosy picture Floyd had painted. 'Oh, Alec, what have I done?'

He looked at her and the anger receded a little from his eyes, leaving only a huge well of misery. His face twisted a little and he said, 'I think you've ruined everything – our whole lives, everything we've worked for and planned. It's all gone.' His shoulders slumped, he hung his hands between his knees and drooped his head. 'I can't talk about it any more tonight. I've had enough. Go to bed, Lizzie. Go to bed and leave me on my own.'

She stared at him. 'But – what are you going to do? Aren't you coming to bed as well?'

'And sleep beside *you*?' he asked. 'No, I don't think I want to do that. I'll doss down here. I'll have to be getting up in a few hours anyway, for work. They want us to do overtime again this weekend so I won't be home for dinner. You can have the day to yourself to do your packing.' He lifted his head suddenly and looked at her. 'Only don't pack anything for the kids, you understand? They're not going anywhere.'

Lizzie did no packing, either for herself or for the children. She spent an uneasy few hours in bed, alternately crying into her pillow and dozing into a jumble of unhappy dreams. Eventually, she slept heavily for a couple of hours, waking to find Gillie at her bedside telling her it was past eight o'clock. When she went downstairs, Alec had gone.

It was Saturday, so there was no school. Often at weekends she would take the children out to Bridge End to see her parents, but she knew she couldn't face her mother. Jane would only need to take one quick look at Lizzie's drawn face to know that Alec had found out about her and Floyd.

Drearily, she set about her daily tasks, giving the children their breakfast, washing Barry but leaving Gillie to see to herself, tidying up, making beds, clearing the grate and laying the fire, brushing their square of carpet even though it had been done during her cleaning frenzy only yesterday evening, trying all the time to keep her panicky thoughts at bay; trying desperately to pretend that everything was normal.

'Mummy, can I go out to play?' Gillie asked. 'Anne Jenkins has got a new skipping-rope.'

Lizzie looked out of the window. The sky was blue, with just a few clouds scudding across it. There was a cool breeze but the children ought to be outside, getting fresh air and exercise.

'Yes, all right. Put on your coat and take Barry with you.'

Gillie made a face. 'Oh, do I have to? He can't skip, and he gets in the way.'

'Yes, you do,' her mother said firmly. 'And don't let him go off with the big boys. He's too young for them. He's got to stay with you. You're not the only one with a little brother,' she added, forestalling further objections. 'Susie Wright has to take hers, so they can play together. Go on, now.'

The children departed, Gillie still grumbling and tugging Barry along by the hand, but once they were out of the house Lizzie's energy seemed to go with them. She sank down on a kitchen chair and leaned her elbow on the table, massaging her forehead with her fingertips. A deep cloud of depression settled over her, and tears trickled down her cheeks.

It was as if she had been running headlong down a road she had never seen before, only to be brought up short by a dead end. There was no happy, sunlit land ahead, no bright future – and if she turned to run back, she would be blocked again, her old life as inaccessible as the new. She was trapped in a small, narrow space with no way out, and darkness was closing in.

Alec's right, she thought miserably. I've wrecked everything.

We've had a good life together, and I've destroyed it. He's forgiven me once, and taken Gillie as his own, and now I've betrayed him again and he can't forgive me. Even if I stay with him now, it will never be the same. And I don't think he wants me to stay anyway. I've destroyed his love as well, and he doesn't want me any more. He just wants the children.

Her other hand moved over her stomach. The baby was kicking, as if it knew its mother was in distress, and she thought of her own mother's advice to her, to think happy thoughts because sadness would affect the unborn child. Lizzie didn't know if that was true, but the thought that she might be making even this new life unhappy added to her guilt. Alec's right about that, too, she thought. I'm not fit to be a mother. But the thought of losing her children as well as her husband tore at her heart, and her chest and stomach seemed to be filled with raw pain, like a huge lump of jagged metal scraping at the inside of her body.

She sat for a long time, hearing the voices of the children playing outside in the street – '*Salt, pepper, mustard, vinegar*' – but unable to form any cohesive thought or idea of what she could do next. Alec was working overtime, she thought dimly, so he wouldn't be home until this evening. Did he expect her to still be here? Did he expect the children to be here, or at June's being looked after until he could bring them home? Was he making plans even now to take them to his parents, or even to hers? Was he going to order her from the house, not knowing or caring where she went?

And if he did, what would she do? Would she go to Floyd and tell him that she would go with him to America? Did she even want to do that any more? And would he want her, without Gillie?

The questions battered at her mind like a storm battering at the windows of a dilapidated house, and she could find no answers. She sat trembling under their onslaught, and would perhaps have sat there all day had not Gillie come bursting in through the open front door and announced that they had a visitor.

'Oh no! Tell them I'm busy,' Lizzie cried, but it was too late. The visitor stood behind Gillie, in the doorway of the living room. It was Floyd.

Chapter Thirty-One

Lizzie lifted her head and stared at the man in the doorway. For a moment or two, she felt as if she was looking at a stranger. As if he had changed in some way, become somehow unrecognisable. But she knew that it was her perception of him that had changed. He knew nothing of what had been happening since they last met, and her heart sank at the thought of yet another painful scene.

'Go back outside and play, Gillie,' she said sharply. 'You're supposed to be looking after Barry.'

'I thought you'd be pleased,' Gillie began in an injured tone, but Lizzie waved an impatient hand at her and she ducked out of the doorway and ran out into the street.

Floyd and Lizzie looked at each other.

'*Aren't* you pleased to see me?' he asked. 'Don't I get a kiss?'

'Floyd ...'

'There's something wrong,' he said, coming further into the room. 'What is it, Lizzie? What's happened?'

'Oh, Floyd, it's been so awful! Alec has found out – about you and me, and everything that's happened. He's in a terrible state over it.'

'Well, he had to know sometime soon, and I guess he was bound to be a little upset.'

'A *little* upset?' Lizzie cried. 'I've ruined his life! I'm leaving him, and taking his children with me. He's going to have to live without us for the rest of his life. Of course he's upset!'

Floyd said, 'And I've lived without you for the past six years. You don't need to tell me what it's like to be upset.'

Lizzie dropped her head on to her hand again. 'I don't know what to do. I never realised how much it was going to hurt him. Or maybe I did and didn't want to face it. But now ... I don't think I can do it. Floyd. I don't think I can hurt him like this.'

There was a silence. The children had started a new skipping game now. Their voices came faintly through the open doors and Floyd turned to close the door to the passage. He stepped into the room and came to stand over her, taking her wrists in his hands.

'Look at me, Lizzie. Now, tell me what you mean. Tell me straight.'

She met his eyes waveringly. 'I – I just don't think I can go through with it,' she whispered. 'He's so dreadfully hurt and angry. He's my *husband*, Floyd – I've lived with him and loved him for years. I can't just smash up his whole life, and take away his family.'

'But you already have,' Floyd said bluntly. 'You've told him, and that's as bad as it can get. Going back on it isn't going to hurt him any less. It isn't going to make it better. Not now.'

'Of course it would. It's what he wants.'

'Are you sure about that? Now that he knows it's me you love – is he really going to want you back?'

Lizzie stared at him. There was a harsh, inflexible note in his voice. She thought of the Floyd she had known in the old days, the laughing airman who had come to Sunday dinner at the farm, who had organised square dances in the hangar, who had made love to her in the woods on VE Day. It had only been the once, and she had regretted it when the euphoria of the day had evaporated. How much more she would have regretted it, if she had known the trouble it would lead to.

And yet – there was Gillie. Without that moment of madness, she would never have had her daughter.

Gillie. She was the crux of the whole thing. If it hadn't been for Gillie, Floyd would have gone home and forgotten the young woman he'd met in England. He'd have married an American girl by now, and perhaps had a daughter, or a son, that he could call his own. He would never have come here, making these terrible demands on her, making her fall in love with him all over again ...

'I love Alec too,' she said uncertainly. 'He knows that.'

'Does he? Does he really believe it – when he knows you've been meeting me on the sly? It's a pretty funny way of show-ing a feller you love him.' His eyes met hers, and they were cold and hard. 'As a matter of fact, I'm beginning to wonder if you'd play the same game with me. Sneaking off to meet someone else and saying all the time that it's me you love.'

'No!' Lizzie cried. 'How can you say that? I'd never do such a thing.' But at the look in his eye and the sardonic lift of his brow, she stopped abruptly, biting her lip. 'It's you who's done this to me,' she said more quietly. 'It's you who's made me unfaithful to Alec. I would never have thought of it for a moment if it hadn't been for you.'

'No,' he said, 'it's you, Lizzie. You're the one who agreed to meet me. Yeah, you said no to start with, but you didn't say it for very long, did you? You came along just the same. You *wanted* to be with me again. You wanted it all – don't try to deny it.'

'I had no choice! If Alec had found out—'

'He'd have beaten the hell out of me,' Floyd said. 'And maybe then I'd have gone away. Or maybe—'

'That's right,' Alec agreed from the doorway. 'Just like I'm going to beat the hell out of you now.'

There was a moment of complete silence. Floyd and Lizzie tore their eyes from each other's faces and turned.

'Alec!' Lizzie gasped. 'How long have you been there?'

'Long enough.' He advanced into the room and she shrank back at the sight of his expression. His face was darkly suffused with blood, his eyes narrowed to slits, his shoulders were tense and his fists clenched. He ignored her and addressed Floyd. 'Well? Shall I do it in here, or shall we go outside?'

'No!' Lizzie shrieked. 'Alec, you can't! *Please*!' She flung herself in front of him. 'It's all right, Alec – I'm not going! I'm not going to leave you. I'm not taking Gillie away. Alec, stop, *please*!'

He thrust her aside and gripped the front of Floyd's coat, jerking the American almost off his feet. For a moment, the two men glared at each other. They were much of a size, and probably of similar strength. Alec was used to manual labour and his muscles were hard and powerful, but Floyd's were toned by physical exercise – riding, swimming and sport. If it came to a fight, it would be a hard and brutal one.

'Please!' Lizzie wept, still trying to force her way between them. 'The children could come in at any minute. Please stop!'

Alec glanced at her and let his hand drop. Floyd stepped back, breathing hard, and straightened his coat. There was a second or two of hesitation and then Alec jerked his head towards the door.

'Get out! Get out of here – and don't you ever show your face in this street again, or I swear I'll kill you.'

Floyd's lips compressed and curled. He moved towards the door and then looked back.

'I'm going this time, but only because of the kids. They shouldn't see their dads fighting. But I'll be back, don't you worry. And next time I'll be taking my daughter with me. And I reckon Lizzie'll come too. And nothing you can do is going to stop me.'

Alec made a deep, guttural sound in his throat and leaped towards him, but the American was through the door and slammed it in his face. By the time Alec reached it, Lizzie was there, pressed against it, her arms spread wide and her hands clutching the architrave on both sides. He tried to prise her fingers away, but it was too late, and when he and Lizzie reached the street, there was no sign of Floyd.

The children were 'dipping' now, to decide who was to hold the skipping-rope next. They were standing in a small cluster, and Gillie was counting.

'Eeny-meeny-miney-mo – and you ... are... *OUT*!'

Alec and Lizzie went back into the house. Lizzie was trembling. She felt sick and faint, and stumbled as she went through the door. Alec put out his hand automatically to save her from falling.

'You'd better sit down.'

She sagged into her chair and he stood looking at her. He was shaking almost as much as she was, with anger and with reaction, and as he pushed back his hair his hand quivered.

'Are you all right?'

'I don't know,' she said in a whisper. 'All this upset – it's bad for the baby.'

'Maybe you should have thought of that before.' He glanced towards the kitchen door. 'I'd better get you a cup of tea.'

'Alec.' She put out a trembling hand. 'Alec – I'm sorry.'

He bit his lip, then said briefly, 'Yes, I expect you are.' But he made no move to take her hand or to touch her in any way, and after a moment he turned away.

Lizzie heard him fill the kettle and light the gas. She felt almost too sick and weak to cry. Sinking her head into her hands, she wondered what would happen next. It seemed as if everything had slipped away from her and she had no control any more. Whatever turn events took now, it had nothing to do with her.

Alec came back with the tea. He put her cup on the kitchen chair beside her and sat down at the table with his own. He didn't look at her.

The silence became unbearable. Lizzie felt as if they would sit there for ever, never speaking again. At last, afraid that the children would come back, she said in a whisper, 'What are you going to do?'

Alec turned and she drew in her breath at the expression on his face. There was bitterness there, and anger, but there were lines of pain she had never seen, could never have imagined, and she knew that the wounds she had caused him now might be too deep ever to be healed. Tears filled her eyes as it dawned on her at last how profoundly she had hurt him, and she wondered how she could ever have been so reckless.

'Do?' he said. 'I'll tell you what I'd like to do, Lizzie. I'd like to kill him. I mean that – I'm not just saying it. I'd like to see him dead for what he's done to me and to our family.'

'Alec – you won't ...'

'I don't suppose I will,' he agreed tiredly. 'But don't bank on it. If I lay eyes on him again, here or anywhere else, I tell you I won't be responsible for my actions.'

'Why not?' she demanded, stung by his words. 'You expect me to be responsible for mine!'

They stared at each other like enemies, and then she remembered that this was the man she had loved and married, and that he had been brought to this pass by those very actions she disclaimed. She dropped her gaze and said, 'I'm sorry. I didn't mean that.'

'I don't know what you do mean any more,' Alec said. 'I don't feel as if I know you. I don't know if I ever did.'

'You did know me!' she cried. 'You knew the true Lizzie. The Lizzie who loved you and married you and—'

'Betrayed me.'

She sagged again. 'Alec, I'm so, so sorry. There's nothing else I can say, but it's true.'

'I dare say you are, now that he's gone. But you heard what he said – he'll be back. And what are you going to do then, Lizzie? Are you going to pack your bags and go with him, like you meant to do this time? Or are you going to tell *him* you're sorry? Seems to me you're sorry for whoever happens to be with you at the time – same as you love whoever happens to be with you at the time.'

'That's not true.'

'No? Tell me what is true then. Oh, but I forgot – you don't know what truth is any more. You've got so used to telling lies that you've forgotten how to do anything else.'

'Alec, please stop this. It's not doing any good.'

'Nothing does any good,' he said. 'Not any more. It's all gone – all ruined. Whatever happens now, nothing is ever going to be the same for us.'

There was another silence.

'I don't know what to say,' she said at last. 'I don't know what to do. The children will come in soon, wanting their dinner, and I haven't done anything for them yet. And I wasn't expecting you back until this evening. Why did you come back early? I thought you were doing overtime all day.'

'Obviously,' he said sardonically, and then sighed. 'Did you really expect me to stay at work, knowing you were packing to go? Taking my kids with you? Because that's what I thought you were going to do. I told you last night you could go, Lizzie, but I knew I couldn't trust you to leave them behind, and I just couldn't take it. I clocked in, and then told the foreman I'd got bad trouble at home and had to come back. He didn't like it, but I told him he could lump it and walked out.'

'Alec! You could lose your job.'

'What would that matter? I'm losing everything else.'

Lizzie stirred restlessly. ''I've got to do something for their dinner.'

'Send Gillie up the street for fish and chips. They'll be happy with that. And then you'd better take them over to your mother. Ask her to take them in – you too, if she'll have you – until we make up our minds what we're going to do.' He turned his scathing glance upon her again. 'Until I make up *my* mind.'

'Alec, I can't do that. I'd have to tell her everything.'

'Yes, you would, wouldn't you. And you know just what she'd say, don't you? She wouldn't have any time for you then, and neither would your father. They're decent people and you've let them down as well as me and the children. You've let us all down. But she'll look after the kids, and she'll probably look after you too, if only for the sake of the baby. *My* baby, in case you've forgotten – at least, I assume it is, but maybe I'm wrong about that too.'

'No, you're not wrong about that,' Lizzie said quietly. 'There's never been anyone else but Floyd, and you know he didn't come back to England until after Christmas.' She paused, then said, 'Please, Alec, don't send me away. Not until we've had a chance to talk properly. The children will be going to Sunday School tomorrow – we'll have time then. If you still want me to leave after that, I will – but please let's give each other one last chance.'

He gave her a long look. The front door opened and they heard the sudden noise of voices as the children shouted out to each other. It was dinner-time and mothers were calling them in for their meal.

'All right,' he said, just before Gillie burst in, with Barry close behind her. 'We'll go through it all again tomorrow. But don't expect too much, Lizzie. The way I feel now, I'd as soon jump off Cobden Bridge as stay married to you.'

Chapter Thirty-Two

'Get her something really nice, won't you,' Ruth said to Sammy as he dressed himself in his motorcycling gear, ready to go and meet Maddy in Southampton. 'A three-stone diamond ring always looks right, to my mind, if you can afford it.'

'Maddy fancies a solitaire. She says you get a better stone for the money.'

'Well, that's true, of course. It depends what suits her finger really, and she does have very small hands. A single stone might look better. Just don't get anything coloured, like an opal – they mean tears and bad luck.'

Sam laughed. 'Me and Maddy aren't going to have any bad luck! I won't take the chance, all the same. Now, we're going to go to the shop as soon as she gets off the train, and then we're going round to Lizzie's. I expect we'll stop there an hour or two, so we should be back by teatime.'

'I'm a little teapot, short and stout,' Silver observed, picking up his cue as usual, and Sammy grinned and gave him a sunflower seed.

'You can spend the day learning to say "Congratulations",' he told the parrot. 'Otherwise you'll have nothing to say to Maddy when she comes.'

'That'll be the day, when Silver's got nothing to say,' Ruth remarked wryly, following him to the door. 'Don't be late, mind. Auntie Jane and Uncle George are coming at six and they'll expect you to be here, ready for the party.'

'We'll be here.' He gave her a kiss and pushed the motorcycle out of the front garden and into the lane. 'Tell Linnet to put on her best frock.'

'She won't need telling. She's more excited about this than you are!' Ruth stepped back as he kicked the bike into life and waved him goodbye. She stood watching him for a moment as he roared off up the lane, and then stayed at the gate, thinking of all the times she had seen him off into a new phase of his life, from the very first time he had walked through it and into hers.

There was the day he'd gone back to Portsmouth to stay with his father and she'd feared that she had lost him; the day he'd gone to school in Southampton, rather nervous and still small for his age; the day he'd started work as Solly Barlow's apprentice and the day he'd gone to join the RAF to do his National Service. Now, he was embarking on the most grown-up and important part yet of his life – committing himself to another person. Not a marriage yet, but the engagement that was a promise just the same.

It would be some time before he and Maddy were able to marry, but things would never be quite the same after today. Ruth and Dan would no longer be the most important people in his life. They were stepping back, to allow Maddy to take her place. And one day, when the first child arrived. they would step back once again; and the same would happen when Linnet grew up and got married and had children in her turn.

Life is full of stepping back, Ruth thought a little sadly, turning to go back into the cottage. But it's full of achievements as well, and Dan and I can both feel proud of what we've achieved with Sammy. He's a fine young man, and he'll make Maddy an excellent husband. They'll have a good, happy life together.

Sam was waiting impatiently on the platform when Maddy's train drew in. As she stepped down, he ran to meet her, catching her in his arms and swinging her round in his excitement.

She laughed and kissed him as he set her back on her feet, but he seemed unable to let her go and hugged her tightly.

'We're getting in people's way,' she said, wriggling free. 'Oh, Sammy, it *is* good to see you. I missed you terribly last weekend.'

'I missed you too. I was afraid you wouldn't come back.'

'Why ever shouldn't I?' She linked her arm in his as they began to walk along the pavement.

'Well, you went to Burracombe, didn't you? I was afraid you'd meet Stephen Napier and decide it was him you wanted, after all.'

'Now that's just silly! I'm very fond of Stephen but it's you I love. Anyway, I didn't see him. He doesn't go home all that much, you know.'

'No, he comes to see you instead,' Sammy said jealously, and she shook his arm.

'Now, stop it! He does come to see me sometimes, but he knows about you and he knows we can only be friends. You're not going to stop me having friends, I hope.'

'I suppose not. I'm not sure he does know that, though. He may think that all's fair in love and war and still try to get you away from me.'

They were out of the station buildings by now and Maddy stopped and looked at him seriously.

'If he does, I'll tell him I simply won't see him any more. I mean it, Sammy. Nothing's going to come between you and me.' They met each other's eyes for a moment and then she laughed and said, 'Look at us, getting all solemn! Come on – this is supposed to be a happy day. You're buying me a ring, remember?'

'As if I could forget,' he said, and gave her a quick kiss. 'The bike's over here. I spent all yesterday evening giving it a really special clean and polish, and your crash helmet's in the pannier. Let's go.'

He started the bike and Maddy slid on to the pillion seat

300

behind him. She wrapped her arms around his waist and they sped off into the centre of the town, stopping outside the jeweller's shop. Sam propped the bike on its stand and they put their helmets back into the pannier. Sammy then took off his black riding jacket, revealing his best sports jacket and a white shirt and tie.

'You're looking very smart,' Maddy said admiringly, and he grinned a little self-consciously.

'Can't go into a posh shop and buy my fiancée an engagement ring looking as if I'd just crawled out from under a stone. Anyway, you always look smashing. I wanted to live up to you.'

She squeezed his hand. 'Let's look in the window first. I don't expect I'll ever go shopping for an engagement ring again – I want to make the most of it.'

They stood at the window, examing the various trays of rings and pointing them out to each other. Maddy liked the solitaire diamonds, but Sam remembered Ruth's words and suggested the three-stone or even five-stone half-hoops, although when he saw the prices he wished he hadn't. He told her about the superstition regarding coloured stones like opals.

'I've heard they bring bad luck too,' Maddy said. 'And pearls mean tears, so we won't have that either. And green's supposed to be unlucky as well, so emeralds are out. I quite like the blue stones, though. Look, that one's just like a sapphire but much cheaper. It's pretty, isn't it?'

'It's a zircon,' Sammy said, peering at the label. 'What does that mean? I've never heard of it.'

They went into the shop and explained rather shyly what they wanted. The man who served them was friendly and interested, and asked Sammy in a low voice what he wanted to pay. He brought out a selection of rings and laid them out on the glass-topped counter.

'Try them on. I'll measure your finger first, so that we know what size you need.' He took a rod of different-sized metal rings from a drawer and slipped them on to Maddy's third finger until he found one that fitted. 'My goodness, you do have tiny hands, don't you? Well, I'll take back all the rings that aren't your size and find some others. Try these on while I have a look.'

Maddy picked up one of the solitaires and slid it on to her finger. It sparkled under the lights and she caught her breath. 'It's lovely. I'll have this one.'

'Oh, you must try some more first.' The man produced another tray. 'These are all your size. Let's see what a half-hoop looks like.'

'What are zircons?' Sam enquired. 'We saw one in the window.'

'Oh, yes. They're not exactly a precious stone, but they're a good choice because you get the large coloured stone in the middle and a better diamond on either side than if you had three diamonds. It's the next most brilliant stone to a diamond, too. The blue isn't as deep as a sapphire.' He glanced at Maddy's face. 'It would match your eyes, if you don't mind my saying so.'

They looked at the zircon rings. Maddy set her first choice aside and tried one on, turning her hand this way and that so that the colours flashed. 'It *is* lovely. Which shall I have?'

'Whichever you want,' Sammy said, having made sure that both were within his price range. 'They both suit you.'

'Oh dear. I don't know …' She tried on the solitaire again. 'It's so important to get it right – I'm going to be wearing it for the rest of my life. I didn't realise it was going to be so difficult.'

'The solitaire is a good diamond,' the man said. 'It will always look good. But the zircon is very pretty too.' He seemed to realise he wasn't being much help, and smiled. 'Take your time. There's no hurry.'

'I think I'll have the solitaire,' Maddy decided at last. 'A blue stone might not always look right with whatever I'm wearing. Diamonds go with everything. I'm sure that's what Fenella would say.'

'I like that one best too,' Sammy said. 'We'll have that, then, please.'

The man took the rings back and went off for a few minutes, returning with Maddy's solitaire in a small velvet box. Sammy paid him, and he handed the box over.

'I don't suppose you want to put it on now. You'll be wanting to find a much more romantic spot!' He smiled at them again. 'Congratulations. I hope you'll be very happy together.'

'Oh, we will,' Maddy told him, her smile almost as dazzling as the diamond in her ring. 'We're going to be very happy indeed.'

They walked out hand in hand, and stopped on the pavement, not quite sure what to do next.

'Tell you what,' Sam said. 'Let's buy some bread and cheese and go for a ride somewhere and have a picnic. The man said we ought to find a romantic spot, so that's what we'll do. Where d'you fancy?'

'Oh yes. Let's go somewhere different – not the Forest. Somewhere in the other direction – Bishop's Waltham, or the Meon Valley. Or Winchester.'

'We'll go that way and see where we end up,' Sammy said. 'We're bound to find a village bakery somewhere selling fresh bread.' He produced the crash helmets and they fitted them on, then settled themselves on the saddle. 'Ready?'

'Ready,' Maddy said, pressing her cheek against his back, and he kicked the engine into life and set off into the traffic.

'So you'll come back about six, then,' Ruth said to her sister. 'And we'll have a special tea to celebrate. Mind you, I still think they're a bit too young and I'm not sure Maddy will really settle down, after the life she had with Miss Forsyth, but they're not rushing into anything. They've got time to find out if it's not right for them.'

'What are they going to be doing for the rest of the day?' Jane asked. 'Off on Sam's motorbike, I suppose. Don't you ever worry about them, Ruth?'

'Oh, we can trust Sammy. He won't do anything he shouldn't.'

'I didn't mean that. I meant about the motorbike. You weren't too keen on him having it to begin with, if I remember rightly.'

'No, I wasn't, but he's a sensible chap and he doesn't go haring about at full speed, especially with Maddy on the back. They just like riding round the lanes, exploring the country-side, and they often stop and have a walk as well. I expect that's what they'll do today. And they're going to pop in on Lizzie and Alec too, and tell them the good news.'

'Hm,' Jane said non-committally. 'Well, I hope it'll cheer our Lizzie up a bit. She's looking as miserable as sin these days.'

'I know. I've been worried about her too.' Ruth hesitated. 'You don't think that American's been round again, do you?'

'What, Floyd?' Jane shrugged. 'I don't know, Ruth. She tells me nothing, these days. And she hasn't said anything to you, I take it?'

'No.' Ruth was thankful to be able to say so, honestly, know-ing how hurt Jane would have been if Lizzie had confided in her. 'I've asked her once or twice if she's seen the doctor – I thought it might be the baby, you know – but she says she's been to the clinic regular and there's nothing wrong there. But she doesn't seem her usual self.'

'Up and down, that's what she is,' Jane agreed. 'One day she's full of the joys of spring and the next you'd think she'd lost a pound and found sixpence. And I'm not sure she's get-ting on all that well with Alec, either. I tell you, Ruth, I've laid awake a good few nights just lately, worrying about them, but it don't do no good.'

'I expect it's just the way she is at the moment,' Ruth said, thinking her sister needed cheering up too. 'Pregnancy can make a woman feel low. That's all it is. Once the baby's here, she'll be right as rain.'

'I hope so.' Jane sighed, then said more brightly, 'Anyway, today's not the day for worrying. We've got a party to get ready for! I'll go home now and make those sausage rolls and cheese straws you want, and we'll bring down some cream as well. Is there anything else you need?'

'I could do with some more eggs,' Ruth said. 'Our hens have gone off lay and I thought I'd hard-boil a few to go with the ham and salad. Sammy was always one for a hard-boiled egg.'

'Right, I'll bring them down as well. I might as well boil them myself, then they'll be ready.' Jane went over to the parrot's cage and tickled the bird under his chin. 'There, Silver, we're having a party. You'll enjoy that, won't you – lots of people to show off to.'

'I'm a little teapot,' Silver informed her, and she laughed.

'You ought to learn something special to say to Sammy. What's that rhyme he used to say – I haven't heard it lately.'

'You mean the one his mother taught him.' Ruth came over to the cage and clicked her tongue at the parrot. 'Come on, Silver. *Sammy, Sammy, shine a light ...*'

'Ain't you playing out tonight?' the parrot continued obligingly, and Ruth laughed and gave him a sunflower seed.

'That's a good boy. Now mind you say it tonight, won't you? Sammy'll be pleased you've remembered.'

'I must go,' Jane said, and Ruth accompanied her to the gate and watched her walk up the track that led to the farm. She went back indoors with a tiny furrow between her brows.

Jane didn't seem all that sure that Lizzie hadn't seen Floyd again. Ruth hoped they were both wrong in their uneasy suspicions, and that Lizzie was simply just feeling the effects of her pregnancy. But she'd seen the look in Lizzie's eyes once or twice – a haunted, secret sort of look – and it had made her wonder.

I hope not, she thought. We don't want any more trouble from *that* quarter. Once you start that kind of thing, there's no knowing where it will end.

Sam and Maddy packed the remains of their picnic into the panniers and put their helmets on. They smiled at each other and leaned together for a last kiss.

'It's been a lovely day,' Maddy said dreamily. 'I'll never forget it, Sammy.'

'Nor will I.' He picked up her left hand and looked at the tiny diamond, sparkling on her third finger. 'You're my fiancée now. I can hardly believe it – I have to keep saying it to myself, over and over again. *Maddy Forsyth is my fiancée.* And one day you'll be my wife – Mrs Samuel Hodges. How do you like the sound of that?'

'I like it very much. But we ought to be going soon, if we're planning to call in on Lizzie and Alec on the way back to Bridge End.'

They settled themselves on the bike and set off for Southampton. They had spent the day cruising gently along the lanes between rolling fields and woods, and had eaten their picnic (fresh, crusty bread, cheese and early tomatoes washed down with ginger beer) on Old Winchester Hill. After the storms and rains of February, the dry March had brought sunshine and warmth, and it was a beautiful spring day. For over an hour, they pottered about amongst the tumuli and barrows of the ancient earthworks, trying to imagine the people who had lived here thousands of years before, until at last Sammy stopped and drew Maddy down to sit beside him in a grassy hollow.

'I think it's time we got engaged properly,' he said, and took the little velvet box from his pocket. Maddy felt her heartbeat increase as he took her hand in his, kissed it and then slid the ring on to her finger. They both looked at it for a moment and a tear dropped from Maddy's eye on to the back of her wrist.

'Do you want me to propose again?' he asked, a little unsteadily, and she shook her head.

'No. You've done that. Oh, Sammy – I do love you so much.' She threw her arms around his neck and they kissed. He stroked her hair and looked into her eyes.

'I'll be a good husband, Maddy. I'll always do my best to look after you and make you happy. And if I ever do anything you don't like, you'll tell me – but whatever promises I make in church, I'll keep.'

'And so will I,' she said, her face serious for once. And then her smile broke out again and she laughed. 'If I'm half as happy when we're married as I am now, I'll have nothing to complain about – nothing.'

They stayed in the hollow for a long time, and then, as the sun began to sink towards the horizon, Sammy glanced at his watch and gave an exclamation. 'Crumbs, we're going to be in trouble! Auntie Ruth's putting on a bit of a party for us tonight – she was talking about asking Auntie Jane and Uncle George down to tea. And I promised we'd go and see Lizzie and Alec on the way, so we'd better get our skates on.'

'One more kiss,' Maddy said, reaching up to wind her arms around his neck again. 'Just one ...'

Dusk was falling as they made their reluctant way back to the motorcycle. It deepened as they rode through the lanes until they were back at the outskirts of Southampton, and the gas lights were coming on as they turned the corner to Lizzie's house.

'Hello,' Sammy said, turning the bike at the end of the little cul-de-sac, 'there seems to be something going on. The front door's wide open – and there's Lizzie. She looks upset.'

Lizzie saw them and ran across the pavement. Behind her came the children, looking wide-eyed with fright. Her face was streaked with tears and her mouth was working, as if she wanted to cry out but couldn't find the words.

'Lizzie!' Maddy cried, jumping off the bike and running to her, while Sammy hastily pulled it on to its prop-stand. 'Whatever's the matter? What's happened?'

'It's Alec,' Lizzie wept, falling heavily into Maddy's arms. 'He's left me! He's gone – and I'm terrified he's going to kill himself!'

Chapter Thirty-Three

'Wherever have they got to?' Jane asked for the fourth time, looking at the clock on Ruth's mantelpiece. 'It's almost seven. It's been dark for over an hour. They knew we were having a party, didn't they?'

'Yes, it was almost the last thing I said to Sammy when he left this morning.' Ruth was trying hard not to worry, but there was a leaden feeling her stomach and her heart was jittery. 'Oh dear, I hope they haven't had an accident on that bike.'

'Sam's a sensible lad,' said Dan, who was also trying not to worry. 'He doesn't take any risks, specially with Maddy on pillion.'

'All the same, things can go wrong.' Ruth stopped, aware of Linnet who had just come into the room. 'What is it, love?'

'I'm hungry,' Linnet said, eyeing the table. 'When can we have tea?'

'We're waiting for Sammy and Maddy. You know that. But perhaps you could start yours, since it's so late.'

'I don't want to sit up at the table all by myself.'

Ruth hesitated, unsure what to do. She caught her sister's eye and Jane shrugged.

'If you ask me, I think we might as well all start. They know what time it is. I expect they've stopped on at our Lizzie's and forgotten all about us.'

'Oh, surely not,' Ruth began, dismayed at the jealous tone in her sister's voice. It had always been Jane's failing, and had caused trouble more than once. Then she said, 'Well, I'd rather that than think they might have had an accident. Look, I'll put the kettle on and make the tea anyway. The potatoes must be as hard as rocks by now. And there are those sausage rolls to heat up as well. By the time it's ready, they'll be here. Can you wait that long, Linnet?'

The child nodded and went to sit on her father's lap. Ruth went out to the kitchen to fill the kettle and returned to set it on the range. She put the tray of sausage rolls into the oven and sat down again. They all looked at each other.

'We might as well have the wireless on,' George said. 'We can hear *In Town Tonight*.'

'That's not on until half-past. They'll be here by then.'

'Let's have it on anyway,' Dan said, turning the switch. 'Anything's better than sitting here staring at each other.'

The kettle came to the boil and Ruth made tea. She waited a few minutes to let it brew, poured it into the cups already set out on the table, and then took the sausage rolls and baked potatoes out of the oven and arranged them on plates.

'We might as well start, then. Maybe you're right, Jane, and they've stopped on at Lizzie's. She and Alec might have persuaded them to stay and have something there.'

'Well, if they have I think they're being very rude,' Jane said tightly, and moved over to the table. They settled themselves around it and Ruth began to offer everyone ham, baked potatoes and pickled beetroot.

'One of my favourite meals,' George remarked. 'If that's your own apple chutney, Ruth, I'll have a dollop, please. And some mustard, when you've finished with it, Dan.'

Dan passed him the jar. Between them the men and Linnet managed to keep a conversation of sorts going, but it became increasingly obvious that neither Ruth nor her sister was saying much, and eventually it petered out into silence. Dan looked at his wife.

'Don't worry too much, Ruthie,' he said. 'Sam's a good rider and he'll always look after Maddy.'

'I know. It's not just him on the road though, is it? It's the other people too. And we don't even know that they got to Lizzie's. Something might have happened earlier – hours ago. They might be ...' She glanced at Linnet and bit her lip. Images of ambulances, hospital beds, even mortuaries, passed through her mind, and at one moment she caught herself thinking of wreaths. Unable to bear the pictures, she jumped up. 'I think we ought to try and find out – ring up the police or something.'

'It's only half-past seven.' As if to corroborate this, the stirring strains of Eric Coates' 'Knightsbridge March' began to play on the radio and the commanding voice of the announcer ordered the London traffic to '*Stop!*' Dan shook his head helplessly. 'I think we ought to leave it a bit longer before we start doing anything like that.'

'But we might be too late!'

'Ruth!' He caught at her arm. 'Calm down, love. We don't know that anything's happened to them at all. They're just a bit late, that's all. It's been a big day for them and they've dropped in to see Lizzie and Alec and stopped a bit too long. Or they might have had a puncture, or something else gone wrong with the bike. They've probably tried telephoning to Jane and George, only they're down here with us. Or they might not be anywhere near a phone box. There are dozens of things that could have happened, without it having to be an accident.' He kept his eyes on her face and then tugged gently at her arm. 'Sit down and finish your tea. It won't do any good for us to get all upset, before we know there's something to be upset about.'

Ruth hesitated, then sat down, rather unwillingly. She gave him a rueful look and picked up her knife and fork, then laid them down again. 'I'm sorry. I just don't feel like eating anything until I know.'

Dan sighed. 'Well, it seems to me the best thing is for one of us to go over to Lizzie's and see what's going on. Can we go in your truck, George?'

311

George nodded. 'I think we ought to do that. It'll put Ruth's mind at rest, if nothing else.' He looked wistfully at his plate, still half-full of ham and potato, and Ruth felt a pang of guilt.

'Finish your tea, George. I know I'm being silly but I can't help feeling there's something wrong. I don't suppose a few more minutes will make any difference, though.' She glanced at the clock again. 'Whatever's happened must have happened an hour or more ago.'

'If anything's happened at all,' Dan said. 'I still don't think there's anything to worry over, but I can't sit here and eat knowing that you're fretting. Look, I've had all I want. We can save the rest for later, when those two are back safe and sound. You go up to the farm and get the truck, George, and I'll be ready by the time you get back.'

'All right, Dan. I'll leave this for now.' The farmer got up and went out, and they heard his footsteps hurry away up the track. Dan finished eating and got up to fetch his coat.

'Oh, but I want to go!' Ruth began, and then looked at Linnet. The little girl was watching them with huge, frightened eyes and she knew she couldn't leave the child. 'I'll go up to the farm with Jane,' she amended. 'You can telephone us there as soon as you know.'

'Course we will.' He felt in his pockets and then picked up his wallet from the sideboard. 'I'll need some pennies for the phone.'

'There are some in my purse. It's in the drawer.' She watched while he took them out. 'You will let us know the minute you can, won't you? I wish I could go too.'

'Well, why don't you?' Jane said. 'Linnet will be all right with me, won't you, my pet? You can sleep in the spare bedroom if you like, and help me feed the hens in the morning.'

Linnet looked from one to the other, her face dubious, and Ruth said, 'I don't know …'

'Look, you're worried,' Jane told her. 'And you'll go on worrying until you've seen Sammy for yourself, I know you will. You go, too – there's room for three on that front seat. Anyway, I'll bet a penny to a pound you'll meet Sammy on the road, before you get anywhere near Southampton. He and Maddy are probably on their way back now.'

'I want to go with Mummy and Daddy,' Linnet said, sounding close to tears, and Ruth made up her mind.

'All right. We're coming with you, Dan,' she said as he came back into the room with his overcoat on. 'I can't stop here and I can't leave Linnet behind. We'll let you know as soon as we can,' she said to Jane, and pushed past Dan to fetch her own and Linnet's coats.

'Well, hurry up,' he said. 'I can hear the truck coming now. We don't want to waste any more time.' He looked doubtfully at Linnet. 'I'm not sure this is a good idea though.'

'Oh, take her!' Jane exclaimed impatiently. 'We all know there's nothing to worry about, and she's only going to work herself up if you leave her behind.'

They all went out, closing the door behind them as George pulled up outside in the truck. He hadn't had it very long and seldom used it after dark, and he had never driven it into the middle of Southampton. As the others clambered up beside him, he looked at them in surprise.

'Blimey, what's this, a Sunday School outing? Suppose we have to bring the other two back as well?'

'Me and Sam can ride in the back,' Dan said. 'We can even get his bike in there if needs be. Come on, George, get her moving.'

George sighed and let out the clutch. The truck jerked forwards. 'Sooner we start, sooner we'll get there, I suppose. Those two lovebirds have probably stopped for a bit of a cuddle, that's all, and lost track of the time. They'll think we've all gone raving mad, chasing round the countryside after them like this.'

'They knew we were expecting them back for tea,' Ruth

said. 'And Sammy knew we were doing something special. He wouldn't have let us down.'

'I still think he's had trouble with the bike,' Dan said. 'Get a puncture somewhere out in the Forest and you could be hours getting help. And I don't suppose we've got any idea where they were planning to go for the day, either.'

'They were going to buy the ring,' Ruth began doubtfully. 'I don't know what they were thinking of doing after that.'

'Well, they'd better have a good excuse when we do find them, that's all,' George said, carefully negotiating a hairpin bend. 'That was a good tea I left half-eaten on my plate.'

It seemed a long time before they were in Southampton and none of them was entirely sure of the way to Lizzie's house. Ruth had only been in on the bus, and Dan and George had only visited the house once in all the time Lizzie and Alec had lived there, since it was more usual for the family to come out to Bridge End. Eventually, after several wrong turns and three unplanned visits to the Civic Centre, they turned the corner into the cul-de-sac and George heaved a sigh of relief.

'I thought we'd found our way into a maze,' he said, and peered into the darkness. 'There – isn't that Sam's bike, standing under the lamp post? I told you they'd be all right.'

'Yes, it is, but what's going on?' Ruth struggled with the door-handle. 'Look at Lizzie – she's crying her eyes out. And it looks as if Sammy and Maddy are getting ready to go. You don't suppose they've had a row of some sort, do you? Oh, how does this thing work?'

'Twist it down,' George advised, and Dan reached across her to help. 'Hurry up, or they'll be gone – they haven't re-alised it's us.' He wound down his window and leaned out. 'Sam! Lizzie! What the hell's going on? Why are Sam and Maddy still here? We've all been worried stiff.'

The little group by the front door turned their heads, startled, and Sammy paused in the act of swinging his leg over the saddle of his motorbike. He stared up at the truck in astonishment.

'Uncle George? What are you doing here?' And then, as Ruth almost fell out of the other door and hurried round the front towards him: 'Auntie Ruth? Dad? *Linnet?*'

'We were worried about you,' Ruth said, clutching his arm. 'When you didn't come home, we thought something must have happened. We couldn't think of anything else to do but come over and see if Lizzie knew anything.' Her eyes went to the weeping figure in the doorway. 'Whatever's the matter? What happened, for God's sake?'

Maddy came and touched her arm. 'It's Alec. He's gone off in a bit of a state and Lizzie's afraid of what he might do. Sammy and I are going to go and see if we can find him.'

'Please!' Lizzie cried through her tears. 'Please, Sammy, just go! You're wasting time – you'll be too late! He's going to jump off, I know he is – and it's all my fault.'

Ruth stared at her. 'Lizzie, what are you saying? Where's he gone? What is he going to do? The words seemed to hit her suddenly. 'You don't mean ...'

'Just go,' Lizzie begged them. 'It's Cobden Bridge. That's where he's gone, I know it is. And it's dark, and it's high tide – and he's always hated the water ever since his ship was sunk. Oh please, Sammy, just go and stop him – *please.*'

Ruth turned and ran back to the truck. She scrambled aboard, hearing the sudden roar of the motorcycle as she fell into the seat, and dragged the door shut behind her.

'Go after him, George,' she panted. 'Quickly! Lizzie's right – if we don't get a move on, we'll be too late.'

Chapter Thirty-Four

There wasn't much traffic on Southampton roads at that time of night, but what there was seemed to get deliberately in the way of the motorcycle and the truck as they wound their way through the streets. Sam, who had got to know the town quite well during the past few weeks, led the way through St Denys to the point where the bridge crossed the River Itchen to Bitterne. In daylight, you could see the boatyards, with yachts and dinghies at their moorings, but now only a solid wall of blackness stretched away on either side.

Maddy was on the pillion seat, clinging to Sammy's waist and weeping against his back. Although the journey took less than ten minutes, it seemed endless and she had plenty of time to relive the horror of the past half-hour, since she and Sammy had ridden into the cul-de-sac, full of joy at their engagement, to find Lizzie at the door in hysterics.

'Lizzie! Whatever's the matter? What's happened?'

In those first shocked moments, Lizzie's words hadn't made any sense. She played them over again in her mind, still unable to understand them properly.

Alec, gone? Alec, *killing* himself? Why? What was wrong? What could possibly have happened to drive him to such despair?

'The way I feel now, I'd as soon jump off Cobden Bridge as stay married to you.'

The words echoed in Lizzie's mind as she watched the two

vehicles pull away. Nobody had suggested she should go too, partly because there wasn't room in either, but mainly because she was pregnant and had two children to look after. And also because nobody had had time to think; they'd all caught the urgency in her voice, and seen that there was no time to ask questions, to argue or discuss. They'd simply gone.

The street was quiet after they'd driven away. The gas lamps cast small pools of yellow light at the foot of their posts; in between, it was dark, yet not as dark as the water would be below Cobden Bridge. Lizzie shuddered and went indoors, unable to stand at the door any longer, but equally unable to stay inside. She stood in the middle of the room, staring at her frightened face in the mirror above the fireplace, biting the knuckles of one fist until she tasted her own blood and thinking over the events that had led to this moment.

She hadn't expected to see Floyd that afternoon, hadn't expected to see him ever again. The thought that she had sent him away, given up all that he had promised her, was tearing at her heart, yet she knew she'd done the right thing and might even, one day, be glad of it. But when she had opened the door to the knock and found him standing on the step, it was as if all her resolve and drained away and she swayed towards him, almost too dizzy to stand, and her voice was no more than a whisper.

'What are you doing here?'

'Lizzie.' He put out his arms and caught her. 'Honey, I had to come. I had to try one last time. I couldn't leave things as they were. When I left you with him, I thought you'd tell him you were coming to me. I've been waiting to hear from you.'

'I told you, Floyd,' she said tiredly. 'I can't do it. I can't leave him, and my family, and everything I know. And I can't do it to the children, either.'

'One of whom is mine,' he said, and pushed her gently to allow him into the house.

Lizzie resisted for a moment, then dispiritedly led the way

into the front room with the small three-piece suite they used only on Sundays and for special occasions. He glanced around dismissively and she felt a spurt of anger.

'Yes, I know it's not what you're used to, and I know you could give me a palace to live in, but this is my home. Mine and Alec's. We chose this furniture together. You might think it's poor, but we like it and we're happy with it. And we're happy with each other.'

'Come on, Lizzie! If you were happy with him, you wouldn't be standing here now.'

'I'm standing here with you now,' she said, her voice quivering with anger, 'because I'm not strong enough to keep you out. You've forced your way in, Floyd. You're a bully, and you're trying to bully me to go away with you. You've been doing it all these weeks. Telling me you wanted Gillie. Telling me you *loved* me. If you really loved me, or Gillie, you'd leave us alone. You'd never have come here in the first place. You'd have stuck to our agreement.'

'I meant to. But when I knew I was coming to Southampton, that I'd be so close to you both, I couldn't help myself. And when I saw you again, Lizzie …'

'Oh, stop it!' she exclaimed. 'I've had enough! Floyd, try to understand – I'm not coming with you, and I'm not letting you see Gillie again. It's over. *Over.*'

His dark eyebrows came together in a frown. 'What's happened, Lizzie? What's changed you?'

'You changed me,' she said. 'You came back and changed me from a happily married woman to someone who didn't know what she wanted any more. But now I do know what I want – and it's not you. It's my husband and my children and my home. *This* home.'

For a moment, Floyd said nothing. His glance wandered about the room, taking in the wallpaper Alec had put up when they'd first moved in, with the patch by the door where Barry had rubbed past when he was still crawling, and the shelf with their wedding photograph in its chrome-plated frame and the little china shepherdess Lizzie had been given for her twenty-first birthday. Lizzie looked too, and saw it all through his eyes – small, shabby, even a little poor – but instead of feeling humiliated, she felt protective. There was nothing wrong with it, she told herself fiercely. It was a home, *their* home – hers and Alec's – and it held all she wanted from her life.

'Alec and I had a long talk last Sunday,' she said quietly. 'I don't know if he'll ever quite get over all this, but he wants me to stay. We're going to try again. I love him, Floyd. I'm sorry for all that's happened and I'm sorry if you've been hurt too, but you knew what you were doing when you came here. Alec didn't ask for any of it.'

'So that's it, then, is it?' he said. 'I'm to walk out of here and never come back. I'm to pretend none of it ever happened, and forget you. And forget my daughter.'

Lizzie shrugged. 'That's up to you. I can't tell you what to remember and what to forget. Just leaving will be enough for me. And leave us alone, Floyd. Wait until Gillie gets in touch with you of her own accord.'

'And what if she never does?'

'I'll do as I promised. I'll tell her about you, when she's old enough, but what she does about it then is up to her. I hope you'll respect that.'

'Oh, yeah,' he said. 'I guess I'm going to have a lot of re-specting to do.'

He stood looking at her for a moment, and then he lifted his shoulders and she knew that the battle was over. Tears rose in her throat as she watched him turn away for the last time and knew she would never see him again. And then he turned back towards her.

'One last kiss then, Lizzie,' he said in a husky voice. 'Just one last kiss, to remember you by.'

Lizzie hesitated. She had been caught like this before, she reminded herself. Then she remembered Alec's face as they had agreed to stay together, and she knew she would not be seduced again. She could stop at one kiss.

She moved into Floyd's arms, and as she did so the front door opened and Alec stepped into the passage.

There was a moment of complete silence. Then Alec turned swiftly and walked out. The words he had spoken only a few days ago seemed to hang in the cold evening air.

'*The way I feel now, I'd as soon jump off Cobden Bridge as stay married to you.*'

'Alec!' Lizzie screamed, pushing Floyd roughly aside. 'Alec, come back! It's not what you think!'

But he was gone. Lizzie ran to the corner of the road, but he was already disappearing at the top of the street. Still screaming, she began to follow him but Floyd caught and held her, stopping her from going any further. She turned in fury and beat her fists against his chest.

'Let me go! Let me go after him!'

'You'll never catch him now. He's running too fast. Think of the baby, Lizzie.' His voice was urgent. 'Think of the children.'

'But I've got to go after him! You don't understand, Floyd – he's going to kill himself. He threatened he would and now he's going to do it, I know he is.'

Floyd stared at her in shock. 'What did you say?'

'He's going to jump off Cobden Bridge,' she wept. 'He said he would, rather than stay married to me. Floyd, you don't understand – he's so unhappy, he doesn't even want to go on living, and I've done this to him. *We've* done this to him.' She tried to twist away. 'I've got to go after him – I've got to stop him.'

'No,' he said firmly. 'You've got to stay here and look after the children. I'll go after him. Where has he gone? Which bridge?'

'Cobden Bridge. It's on the way to Bitterne. We went there

once, the afternoon we ...' She could not go on. 'We looked at the boats,' she said dully.

Floyd nodded. 'I remember. OK, Lizzie, you go back indoors and I'll go after him. I'll stop him somehow – and I'll tell him what you've been saying. I won't let him do this, I promise. Now, go back to the children.' He turned her and pushed her away from him. She caught her breath and started after him, but he warded her off with one hand and then began to run. In a few moments he too had turned the corner at the top of the street and disappeared.

Lizzie stood for a moment with her hand at her mouth, tears streaming down her cheeks. Then the baby inside her kicked and she remembered Gillie and Barry, playing at home in the back room of the little house. She turned and walked heavily back. It was just as she reached the door that she heard the sound of an engine and turned to see Sammy's motorcycle come round the corner.

They caught up with Floyd just before they arrived at Cobden Bridge. Sam and Maddy passed him without realising who the running figure was, but Ruth saw him in the headlights and cried out to George to stop. He shook his head.

'We can't waste the time. You heard what Lizzie said. We might be too late as it is.'

Ruth put her head out of the window and shouted to the American as they drew level with him. 'Floyd! It's us – we're on our way.'

She saw the pale shape of his face as he looked up, and the brief wave of his hand. His voice came faintly over the sound of the engine. 'For God's sake, stop him ...' Then they had left him behind, fading into the darkness.

'How much further?' Ruth asked desperately. 'We're going to be too late, I know we are.'

'Another minute or two, that's all.' Jane gripped her arm.

'Oh, that *stupid* girl! I knew she was playing with fire, I knew it all along. And in her condition, too!'

'Stop it, Jane!' George ordered harshly. 'This isn't the time ... here we are.' He swung on to the bridge and the truck jerked to a halt. In only a second, the doors were opened and they tumbled out on to the road.

The mototcycle was already there, with Sammy propping it on its stand. Maddy stood beside it, tears streaming down her face and Ruth ran to her. Jane and Sam started across the road, but George put out his hands and stopped them.

'Don't rush at him. You can see he's only just balanced on the wall. If we scare him, he'll go over.'

'He's going anyway,' Jane whispered. 'Oh, George – that poor man.'

'I'll talk to him.' George began to cross the road. They could see Alec, crouched on top of the wall, a dark shape against the faint glimmer of the sky. His face was turned away, as if he were staring down at the inky water, summoning up the courage to let himself go. Ruth could almost feel his despair, the trembling of his body, the sickness in his throat. She caught Dan's hand, gripping it tightly, and he squeezed back. They stood in a little group – herself, Jane, Sam and Maddy – and then she felt a tug on her skirt and turned to see Linnet's frightened face.

'Linnet! Get back into the van, there's a good girl.'

'What's happening? Why is Uncle Alec standing on the wall? He'll fall off.'

'Of course he won't. Your Uncle George will get him to come down and then we can all go home.'

'I thought we were having a party,' the little girl said, bewildered. 'I'm cold.'

'Get back in the van,' Ruth repeated, and gave her a gentle push in the direction of the truck.

'Is Uncle Alec coming to the party?'

'I don't know. He's not very well. Linnet, get back into the van – *now*.'

'You get in with her,' Dan said. 'There's nothing you can do out here. I'll go and help George.'

'Dan, be careful,' But even as she spoke, things began to happen very quickly, and she never knew in just what order they took place. She had no more than a jumble of memories – of Linnet, tugging at her hand, of Dan starting across the road, of Sam and Maddy watching helplessly as George and Jane tried to persuade their son-in-law to come down. And then, in a dark kaleidoscope of tumbling pictures and roaring sound, Linnet's hand twisting out of hers as the child ran after her father, the rumble of a lorry coming across the bridge, shouts and screams from Maddy and Sam, the screech of brakes close beside them, the crunch of glass and metal as the vehicle swerved to avoid the people so suddenly in the road and struck the wall; and, finally, the silence.

And, following the silence, a bitter sobbing from somewhere nearby, and a shriek that seemed to split the night air like the rip of fabric, a shriek that went on and on until someone came up to Ruth and struck her sharply on the face and she realised that it was her own voice.

Across the road, Alec climbed down, shaking, from the parapet of the bridge, supported by George and Jane. And on the road itself was a small cluster of figures. The lorry-driver, panic-stricken; Maddy, crumpled beside the huddled body of Linnet, terrifyingly close to the bonnet of the lorry. And Sammy, sprawled face down a yard or two away, his blood already seeping into the dust of the road.

When Floyd arrived, there was nothing he could do but to sprint to the nearest telephone kiosk and call an ambulance.

Chapter Thirty-Five

'It's all my fault,' Alec sobbed. He was sitting in his usual armchair at home, curled like a baby into its cushions, his face buried in both hands, his shoulders shaking. 'None of this would have happened if I hadn't rushed off like that.'

'None of it would have happened if I hadn't been here when you came home,' Floyd said bitterly. 'Or if you hadn't seen me with Lizzie. Or if I'd never come back in the first place.'

'No,' Lizzie said. She was on a chair beside Alec, her arms around his trembling body, her tears falling on his hair. 'Nor if I'd had the sense to tell you to go away, and mean it. It's our fault. But it's happened now, and it's no good going over it all.'

Floyd looked at them and hesitated. 'Is there anything I can do? I don't care what it is.'

'Yes,' Alec said. 'Go away. Don't ever come here again. That's what you can do.'

Floyd bowed his head. 'I know. I'm just making things worse. But – heck, I can't just walk away. There must be something.'

'You could go to the hospital and see what's happening,' Lizzie said. Her voice quivered and her face was white with fear. 'I can't leave Alec or the children, and God knows how long it'll be before anyone can come back. Do that, Floyd, will you?'

'Sure.' He started towards the door and paused again. 'Can I make you some coffee before I go? Or tea? Don't they say that's good for shock?'

'I'll do that.' She looked at him with desperation. 'Please, Floyd, find out what's happening. And come back and tell us. If either of those two die . . .'

'OK. I'll come back as soon as I've got some news.' He moved swiftly to the door, putting out one hand to touch her hair as he passed, then withdrawing it quickly. 'Get him some tea, Lizzie, and get some for yourself. You both need it.'

He went out. The door closed and the room was silent except for Alec's muffled sobs. Lizzie bent her head and laid her face against his hair, wet from her tears. Her arms tightened around his shoulders.

'Alec, you know I love you, don't you?' she whispered. 'All the time, it was always really you. I think I just went mad for a while, but deep down I always knew I'd never leave you. I'm sorry – I'm so, so sorry.' There was a short silence, then she said, 'What you saw when you came in – he was saying goodbye. I told him I wasn't going with him and he believed it at last. I didn't want him to kiss me. I just wanted him to go. That's all it was. Really and truly, that's all it was.'

Alec's trembling slowly lessened. He turned slightly in her arms, and lifted his head. His eyes, red and swollen, met hers.

'I swear it's true,' she said quietly. 'I wasn't going to leave you. I was never really going to leave you.'

'You put me through hell,' he said hoarsely. 'I didn't want to live any more. But when it came to it – on the bridge – I didn't want to die either. I was scared, Lizzie. I didn't know what to do. I didn't know which way to go. Living or dying, it seemed a nightmare either way.'

'I don't know what I can say to tell you how sorry I am,' she whispered. 'There ought to be a bigger word for it.'

'There aren't big enough words for any of this,' he said. 'I don't even know what happened, not really. It just all seemed to happen at once. Mum and Dad, trying to get me down from the bridge – and it was as if I was nailed there, Lizzie, I

325

couldn't seem to move at all, one way or the other. And then people rushing across the road – I couldn't even see properly who they were. Maddy and Sam – and Linnet. What the hell was *Linnet* doing there? And then that lorry, smashing into them – and all the noise – the brakes, the engine, the screaming ...' He shuddered and buried his face in his hands again. 'Oh God, Lizzie, if any of them are badly hurt ...'

'They're in the hospital,' Lizzie said, trying to keep the dread from her own voice. 'The ambulance got them there as quickly as possible. They'll be in good hands.'

'All three of them,' he said, as if she hadn't spoken. 'Maddy and Sam, and Linnet. Lizzie, if anything happens to that kiddie, I swear I won't want to go on living.'

'Alec, don't say that! We've got our own little ones – they depend on you, Gillie, and Barry, and the new baby. They need you. *I* need you. In any case,' she went on determinedly, 'they're not going to die. None of them. They're going to be all right.'

Alec stirred restlessly in her arms. 'Where's that blasted Yank? He ought to be back by now.'

'He won't even be at the hospital yet,' Lizzie said. 'And then he's got to find out where they are. He won't be back for a while yet.' Gently, she removed her arms from his shoulders. 'I'm going to make some tea. He was right about that, anyway; we both need it. All we can do now is wait – and pray.'

'It's a long time since I said any prayers,' Alec said ruefully. 'But I reckon that's what I was doing when I was on that bridge.' He sat up a little and leaned forward, his hands dangling between his knees and his voice dispirited. 'I don't even know what I was praying for – but it wasn't this.'

When Floyd finally found the others, they were sitting in a frightened row in the hospital corridor. He walked quietly along the stone-flagged floor and touched Dan on the shoulder.

Dan, whose other arm was around Ruth's shoulders, looked up and started to his feet. Until tonight, he had never met Floyd, and had barely seen him during the confusion on the bridge. He gripped the American's arm.

'How are they?'

'No – I'm not a doctor.' Floyd shook his head in confusion. 'I'm Floyd Hanson – I'm the cause of all this. I came to see what's happening.'

'Floyd.' Jane got up too, seeing that her sister was too weary and too upset to speak. 'How's our Lizzie?'

He rubbed his face. 'She's in a bit of a state. And Alec's worse. I wanted to do something – make tea, whatever they needed – but she asked me to come here and find out what's going on. Has there been any news yet?'

Jane shook her head and sat down again. 'A nurse told us they took them all away as soon as the ambulance came in. She didn't know any more than that. We've just got to wait.'

'Oh, God.' He sat down next to Dan. 'D'you mind if I stay too? I promised I'd go back as soon as there was any news.'

Jane shrugged. Dan tightened his arm around Ruth's shoulders as she leaned against him. George, at the far end of the row, looked past the others at Floyd.

'I'm glad you realise it's all your doing. Our Lizzie and Alec were all right until you came back. Why you had to do that, I'll never understand – messing up a decent little family. And now there's three innocent young people lying in there at death's door—'

'George!' Jane slapped at his arm. 'Don't say that! Don't say it!'

'Well, it's time someone told him the truth. Coming here, getting between husband and wife, creating trouble where there weren't none before. That's been the worst of the Yanks, all along – over-paid, over-sexed and over here, that's what folk used to say during the war, and by God it's true. It was true then and it still is, and always will be.'

'That's just stupid talk!' Floyd retorted. 'There's bad Yanks, yeah, sure, but there's plenty of good ones too and I used to think I was one of them.' His body sagged as he added in a lower tone, 'I'm not so sure now.'

'Neither am I,' George said bitterly. 'And if I'd known what you were going to do when they first asked us to take in American servicemen and give them a taste of family life in England, I'd never have let you over the doorstep.'

'I never meant to abuse your hospitality—'

'That's what you did, though, isn't it! You took advantage of our Lizzie. Dances in the hangar – walks on Sunday afternoons. And her with a husband in a German POW camp. And you say you're a good Yank? God preserve us from the bad ones, that's all I can say.'

'We never did a thing wrong until VE Day—'

'You did it then, though, didn't you? And you came back again and made everything worse.' George paused, staring down the endless corridor. 'I got over what happened on VE Day – our Gillie's a part of the family, and a welcome one. It's what you've done *now* that's caused all this. Upsetting our Lizzie – driving Alec to try to kill himself.' Suddenly unable to control his turbulent emotions, he leaped to his feet. 'Why, you're nothing but a common murderer!'

'*George!*' Jane jumped up too, holding him back as he advanced towards the American. 'George, stop it! You're doing no good – and you'll get us thrown out. This is a hospital, for goodness' sake!'

'Yes, sit down, George.' Dan helped her to push George back on to his chair. 'Things are bad enough without you starting a fight. I'm not saying you don't have justice on your side, but Jane's right, this isn't the place to settle matters. And you're upsetting Ruth, too – look at her. My Sam and our Linnet are in there somewhere, not to mention young Maddy, and God knows what's happening to them. Now, *sit down.*'

Scowling, George did as he was told. Floyd, his face pale, looked from one to the other of them.

'I guess I'd better get out. I'll wait outside. If one of you'll bring me news when you get any, I'll go back and tell Lizzie.'

'And that you will not!' George exclaimed, half on his feet again. 'You'll keep away from my daughter from now on, do you hear? If anyone goes back to her, it'll be me or her mother. You don't go anywhere near that house ever again.'

'I promised—'

'And this is one promise you'll break with my blessing,' George responded. 'It's news she wants, *good* news, not the chance to see your face again. And I'm bloody sure Alec won't welcome you, whatever you may say.'

Floyd inclined his head. 'I guess not.' He stood up slowly and looked down at the row of anxious faces. 'There's not much point in me hanging around, then,' he said heavily. 'I may as well leave. But I still want to know what happens. You will let me know, won't you?' He glanced at Ruth and Dan. 'I sure hope it's not bad news.'

'Oh, you'll be told,' Dan said wearily. 'It was a traffic accident, remember? The lorry driver's with the police now and they want us all to go round to the station in the morning. That includes you, too. You'll find out all right.'

'I see.' The American looked at them again, hesitating, then said, 'I guess I may see you there, then. And – well, you might not believe this but – I'm really sorry. I know I've been a fool.'

Nobody spoke. He waited for a moment, then began to walk slowly back down the corridor. They watched as he disappeared around the corner, and then Ruth drew in a long, shuddering breath and buried her face against Dan's shoulder once more.

'He was a decent enough boy,' Jane said after a moment. 'He never meant any of this to happen. It just got out of hand.'

George said nothing. The silence returned. And then, at

last, a door opened and a doctor appeared, walking towards them with a heavy tread. They all stared at him and then, slowly, rose to their feet to hear what he had to say.

Chapter Thirty-Six

'What a day for a funeral,' Ruth said, staring unhappily out of the window. 'Even the sky is crying.'

Dan came up behind her and laid his hands on her shoulders. She leaned back against him, the tears running down her cheeks, and his hands tightened as he bowed his head to rest his cheek against her hair.

'I don't know how we're going to get through this,' she said, her voice trembling.

'Neither do I. But we will, somehow.' He blew his nose. 'I've felt like this before – when my Nora was buried. And when I heard that Gordon had been killed. There was never no funeral for him, but they had a service of remembrance in the cathedral and I went along to that. I didn't think I could get through it then, either time, but I done it somehow. And we've got each other now, Ruthie. We'll do it.'

'I suppose so. But it's so unfair. People shouldn't die like that – so young, with their whole lives before them. And it's such a waste.' Her voice broke and she turned to him, clinging to his broad shoulders and weeping. 'It's such a terrible, terrible waste.'

Dan patted her back. He was close to tears himself, but knew that once he gave way he would lose all control. Later, perhaps, after it was all over, he could let go, but not until the whole miserable business was done and everyone gone away again. Not until then.

'I know,' he said into her hair. 'I know.'

'Why did it have to happen?' she sobbed. 'Why did they have to run across the road like that? Why was that lorry there at just that moment? Why did poor Alec feel so desperate? Why couldn't Floyd have stayed away? It was him brought all this trouble on us, Dan. It was all his fault.'

'It's no use going on like that, Ruthie. It don't do any good.' Dan felt helpless. In the past, it had always been he who was likely to fly into a temper, but since meeting Ruth he had learned a different way. It was her common sense and calm wisdom that brought reason into their discussions. Now, in her anguish, all that seemed to have deserted her and it was for him to apply the lessons he had learned.

All the harder, because of his own deep, grinding pain.

'It's nearly time to go,' he said quietly. 'I can hear the bells.'

Ruth raised her head and listened. The six bells of the village church had begun to ring, slow and sonorous, every other round muffled to denote a death. At the same moment, she heard the clip-clop of horses' hooves and George Warren's haywain, draped in black tarpaulin nailed to the sides but still billowing in the wind, appeared in the lane outside. Behind it was the smaller cart, also draped in black, with her sister Jane walking beside it, holding up a large, black umbrella.

'All right, Ruthie?' Dan asked gently, and she straightened her shoulders and nodded. 'Let's go.'

They walked out of the door together and paused a moment, gazing at the haywain with its black-swathed burden almost obliterated by the wreaths that covered it. Ruth felt the tears rise again in her throat and clutched Dan's hand so tightly that her wedding ring bit into the skin of both their fingers. For a moment, she hesitated, certain that she could not go a step further on this terrible journey; then she felt Dan's hand on her shoulder, gently urging her on, and her feet seemed to step forward of their own accord.

'Hello, Ruth,' Jane murmured. Her eyes were red and her

face pale. She held out both hands to her sister, and Ruth walked into her arms. They held each other tightly, and then let go. Ruth climbed up into the cart and took her seat, and Jane followed. Dan took his place behind the haywain and they moved off.

'Everyone in the village is going to be there,' Jane said softly, and as the little cavalcade progressed through the narrow lanes people came out of the cottages and fell in behind the second cart. All were wearing black and some carried umbrellas; most of them looked as if they had been weeping for the young soul so suddenly taken from them. They walked silently, past the house where the Woddis sisters had lived, past the cottage where little evacuee Martin Baker had been so harshly treated, past the Greenaways' farm where Jess Budd and her family had been made so welcome, past Solly Barlow's forge, closed for the day out of respect, past the vicarage where Stella and Muriel Simmons had played with Tim and Keith Budd. And all along the way, the procession grew longer, joined by people Ruth and Dan had never expected to see on this day.

'There's Jess and Frank Budd, and Tim,' Ruth whispered in amazement. 'And Jess's sister Annie, and her hubby. And Tommy Vickers and his wife. Oh, how kind of them to come.'

'They've been good friends all through,' Dan said. 'Good to me and Sam, and good to young Maddy and her sister. And they really took to Linnet at the wedding.'

Ruth nodded, tears brimming from her eyes again. She could not look behind her at the gathering crowd, but she knew that the queue must be growing and would fill the church. And still the bells rang, their normally joyous notes a mournful threnody in the still air.

At the lych gate, the two carts stopped to allow the congregation to go into the church first. They filed past, heads bowed, and Ruth watched them with tears in her heart. As Dan had said, the whole village was there, all except the youngest children, and every seat would be taken.

The four pall-bearers – George, Dan, Alec and Solly Barlow – came to the side of the haywain and lifted down the coffin. They shouldered it for a moment, found their feet, and then marched slowly through the door, followed by Ruth, Jane and Lizzie. Just inside, they were joined by a frail Maddy, her sister Stella and Felix Copley; and so, as the sad chimes ceased and the organ's slow notes commenced, Sammy Hodges began his final journey.

Only the family and closest friends were to come back to the cottage, but everyone in the village wanted to give their condolences to Ruth and Dan; everyone wanted to shake their hands or touch their arms, or speak a halting word or two of sorrow. It seemed to go on for ever, this shaking and touching and sad, sad smiling, yet to Ruth it was like moving through a dream, a shifting kaleidoscope of faces, and she felt only a dim surprise at their tears; her own seemed to have ebbed, like the tide after a giant wave, receding only to return later in an even greater flood. But for now, she was safe.

Jess Budd was before her, with Frank at her side and their elder son, Tim, close by. 'Ruth – we had to come. We're so sorry.'

'You were good to Sammy,' Ruth said. 'He used to tell me about how you looked after him in April Grove, after his mother died.'

'He was a dear little boy,' Jess said. 'And he grew into a grand young man. That was your doing, Ruth – yours and Dan's.' She glanced at Sammy's father. She'd never known him well – he'd been more Frank's friend than hers, and not what you'd really call a friend, even then – and she'd never liked him all that much when he'd lived at the other end of April Grove, but she understood now that it was his difficult life that had made him a difficult man. Since coming to Bridge

End, first to see Sammy and then to marry Ruth, the real Dan had emerged, and he was almost as fine a man (only 'almost', because nobody could be quite as fine) as her own Frank.

'Sam was grand on his own account,' Dan said. 'He had a good mother to start with, and Ruth took over where my Nora left off. I don't take no credit for it.'

'You shouldn't talk like that,' Frank said. 'None of us had much chance to be a father to our boys during the war, but you've done well since then, Dan, and don't deny it.'

'Will you come back to the house?' Ruth asked them. 'Jane's done a ham salad and some sandwiches and a fruit cake. We'd be pleased to have you.'

But Jess and Frank shook their heads. 'We're going to have a bite of dinner with the Greenaways and then we're catching the train back to Pompey. We don't want to intrude, but we did want to come, to pay our respects. And you've got enough people round you now.'

'Come again, then,' Ruth begged them. 'Come in the summer one day. For Sunday dinner. You're always welcome. You could come out on that tandem you've got.'

Frank grinned. 'All right, we'll do that. We've got a little motor on it now.' They turned away, but Tim stepped forward in their place.

'I wanted to tell you something,' he said. 'It's not to do with Sammy – it's about when Keith and me were here in the war. When your dad died, Mrs Hodges.'

'My father? I didn't even know you knew him, Tim.'

'We didn't, not really. We used to wave to him when he was sitting in the window, looking out, that's all. But the day he was buried – well, I expect you remember what it was like that day. Cold and snowy. And Keith and me and Brian Collins, we weren't at school in the afternoons so we got Reg Corner's dog and a couple of tea-trays and said we were going on an expedition to the North Pole. You know what kids are like.' He blushed a little at the memory of his childish adventures.

335

'But then Brian said he wanted to see the grave before – well, before the coffin was put into it. And we went and had a look, and Keith fell in.'

'Fell into the grave?' Ruth echoed. 'Into *Dad's* grave?'

'That's right. He was scared stiff – he thought he'd be buried alive under the coffin – and we had to get a ladder to fetch him out. And the dog was barking, and we were all in a panic in case you came out of the church and caught us there. We only just got away in time.' Tim stopped as Ruth started to laugh. 'It didn't seem funny at the time, I can tell you!'

'I don't suppose it did,' Ruth said, her laughter mingling with tears. 'You know, I remembering hearing the noise and wondering what was happening outside, but when we came out there was no sign of anyone. Just one of Edna Corner's tea-trays leaning against the wall, so we knew it was you pair, up to something you shouldn't have been. Neither of us said a word, though – she must have slipped back later on and picked it up. So Keith fell into the grave and thought we'd drop poor old Dad on top of him, did he? Poor little chap! I bet that cured him of snooping around in graveyards.'

'It did,' Tim said, grinning. 'He had nightmares about it for weeks afterwards and we could never tell anyone why. In fact, I don't think either of us has told anyone, to this day. But I thought you'd like to know about it.'

'Yes,' Ruth said, wiping her eyes. 'You were right. It wasn't Sammy, but it was just the sort of mischief he might have got into, with you little terrors leading him on.' She turned as someone else came to stand beside her, and took Maddy's hand. 'Oh, my poor love.'

Maddy looked at her wordlessly. Her face was white and her eyes looked like bruises. One arm was in a sling, and Ruth knew that beneath her small black hat some of her golden hair had been shaved off to cleanse the gash in her head. She had been in hospital until yesterday, and would have been kept in longer but had begged and pleaded to be allowed out, to come to her fiancé's funeral. She looked thinner than before, and almost transparent in her grief.

'Maddy, you look frozen,' Ruth said. 'You need to get into the warm.'

'I came to say hello to Tim.' She looked gravely at the tall young man. 'You were a good friend to Sammy. I just wanted to say thank you.'

'There's no need,' he said uncomfortably. 'Boys are only friends if it suits them. I liked Sam and he liked me and Keith. That's all there was to it.'

'Well, thank you all the same,' she said, and shivered suddenly. 'I think I will go to the house now, though, Auntie Ruth. Goodbye, Tim.'

He nodded and she turned away. Dan tood her arm but Ruth paused a moment longer, sensing that there was something else Tim wanted to ask.

'Nobody's said just what happened,' he said quietly. 'How did Sammy end up getting knocked down by a lorry? And how did Maddy get her arm broken? And what about your Linnet – someone said she was there too. What was it all about, Mrs Hodges?'

Ruth sighed. 'It was a bit of a muddle, Tim. I can't tell you all the story – but we were all on the bridge together. And then Linnet ran out into the road. Maddy ran after her, and Sammy must have seen the lorry coming and tried to save them both.' A shudder ran through her. 'He did save them both – he pushed them out of the way of the lorry. But then he fell. The driver didn't have a chance. Everyone said that, and the police agreed. Neither he nor Sammy had a chance.'

Everyone had gone at last. The last sandwich had been eaten, the last crumb of fruit cake finished up, the last glass of sherry emptied. Jane and Lizzie had done the washing-up and gone back to the farmhouse, where the children had spent the day with one of the village girls. Linnet, shaken but in one piece, was staying there for a second night and would come home tomorrow, to the cottage where Sammy no longer lived, and start life without her big brother to tease and pamper her.

Ruth and Dan sat together on the sofa, gazing into the fire, still trying to come to terms with all that had happened.

'Only a week ago, we were planning an engagement party for him and Maddy,' Ruth said in a dry, husky voice. 'How can life change so quickly?'

'We've both been through that before,' he replied. 'You and your Jack – me and Nora. Only it wasn't so sudden, with her, and you never even knew about Jack until weeks afterwards. It still seems sudden, though, when it happens. One minute they're there – or you think they are – and the next, they're gone. They're not part of the world any more. And somehow, you got to get used to that. You got to get used to living without them.' There was a long pause and then his voice cracked suddenly as the tears broke through the dam he had built against them. 'It don't get any easier, though. And this is the hardest one of all.' He turned to her, his dark face contorted with grief, and she pulled him into her arms and held him as tightly as she could. 'Our Sam's gone, Ruthie – our lovely boy has gone.'

Ruth fought back her own tears, which Dan had allowed her through all the past week. This was not her time; it was Dan's, and he must be given full rein, or the grief would sour inside and turn him back to the bitter man he had been when she had first met him.

'It's such a waste,' he said, echoing her own words. 'He was still no more than a boy. He could have done so much. It's such a bloody *waste*.'

'Dan,' she said at last, 'you mustn't think like that. Look at all the people who came to the church today. People who knew Sammy and loved him. How can a life be wasted when so many people want to say goodbye? And think of this too.' She looked into his eyes. 'He died a hero. Both your boys died heroes, Dan. At least you'll always have that.'

338

'I know,' he said. 'But he'd have had a miserable life if it hadn't been for you, Ruthie. Both of us would have had a miserable life if it hadn't been for you. You gave us both a lot of happiness over the last few years. And you gave us Linnet, too. I dunno what me and Sam would have done without you, and that's the truth.'

There was a silence. They sat holding each other tightly, trying to make sense of the tragedy that had befallen them. Then Silver, who had been unnaturally quiet, ruffled his feathers and spoke in the voice Sammy had used when he was just eight years old:

> *'Sammy, Sammy, shine a light.*
> *Ain't you playing out tonight?'*